BOBBI SMITH

BRIDES OF DURANGO: ELISE

LEISURE
BOOKS

$5.99 US
$6.99 CAN
$12.95 AUS

50599

9 780843 945751

ISBN 0-8439-4575-3

A DEMANDING KISS

"Good old Ben might have let you put yourself in harm's way, but I am not Ben! I am your new editor. I own the Star! No story is worth getting hurt over."

"You're right about one thing—you're not Ben! You're not really an editor, either! I know what makes a good story, and you just ruined everything by interfering with your high-handed ways!"

"Interfering? I saved you from being attacked!" Gabe growled, closing on her. "Or maybe you really wanted to do all the research and make your story completely accurate!"

"Why, you—" Elise was hurt and angered by his insinuation. Without thought, she slapped him.

The last of his iron-willed self-control snapped, and he reached back to push the door shut. "Since you think I interfered with your work and you want to do more research, let me help."

He took her by the shoulders and dragged her to him.

As Elise gazed up at him in the darkness of the night, Gabe looked different to her. No longer was he the mild-mannered boss. Tonight, he appeared as some fierce, avenging warrior, and she gasped softly as his mouth claimed hers in a demanding kiss.

Elise resisted for a moment, angered by his daring, but then his kiss gentled. Instead of dominating her, it became persuasive, coaxing. His lips moved seductively over hers, evoking a response that overruled her outrage at him.

BRIDES OF DURANGO: ELISE

BOBBI SMITH

LEISURE BOOKS　　　　NEW YORK CITY

*This book is dedicated to Alicia Condon,
the world's best editor!*

A LEISURE BOOK®

September 1999

Published by

Dorchester Publishing Co., Inc.
276 Fifth Avenue
New York, NY 10001

ISBN 0-8439-4575-3

The name "Leisure Books" and the stylized "L" with design are trademarks of Dorchester Publishing Co., Inc.

Printed in the United States of America.

ACKNOWLEDGMENTS

I'd like to thank Gwen Morton for all her help and support.

I'd also like to thank some wonderful people at Anderson News—Bill Golliher, Becky Rose, Aileen Schrade, Bill Davis, James Hollis, Varina Shortt, Diane Hopkins, Charmaine Thessin, Vicki Church, Nick Ursino, Wayne Mathias, Phil Pepalis and Norvel Carrick. Thanks for everything! You're terrific!

"Hi" to all my friends at the Nancy's Trade-A-Book stores in Jefferson City and Columbia, Missouri—Nancy Heidbreder, Nita Pierce, Patty Harrison, Olga Bolden, Kristin Krebs, Becky Asher, Cheryl Elliston, Jennet Wilson and John Harvey.

BRIDES OF DURANGO: ELISE

Prologue

Colorado, 1883

"We're getting close," Sheriff Trace Jackson warned his posse as he dismounted to check the trail they'd been following. "These tracks are only a few hours old."

"Good," Deputy Paul Andrews said as he reined in beside him. "I can't wait to catch up with the murdering bastards."

"You're not alone," Trace agreed grimly.

The four other members of the posse muttered their agreement. They had been on the trail of the notorious killer Matt Harris and his gang for the better part of a week now—ever since Harris had gunned down an unarmed man in an attempted robbery back in their town of Eagle Pass. The dead man, Ed Rankins, had been a good friend to Trace and the

11

others. They were looking forward to seeing the Harris gang pay for their savagery.

Trace lifted his dark-eyed gaze to study the surrounding hills. His expression was wary. Harris was close by—he could almost feel it.

"Let's keep a sharp eye out. I don't want—" he began, but it was then, in that moment, that he saw the glint of the sun off a rifle barrel among the rocks on the hillside ahead of them. "Take cover!"

Trace drew his gun and began firing just as the outlaws' first shots rang out.

The Harris gang's murderous barrage rained death down upon the lawmen. Bullets slammed into Trace as he dove for the cover of a nearby boulder. The rest of the posse wheeled their horses around trying to escape, but Harris's men seemed to be everywhere. The lawmen got off only a few answering rounds before they were slaughtered.

When the gunfire died down, Matt Harris emerged from his hiding place, laughing and cheering loudly in his victory.

"And Trace Jackson always prided himself on being such a good lawman and tracker," he sneered. "He don't look so damned good right now, does he, boys? All he looks is dead to me!"

Harris mounted his horse and rode down to inspect the carnage they'd wreaked. His men followed his lead. While they went to check each of the deputies to make sure they were dead, Harris rode straight to where Trace lay facedown and unmoving in the dirt. He smiled as he saw the blood that had pooled beneath the sheriff's head, and the blood on his shirt from another bullet wound. He glanced over at

Terp Wilson, his closest friend, who had ridden up beside him.

"Damn, I'm good," he gloated. "I got him twice—a head shot and his shooting arm!" He chuckled, pleased with his own marksmanship. "Sheriff Trace Jackson ain't so high and mighty anymore."

"You done good," Terp agreed. They'd always been concerned about Jackson. He'd had a reputation as a tough lawman who always brought in his man. It was good to know that they wouldn't have to worry about him anymore.

Harris drew his six-gun and aimed at Trace's back. Without remorse, he shot him again, then slowly holstered his gun.

"What did ya do that for if he's already dead?" Terp asked.

"Because it felt good," Harris said, grinning. "Now, let's get the hell out of here. I want to find me some whiskey and a willing woman. I want to do some celebratin'!"

As he rode away, Harris was still smiling. He knew what wiping out Jackson and his whole posse would do for his reputation. From now on, only fools would dare mess with Matt Harris.

The pain was unrelenting and maddening, and because of it, Trace knew he wasn't dead. If he'd been dead, he wouldn't have been in such torment. It took all his energy just to open his eyes, and he was immediately sorry for the effort. The glare of the sunlight stabbed at him, leaving him longing for unconsciousness again. In unconsciousness, there would be no agony. In unconsciousness, there would be peace—and the absence of pain.

"So you're finally wakin' up, are ya?"

The sound of the man's voice startled Trace. He struggled to look around, thinking the man might be one of Harris's gang. He was relieved to find that he was a stranger.

"Good to see you're awake, Sheriff," the wildly bearded old man said, giving him a toothless grin. "You had me wonderin' for a while there—I was thinkin' and afearin' you might not make it."

"Water—" Trace said hoarsely as he let his eyes close, exhausted.

"I'll get you some right now."

A moment later the man was back beside him with a dipper of water.

"Okay, young fella, let's see if we can get you to drink some of this," the old man urged, helping to lift his head as he held the dipper to his lips.

Trace drank thirstily. After a few good swallows, the old man drew back.

"Take it easy—that'll be enough for now," he said as he took the water away. "You don't want to drink too fast after what you been through. My name's Gibby, by the way. Gibby Pruett."

"Thanks, Gibby. I'm Trace Jackson." Trace gave a guttural groan as he lay back. He didn't want to rest. He had to get up. He needed to find his men and go after Harris. "Where am I? And my men? Where are my men? Are they here?"

Gibby's expression darkened. "Your men are dead, Sheriff."

Trace closed his eyes against the agony that tore at him. *They were all dead.*

14

"You was the only one left alive, so I brung you up here to my cabin," the old man went on. "It ain't nothing short of a miracle that you was still alive and kickin' when I found you, seein' as how you had two bullets still in you and your head grazed by another one."

Trace opened his eyes again to look at the man who'd rescued him. A burning, deadly fervor was mirrored in their dark depths.

"How long . . . ?" was all he could manage.

"Been almost a week now that I've been tendin' to you. I done buried the others."

Trace drew a deep, ragged breath. "I owe you, friend."

"You don't owe me nothin'. Jes' get better, that's all. What town are you from? Do you want me to get word to anybody back there about you being alive?"

"No!" Obviously, Harris had left him for dead. He wanted the outlaw and his gang to keep on thinking he was dead. It was going to take him a while to recover from his wounds, but when he did, he was going to finish what he'd started. He was going after the Harris gang—and he wouldn't quit until they'd been brought to justice.

"No?" Gibby was surprised. "Ain't you got nobody who'd be worryin' about you?"

"No. No one." Trace slowly shook his head. Paul and the rest of his deputies were dead. Harris had killed them all. He thought of Anna, the woman he'd occasionally seen in town. She had known from the start of their relationship that it would never be serious or binding. No words of love had ever been spoken between them, and he had wanted it that way. He had no room in his life for a commitment. His dedication had been to his job as a lawman.

"You sure there ain't somebody who'd want to know about you? Don't you have family?"

"I don't have any family, and if the rest of the folks in town think I'm dead, then we'll leave it that way." He turned to the old man, his eyes glowing with the fire of his intent. "As far as everyone's concerned, Sheriff Trace Jackson from Eagle Pass was killed in an ambush by the Harris gang along with the rest of his posse. There were no survivors."

Gibby saw the fierceness of his emotions and nodded. "I won't tell nobody that you're here."

"Thank you." Fury and hatred filled Trace as he lay there, searing him with the need for revenge and giving him the will he needed to live. "How bad am I?"

"You was lucky that the one bullet only grazed your head. The other two . . . well, I hate to tell you this, but you ain't gonna be so fast on the draw right-handed anymore."

Trace tried to lift his right arm, but could barely move it. He ground his teeth in frustration at discovering his own weakness. Somehow, he was going to have to find a way to deal with it. When he glanced over at Gibby, his expression was cold and deadly. "If my right arm's this bad, then I guess I'll just have to learn how to shoot left-handed."

Their gazes met and locked.

The old man could see reflected in his dark eyes the depth of the raw, savage emotion that motivated him. Gibby was glad he wasn't part of the gang who'd done this to Jackson, for he knew they were going to pay.

"I'll help you any way I can," Gibby offered.

"I'll see to it that you're paid for your help."

"You don't need to pay me. Just get the ones who did this behind bars where they belong."

Trace nodded, grim in his determination. It wasn't going to be easy, but he would get his strength back, and once he did, he was going to finish what he'd started. He was going to bring in Matt Harris. Harris believed Sheriff Trace Jackson was dead, and that was going to be his fatal mistake.

Trace would see to it.

Chapter One

Durango, Colorado—Two Months Later

Elise Martin knew she was making quite a spectacle of herself waiting at the Sanderson Stage Depot in the middle of the afternoon in her wedding gown and veil, but she didn't care. The wedding ceremony was scheduled to take place in less than an hour, and the stage on which she hoped her fiancé, Ben, would be arriving was running late. Her pace was restless as she stared off into the distance hoping to catch a glimpse of the Durango-bound stagecoach.

"Miss Elise? Is there anything I can do for you? Any way I can help?" Tom Bradshaw, the station manager, asked. He was concerned, for he knew how important this day had to be for her—it was her wedding day. Certainly, she did look lovely. He'd always thought Elise quite a pretty young woman with her dark hair and green eyes, but now in her gown of white satin and lace, she was downright beautiful. She should have been primping and preparing for her vows instead of waiting around the stage depot for a fiancé who looked like he wasn't going to show up. Tom hoped he would get there in time. Though Tom wasn't a close acquaintance, from what he'd heard about her, he knew that Miss Elise was a lady, and she deserved better than this.

"Not unless you can hurry the stage up," Elise told him a bit shortly. As cool and composed as she usually prided herself on being, she hated to admit that the steadiness of her nerve was being severely tested by this unexpected turn of events. Ben should have been back days ago. *Where was he?*

"I don't know what could be holding them up today. The weather's been good. They should have rolled into town over two hours ago. What time is your wedding due to start?"

"Preacher Farnsworth is set to perform the ceremony at four. That doesn't leave us a lot of time."

Tom couldn't think of anything reassuring to say to her, so he disappeared back inside, leaving the would-be bride to wait by herself. He knew there was nothing he could do to change things, so it was better just to stay out of harm's way.

Elise stopped pacing and drew a determined breath as she contemplated the possibility that the stage just might not make it into town in time. She had to have an alternative plan of action. She had to think of some way to salvage the situation—and fast! She'd worked too long and too hard making everything come together at just the right time and place today, and she refused to let it all fall through.

Had she been a man, Elise would have sworn aloud her frustration in the vilest language possible. She was a lady, though, and she reminded herself to behave like one. Certainly, she did look the part in her bridal gown and veil. It was just that standing there all alone in front of the stage depot waiting desperately for a stage that might not come didn't sit well with her—not now, not today. This was to have been the most exciting day of her life, but she hadn't intended the excitement to be her not knowing when Ben was going to show up.

"Elise!"

Elise turned at the sound of her name being called to find her grandmother hurrying toward her. She was holding the wedding bouquet in one hand and waving a slip of paper in the other.

"What is it?" Elise moved to meet her. She wondered what had happened to bring her grandmother to the depot at almost a run. It had to be important.

"This telegram just came! I knew you'd want to see it right away!" Claire Martin told her a bit breathlessly as she reached her side and handed her the missive. "It's from Ben!"

Elise tensed at the news. Ben should have been here! Why was he sending her a wire? Did this telegram mean he wasn't on the stage? She quickly read the short message.

"Oh, no," she said in quiet misery as she looked up from the telegram. "Did you read it already?"

"Yes. What are you going to do now?" Claire knew the wire was devastating to her plans. Ben Hollins, her would-be fiancé and the owner and editor of the *Durango Weekly Star*, had lost the newspaper in a poker game, and he would not be returning to town—ever.

"I don't know," Elise muttered in total frustration.

Ben's timing couldn't have been worse. The preacher was waiting. The guests were already arriving for the ceremony. She was in her wedding dress. Everything was set, and now he wasn't going to show up at all! She could have screamed, but the sound of a stagecoach in the distance finally pulling into town stopped her. Her expression grew even more determined.

"I don't think I like that look on your face," Claire said worriedly. "What are you planning to do?"

"There's only one thing I can do," she told her grandmother with as much bravado as she could muster as she lifted her gaze to watch the stage roll in.

"What's that?" Claire couldn't imagine what she was contemplating, but then, that wasn't unusual with Elise. Her granddaughter was always surprising her with clever, brilliant ideas, and if ever she'd needed one, this was the time.

"I'm going through with this wedding just as I planned. I'm going to get married—today."

For once, Elise did manage to truly shock her. Claire paled at her declaration.

"I don't understand. Ben's not coming in on that stage. You can't have a wedding without the groom."

"I know Ben's not coming, but somebody else just might. We'll have to see . . ."

Elise focused on the stagecoach as it drew to a stop before her. She took a deep breath and said a silent prayer. She never liked to admit to being in less than total control of any given situation, so she girded herself for what was to come. This wasn't going to be easy, but she would do it. Somehow, in the next few minutes, she was going to find herself a new fiancé and then she was going to get married. It would be that simple—she hoped.

The door to the stagecoach flew open. Straining to get a look, Elise could see that there were only three people inside—two men and a woman.

The middle-aged woman was the first to descend. Seeing Elise in her wedding gown, she eyed her with open curiosity, but Elise ignored her reaction. Elise didn't care what the woman thought. There was only one thing she cared about and that was finding a husband—fast.

A white-haired old man started to climb out next, his movements slow and almost arthritic. He gave Elise the same amazed look that the woman had, but Elise looked past him. He definitely didn't fit the bill. She needed—

It was then that she saw him more clearly—the third and final passenger. He was half standing behind the elderly gent, waiting for his turn to descend from the stage. He was bespectacled and probably not older than thirty.

With just that one look, Elise knew she had found the man she needed. This was the man she was going to marry. He was dark-haired, dark-eyed, and tall without being gangly. His shoulders were broad, but in the loose-fitting suit he was wearing she couldn't tell much else about his physique. He didn't look to be much of an outdoorsman, though, so she assumed he was probably thin and not too strong. Not that it mattered to her one way or the other if he was strong or not. She didn't need any muscles right now. All she needed was a reasonably young man who was alive and breathing. The fact that this one looked to be most unassuming and mild-mannered in his suit and bow tie made him even more perfect for her. He would definitely be easier to handle than any of the rougher cowboys would have been.

Without further hesitation, Elise made her decision and made her move. She didn't have any more time to waste. She smiled warmly and threw herself straight into the man's arms, crying out, "Darling! Thank heaven you have finally gotten here!"

To say the stranger was shocked would have been an understatement, but Elise gave him no time to protest her display of open affection. She kissed him fully on the lips to silence any comment or complaint he might have had about the warmth of her welcome as she hugged him close.

As she embraced him, Elise was surprised to find that the stranger was much more solidly built than she'd thought. He was hard-muscled and strong beneath her hands. Had she not been so frantic in her plotting, she might even have enjoyed the "spontaneous" kiss, but there was no time to think about that right then. She had only one thing on her mind—she had to get her new "fiancé" to Preacher Farnsworth's tent as fast as she could.

"I thought the stage would never get in!" she breathed excitedly when she ended the kiss.

The man had stiffened as if to resist her unexpected sensual assault. He tried to draw away from her, but she held on to him as if her life depended on it.

"What? I—" he began.

"I know," Elise interrupted him, refusing to be deterred from her purpose. "I've missed you, too!" Then she whispered in his ear for only him to hear, "I'll pay you ten dollars, if you'll just play along with me for a while. My name is Elise Martin and, for right now, yours is Ben Hollins."

A strange look momentarily passed over the man's face, but he quickly masked it. Instead, he gave his would-be bride a lopsided grin.

"Sweetheart," he said with open affection, and then he kissed her this time. His lips moved over hers in a possessive exchange as his arms came around her and drew her closer to him. "I'm sorry the stage is so late. If I'd known the kind of welcome I was going to get, I'd have taken over the reins and done the driving myself just so I could get here to you sooner."

Elise was surprised by his unexpectedly amorous move. She found herself crushed to the hard width of his chest until the kiss was over, and then she deliberately moved out of his arms, trying to regain her wits. She was more than a little breathless as she took a step back to look up at him. "All that matters is that you're here now, darling. There's still time, but we'll have to hurry. Preacher Farnsworth is waiting for us!"

"Elise!" Claire had looked on in disbelief as her granddaughter all but threw herself into this complete stranger's arms. She had been shocked by all that had transpired. What was Elise thinking? She had actually kissed this stranger right there in public! Surely Elise didn't think she could just take this man from off the stagecoach and—

"Come on, Grandmother, dear," Elise said, shooting her a sidelong glance that spoke volumes as she reached out to take her "fiancé's" hand. "Ben and I can't be late for our own wedding. You two can renew your acquaintance after the ceremony. Don't you agree, Ben?" Her gaze met and locked with his as she gave him a challenging look.

"Whatever you say, dear," he said agreeably, allowing her to lead him away.

His answer confirmed that her first assessment of his character had been right. *He would be easy to handle.* Elise felt her confidence in her own judgment return with a vengeance. It had been momentarily shaken by the powerful kiss he'd given her, but she *had* asked him to play along with her, so he was probably just doing what he thought she wanted him to do. Obviously, he needed the money she'd offered him and was willing to go along with whatever she had planned to earn it.

"It's not far to the tent. We've still got just enough time for everything to go smoothly," she told him as she led the way, rushing along toward the other end of town.

"We're going to a tent?" He looked startled.

"Preacher Farnsworth is a traveling minister. There was no other way for him to perform the ceremony," she quickly explained, not bothering to go into any detail. Elise knew she had no time to waste on details right now, and besides, all he needed to do was stand there. She would take care of the rest. She lowered her voice as she continued to explain, ignoring the looks of those on the streets of town who turned with open interest to watch their progress. "This isn't going to be difficult at all. All you have to remember is that your name is Ben Hollins and I'm your fiancée, Elise Martin. This is my grandmother, Claire Martin, by the way."

"Ma'am," he said in a most gentlemanly fashion to the elegant older lady who was trying to keep pace with them.

"Ben." Claire nodded and gave him a most quixotic smile. She wondered why he was going along with her granddaughter so readily. True, he wasn't your average cowboy, but he didn't look altogether slow-witted, either. In fact, she could have sworn that she'd seen a bit of a twinkle in his eye earlier, but then she decided it might just have been a reflection off his eyeglasses.

"Just follow my lead, *Ben*, and everything will be fine," Elise went on, all the while silently praying that what she was telling him would be the truth.

"Yes, ma'am," he answered politely. "Whatever you say. That ten dollars is going to come in real handy."

Claire listened to the exchange and smiled to herself in amazement. She didn't know how Elise managed to solve even the most difficult of problems with such seeming ease, but she did it. Her talent was definitely a gift. Of course, this young man being on the stage was a gift, too. If it hadn't been for him, heaven only knew what scheme Elise would have had to concoct at the last minute to save the day. She edged closer to her granddaughter and spoke quietly. "I can't believe things are working out so smoothly."

"It isn't over yet," Elise cautioned, unwilling yet to allow herself to believe that things were going to turn out fine.

"I know, but your new 'Ben' here seems to be a very nice, very agreeable young man," she confided. "Thank goodness he arrived when he did, but what are you going to tell people? Everyone's going to know immediately that he's not the real Ben."

"Just pray that no one says anything too loudly or causes any kind of disruption. Preacher Farnsworth has never met the real Ben, so he won't have any idea that I've switched grooms."

"I hope you're right."

"We're about to find out."

The tent loomed ahead of them, and they could see their friends going in the main entrance in anticipation of the ceremony to come.

Elise now regretted having invited so many people, but she'd known at the time she started making the arrangements that there was no other way. Everything had to be set up perfectly, and it had been. Just because her groom hadn't shown up was no reason to cancel the ceremony!

Elise stopped a short distance away, just out of sight of the arriving guests.

"Grandmother, you go on in. I'll show Ben where to wait, and then we'll be ready."

"Are you sure you're going to be all right? Do you need any help with anything?"

"I'll be fine."

"All right, dear," Claire agreed reluctantly. "Here are your flowers."

She pressed the bouquet into her hand.

"Did you bring the ring?" Elise asked, suddenly fearful that they didn't have it with them.

"Yes, it's right here." Claire took the ring out of her pocket and handed the plain gold band to her with a wry smile. "Your Ben is going to need this."

Elise smiled back, confident now that everything was in order. "Thank you."

"You are a beautiful bride, darling," Claire told her with emotion as she gave her a soft kiss on the cheek. She hurried away into the tent to join the others waiting for the wedding to begin.

Alone with "Ben" at last, Elise turned to face him. "Here's the ring. Now, come with me."

"Ben" slipped the ring safely into his jacket pocket and followed her to the rear of the main tent, where there were several curtained-off areas.

"That's Preacher Farnsworth over there," Elise told him, pointing out a distinguished-looking man in a dark suit standing a short distance away. "Go on over and introduce yourself, while I slip in here and freshen up a bit. It's been quite an exciting day already, and I doubt it's going to get calmer any time soon. Do you remember your name?"

"I'm Ben Hollins," he repeated dutifully. "And you're Elise Martin, my fiancée."

She was relieved that, at least, he'd paid attention to what she'd told him. "Good. Then go on. I'll see you in a very few minutes inside at the altar."

The stranger frowned a bit at her instructions, but nodded and made his way to greet the minister.

Elise entered one of the curtained-off areas. The preacher had told her the day before to wait there for the ceremony to begin. There was a small mirror and a table and chair in the makeshift room, so she took the time to adjust her veil and then paused to study her own reflection.

She wondered if she looked as pretty as her mother had when she'd worn this dress in her own wedding all those years before. She wondered, too, if her parents would have been proud of her today. She hoped so. She wanted to make them proud of her. Of one thing she was certain: When all was said and done, this wedding was going to be the talk of Durango for some time to come.

"Elise? Are you about ready?" George Lansing called out to her from outside the curtained room.

"I'm as ready as I'll ever be," she answered.

Elise put down the mirror and went to hold the curtain aside to greet the man who was to walk her down the aisle. George was the owner of the mercantile in town and a close friend to both her and her grandmother.

"You look lovely," he told her as he stepped inside to speak with her more privately. His gaze went over her with warm appreciation.

"Thank you."

"Shall we?" He offered her his arm, and she took it. "Where have you and your grandmother been? It was getting so late that I was starting to worry about you. I was afraid something had happened."

"Things did get a little complicated," she began.

"What's wrong?"

"There has been a slight change in plans, but I think everything is going to turn out all right anyway."

"What kind of a change?" he asked cautiously.

Elise looked him straight in the eye. "Ben didn't make it in on the stage."

"What?" He was shocked. "Then who—?"

The music started in the tent, signaling the beginning of the ceremony, and Elise knew they had to hurry.

"I'll explain it all to you later. I managed to get a stand-in for Ben, so we should be all right—I hope."

"No wonder you were running behind schedule." George chuckled and shook his head in good-humored disbelief. Elise was one amazing young woman.

He guided her from the makeshift dressing room, and they headed for the main entrance of the tent.

"Here we go."

She smiled brightly up at him, glad that the ceremony was under way and on time.

"This is the easiest part," she told him quietly. "And it will all be over in no time. You'll see."

"I hope you're right."

"Oh, I am. And then just wait until tomorrow." Elise's eyes were aglow at the thought of what the next morning would bring.

They paused just outside the entrance, as they'd practiced the day before. George patted her hand reassuringly, and Elise smiled up at him, ready for what was to come.

They started down the aisle.

Chapter Two

Claire had taken her seat at the front of the congregation after making her way down the aisle, greeting friends along the way. She'd noticed that even Julie Stevens had chosen to attend, and that had pleased Claire. The young woman's presence meant that Elise and Ben's wedding was being considered quite a social event by the town. Claire had smiled at the thought.

Julie was the daughter of Lyle Stevens, a banker and one of the town's richest men. She was certainly a beauty and more than a bit spoiled by her doting parents. Though she was not one of Elise's close friends, Julie was known for always being at the right place at the right time, and here she was at the wedding. Claire was thrilled that everything seemed to be turning out just the way Elise had hoped it would. Now, if only her granddaughter's luck held.

Claire had turned her attention to the altar as she waited for the ceremony to begin. It had been then that she'd noticed the new "Ben" standing with the preacher off to the side, just out of sight of the rest of the guests. She'd been surprised to find that he appeared very calm and collected. There weren't many men who would have gone along with Elise in a situation like this. She'd found herself wondering if he was a very smart man to have agreed to this, or if he was a little less than brilliant and just in desperate need of money. Claire supposed that it didn't really matter. What mattered was that he was there, and everything was going to come off as Elise had planned—she hoped.

At that moment, Preacher Farnsworth led the way out before the congregation with "Ben" following along behind him.

Claire could hear the murmurs of surprise among those gathered as they tried to figure out who the stranger was with the minister.

Julie Stevens was not happy as she sat waiting for the wedding to begin. She couldn't believe this was happening to her! She couldn't believe that she was going to sit there and watch Ben Hollins marry Elise Martin!

Tears of frustration and outrage threatened to overwhelm her, but, accomplished actress that she was, Julie controlled them with an effort and hid them behind a pleasant smile. She was not about to let on that she was upset about this match. She would play the lady. She would smile and greet everyone as if she hadn't a care in the world. She would never let anyone know that she had been powerless to stop the man she loved from marrying another woman.

It was then, as Julie was lost deep in thought, that Preacher Farnsworth walked out before the congregation with a tall, dark-haired man wearing eyeglasses behind him. She watched as the preacher and the stranger came to stand facing the aisle and the tempo of the music changed. Julie looked around for Ben, but saw no sign of him. She frowned and glanced over at her mother and father.

"Where's Ben?"

Adele Stevens was looking confused, too. "I don't know, dear," she whispered back. "Who is that young man? I've never seen him before."

"I don't know," Julie answered in hushed tones.

All around them, people were wondering the same thing. A low murmur of puzzlement and surprise ran among the guests.

Preacher Farnsworth gave no indication that he'd noticed the unrest in the congregation. He kept his focus on the bride as she started up the aisle on George's arm.

The murmuring in the congregation changed from questioning to excited as Elise appeared.

Claire turned in her seat to watch her granddaughter's progress. Her heart quickened at the devastatingly lovely picture she made. She didn't know why Elise had never married, and she sighed to herself wistfully. *If only . . .*

Elise clung tightly to George's arm as they slowly made their way up the aisle. She was relieved to see that "Ben" hadn't changed his mind and backed out on her at the last minute. She would have had a lot of explaining to do if that had happened. Things were going to be exciting enough as they were.

Elise found herself studying the groom critically as they drew ever closer to the altar. For some reason, the man who stood next to the minister watching her walk up the aisle seemed very different from the one who'd gotten off the stage just a short time before. Suddenly, he seemed taller and more powerful. His shoulders were broader, and he was holding himself with pride.

As she neared the front of the makeshift church, Elise suddenly wondered how she could have thought him less than brilliant. When he acknowledged her with a slight nod and a twist of his lips that could almost have passed for a smile, she felt a quiver of awareness in the depths of her soul. She had the strangest feeling that he was taking this whole wedding very seriously, and she swallowed, suddenly a bit nervous about what was to come.

George felt the rising tension in her, and he patted her hand again, hoping to reassure her when they finally came to a stop before the preacher.

"Who gives this woman to this man in Holy Matrimony?" Preacher Farnsworth asked, gesturing from Elise to "Ben."

"I do," George intoned solemnly, and he handed Elise over to her would-be groom. George's expression betrayed no surprise as he did so.

"Ben" reached out to take her hand in his, and Elise had to stifle a gasp at the warmth and strength of his grip. A shiver of awareness thrilled up her spine. She looked at him again in surprise, and she was lost in the wonder of his dark-eyed gaze. Only the preacher's words jarred her back to reality.

"Let us begin," Farnsworth said as he started the ceremony. "Dearly beloved, we are gathered here this day to join this man—Ben Hollins—and this woman—Elise Martin—in Holy Matrimony."

Julie and her parents exchanged sharp, puzzled looks, as did many of those gathered to witness the nuptials.

"But that's not Ben," Julie said softly, completely confused by what was taking place.

The troubled murmur passed through the congregation, but when the preacher didn't pause in his recitation, everything soon quieted down.

Elise kept her attention on the preacher as she waited for what was to come next. It wouldn't be long now. She was sure of that. She had everything worked out perfectly.

"Today is the day you both have waited a lifetime for," the preacher was saying.

Today is the day, all right! Elise thought. Of that, she was certain. Actually, it seemed she *had* been waiting a lifetime for just this moment.

"Today marks the end of one way of life—" Farnsworth preached.

Elise smiled, knowing there was more truth to his words than he could ever imagine.

"—and the beginning of a new, more fulfilling existence."

If all went as planned, today would be the beginning of a new existence for sure, Elise mused. She wasn't certain just how fulfilling it was going to be, but any minute now, she was going to find out.

She managed to glance out of the corner of her eye toward the tent's main entrance. There was no one there. A sense of foreboding came over her, but she pushed it away. Everything that could have gone wrong had already gone wrong. She just had to be patient a few more minutes—

"You must love one another!" Farnsworth continued, exhorting them. "No matter what the future may bring, you must cling to each other! You must be each other's strength! You will be one in the eyes of God!" His style of preaching was loud and forceful. "Say 'Amen'!"

"Amen!" everyone echoed in unison.

"Let us now recite the vows which will bind you—the vows which will make you husband and wife in the eyes of God, forever and ever—Amen!"

"Amen!" everyone echoed.

Farnsworth looked straight at "Ben." "Repeat after me. I, Ben, take you, Elise, to be my lawful wedded wife—"

"I, Ben, take you, Elise, to be my lawful wedded wife," the stand-in "Ben" repeated dutifully.

Elise couldn't believe this was happening. They were actually exchanging vows! She managed a tight smile that looked to all the world to be simply a nervous one, yet her thoughts were racing. Never in all her planning had she imagined that the wedding would progress this far. It should have been over long before now! What was taking so long? Frantically, she realized there was nothing she could do about it.

She was determined to see things through to the end. She couldn't quit now. She'd come too far to give up and walk away.

"To have and to hold—"

"To have and to hold—" "Ben" said slowly, his dark eyes upon his "bride."

Nervous tension gripped Elise as she felt "Ben" staring at her, but she kept smiling, refusing to panic. She cast another surreptitious glance down the aisle. *Where was Marshal Trent? He should have been there by now!*

As Preacher Farnsworth said the vows, "Ben" repeated each sacred promise in a calm, confident tone.

" 'Til death us do part," he said.

" 'Til death us do part," "Ben" finished solemnly.

And then it was Elise's turn.

Preacher Farnsworth turned to her and gave her an encouraging smile as he began, "I, Elise, take you, Ben, to be my lawful wedded husband—"

Elise was certain she seemed the perfect example of a frightened young bride as she echoed the preacher's supposedly binding words.

"For better or worse."

"For better or worse."

Each moment of the ceremony seemed to last an eternity as she echoed his urgings.

" 'Til death us do part," Farnsworth finally concluded the recitation.

" 'Til death us do part," she repeated slowly, not chancing a look at her "husband." She could just imagine what was going through his mind. He probably thought he'd gotten himself tangled up with a crazy woman, and right then, he wouldn't have been too far wrong. The situation was definitely not turning out the way she'd envisioned it would.

"You may present her with the ring," the minister told him.

"Ben" drew the plain golden circle from his pocket. He took her trembling hand in his and slipped it on her finger.

Elise studiously avoided meeting her "groom's" gaze. She stared down at the wedding band on her hand and tried to keep from frowning. She couldn't believe this had happened to her—and after all her meticulous planning. She should have realized when Ben's telegram had come that her carefully laid plan was in a shambles, but by then it had been too late to call the whole thing off. She'd been too close to her goal to just walk away. She'd had to go through with it, and she had.

But now—

"I now pronounce you man and wife. Mr. Hollins, you may kiss your bride."

"My pleasure," "Ben" said in a deep voice that held just a hint of amusement. Without further ado, he swept his "bride" into a loving embrace.

Before Elise could even think of resisting, her "husband" gave her a possessive kiss that left her grandmother, George, and the rest of the onlookers tittering with delight. His lips moved over hers with such persuasive intent that, for just an instant, she forgot her real reason for being there. Swept away by the power of his touch, she was thoroughly caught up in the sweet heat of his mouth on hers and the strength of his arms around her. His kiss evoked an answering response in the womanly depths of her that she'd never experienced before. Her heartbeat quickened to an erratic rhythm.

When "Ben" finally ended the exchange and put her from him, Elise found herself momentarily disoriented. She hadn't been sure what kind of reaction to expect from her stand-in groom, but his potent embrace had left her stunned. She gazed up at this man she'd just married, in his eyeglasses and bow tie, and blinked a bit dazedly. She wondered how this unassuming-looking man's kiss could have affected her so. He looked as if he'd been totally unmoved by the experience, and for some reason, that realization irked her.

Logic reasserted itself within Elise as the preacher spoke the next words.

"Ladies and gentlemen, may I present to you Mr. and Mrs. Ben Hollins."

Applause rippled through the gathering, along with more muffled whispers.

"Elise?" "Ben" held out his left arm to her in a gentlemanly fashion, ready to escort her from the tent.

Trapped by circumstances beyond her control, Elise could only play along. She took his arm and was again amazed at how powerful he felt beneath her touch. She had no time to dwell on the thought, though, for at that very moment the marshal of Durango, Jared Trent, appeared in the doorway of the tent and blocked the aisle.

"Hold it right there, Farnsworth," the law-man dictated in stern tones.

"What—?" the preacher blurted out, shocked by this interruption of his ceremony.

"You're under arrest, Byron Farnsworth. I'm taking you in for robbery. We've already got the rest of your gang locked up down at the jail."

A roar of disbelief and shock erupted from the congregation at his announcement.

Elise offered up a quick, silent prayer of thanks that the marshal had finally gotten there. Relief flooded through her. Everything had worked out the way it was supposed to. Her suspicions about the evil preacher and his gang had been right. It was over! She'd done it! Excitement coursed through her.

Farnsworth had been passing himself off as a man of God, but in reality, he had been a suspect in numerous robberies. He had no intention of being arrested, however, and in that moment, he snarled an ungodly oath and made a desperate move.

"Like hell I am!" the evil preacher swore. He drew a derringer from his coat pocket and grabbed Elise by the arm, hauling her toward him.

"Don't!" she shrieked in outrage.

Farnsworth ignored her scream and clutched her in front of him, using her for a shield.

"I'm not going anywhere with you, Trent!" he declared. "You're going to let me ride right out of this town, the same way I rode in—a free man!"

"Oh, no, I'm not." The marshal's tone was harsh, his expression just as deadly. Though Jared Trent had not been the town's lawman for long, he was very good at his job. There was no way he was going to let Farnsworth get away.

"Let me go!" Elise continued to struggle in her effort to be free of him, but Farnsworth's hold on her was bruising. She tried to kick out at him, but the fullness of her skirts hindered her efforts. Terror threatened, for she realized how dangerous her situation was. In the space of a heartbeat, she'd gone from elation at her victory in trapping him to icy fear for her own life and the lives of those around her.

"Shut up and hold still, bitch!" Farnsworth commanded. "I'd hate for your wedding day to end with a funeral!"

Elise refused to submit to him. She continued her struggle, but found there was no way to free herself. She was pinned helplessly against his chest.

She looked up and caught sight of her grandmother sitting in the front row. Claire was trembling visibly in fear and clutching at George beside her. Terror was etched in both their faces as they watched in horror what was transpiring.

"Ben," too, was watching what was happening. The minute Farnsworth had grabbed Elise, he had known they were in trouble. He'd quickly assessed the situation and knew from the look in the preacher's eyes that it wasn't going to be easy for him to stop the man, unarmed as he was. Still, he realized he had to try something. He couldn't risk letting anything happen to Elise.

"Let my wife go," he spoke up. He was still playing his role as the groom, but there was something in the tone of his voice that proclaimed authority.

Those gathered in the tent were silent at his command, and Farnsworth glanced over at him. He was frowning slightly, surprised by the fierceness of his tone.

"Don't even think about trying anything!" Farnsworth threatened.

The congregation had been stunned by this unexpected display of savagery from a man they'd thought was a moral leader, and now they were even more shocked by the confrontation taking place. They could see the angry determination in "Ben's" eyes and wondered what he and Marshal Trent were going to do. They seemed to be collectively holding their breaths as they watched the fearful situation unfolding before them.

"Let her go, Farnsworth!" Marshal Trent ordered, taking a step closer.

"Stay away from me!" the evil preacher commanded, swinging the gun from left to right in a threatening manner. "Both of you, back off!"

But neither "Ben" nor Marshal Trent obeyed.

The marshal remained blocking the main aisle. "You're not going anywhere, *preacher*. It's over. You may as well give it up."

"I ain't giving anything up! Somebody's going to end up hurt—maybe dead—if you don't let me out of here right now!" he threatened, a rising note of hysteria in his voice.

"Ben" had heard all he needed to hear. He'd dealt with his kind before—the desperate, the scared, the deadly. He knew what men like Farnsworth were capable of, and he knew he had to act—and act quickly—before someone really did get hurt. "Ben" was reasonably certain that Farnsworth had totally discounted him as a real threat, and that was a serious error in judgment on the outlaw's part that gave him just the edge he needed.

"Preacher Farnsworth, I don't know what this is all about," "Ben" began, "but I'm sure it's all a mistake. Please—release my wife, and we'll talk to the marshal about it. I'm sure everything will be fine." He tried to sound conciliatory.

The preacher tightened his hold on Elise as he glared at "Ben." "What do you think I am? A fool? Your new little wife is just the ticket I need to get out of town. She's going with me. I'm not letting her go free until I'm far away from here!"

"Look—why don't you take me instead? I'll ride with you. Just let her go," "Ben" offered, assessing the other man's strength and agility. Whatever he tried, he was going to have to catch him unawares. He needed the element of surprise on his side.

"No! Now back away, or I'll shoot you right where you stand!" Farnsworth threatened, pointing the derringer at him.

"Ben" glanced toward the lawman, who was standing, revolver in hand, waiting for Farnsworth's next move. The town marshal didn't look like the kind who would overreact, but "Ben" still feared what might happen if shooting erupted in such close quarters with so many people around. He put his hands up, deciding to play the intimidated coward.

"All right, all right—don't shoot me!" He took what appeared to be a faltering, nervous step backward and faked tripping and losing his balance. He managed to lurch awkwardly, and then he deliberately fell toward the outlaw.

Chapter Three

"Ben" threw himself bodily into the outlaw's gun arm, leading with his left shoulder.

"What the hell!" Farnsworth swore, as "Ben's" unexpected tackle jarred him violently.

The preacher tried to dodge out of his way, but at that strategic moment, Elise reacted on instinct. She elbowed him in the stomach with all her might. Farnsworth grunted in pain and was forced to let her go. Suddenly, he was desperate to hold the others off as he made an escape. He fired off a wild shot, hoping everyone would panic so he could elude the lawman in the rush and make his getaway. But no one panicked, and before he could make a run for it, Marshal Trent was there before him, his gun aimed at the middle of his chest at pointblank range.

"I know you've got one shot left, Farnsworth, but don't even think about trying anything or you'll be meeting your maker right here today. I can turn this wedding into a funeral real quick," the marshal snarled. His fierce expression showed that he meant what he said. "Now, drop the gun."

The preacher was cursing obscenely as he obliged. Marshal Trent picked up his gun and marched him unceremoniously from the tent. The wedding guests looked on, amazed by all that had transpired.

Claire was the first to recover from the shock. She jumped to her feet and ran to her granddaughter, embracing Elise and hugging her close.

"Elise, darling! Are you all right?" Claire cried.

"I'm fine," Elise said breathlessly as she watched the lawman lead the outlaw away.

"Thank God! You could have been killed!"

"But I wasn't." She started smiling now, pleased with the way everything had finally turned out. There had been a few moments there when she had honestly feared for her life, but Marshal Trent had come to her rescue just in time.

"I am so proud of you," Claire went on, forgetting about the terror and celebrating her success. "You were right about everything! Farnsworth was an evil man—a very evil man!"

Elise's eyes glowed with pleasure at her praise. She'd worked for weeks to bring this whole plan to fruition, and she'd done it. She looked up to watch the lawman and the phony preacher disappear through the main entrance of the tent. "And to think he got away with his deception for this long—Marshal Trent must have caught his men in action."

"I'm so happy for you. In all the towns Farnsworth's performed his ministry, no one else had any idea that he was really the leader of a gang that was robbing the people in his own congregations. It's easy to understand how he got away with it for so long. Who would think that the man of God was really a low-down, dirty thief?"

"I can't wait to get to the office and write this story! I bet this will be the *Star*'s biggest printing ever!"

"Elise?" "Ben" spoke up somewhat tentatively from where he was standing off to the side, pretending to be a bit unsettled by all that had happened. "Are you all right?"

Elise had forgotten about her "groom." She turned to him a bit embarrassed as everyone came hurrying forward to bombard her with questions.

"I'm fine. What about you? That was a nasty fall you took. Did you hurt yourself?" she asked, trying to talk to him while all her friends from town surrounded her. She couldn't believe that he'd been so uncoordinated as to fall that way and make such a fool out of himself at such a dangerous moment.

"No, not at all."

She nodded, glad that he was all right. "Thank goodness Marshal Trent was here or you might have gotten yourself shot. Farnsworth was every bit as horrible and dangerous as I suspected he was. He meant business today. His warnings that he'd shoot us weren't empty threats."

"And you lived to tell about it!" George proclaimed proudly, drawing her attention away from her new "husband."

"Thank heaven she lived to tell about it!" Claire said emotionally. She had been horrified by the evil man's actions and by her own inability to do anything to help the situation.

"Elise! What was this all about?" Lyle Stevens demanded, his wife Adele and daughter Julie standing beside him. "And where's the real Ben?"

Those nearest to Elise closed in, echoing Lyle's questions. She was even further distracted from thoughts of her stand-in "Ben."

"Ben" looked on for a moment longer, listening to all the questions and watching her with the crowd; then he quietly moved away. No one noticed him leave the tent.

Elise responded to everyone's inquiries. The more she talked about the way they'd managed to capture the outlaw preacher, the more excited she became. For although things had started off so badly, she had exposed Preacher Farnsworth for the terrible thief that he was.

Elise could just see the headline for the next edition of the *Durango Weekly Star*: PRETENDER IN THE PULPIT! FARNSWORTH A FRAUD! A CONSPIRATOR OF THE CLOTH! Headline after possible headline played in her mind as she explained things to her friends. She found herself wondering which one would sell the most newspapers.

"How on earth did you figure all this out?" one amazed woman asked.

"I was reading some newspapers from out of

state several months ago and noticed a strange connection between visits by the Preacher Farnsworth and a string of robberies. At first I thought it was coincidence, but then I did some more checking, and I began to realize it was too perfect, too organized. That's when I approached Marshal Trent about setting this trap for him. I had Marshal Trent's full cooperation and support. I couldn't have done it without him."

Everyone murmured their agreement. They all respected and admired their marshal.

"But where's the real Ben?" Lyle Stevens asked.

"And what happened to your Ben?" someone asked.

Everyone looked around and realized the new groom had disappeared.

"I don't know where my stand-in went," she said, surprised that he'd left without waiting to be paid. She still owed him the ten dollars, and she was more than willing to pay up. It had been worth every cent she'd promised him to have this story. "But the real Ben . . . "

Everyone waited, curious to hear where the well-known editor/owner and supposed groom had gone.

"I got a telegram from him just before the wedding was to take place. In it he said that he wasn't coming back to town—ever."

"Why? What happened?" another woman asked.

No one noticed that Julie had gone pale at her announcement.

Elise quickly related the news about how

Ben had lost the paper in a card game.

"You must have been frantic, what with the wedding all set and everything."

"Frantic is too mild of a word for what I was feeling. I was quite a sight standing at the stage depot in my wedding gown," she told them with a slight smile. "I'd convinced myself that Ben would be showing up on the stage that was overdue, but then Grandmother brought me his telegram."

"Did Ben even know about the wedding? He'd been gone for quite a few weeks already, hadn't he?"

"He'd left Durango to take care of some family business before I found out the truth about Farnsworth. I hadn't had the opportunity to tell him that he had proposed to me and that the arrangements had been made for him to marry me today. I just kept expecting him to come back to town and go back to work. When I started this, I felt certain he'd get here in plenty of time." She was smiling broadly as she related the tale.

The crowd chuckled good-naturedly. "Are you ever going to tell him what happened?"

"Maybe—if I ever see him again."

"Did he say who the new owner of the paper is?" George asked.

"No, but I imagine I'll be finding out any time now."

As she'd stood in the crowd listening to Elise's explanations of all that had happened, Julie couldn't believe what she'd heard. Elise and Ben's wedding had been a hoax from the start. None of it had been real. He didn't love Elise and had never planned to marry her. Her mood brightened a little bit, but she was still upset by the news that Ben was not returning to town.

"Who was the Ben Hollins you 'married'?" Julie asked.

"He came in on the stage this afternoon. I was standing there at the depot wondering what I was going to do without the real Ben when he climbed down. I knew the moment I saw him that he'd be perfect."

"And he agreed to pose as your finacé with no questions asked?"

"Yes. He was wonderful. I couldn't have done it without him. He was a big help."

"What's his real name?"

Elise frowned. "You know, everything happened so quickly, I never got the chance to ask him."

Everyone laughed and joked about her marrying a complete stranger.

"You certainly were lucky that he showed up when he did," George remarked.

"I'll say. I wasn't quite sure what I was going to do without a groom."

Those gathered around Elise laughed again.

"I wonder . . . " one woman said thoughtfully. "Are you and your substitute groom legally married now? I mean, you did say your vows and all."

"Farnsworth could hardly be called a man of the cloth. He was the leader of a gang of thieves," Elise replied easily, trying to ignore the nagging thought that the woman might be right. After all, in all of her planning, she had been certain that they would be interrupted long before the final vows had been exchanged.

She quickly dismissed her worry, though. "Had he been a proxy for Ben, I might be married to the real Ben Hollins right now, but I don't think the vows we exchanged today were binding in any way. The whole point of faking the ceremony was to bring a bad man to justice, and that's exactly what we accomplished."

"I can't wait to see the next edition of the *Star*," Claire said proudly.

"I can't wait to write it!" Elise beamed. "Speaking of which, I'd better get to the office and go to work. You can read all the details of what happened today in tomorrow's issue."

A buzz of excitement ran through those who had come to talk with her.

Elise started from the tent, ready to get to her desk and start writing copy. She was thrilled that her investigation had panned out just the way she'd hoped it would. All her hard work had been worth it! It was just a shame that the real Ben Hollins hadn't been here to witness her triumph and share in the glory. He would have been proud of her. She hoped the new owner—whoever he was—appreciated her accomplishment.

Sales of the *Star* would be soaring after this next issue. Elise was sure of it, but she knew she couldn't rest on her laurels. She would have to find a way to top this exposé. It wouldn't be easy. Stories like this one about Preacher Farnsworth came along once in a blue moon, but somehow she would find a way to keep things exciting so they would sell more papers. There was a lot of competition in town among the several newspapers, and she wanted the *Star* to be the best of them all.

The realization of her success kept her spirits soaring. She reveled in the praises the crowd heaped upon her. Still, Elise knew not to take all their compliments too seriously. A newspaper reporter was only as good as her next story.

Her grandmother's call brought her up short just as they were starting outside.

"Darling, don't you think you should go home for a moment and change into something a little more suitable before you go to work?" Claire asked, trying not to laugh over her granddaughter's enthusiasm for her job.

Elise laughed, chagrined. "You're right. I am just a little overdressed for the occasion."

They started for home so she could change clothes.

"You know," her grandmother began with a chuckle, "this is your wedding night. Are you sure you want to go to work?"

"I'm sure. I'm going to be spending most of the night at the jail interviewing Marshal Trent and his deputies. Andy rode with the deputies, so I should have some good inside information from him. I hope he'll be waiting for me at the office so that once I've talked to the lawmen, I can go straight there and write the article right away. I don't have a minute to lose. We need to meet our deadline to get the paper out on time."

"Somehow, having you visiting the jail and then going to work at your desk were not quite what I had envisioned for you on such a momentous occasion," Claire teased.

"Me either, but since this wasn't a real wedding, I suppose it's best that I don't have a real wedding night, either."

"You're absolutely right about that—especially since you don't even know your 'husband's' real name."

"I'll have to go find him in the morning, so I can pay him and thank him for all he did to help me."

"He did do a fine job. I was worried when the time came for you to say your vows. It's amazing that he didn't protest and try to get out of the ceremony."

"Everything turned out perfectly, though."

"Yes, it did. I'm very proud of you, darling."

Elise slanted her a smile. "Now all I have to do is find a way to top this story."

Claire gave her a worried look. "That's not going to be easy, and you were in a lot of danger today. Things might have taken a terrible turn if it hadn't been for your 'groom's' quick action."

"My groom's quick action? What quick action?" Elise frowned at her, puzzled by her remark. " 'Ben' didn't do anything except trip and almost fall down."

"You're wrong about that. If your 'Ben' hadn't deliberately fallen into Farnsworth the way he did when he did, somebody most assuredly would have gotten hurt."

"But the marshal—"

"Marshal Trent was wonderful, but 'Ben' was the one who really stopped Farnsworth. If he hadn't made his move right then, that horrible man would have dragged you away with him. God only knows what might have happened to you next."

Elise was amazed by her grandmother's perception. "But I thought 'Ben' just stumbled and accidentally fell against him."

"Oh, he did 'just stumble,' but his timing was everything. Surely, as mild-mannered as he is, he wouldn't have gone for a major confrontation, especially since he was unarmed. No, he used his brains instead of his brawn. He did some quick thinking, and he managed to save you quite handily. We were very lucky he was on that stagecoach today. I don't know of another man who could have handled everything so well—not even the real Ben Hollins."

Elise said nothing more, allowing her grandmother to think that she was in agreement with her. The truth be told, though, for all that her stand-in groom had been agreeable to helping her in her dilemma, she honestly believed his actions during what could have been a terrible shoot-out had been strictly accidental. He was a very nice man, but she was certain that he was not the hero of the day as her grandmother seemed to think he was.

Chapter Four

While Elise had been surrounded by her wedding guests, Trace had quietly slipped away. He'd picked up his bags at the stage depot and made his way to the hotel.

"Good afternoon," the clerk greeted him, sliding the hotel register across the counter toward him. "Just sign in here. Will you be staying long?"

"For a few days, at least," he told him as he registered under the name of Gabriel West. It had been his grandfather's name, and he intended to keep using it until he was ready to go after the Harris gang. That was why he'd adopted the disguise, too. The longer everyone thought Trace Jackson dead, the better. He wanted to catch Harris by surprise.

"Welcome to Durango, Mr. West. I hope you enjoy your stay."

"It looks like it's going to be an interesting one," he remarked, thinking of all that had happened just since he'd gotten off the stage. His had been quite an unusual welcome.

"Well, good. If you need anything, just let me know. Your room's at the top of the stairs and to the left."

Trace thanked him and made his way upstairs. The accommodations weren't plush, but they were clean and comfortable, and that was all he needed. He would look for a more permanent residence once he'd assumed his position as editor/owner of the *Star*.

Trace smiled to himself at the thought of taking over the paper. He wondered what Elise's reaction was going to be when she discovered that she'd ended up "marrying" her boss just as she'd originally planned.

Evidently, everything Ben Hollins had told him about Elise Martin that night after the poker game had been true. He'd warned him that she was one helluva newspaper woman who would go to just about any lengths to get her story, and now he knew Ben hadn't been exaggerating.

Trace hadn't expected to run into Elise so quickly upon arriving in town. He'd been surprised to see a bride at the stage depot, and even more surprised when she'd greeted him with that very pleasant kiss. But once she'd whispered her name to him and asked him to cooperate, there had been no way he could refuse. Elise—his reporter—had been up to something, and he'd played along to find out exactly what.

Trace was glad that he had. Though her methods had been unorthodox, they'd gotten results. She'd helped to bring in an outlaw who'd been causing trouble throughout the state. He was glad that he had been able to play a small part in it.

Setting his bags aside, Trace started to shrug out of his jacket. Just that movement left his right arm and shoulder aching, though, and he shook his head in disgust as a great weariness settled over him. He couldn't believe he was still so weak. It had been a good two months since the ambush, yet, even now, any great physical exertion left him exhausted. Though he'd tried to make his attack on Farnsworth look like an accident, driving his shoulder forcefully into the preacher's gun arm had jarred him, and now he was paying the price.

Drawing a ragged breath, he finally managed to take off the coat and rid himself of the tie and his eyeglasses. He hated the damned things, but he could not dispense with them yet—not until he was ready to face Harris down.

Trace began to massage his injured right shoulder and arm, knowing it wouldn't help, yet hoping that it would. He smiled grimly to himself as he walked to the window to look out on the streets of Durango. It seemed to be a decent enough town, but he didn't like being here. He would much rather have been on Harris's trail, tracking him down. For the time being, though, there was nothing else he could do. He silently swore at the fate that had brought him to this. He flexed his right arm, longing for relief, but was rewarded with more stabbing pain.

Grimacing, Trace wondered if he would ever be the same again. Even as he thought it, he already knew the answer. The Trace Jackson who had been known for his fast draw didn't exist anymore. He was a different man now. He had always believed in truth and justice and that in the end, good would prevail. But now he wasn't so sure. He'd become a driven man. His only motivation was to catch up with Harris and avenge his friends' deaths.

As memories of that fateful day besieged him, Trace suddenly needed to get out of the small room. He felt the need for a drink. He slowly put his coat back on, donned the spectacles, and left the hotel to find the nearest saloon. A shot or two of whiskey would definitely ease the pain in his shoulder—and the pain that haunted his heart.

The Mother Lode Saloon was relatively quiet as Trace made his way to the bar. He ordered a whiskey, then sat at a table near the back. He took a deep drink and waited for the liquor to work its magic on his body and soul.

"My name's Penny. Is there anything I can get for you today?" a blond-haired bar girl purred as she came to stand before him in her tight-fitting, very revealing satin dress.

Trace downed the rest of his drink and pushed the glass toward her. "Just a refill on my whiskey will do me fine," he answered, glancing only briefly at the tempting view offered by her low-cut bodice.

"Are you sure that's all you need?" Penny gave him a enticing look, wanting to attract him. She could tell immediately that he was different from the other men who patronized the bar, and she found him intriguing with his nice-looking clothes and eyeglasses. For all that he didn't look like one of the usual ranch hands or soldiers who were her regular customers, she wondered what he would really be like if she got him alone upstairs. She sensed there was more to this man than met the eye, and she wanted to find out if her instincts were right.

"I'm sure," he answered, his tone dismissive.

"Too bad," she sighed, picking up his glass. "We could have had some fun together tonight."

Trace watched her walk away, her hips swaying in suggestive invitation. He found himself smiling as he thought that, by all rights, it really was his wedding night and he should have been somewhere having some fun. Well, he conceded, at least it was Ben Hollins's wedding night.

Trace wondered if his "bride" had given any thought to this being their wedding night. As caught up as she'd been in her excitement over the preacher's arrest, he doubted it. Elise Martin had wanted her story, and she'd gotten it. That had been all that had mattered to the *Star*'s reporter.

Thoughts of Elise made him smile even more. Ben had used the term "firebrand" when he described her, and now he understood why. When it came to tracking down her story, she had been relentless. In the face of near disaster, she hadn't panicked, but had kept her wits about her. She had been determined that the wedding was going to go on no matter what, and she'd accomplished it—even going so far as to marry a total stranger to get it done. His smile broadened as he thought of the kiss he'd given her after the ceremony. It had been quite exciting, and he wondered if the rest of his stay could possibly measure up to his first day.

Trace's thoughts about Elise were interrupted as Penny returned with his whiskey.

"Here you are, honey," she cooed, leaning forward as she set the drink before him to give him an even better look at her ample breasts. "You change your mind about wanting anything . . ." She paused for dramatic effect. "Anything at all, you just let me know."

"I will," he promised, handing her the money for the whiskey plus a decent tip.

She smiled at him as she put her tip money down her bodice and laughed throatily as she moved away. "It'll be safe there—for the time being."

Trace nursed his second drink and tried to relax. Several new customers came in and began relating the news of Farnsworth's arrest to the others at the bar. He didn't recognize any of the men as having been at the wedding, so he knew that word of what had happened was quickly spreading around town. When the men told the others that the female reporter from the *Star* had been a part of the investigation, everyone was eager to read the *Star*'s next edition so they could get the whole story. It was obvious that Elise knew how to drum up interest and sell newspapers. He was impressed.

It was growing dark outside when the throbbing in Trace's arm and shoulder finally began to ease. He quit the bar and returned to his hotel room, glad for the reprieve from the pain. He was looking forward to getting some rest. There was a lot that had to be done tomorrow, and he needed to be ready. He had to establish himself at the paper, find a more permanent place to live, and locate a site where he could practice shooting without anyone being the wiser to his motive. Of the three, the last was most important to him. For all that he could carry a sawed-off shotgun with him, he would feel more in control once he was able to use his sidearm again.

Trace's reputation as a deadly gun had helped keep things quiet in Eagle Pass. Few had dared to start trouble in his town, knowing the justice he would immediately mete out. His remarkable accuracy and his quick-draw ability had ended with the ambush, though. Ever since he'd been strong enough to stand, he'd been trying to train himself to shoot left-handed. He'd improved a lot from that first day he'd picked up his sidearm again, but he was still a far cry from being as good as he had been. Still, he wasn't going to quit until he was close to being that fast and accurate once more.

Trace settled back in his room and, leaving his spectacles on the bedside table, he lay down. He was glad that no one in town knew who he was, and he was going to make sure it stayed that way. As far as anyone in Durango was concerned, he was Gabriel West, the newspaper editor. When the time came for Trace Jackson to make his move in pursuit of the Harris gang, Gabe West would simply disappear.

There were only two people in the world right then who knew Trace Jackson was still alive. Gibby was one, and the other was Will Campbell, the deputy he'd left behind in Eagle Pass to keep watch over the town while he and the posse went after the gang.

Trace's expression darkened as he remembered his reunion with Will. It had been about four weeks before, when he'd finally recovered enough to make the long trip into town. He'd deliberately ridden into Eagle Pass late at night, and he had taken great care not to allow himself to be seen. Everyone thought he was dead, and he wanted it to stay that way. He'd sought his deputy out at the jail, knocking quietly at the back door that opened into the unlighted alley.

"Who is it?" Will had demanded cautiously, not opening the door right away.

Trace had not answered. He'd waited in silence until Will finally unlocked the door and then held up the lamp he'd carried with him to take a look around. Trace would never forget the look of astonishment on his friend's face when he'd first seen him there half hidden in the shadows of the night.

"Trace—" Will had been completely shocked to find his friend standing before him.

"So you're the new sheriff, are you?" Trace had asked, giving him a half smile.

"Oh, my God! You're alive!"

"We need to talk privately," he'd told Will quickly, glancing around to make sure no one was watching them. "Can we go in the back room where no one will see us?"

Will had quickly regained his wits and stood aside to let Trace enter. He had closed and locked the door securely behind him. "Of course we can, but why? Everybody in town was devastated by what happened. Everyone thinks you're dead! Let's let everyone know you're all right—"

"No! That's why I came here now—at night. You're the only one I want to know that I'm still alive. As far as everyone in town is concerned, I was killed with the rest of the posse."

"But why?"

"Because the Harris gang thinks I'm dead, too."

"You're going after them," Will had stated with certainty, finally understanding his motive for secrecy.

"You're damned right I am," he'd told him. "And I'm not going to stop tracking them until they're all either dead or in jail."

"But what happened to you? Where have you been all this time?"

"I was shot three times and as close to dead as I ever care to get. Gibby Pruett found me and saved me. He hid me out and took care of me."

"But I talked to him when he came into town to report the ambush. He'd said that he'd buried all of you."

"That's what I told him to say. I didn't want word to get back to Harris that I was alive. I want to surprise him the next time I see him."

Will had completely understood. "What can I do to help you?"

"Nothing for right now. I'll be in touch."

"You need anything, anything at all, just let me know. Here—" His friend had dug into his pocket and given him all the cash he'd had on him. "It isn't a lot, but it'll help some."

"Thanks."

They'd shaken hands, and Trace had disappeared back into the night. He hadn't returned to Eagle Pass since. There was no need. The life he'd led there was over.

Trace had remained hiding out with Gibby for several more weeks until they'd journeyed into a different town to get supplies. It was there that he'd won a large sum of money along with the *Durango Weekly Star* from Ben Hollins in the poker game. He'd used his grandfather's name when he'd first sat in on the game, and after his big win, he'd decided to just keep using it. He needed anonymity for now. Before leaving for Durango, Trace had bought the clothes and eyeglasses he needed for his new identity. Durango was a busy, growing town, and he hadn't wanted to risk running into someone who might recognize him.

The unexpected opportunity that winning the paper afforded Trace couldn't have come at a better time. Working at the newspaper, he would be able to keep track of the Harris gang's activities while he continued to perfect his shooting skills and get his full strength back.

Trace's thoughts settled on the *Star* again— and on his "bride." It had been interesting, to say the least, getting caught up in the trap she'd set for the outlaw preacher. Had she been a man, he could have used her as a deputy back in Eagle Pass. From the talk he'd heard in the saloon, they were going to sell a lot of papers because of her efforts. He found himself anticipating the next morning, when he would make his first appearance at the *Star*'s office as the new owner/editor. He was looking forward to seeing Elise's expression when he finally introduced himself to her. It would prove interesting to see what she thought about having him for her boss.

"How did it go?" Andy Roland asked Elise when she returned to the *Star*'s office late that night.

"Marshal Trent was a great help. I've got all the details I need now," she told him excitedly as she patted the notebook she carried with her. She'd just spent two hours going over all that had happened with the marshal before he'd shown up at the wedding to arrest Farnsworth.

"Did you try to talk to Farnsworth, too?" the young man asked. He was only eighteen, but he already knew that he wanted to be a reporter. Currently, he was stuck doing the hard physical work at the paper, but he intended to work his way up eventually. Following Marshal Trent around earlier that day had been the highlight so far of his journalistic career.

"The marshal let me go back to the cell area where they're holding him, but Farnsworth wouldn't say anything."

"Aren't the men who did his dirty work a dangerous-looking bunch?" Andy asked. He'd been along when some of the arrests had been made.

"It's no wonder no one else ever caught on to the connection between them before. They hardly look like the types Farnsworth would be dealing with."

"But if he really was a preacher, those are the kinds of men he should be going after to save," Andy remarked with thoughtful insight.

"If Farnsworth had been a smart man, he would have tried to save them, but I don't think he's going to be saving anybody anytime soon—including himself. He's guilty, and we've got the proof for all to see right here in the *Star*. How many extra copies are you planning to print?"

"Another five hundred, I thought. Is that good enough?"

She nodded. "We can always go back to press if we have to. Too bad Ben isn't here to see this. He would have been very proud of us."

"He'd have been proud of you," Andy corrected, giving her full credit. "You always told him you were going to get him a big story, and you did."

"It has been exciting. I still can't believe that everything turned out so well—especially after getting his last-minute telegram that way."

"You were saying earlier that Ben lost the paper in a card game, but you didn't say who he'd lost it to. Do you know who our new boss is?"

"Ben didn't say in the wire. I guess we'll just have to keep things going on our own until the new owner decides to show up. And speaking of keeping things going, I'd better get this article finished so you can start the presses."

"I'll be ready whenever you are," Andy assured her. "From the looks of things, we're going to be here all night and maybe part of the morning."

She nodded. "We can't afford to run late. We've got to be on the street with this edition first thing tomorrow. We don't want to give anyone else the chance to beat us out with the story."

"Don't worry. This is your scoop. We're going to be the first and the best." He gave her a confident smile.

"Then I'd better get to work."

"By the way, who was the man you 'married'?" Andy asked, curious since Ben hadn't shown up in time. With all the talk about the arrest of the preacher and his gang after the ceremony, she hadn't said a word about her stand-in groom.

"I didn't get his name."

"You didn't even know his name, and you married him?" Andy was surprised.

"When a reporter is desperate, she'll go to any lengths to get her story—remember that!" She laughed. "Don't worry. As soon as we get done with this edition, I'll go find my 'husband' and thank him. I'm sure he's staying at one of the hotels in town. It shouldn't be too difficult to locate him, but right now, that's the least of my worries. We've got a paper to put out."

As Elise started to write the story, thoughts of her "groom"—and his kiss—interfered. It had been strange that her stand-in Ben had played along with her charade so completely and without question, only to disappear without a word—especially after the kiss he'd given her. As she recalled her reaction to his embrace, she was still a bit disconcerted by the feelings it had evoked in her. This man had been a total stranger, and yet she had responded to him as she'd never responded to any other man's embrace. Not that she'd had that much experience with men and kissing, but she had kissed a few of her suitors and none of their embraces had had anywhere near the effect of his. Surely, it had simply been the excitement of the moment that had caused her to react that way to him. That had to be it.

Elise realized as she tried to turn her attention to her writing again that she still owed "Ben" the money she'd promised to pay him for his help. As mild-mannered as he'd seemed, she figured he'd probably just been too timid to cause a scene there at the depot, and once the ceremony had started it had been too late for him to back out. She owed him the money, however, and she would pay her debt—once she'd finally finished her article for the paper.

Chapter Five

If Elise had taken time to think about it, exhaustion would have been too mild a word for the way she was feeling as she watched the *Star* come off the press in the early-morning hours. Her elation over the new edition tempered her weariness. She and Andy had gotten the paper out in record time.

PRETENDER IN THE PULPIT! The headline screamed.

A SNAKE IS DISCOVERED IN THE GARDEN OF EDEN! CHECK YOUR MARRIAGE LICENSES! PREACHER FARNSWORTH WAS A FRAUD! read the opening lines of her in-depth exposé on the outlaw preacher.

Elise picked up a copy and read it over quickly. When she looked up at Andy, she gave him a dazzling, triumphant smile.

"This is amazing! We actually did it!"

"We're going to be giving some of the other more established papers in town a run for their money now," Andy stated firmly, secure in the knowledge that they had just put out the best edition of the *Star* ever.

"It's about time, too. We've been doing good work all along, but we never had such a great opportunity before! This lead story is such a shocker."

"You did a fine job, Elise," Andy complimented her. "Without your persistence, the truth about Farnsworth would never have been uncovered, and the men working for him would never have been caught."

"Who would have thought that someone would be low enough to pass himself off as a man of the cloth and all the while be directing a gang of thieves?"

"He's going to be paying for it now that Marshal Trent's arrested him. The trial should take place reasonably soon, I would think."

"Yes, and that's going to make great copy, too! It feels good to know that we helped out the community. The bad news is that this one great story isn't going to sustain the paper forever. We can't just sit back on our laurels now. We have to keep coming up with new, exciting ideas, so everyone learns to count on the *Star* for the most important news!"

Elise's enthusiasm for going after a big story never wavered. She loved the thrill of hunting down the facts, of uncovering the truth about people and situations. Reporting was in her blood. She lived and breathed the newspaper. It was her life.

"That's easier said than done," Andy said, a note of weariness sounding now in his voice.

"There's no time for you to get tired on me now, Andy."

"Not even for the rest of the weekend?" he asked with a laugh.

"You know what I mean," she countered. "We'll have to work harder than ever. We have to keep topping our last success. We have to keep going after the most exciting and most outrageous stories. That's what will keep the *Star* selling like hotcakes."

"I know you've been working on Farnsworth for months and with Ben's blessing, but what's going to happen when the new owner shows up? What if he comes in and wants us to do something totally different?"

"Why would he? If what we're doing is successful, he'll support us one-hundred percent." Her expression faltered a bit as she considered the possibility that Andy might be right. "The object is to sell newspapers, isn't it?"

"Yes, but as the new editor, too, the owner might not see things our way."

"We'll see, but I wouldn't worry too much about that if I were you," she reassured him. "When our new boss finally does show up— whoever he is—he's going to be very pleased with what we've accomplished here in Durango."

"He might be, or he could just close the paper down without a thought and move on."

Though Andy had been in the newspaper business only a short time, he had already witnessed the comings and goings of several papers in the area. Newspaper owners always had the option to pack up their presses and head on to another town whenever it suited them. The uncertainty of not knowing who their new boss was and what they could expect from him was unsettling.

"No one is going to shut down the *Star*. We've worked too hard to build it up, and we're too good at what we do for him even to consider walking away. I just wish that I'd known how Ben felt about the paper. If I'd had any idea that he'd wanted out of the business, I would have bought the *Star* from him."

"I don't think he wanted to get rid of the *Star*," Andy commented, thinking of their past editor's devotion to the newspaper. "I think he believed his poker hand couldn't be beaten, so he bet everything he owned to make a big killing."

"And got killed in the process," Elise finished glumly. "I enjoyed working with Ben. He was a good man. I'm going to miss him."

"So am I," Andy agreed.

"I wonder what our new owner will be like?"

"Well, one thing's for certain," he began. At her questioning look, he finished, "Our new boss is certainly a lot better gambler than Ben ever was."

"Yes, he won us, and it looks as if he did it all fair and square. Let's just hope he's pleased with what he's acquired, and there's no reason why he shouldn't be. Do you know how many additional papers we're going to sell today all because of Farnsworth's arrest?" Her excitement returned as her thoughts turned to her lead story.

"So, the secret in making our new boss happy and keeping the *Star* going here in

Durango is to have great reporting so we can sell a lot of papers. Since it's so simple, why don't you tell me what your next story is going to be? You're going to have to top 'Pretender in the Pulpit'."

Though she was smiling, Elise's exhaustion finally won out. Her shoulders slumped at the thought of coming up with a new angle on another story for the following week right away. "Right this minute, I have absolutely no idea what I'll be writing about, but I'll think of something good before our deadline—you just wait and see."

Just then they heard the sound of someone entering the outer office, and they exchanged quizzical looks. It was still quite early in the morning, and it was most unusual for anyone to show up at this hour. Together, Elise and Andy started to walk to the front to see who had come in.

"Hello?" a man called out.

"Can we help—" Elise started to speak and then stopped in mid-sentence. Standing before her just inside the office door was "Ben." "Oh . . . Hello."

"Hello." Trace saw her come out of the back room with the young man right behind her, and he smiled. When last he'd seen her, she'd been wearing the wedding gown and veil and had looked delicate and ethereally beautiful to him. Now, wearing a blue, high-necked, long-sleeved daygown, she looked like a much different woman. She was still lovely, but in a more subtle way. Her lustrous dark hair was drawn back in a severe bun that was secured at the nape of her neck. It was a harsh style that on some women would have proven unflattering, but on Elise it only served to emphasize the beauty of her high cheekbones and the slender line of her neck. "I thought I might find you here. Nice office," he remarked, looking around.

"I'm so glad you stopped by," she said quickly, a light flush staining her cheeks. She was embarrassed that he had found her before she could find him to pay him the money she owned him.

Andy noticed her reaction and knew exactly who the stranger was. "You must be 'Ben.' "

"Actually, my name's Gabe, Gabe West, but yes, yesterday for a short while I was 'Ben.' "

"And I'm Andy Roland. I work here. From what Elise has told me, it sounds like you did a fine job yesterday. It's nice to finally meet you and find out your real name." Andy grinned at him as he extended his hand.

"It's nice to meet you, too."

The two men shook hands.

"Gabe?" Elise said his name slowly, as if testing the sound of it. "Where did you disappear to last night? I was looking for you and didn't know where you'd gone."

"I had to get my things from the stage depot and find a hotel room for the night."

"Neither one of you had a very exciting wedding night, did you?" Andy said with a laugh, looking at both of them.

The memory of this man's passionate kiss after they'd been declared man and wife deepened her blush. Even though she had "married" him, he really was still a stranger to her. Not wanting to think about his kiss or the effect it had on her, let alone talk about any wedding nights, Elise changed the topic. "I had planned to look for you later this morning, once we'd finished getting the paper out. I wanted to make sure you were paid for helping out as you did. I really appreciated what you did. If you'll wait here for a moment, I'll get the money for you."

Before Trace could say anything more, Elise retreated into the back room to get her purse. She was eager to pay him off, so he would leave. He'd served his purpose in her plan, and there was no need for them to have any further contact. All she wanted to do was go home and get some rest.

When Elise returned to the outer office with the money in hand, she found Gabe reading the new edition of the newspaper with great interest.

"Here's your money," she offered.

"Thanks. I'm glad I was able to help," he said as he looked up from the headlines to take the ten dollars from her. "It looks like things turned out just fine, judging from your article. I must compliment you. Your choice of headlines is very intriguing. Your idea to do an investigative report on Farnsworth was very successful."

The smile he gave her made Elise pause. He seemed almost handsome when he looked at her that way. She gave herself a mental shake at the thought. This was just her stand-in Ben. Even though the kisses he'd given her the day before had surprised her with their intensity, he was still a mild-mannered sort, nothing like the kind of men she was attracted to. She liked

76

strong men—men who stood for something. Gabe West was a nice man, and he'd come in handy yesterday when she'd found herself in a tight squeeze, but she had no interest in continuing a relationship of any sort with him. She was, however, pleased by his perceptive remarks about the *Star*.

"You played a large part in helping me pull the whole thing off. If you had balked at helping me at the stage depot or had refused to say the wedding vows and caused a scene yesterday, things wouldn't have turned out so well. I still can't believe that everything went as smoothly as it did after all the turmoil of worrying about whether the real Ben would show up in time or not."

"You should be very proud of what you accomplished."

"I am thrilled that Farnsworth and his men were arrested, but it certainly didn't go as I'd planned. I was supposed to 'marry' my boss, Ben Hollins. He was expected back from a business trip early in the week, but he was detained for some reason. Right before your stagecoach arrived, I received that telegram from him informing me that he wouldn't be returning at all. Your arrival yesterday afternoon was most timely."

"It was the first time I've ever gotten to rescue a damsel in distress."

Elise stifled a groan at his statement. She wasn't a damsel and she hadn't been in distress—well, not really. Just because he'd helped her out of a tight spot, she hoped he didn't think there was anything more to their relationship. Their marriage had been neither legal nor binding, and she'd paid him what she'd owed him in full.

"Is there something else we can do for you?" Elise asked cautiously. She deliberately used "we" and kept her tone cool, not wanting to encourage any more familiarity than they'd already established. He had helped her out; she had paid him; now it was time for them to go their separate ways.

"As a matter of fact"—Trace glanced around, studying the interior of the office—"there are a few things I needed to speak with you about."

"What?" she asked, unable to imagine what more he could possibly have to say to her.

Andy was growing more and more confused by their conversation, so he said nothing and just listened.

"I suppose I should explain. You see, we're going to be spending a lot more time together, you and I."

Elise suddenly felt uneasy. "You realize that the wedding ceremony wasn't binding and—"

He slanted her a knowing grin. "Certainly. If Farnsworth wasn't a real preacher and I wasn't the real Ben Hollins, then the ceremony wasn't real either, and we're not man and wife," he stated easily, enjoying her discomposure.

"Then I don't understand—" She was frowning, unable to imagine what it was he wanted with her.

"Here. Read this. I think it will explain everything."

Trace took a letter out of his jacket pocket and handed it to Elise. It was the note the real Ben had written, advising them that Gabriel West was the official new owner of the *Star*.

Trace waited quietly while both she and Andy read the short missive.

"I won the paper from Ben Hollins in the poker game. I'm the new owner of the *Star*."

Elise was stunned. She looked up at him in disbelief. *"You're* the new owner?"

"That's right. I'm the *Star's* new editor-in-chief, and I must say you've done a fine job with this issue. Ben told me you were good, Elise, but I didn't realize just how good you were until now." He paged through the newspaper with interest.

"But—" She found herself almost speechless.

"That's why, when I got off the stagecoach yesterday, I went along with you without saying anything. Ben had cautioned me about the lengths you would go to to get a story, and once you'd told me your name, I knew that yours was no ordinary wedding. I was sure something important was about to happen, and I was right." He didn't mention that her welcoming kiss had been more than a little influential in helping him make his decision.

Elise suddenly felt embarrassed and humiliated. Yesterday, she'd imagined that this man was a little less than intelligent, and now, here he was—her new boss! She struggled to recover her composure so she could deal more rationally with all that was happening to her.

"I take it you worked straight through the night to get this issue ready?" Trace asked.

"Yes. We just finished up a few minutes ago."

"Good. I'm impressed with the quality of your work. I was in the Mother Lode Saloon last night and heard some of the talk about the incident. It seems the townspeople can't wait to get their hands on today's paper. Ben was right about you, Elise. You are good—very good."

"Why, thank you."

"There's no need to thank me. I'm just telling you the truth. Andy, I take it she couldn't have done this without you?"

"We work very well together, sir."

"Not 'sir'—Gabe will do—and good job. Now, which room was Ben's office? I may as well get to work and see what needs to be done."

"The room off to the right was Ben's," Elise directed, and then asked, "Have you had much newspaper experience? Do you know a lot about it?"

"I don't know anything about the newspaper business," he admitted openly as he moved into Ben's office. "But I plan to be a very fast learner."

Elise and Andy glanced at each other in amazement as Trace walked away.

"So your 'husband' is now your boss?" Andy asked as he grinned at her.

"Oh, be quiet!" she told him, not appreciating his sense of humor right then.

Elise wasn't sure whether to be annoyed with Gabe West or not. He had had ample opportunity to introduce himself as the new owner of the newspaper the day before when he'd been playing along with the entire wedding charade, and he hadn't said a word. One part of her said she should just be glad that he'd helped out the way he had, but another part of her didn't like surprises—especially when they dealt with her career.

After debating with herself for a moment, Elise finally decided to follow Gabe into Ben's office and talk with him some more. She found him already sitting comfortably at Ben's desk, and she felt a pang of regret that she would never find Ben there again.

Elise had liked her former boss very much. They had gotten along very well together. He had tutored her and helped her develop her skills to become the reporter she was today. Seeing this man trying to take his place didn't sit well with her. Ben had been a knowledgeable newspaperman and a very supportive boss, while this new owner had already admitted that he had no experience whatsoever. The thought troubled her.

"Did Ben say what he was going to do next or where he was going?" she asked.

Trace looked up from the stack of correspondence he'd been sorting through. "No. We only talked for a short while after that last game. He wasn't in the best of moods after my four of a kind beat his full house."

"I don't doubt it. He did love this paper." Her tone was regretful.

"Then he shouldn't have risked it in a game of chance," Trace told her. "You should never wager what you can't afford to lose."

"So you're a professional gambling man, are you?" she countered, feeling the need to somehow defend Ben.

Trace's gaze met hers. He was careful to keep his expression unreadable. "Actually, my winning the newspaper was simple luck. I don't believe in taking unnecessary risks. Life is a big enough gamble as it is. I like sure things."

"What did you do for a living before you came here?" Elise asked, a bit curious about him and wanting to know more if she was going to be forced to work with him every day.

"I've done a number of things over the years," he answered, being deliberately evasive. "Most recently, though, I've just been traveling, trying to see the country. It looks like I'll be putting down roots here in Durango for now, though. Speaking of which—" He was glad to change the topic. He didn't want to answer any more personal questions. "I'm staying at the hotel right now, but I'll need to find something more permanent. Do you have any suggestions?"

"What about Ben's old house?" Andy asked from where he'd come to stand in the doorway. He wanted to let them know it was time to get the papers out for distribution.

"Ben had a place of his own?" Trace asked.

"He rented a small house on the outskirts of town. I can check on it for you," Elise offered.

"I'd appreciate it."

"Is there anything else we can do to help you right now? If not, I'd like to call it a day. Andy and I have both been working since the wedding yesterday."

"No, I'll be fine. You two go ahead. I've got a lot to learn, so I was just going to look through back issues of the newspaper and then go over the books to see how we stand financially. When will you be in the office again?"

"Andy takes care of things here most days. I'm in and out of the office, depending on what's happening that's newsworthy around town."

"Since this is Saturday, let's plan to meet on Monday, say three o'clock? By then, I should have a better idea of what needs to be done around here."

Elise didn't like the sound of that, but she held her tongue. He'd already admitted that he didn't know what he was talking about when it came to the newspaper business, so there was no point in trying to discuss anything more with him right then. "All right, I'll see you Monday afternoon."

Elise and Andy quit the office and walked slowly through town together on their way home.

"What are you thinking?" Andy asked. He could tell by her unusual silence that something was troubling her. "What's bothering you?"

She glanced at him, her expression a bit angry. "I'm not sure what I think. Gabe has just waltzed right in and taken over. He played Ben's part in the wedding; he's sitting at Ben's desk; he's reading Ben's mail, and now he might end up actually living in Ben's house."

"Gabe is our new owner. We can't hide from that."

"I know," she said tightly. "I guess I'm reacting this way because he could have told me the truth yesterday, but for some reason he didn't."

"Maybe he just wanted to watch you in action. He said Ben had talked to him about you, and you have to admit you can be pretty impressive when you're on a story. I mean, there you were in a wedding dress desperately looking for a groom—"

"I wasn't desperate. Well, not too desperate," she corrected. "I still had almost an hour left before the ceremony was to begin."

Andy laughed outright at her. "Everything's worked out all right. That's the important thing. Marshal Trent caught Farnsworth and his gang, and we made our deadline. The papers are being delivered even as we speak. It's been a good week—a very good week."

"It has, hasn't it?" Her mood lightened a bit as Andy put things in better perspective for her.

"Very. I can't say that I'm glad Ben lost the paper in a poker game the way he did, but Gabe doesn't seem like he's going to be too hard to work with. At least, he's not going to pack up the presses and leave town. He's going to keep the *Star* running, and that means we're both still employed."

Elise knew everything he was saying was right. "I guess I'm just tired."

They stopped in front of her house.

"You have every right to be tired, but don't pat yourself on the back or let yourself relax too much. We've got another paper to get out next week, so you'd better start thinking of what you're going to be reporting on next."

"I'll worry about that on Monday, Andy," she told him with a weary laugh. "I'll see you then."

Chapter Six

Alone in the office, Trace worked at cleaning off the top of Ben's desk as best he could. He reviewed all the correspondence and sorted through the unpaid bills. That done, he started to go through the desk drawers and was surprised when he discovered a half-full bottle of whiskey and a six-gun in the bottom drawer.

"Ben, you had damned good taste in liquor," he muttered to himself as he noted the brand name of the whiskey. "And working around here, you probably needed both the whiskey and the gun."

Trace smiled grimly at the thought. He was certain that if the good Preacher Farnsworth managed to break out of jail right then and got to a gun, they would be in for some trouble at the office. It wasn't unusual in the wilder Western towns for an offended party to call out and duel with an editor. Some editors had even been shot down in cold blood and killed for what they printed in their papers. He wondered if Elise took any precautions for her own safety. He intended to make sure that she did when he spoke with her on Monday.

Ben's private stock was tempting right then, but Trace denied himself. Instead, he took up the handgun and checked it over, making sure it was in good working order. Ben's choice of weapons was as excellent as his taste in liquor. The sidearm was in good condition and had been left in the drawer fully loaded—just in case it was needed in a hurry.

Intrigued by Ben's practice of keeping a gun so close at hand, Trace laid it aside and got up from the desk to go get a stack of back issues of the paper from where they were kept on file in the outer office. He wanted to familiarize himself with Ben's editing. He wanted to study his predecessor's style and learn from it. He also wanted to see what else Elise had been reporting on. By the time he was done reading everything, he planned to know what the town was really like, who its most prominent citizens were, and what the lead stories had been for the last year. Trace settled back in at the desk and started to read.

It was late in the afternoon when Trace came across the paper with the headline DEADLY HARRIS GANG STRIKES AGAIN. He quickly scanned Elise's article detailing the gang's robbery of a Pueblo bank and their cold-blooded murder of several of the bank's employees. That robbery had happened just three weeks before they'd ridden into Eagle Pass.

Suddenly, Trace needed to know what she'd written about the gang's murderous attempted robbery in his town. He sorted through the papers until he found her report on that tragic day.

MURDER IN EAGLE PASS, the headline screamed.

Trace read over her report of the failed robbery attempt and Ed Rankins's murder. It was accurate, and he was surprised when he read on:

Sheriff Trace Jackson and his deputy Will Campbell arrived on the scene in time to foil the robbery attempt. During the ensuing escape by the Harris gang, however, unarmed citizen Ed Rankins was killed, shot down by the fleeing outlaws.

Sheriff Jackson is renowned for his no-nonsense law enforcement. He immediately formed a posse to go after the gang.

It is this reporter's opinion that the Harris gang's days are numbered. It is a well-known fact that Sheriff Jackson always gets his man. He is one of the most respected—and feared—lawmen in the state.

Elise's praise left Trace feeling cold and disgusted with himself. If he'd been such a damned good lawman, he would have arrested the Harris gang in town before Ed got shot. If he'd been such a damned good lawman, the members of his posse would be alive, and Harris and his men would already have been hanged.

The memory of his friends' murders infuriated him, and he all but threw the edition of the *Star* down.

Suddenly, it didn't matter to Trace how early it was. He didn't care. He needed a drink. He got a glass from the tray that held the water pitcher nearby and sat back down at the desk. Taking Ben's bottle out of the drawer, he poured himself a stiff drink and stared at the amber liquid for a long moment, his emotions in turmoil.

Trace picked up the paper again and reread Elise's article.

> It is a well-known fact that Sheriff Jackson always gets his man. He is one of the most respected—and feared—lawmen in the state.

He gave a derisive laugh, downed the shot of whiskey, and poured another. He didn't like feeling helpless. He was a man accustomed to going out and getting things done, but where the Harris gang was concerned, nothing was going to happen fast. It was going to take time to track the outlaws down.

And Trace Jackson had never been a patient man.

Taking up the following week's edition, Trace began to read again. He finished skimming that copy and reached for the next. He stopped and stared down at the headline.

ENTIRE POSSE SLAIN! EAGLE PASS SHERIFF TRACE JACKSON AND HIS DEPUTIES AMBUSHED AND MURDERED BY THE HARRIS GANG! KILLERS STILL ON THE LOOSE!

He drew a deep breath and kept on reading.

> As we reported several weeks ago, the Harris gang's attempt to rob the bank in

Eagle Pass was foiled by Sheriff Trace Jackson. Ed Rankins, a local citizen, was shot and killed during their escape. Sheriff Jackson immediately mounted a posse to track them down.

Word has just reached us that the lawmen riding in the posse were ambushed and slain. There were no survivors. Gibby Pruett, a miner on his way into town for supplies, found their bodies on the trail.

The deaths of Sheriff Jackson and his men is a tragedy for Eagle Pass and for the state of Colorado. By reputation, Jackson was known to be an honorable, dedicated, courageous man. He will be sorely missed. It's a shame that there aren't more good men like him around.

Will Campbell has been named the new sheriff of Eagle Pass.

Trace downed his second shot of whiskey as he stared at the article. Honorable, dedicated, courageous—he didn't feel like any of those things right now, and he wondered if he ever would again. He wondered, too, how much longer he was going to have to wait before he got to have his final showdown with Harris.

Picking up Ben's gun, Trace savored the weight of the weapon in his hand. It felt good to be holding it. He'd left his own sidearm in the hotel room. There had been no point in wearing it to the office. But now, thinking about Harris and all the terror he'd wreaked, Trace realized that he was looking forward to the day when he would come face-to-face with the murderer.

Trace had never looked forward to killing a man before. He'd always used his weapon only when he was forced to. But now, with Harris, things were different. He wanted to see the outlaw dead, and for the first time in his life, he was going to enjoy doing the shooting. It was personal.

Reaching into his jacket pocket, he took out a small item wrapped in a handkerchief. He laid it on his desktop and carefully unwrapped it. He sat there, staring down at his sheriff's badge, remembering the last day he'd worn it. He knew he should feel guilty about the emotions he was experiencing about Harris, but he didn't. Before their confrontation was over, one of them would be dead.

Trace drew a ragged breath as he took off his spectacles and set them aside, then wearily rubbed his eyes. He would know no peace, have no rest, until justice had been done.

The badge made him think of Eagle Pass. It had been his home for over six years. He missed the town and the friends he'd made there, but there would be no going back until he could return with the news that Harris and his men would no longer be robbing or killing anyone. Only when he could tell the townspeople that Harris and his men were dead and buried would he return.

Trace's hand closed over the badge, his fist clenched with the fierceness of his emotion. The sharp edges of the star cut into his palm, but he barely felt it. He wondered if there would ever be a day when he would wear it again. He had no answer.

"I didn't know you were going to be staying

here at the office all day," Elise said as she came to stand in the office door. She stopped in mid-sentence and stared at her new boss. With his eyeglasses off and his expression so dark and serious—almost dangerous—Gabe looked like an entirely different man, and this man was a complete stranger to her. "Oh—I'm sorry. I didn't mean to interrupt you." She felt suddenly awkward, as if she'd walked in on something private.

Trace tried to hide his own shock at Elise's sudden appearance. He quickly donned his eyeglasses, then shoved the badge deep into his pocket. He faced her and gave her a weak smile, reassuming his Gabe West manner. "There's a lot I need to learn if I'm going to be running this paper. So I decided to stay late," he answered. "What brings you here? I thought you wouldn't be back in until Monday."

The sight of him once again in his glasses, looking innocuous, left Elise disoriented and a bit confused. She wondered vaguely how he could have changed so quickly or if she'd just imagined that he'd looked so different. She'd always considered herself an astute judge of people, and the difference in him troubled her. "I had a message for you."

"Oh?" Trace asked rather abruptly, wanting her to leave. He wasn't in the mood for company or light conversation. He was angry with himself for letting his guard down so carelessly. She'd managed to enter the outer office and approach the door without his even hearing her. The realization that he'd been so negligent infuriated him. If he planned to go after Harris, he had damned well better be more aware of his surroundings. A mistake like this one could cost him his life on the trail.

"Ben's landlord, Charles Rodgers, came to see me this afternoon. He'd just gotten a wire from Ben letting him know that he wouldn't be coming back and instructing him to ask me to pack up and ship his personal things to him. So, while Charles was there, I asked him if he wanted to rent the home again and I told him about you. He said he'd like to meet with you—if you're interested," she explained quickly, sensing his curtness and thinking he wanted to be alone.

Her offer distracted him from his darker emotions. "Did you say earlier that the house is out of town?"

"It's not too far. It's an easy ride."

"Yes, I would like to take a look at it, if that's all right with you? Would you have time to show it to me?" He glanced out his window to see that it was near sundown.

"It's too late to go tonight, but we could ride out there tomorrow, if you'd like. That would give me time to pack up Ben's things while we're there."

"That sounds fine. Thank you."

"It'll be good to have company while I'm working on Ben's things. And I have another offer for you."

He gave her a quizzical look.

"My grandmother and I are attending the church social tonight. There will be dinner and some other activities, and my grandmother thought you might want to join us. It would give you the opportunity to meet some of the townsfolk—Charles included. He did say he would be there."

"What time does it start?"

"It's already going on. I've got to meet my grandmother there in a few minutes. Would you like to go?"

Trace looked down at the papers strewn on his desk. "Just let me put some of this in order."

"I see you found Ben's gun—and his whiskey," she remarked, coming farther into the office. "He always kept the gun handy, just in case there was any trouble."

"Did he ever have cause to use it?"

"Several times, actually. One crazy miner came charging in here, accusing Ben of lying about him in an article in the paper. He was just about ready to smash the place up when Ben drew the gun on him. He backed down real fast once he saw that Ben was armed. Another time, two men confronted him out on the street and tried to beat him up for something he'd printed. Ben managed to break free and run in here to get the gun. They came after him, but backed down when they saw that he had a weapon. Sometimes people can't bear to see the truth about themselves in print. It can get ugly—and deadly."

"Let's just hope we don't get anybody too excited around here any time soon," he said, deliberately acting as if he were scared to be handling the gun as he put it back in the drawer.

"It might not hurt you to learn how to handle one—just in case," she advised.

"I suppose it couldn't," he agreed with her. "It's been a while since I've used one."

"If you need any help, I can give you a few pointers. I learned how to shoot when I was a

93

little girl. My father thought it was important that I know how to defend myself."

"Smart man, your father."

"Well, if you want to start practicing, you'll have plenty of room once you're settled in at Ben's."

"Good. If we're going to continue to publish articles in the paper that are as rousing as your story on Farnsworth, we're going to have to be ready for all kinds of trouble." He gave her a smile.

"Let's just hope not too much," she said. "So, are you ready to go to the social? I hate to think of you sitting here all alone just going through the papers for the rest of the evening. You haven't eaten yet, have you?"

"As a matter of fact, I haven't had anything to eat since this morning. I'd enjoy going and meeting everyone—if you're sure I won't be intruding on your plans." He really wasn't in the mood to do much socializing, but if it gave him the opportunity to set himself up in a house, he'd do it.

"No, you won't be intruding. My grandmother will be pleased. Since I told her this morning exactly who you were, she's been looking forward to seeing you again."

"It'll be my pleasure." He put the cap on the whiskey bottle and stowed it in the drawer with the gun, then stood up.

Elise came to stand by his desk. "Which edition were you reading?"

"The one about the ambush by the Harris gang."

She suppressed a shudder. "They're a savage bunch. I still can't believe that they were able to

94

ambush and kill Sheriff Jackson and the posse from Eagle Pass," she told him, staring down at the headline of the paper he'd just been reading. "They were such good men."

"Did you know any of the people from Eagle Pass? The article sounded as if you were acquainted with them."

"I'd never met Sheriff Jackson, but his reputation was well known. He was one tough lawman. It's so hard to believe that the Harris gang can rob and kill like that, and get away with it. It seems no one can stop them. Surely there must be someone out there who can bring them in. I thought Jackson was the man to do it, but—"

"They really were ambushed that way?"

"From what I heard," she told him sadly. "The carnage must have been unbelievable. As good as Sheriff Jackson was, I can't believe he died without putting up some kind of fight."

"So where are Harris and his men now?" he asked, trying to sound conversational. "Have you heard any news of where they might be hiding or planning their next crime? I hope they're not planning on coming to Durango."

"I haven't heard a word about where they are or what they might be up to. I wish I had. I'd tell Marshal Trent. I'd love to be the one who helped bring them in. The Farnsworth arrest was good, but the Harris gang—" Her eyes were aglow. "We'd sell a lot of papers with that for our lead story."

"As bloodthirsty as that gang is, I would be careful what I wished for," he cautioned her, deliberately making himself sound nervous about the idea of dealing with such killers. "Men like Farnsworth are one thing, but this Harris—"

"Don't look so worried, Gabe. You've got your gun right there in the drawer, and I've got mine in my purse," she told him, opening her drawstring purse to show him the derringer she carried. "If the Harris gang ever shows up, between the two of us, we'll be ready for them."

"If Jackson and his posse couldn't bring them in, how do you think that we could?"

" 'The pen is mightier than the sword,' " she quoted, smiling excitedly at the thought.

"I've never known a pen that could shoot straight," he countered, still playing timid. He wanted nothing more than to face down the gang, but when the time came, he didn't want Elise anywhere around. He didn't want to risk her getting hurt.

"That's beside the point. Just think how it would look if we were the ones who managed to help bring them in!"

"And just how to do you propose to do that with just a two-shot derringer and a newspaper?"

"Don't forget—you've got a gun, too! If the time comes when we get the chance, I'm sure we'll think of something." She sounded confident.

" 'We'll' think of something," he repeated, nervously clearing his throat. "Let's think about this for a while. For all that Farnsworth was a miserable excuse for a human being and deserved to be arrested and put in jail, his worst crimes were robbery and impersonating a preacher. With Harris and his men, you'll be dealing with a whole different kind of criminal.

Judging from what I just read in your accounts, they're nothing but cold-blooded killers."

"You don't have to be afraid, Gabe," she reassured him with a smile. "I don't even know where they are right now."

"Good," he answered, sounding relieved, and he was. "Let's keep it that way. Dealing with them would mean nothing but trouble for us."

"We'd increase our circulation," Elise said, taunting him with the idea.

"We might end up dead, too, just like everyone else they've come into contact with."

"Or we might be the ones who finally manage to trap them—just like I trapped Farnsworth." She could just see the headline in her mind, and the prospect excited her even more. "Where's your sense of adventure? These men are murderers who should be behind bars! If we can help put them there, it would be wonderful—for us and for the whole state of Colorado."

"Yes, it would be, if there were some guarantee that you wouldn't get hurt in the process."

"Nothing happened with Farnsworth."

"It could have. Or have you forgotten already how he was threatening you?"

"Oh, I wasn't going to get hurt. Marshal Trent was there," she answered simply and then added, "And, of course, you helped, too."

The fact that she gave more credit to Trent for saving her that day for some reason annoyed Trace. All the lawman did was walk up and point his gun at Farnsworth.

"You did manage to come away from your encounter with the preacher unharmed, but from everything I've read about Harris, I doubt you'd be as lucky with him. Harris wouldn't try to talk his way out of a trap. He would shoot his way out."

Elise saw a sudden glimmer of fierceness in Gabe's eyes and was surprised by it. It seemed so at odds with his usual personality. "All right, I won't go looking for trouble."

"Good."

"Now, shall we go to the social? I doubt seriously that Harris or any of his men will be there."

"Let's hope not, anyway."

"Have you ever been to a box dinner before?" Elise asked as they left the office and made their way to the church. "It's an auction, you know."

"I've been to a few. Did you cook a dinner?"

"Yes, my grandmother took it over with her when she went. Why are you so surprised?" she asked, noticing his quick sidelong glance.

"Somehow, I never pictured you as a cook."

"Truth be told, I never wanted to be one, but my mother insisted that I learn all the necessary elements of running a household, so I learned to cook at a very young age."

"Ah, but are you good?" Trace asked.

"Why? Are you planning to bid on mine?"

"You never know," he answered with a grin. He knew that at church box dinners, the woman who made the dinner had to sit with the man who bought it.

As they neared the church, they could see the crowd gathering.

"It looks like the social is going to be quite a success," Trace remarked.

"They usually are. Everyone has to eat, and if we can raise money for the church this way, why not?"

"Whose dinners are the most popular?"

"It's a known fact that my grandmother and Mrs. Buxton are the two best cooks in town. Their meals cause the biggest bidding contest. One year, George bid twenty-five dollars for my grandmother's dinner."

"What was it?"

"Stew and her famous apple pie."

"She must be a really good cook to get the bidding up that high. I just might bid on hers."

Elise laughed. "She'd be delighted to have you join in the bidding war. In fact, she'll be delighted that you just showed up. She wondered what happened to you after the wedding when you left without saying anything. This morning, when I told her that you were the new owner of the *Star*, she was most amused."

"She was?"

"Oh, yes. She figured you had to be one very nice man to play along with us at the stage depot and at the wedding ceremony, and then to learn that you were my new boss—well, I think her exact words were, 'Your stand-in Ben is not only a good sport, he must be an excellent poker player, too.'"

Trace laughed. "I may not be so much an excellent player, as I was just plain lucky that night."

"So you think you were lucky to win the paper?" Elise glanced over at him.

"From what I read today and the success of your investigation, I'd say the newspaper is a fine investment."

"I hope so. I know Ben was concerned about the falling number of subscriptions."

"Then we'll just have to work at making the *Star* better," he said with conviction, although he wondered how long he'd really be there to worry about it.

Chapter Seven

When Elise and Trace reached the church, they were warmly welcomed by Reverend Ford, the pastor. Elise quickly introduced Trace and then they moved on.

Claire had been with George tending to their baskets of food when she saw the two of them coming and hurried over to greet them.

"Ben! Or should I call you Mr. West?" Claire asked with a smile. "It's so good to see you again—my almost grandson-in-law. I'm so glad Elise was able to convince you to join us tonight."

"My pleasure, Mrs.—" Trace found himself drawn to the older woman's friendliness and genuine good nature. His paternal grandmother had helped to raise him after his mother died when he was young, and he truly enjoyed being around older people.

"Just call me Claire," she interrupted, beaming up at him. "Claire will be just fine, and thank you so much for helping Elise yesterday. The wedding would have turned into a complete disaster without you. You were wonderful, stepping in as you did."

"Well, it's not every day a man gets off a stage in a strange town and walks straight into the arms of a beautiful bride."

"Elise did look lovely yesterday. Maybe someday she really will be a bride." Claire sighed. She had long thought Elise should find a good man and settle down. At twenty-two, her granddaughter was past the most marriageable age for a woman. Claire hated the prospect of the career-driven Elise becoming an old maid.

"When the right man comes along, I'll marry him, Grandmother. Until then, I'm more than happy to concentrate all my energy on my job at the newspaper," Elise put in. She knew how her grandmother felt about her unmarried state, and she didn't even want to think about that tonight.

"Even though it wasn't a real wedding, you two did make quite a handsome couple. Didn't you think so, George?" Claire asked as he joined them.

"Yes, they did. They certainly had Preacher Farnsworth fooled, too. He believed it was a true marriage. It was a good thing he'd never met the real Ben Hollins before the ceremony."

"Thank heaven for that. Just think what might have happened if Farnsworth had discovered the deception beforehand. It could have been even more dangerous than it was when Marshal Trent showed up, and that was frightening enough."

"It's hard to say what the man might have done, as desperate as he was," George agreed.

"Whatever he'd tried, I'm sure Gabe would have thought of something to help save the day." Claire looked up at him, her gaze upon him admiringly. For all that he looked more bookish than physically fit, she knew he was a most intelligent, very brave young man. "You certainly came to the marshal's aid, tackling Farnsworth when you did. God only knows how many people would have gotten hurt if you hadn't helped out."

"I'm just glad everything turned out all right," he told her.

Elise still found it difficult to believe that Gabe had helped Marshal Trent that much by tripping and falling into the preacher, but she wasn't going to argue the point tonight. She was there to just relax and enjoy herself for a while.

"Everything turned out wonderfully with the wedding, but now, young man, it's time to show you what we ordinarily do for an exciting time in Durango," Claire teased. At his questioning look, she went on, "It's almost time for the box dinner auction. We're a very Wild West town, you know."

Trace grinned at her. Durango hadn't been in existence very long, and it hadn't experienced the roughness of life that affected so many other Western towns. "From what I heard about how good a cook you are, I bet there have been more than a few standoffs over who was going to win your dinner."

"That's right, but I've never had to shoot anybody yet," George confirmed with a laugh.

"Elise said the bidding can get pretty expensive."

"Claire's home-cooked meals are worth every penny you pay for them."

"I'll remember that," Trace told her. He fully intended to bid on Claire's dinner, but as much as he would have liked to dine with her, he knew that ultimately he would stop bidding so George could win. "So this whole auction is for charity?"

"All the monies raised go to the orphans' home that the church supports," Elise told him. "As soon as Reverend Ford gets ready, he'll have Mrs. Stevens call us up to the front table and start the bidding. She and her daughter, Julie, are running the fund raiser for the orphanage this year."

"Why, there you are, 'Ben'!" Julie said as she spied them across the grounds and went to speak with them. "I was wondering if I'd ever get to see you again."

Trace looked in her direction to see a very beautiful young blonde coming their way. "Hello."

"Hello," she said in a rather sultry voice, eyeing him with open interest. She'd done a lot of thinking overnight, and her anger and heartbreak over Ben disappearing had been replaced by curiosity over this new man in town. "I'm Julie—and I know you're not really Ben."

Trace laughed aloud. "No, I'm not, and it's very perceptive of you to notice. My name's Gabe West."

"I'm sorry I didn't get the chance to speak with you after your wedding. Things were a little confused there for a while."

"So you were there—I thought you looked a bit familiar."

Julie's smile widened, and she gave a toss of her blond mane. He had noticed her. The knowledge only reinforced the decision she'd made earlier that day: *She wanted to know more about this man—much more.* "Oh, yes. I wouldn't have missed Elise and Ben's nuptials for the world, but you can imagine my shock when you were the one who came out with Preacher Farnsworth. Yours was quite the most exciting wedding I've ever attended."

"It did have its moments," he agreed, his expression darkening as he thought of Farnsworth's desperate attempt to escape using Elise as his shield.

"Well, it's delightful to meet you, Gabe." She said his name with soft emphasis as she touched his arm in a familiar way. "And I hope you enjoy your stay with us in Durango. Will you be staying here long?"

"It certainly looks as if he will be," Elise interrupted her. There was something about Julie that irritated her, but she could never decide exactly what it was.

"Why, Elise." Julie turned her attention to the other woman. The day before she would have had difficulty speaking to her, believing she was truly marrying Ben, but now she smiled at her with ease as she said, "Congratulations on your success yesterday. You must be quite pleased."

"Yes, we are. We helped to put an outlaw and his men behind bars."

"We?"

"Gabe, here, is the new owner of the *Star*. He's the man who won the *Star* from Ben in a poker game."

"You're the new owner? That's wonderful! It's so good to know that you really will be staying on in Durango!" Julie was truly surprised by this bit of news.

"I'm going to enjoy living here, I'm sure," Trace said. "I plan on working with Elise and Andy to make the *Star* the best newspaper in town."

"I'm sure you will, Gabe," Julie told him.

Elise watched the interplay between the two, and for some reason, found herself grinding her teeth in irritation. Not that she cared one way or another about Gabe. It was just that Julie was such an accomplished flirt that she always had men falling all over themselves trying to impress her. Even Ben had not proven immune to her charms. She was talking to Gabe now in the same way she used to talk to Ben, and he seemed to be as smitten as Ben had been with her flirtatious ways.

"Do you know whose dinner you're going to buy tonight?" Julie asked him.

"When everything smells so delicious, it's not going to be an easy decision," he replied evasively. "But I have it from reliable sources that Claire and Mrs. Buxton are the two best cooks in town."

Julie tried not to look annoyed by his answer. "If it's only food you're looking for tonight," she said in a softer voice, leaning toward him, "then you'll be quite pleased with anything those two ladies cook up. But remember—there's more to the social than just eating a dinner. There will be dancing afterward."

"Oh, I see." And he did. He recognized the look in her eyes, and he had to admit that she was an attractive woman. Right then, though, he couldn't risk getting involved with any female. He had only one thing on his mind, and that was getting ready to take on Harris.

"Ladies and gentlemen!" came the call from Adele Stevens as she accompanied the Reverend to the head table. "It's time for the fun to begin."

Julie knew she'd be needed to help her mother with the bidding, so she excused herself. She looked up at Gabe and said with meaning, "I hope I'll get to see more of you later."

"I'll be here."

"Good." She hurried off.

Elise watched Julie walk away and was glad she'd gone.

"Is everyone hungry and ready to eat?" the Reverend called out.

A rousing "Yes" came from those gathered around.

"Then without further delay, let's start the bidding." He walked to the first table that had a meal displayed for all to see.

"This is Miss Charity Hancock's box. For tonight's festivities, she's cooked stew for her main dish, and she has a thick, delicious pudding for dessert. "What bid do I have for our first meal tonight?"

The bidding started at a reasonable rate, for no one wanted to buy anything too cheaply. The idea was to raise money for a good cause, so everyone wanted to pay as much as they could afford to help out. After some bidding back and forth, her dinner was sold for five dollars. The woman was pleased with the amount—and with the man who'd bought it. They walked off together arm-in-arm carrying her basket with the food in it. The Reverend went on to the next woman's meal.

"Five dollars is about average for a dinner," Elise confided to Gabe as they watched all that was transpiring.

"No wonder you were so impressed with the twenty-five that was paid for your grandmother's."

"Oh, no!" she said suddenly, tersely.

The dramatic change in her tone surprised Gabe, and he glanced down at her sharply. "What's wrong?"

"I'm going to be up for auction in a few more minutes, and Clint Parker just got here." She all but groaned.

"Who's Clint Parker?" Gabe asked, wondering at her reaction to him.

"He's one of the ranch hands on the Double Bar M Ranch."

"And?" Her description had done nothing to explain her reaction to the man.

"And he always comes to these auctions to buy my dinner." She saw Clint watching her, and she did her best not to make eye contact with him. She concentrated instead on what she was saying to Gabe.

"So you don't want this Clint to buy your dinner? I thought that was the purpose of this whole thing—to get people excited about the auction."

She gave him a strained look. "That's the problem. Clint gets excited all right. He fancies himself in love with me."

"I take it you don't return his feelings."

"No, and from the look on his face, I'd say he just found out that I didn't officially marry Ben yesterday. It's going to be a very long night."

Trace said nothing, but looked on quietly as the cowboy shouldered his way through the crowd, making his way toward Elise. Clint Parker was a big, powerful-looking man. Trace could see that the other man's gaze was riveted solely on Elise, and there was a look of open hunger in his eyes.

"Well, hey, darlin', what's this I hear that your wedding wasn't real?" Clint asked, grinning broadly as he strode up beside her. "It just about broke my heart when I heard you were getting married—to somebody else."

Elise was as ready for him as she would ever be. "That's right, Clint. I set the whole wedding up as a trap to catch Preacher Farnsworth and his gang."

"You had me worried there for a while, sweetheart. I thought you were really going to go through with it. You know you could have used me in the ceremony," he said, his voice thick with meaning. "I would have been happy to help you out."

"The next time I plan a wedding like this one, I'll make sure to ask you."

"Good, and maybe your next one will be a real one with a real preacher," he said, grinning lustily at her, imagining all the fun he would have had with her as his bride. "You could do a lot worse than ol' Clint, you know."

"I'm sure I could," she answered, although right then she doubted it. She was already dreading the rest of the night to come. She knew he would be hovering nearby all evening long. "Clint, this is the new owner of the *Star*, Gabe West. Gabe, this is Clint Parker."

The two men acknowledged each other.

Clint turned his attention back to Elise and winked at her knowingly. "How soon is your dinner going to be up for bids? I'm real hungry tonight."

"I think there are two or three more before mine."

"I'll just have to wait around for the fun to start, then," he declared, determined to buy her dinner and spend the rest of the social with her.

Elise managed a smile, but it wasn't easy. "I don't imagine it will be long, the way things have been going."

Even as she spoke, the Reverend was concluding the bidding on another dinner and getting ready to move on to the next.

Trace watched as Mrs. Buxton's was the next to be offered. The bidding was hot and heavy, and she was finally auctioned off for twenty-two dollars.

"Not a record, but a wonderful amount!" Reverend Ford announced with pride. "Thank you, Mrs. Buxton. And now for your stiffest competition. Gentlemen—it's time to bid on Claire Martin's dinner. Claire, would you care to come up here and join me?"

Claire made her way to stand with him at the table over the food she'd prepared. Everything looked delicious, especially her apple pie, and Trace easily understood why hers went for such a high price.

"Do I hear an opening bid, please?"

"Ten dollars!" George shouted out, wanting to impress Claire with his fervor.

"Twelve!" another man countered.

"We have twelve dollars. Do I hear any other bids?"

Trace was watching Claire and knew the friendly competition between her and Mrs. Buxton meant a lot. He called out, "I bid eighteen!"

A rousing round of applause swelled through the crowd. Elise didn't say anything, but she gave him a questioning look.

"It's for your grandmother's dinner," he said simply.

Clint looked over at him and, immediately judging him by his clothing and eyeglasses, dismissed him as totally harmless. He grinned at him as he asked, "So you like to eat dinner with little old ladies, do you?"

"I like good food, and Elise tells me that Claire's cooking is the best."

As they were talking, George bid again, running it up to twenty dollars.

"Twenty-two," Trace countered, drawing looks from all in attendance.

The tension mounted, for they were even with Mrs. Buxton's price now. Everyone waited, breathlessly, to see if George or anyone else would top his bid. The silence was deafening.

"What the hell—uh, er, pardon me, Reverend," George mumbled. He turned red when he realized what he'd said. "I bid twenty-five dollars. I paid it last year, I might as well pay it again."

The crowd roared with good-natured laughter over his slip of the tongue. They all knew

George was an honest, God-fearing man. Everyone waited to see what the new owner of the newspaper would do next.

"You going to bid again?" Clint asked.

"Do I hear another bid?" the Reverend asked.

Trace was wondering whether to push the bidding any higher, when Elise shifted a little nearer to him.

"I think I may need your help in the bidding tonight, if you know what I mean." Her green-eyed gaze mirrored the desperation she was feeling as she glanced toward the other man, letting Gabe know without saying a word that she was hoping he would save her from having to spend the evening with Clint.

Trace frowned for a moment at the thought that she needed to be rescued from the cowboy. As he thought about it, though, he actually found the situation mildly amusing. This was the same woman who'd taken on an outlaw preacher the day before and had seen him sent to jail. Yet today, she wanted to be saved from an ordinary ranch hand. "You know," he told her, grinning down at her easily, "I did get paid recently, so I do have an extra ten dollars I can spend on dinner tonight."

Elise didn't say a thing. She saw the twinkle in his dark eyes and hoped it meant what she thought it meant. She turned her attention back to the bidding on her grandmother's meal.

"I have a bid of twenty-five dollars. Do I hear another?" Reverend Ford called out one last time, looking Trace's way. "No? Then you're the lucky man, George. Come on up here and get your dinner."

Trace watched with pleasure as George picked up Claire's basket and escorted her away to one of the tables where they could relax and dine together.

"Looks like you ran out of money," Clint remarked smugly. "Too bad."

"There are a few more dinners left," Trace reminded him casually. "I don't think I'm going to go hungry."

"Looks like it's my turn now," Elise said as she started forward to stand with Reverend Ford.

"Don't worry, darlin', I'll take care of you," the cowboy promised boldly. He'd been saving his pay for weeks now just to have enough to bid on her dinner. He didn't get into town to see her very often, so he had to take full advantage while he could.

Elise approached the Reverend. As she neared the table, he put his hands up in the air.

"Don't arrest me, Elise! I really *am* a preacher!" he quipped.

Everyone roared with laughter.

Elise blushed as she laughed along with them. "Don't worry. My days of arresting preachers are over. You're safe with me."

"That's good to know. Congratulations on your accomplishment. That was a very brave thing you did yesterday. I'm glad it turned out all right."

"So am I."

"Shall we open the bidding for Elise's dinner?"

"Five dollars!" Clint shouted eagerly. He'd been waiting for just this moment, and he was ready.

Several others continued the bidding. Trace waited, watching to see what would transpire.

After several more offers, Elise's meal was up to nine dollars, with Clint having been the one who'd offered it. Trace glanced at Elise and noticed the tenseness about her. No one else seemed to be aware of it, but he could tell.

"I bid ten dollars," Trace jumped in.

Clint cast him a puzzled look and upped the bid. "Twelve."

"Fifteen," Trace countered.

The cowboy was not pleased. "Sixteen dollars," he bid, glaring at his competition.

"Seventeen."

"This one's mine," Clint told him.

"I don't think so."

"Eighteen," Clint upped it again, feeling rather proud of himself.

A murmur went through the crowd. They were used to a competition between Claire and Mrs. Buxton, but no one had ever driven up the prices of a younger woman's meal before. Most found it quite interesting. They were waiting eagerly to see who was going to come out the winner in the bidding war—Clint or the new man in town.

"Twenty dollars." Trace topped him.

Clint was growing angry. He knew Gabe had at least twenty-two dollars on him, for he had bid that much earlier for Elise's grandmother's dinner. "Twenty-two!"

"Twenty-five."

Clint was shocked. He'd had no idea the other man had that much money. He had all his savings with him, and from the looks of things, he was going to have to spend every cent of it right now to get rid of the other man and claim Elise as his own for the evening. Irritated but determined, he called out his final bid, wanting to end the bidding right then. "Twenty-six dollars!"

Those gathered around gasped at the amount. Twenty-six dollars was a lot of money. No one had ever gone that high for a dinner before.

Reverend Ford was astonished. "That's twenty-six dollars—"

Trace looked over at the ranch hand and knew what he had to do. "I bid thirty dollars."

Clint's jaw tightened in frustration at his offer. There was nothing more he could do. He had only twenty-six dollars to his name.

"Clint?" The reverend looked to the ranch hand to see if he wanted to up it again.

Clint just shook his head, his expression grim. The bidding war was over, and he'd lost. He looked over at Gabe resentfully.

Trace looked him in the eye. "I like having dinner with young ladies, too."

"Young man, come on up here and get your dinner!" the Reverend exhorted him.

Trace went to stand beside Elise. He could see the look of relief in her expression, and he was glad that he'd won.

"Enjoy your dinner! Your bid set a record for the auction. We thank you for your generosity, sir."

"It was worth every cent, I'm sure," Trace told him.

Chapter Eight

Julie watched as Gabe escorted Elise to join
Claire and George at their table. She couldn't
remember when she'd ever suffered so many
disappointments in such a short period of
time. It had been upsetting enough to attend
the wedding the day before, thinking the real
Ben was going to marry Elise, only to find out
that the whole ceremony had been a sham.
Then to discover that Ben had gambled away
the paper and was never coming back to
Durango—well, that had just about broken her
heart. She had thought she meant something
to him. She had thought that he cared about
her. Obviously, she'd been wrong.

Gabe West's appearance in town, though,
had turned Julie's disappointment to delight.
Since she'd been educated back East, and Gabe
looked like an Eastern gentleman, she was sure

that he was just the type of man she needed—especially after Ben's heartless defection. She had fully expected Gabe to bid on her dinner, but once again, fate had intervened in the person of Elise.

Fighting back the jealousy that threatened, Julie managed a smile when she heard Reverend Ford call her up to the front for her turn in the auction.

"We have Julie Stevens's dinner next. Which one of you fine young gentlemen would like to have dinner with our Julie?" he announced.

The bidding started. It went steadily upward, and Julie kept a smile on her face for the duration of the sale.

"I bid twelve dollars!" Clint spoke up.

Julie supposed she should be pleased that at least several men were bidding for her dinner, but she also remembered that Clint had bid much more than twelve dollars, on Elise's dinner, and her jealousy was piqued again. The thought kept her mood somber.

"Do I hear a bit higher than twelve?"

No one responded.

"Miss Julie's is sold to Clint Parker!"

Clint was irritated as he started forward to claim his dinner and his date. He kept his dark mood carefully concealed, though, behind a benign smile. He didn't want anyone to suspect that he cared one way or another that he'd lost out in the bidding war for Elise. He could have just walked away from the social, but he'd wanted to stay around for the dancing part. He would dine with Julie, but as soon as he got the chance, he would get away from her and find a way to spend some time with Elise. He wasn't going to get to have dinner with her, but he could at least have one dance.

"Congratulations, Clint. You two enjoy your dinner!" Reverend Ford told him before moving on to the next entry and continuing with the auction.

"Shall we find a table somewhere quiet?" Clint suggested as he picked up her basket.

"That sounds wonderful," Julie agreed, following along behind him as they headed to one of the more remote tables to share their meal.

They settled in away from everyone, and Julie began to spread the food out.

"Are you a good cook?" Clint ventured out of curiosity, looking at the fare she was unpacking.

"Well—what I lack in cooking ability, I make up for in dancing," Julie said, managing to smile at him as she tried to make the best of a frustrating situation. Of all the men she could have ended up with, Clint was not even close to her first choice, and she knew from the way the bidding had gone that she wasn't his first choice either. All of which didn't make for a wonderful evening for either one of them.

"I'm looking forward to finding out just how good you are, once we're done eating," he said, telling Julie what he thought she wanted to hear as he waited for the opportunity to go after Elise.

Julie noticed how Clint kept glancing Elise's way, and she was not the least bit offended.

"So you like Elise, do you?" she asked rather pointedly, seeing no reason to pretend.

The easygoing manner he'd been faking slipped at her remark. "Her new boss, that Gabe West, must think he's pretty smart outbidding me like he did—the bastard." He suddenly realized what he'd said as his temper flared again, and he quickly apologized. "Sorry."

"Don't worry, I know what it's like to want something and not be able to get it. When the dancing starts, we'll have our dance and then you go ask Elise to dance. Just because Gabe bought her dinner doesn't mean he can keep her to himself all night long," she encouraged him.

Julie definitely had an ulterior motive to her plan. Once Clint was dancing with Elise, Gabe would be all alone and she would seek him out. She wanted to learn more about him. He intrigued her, and she wondered what his background was. Surely, dressing and acting the way he did, he was a gentleman from back East somewhere.

Trace found Elise's dinner to be delicious, especially her freshly baked bread. He'd smothered it in butter and enjoyed every soft, delicious bite. He discovered to his pleasure that Claire had shared her apple pie with her granddaughter, so they all feasted on the delicious dessert together.

"So what do you think of our town so far, Gabe?" George asked as he finished off his last bite of pie.

"I'm impressed," Trace told him. "It's very friendly."

"Durango is a good place to live," Claire agreed. "It's very safe. It doesn't have all that wildness that other towns have. I shudder every time I think of some of the horrible things that go on. Why, just reading those stories in the *Star* about what that outlaw named Harris and his gang have done is enough to make you really appreciate Durango and Marshal Trent."

"We have been very blessed here," Elise agreed.

"So far," Trace cautioned. "Let's just hope it stays that way."

"You're right. The last thing we need is Matt Harris riding into town," George agreed.

Trace's expression darkened at the thought of the murderer. He wished things were different. He wanted to be on the gang's trail, tracking them mercilessly until they were brought to justice. He resented being forced to bide his time in Durango. He hated the fact that while he was sitting there in an office pretending to be a newspaper editor, they were still on the loose, free to rob and kill.

"That gang sounds just awful, doesn't it, Gabe?" Claire said, seeing the change in him and thinking he was intimidated by the prospect of dealing with such bad men. "You've probably never run into criminals of their kind before, have you?"

"I read about them in the paper as you did, and I'm looking forward to the day when men like Harris no longer terrorize the West," he said grimly.

"What do you think it's going to take?" Elise spoke up. "If Sheriff Jackson from Eagle Pass couldn't stop them, who can? These outlaws are amoral and deadly. It seems they know no fear."

"The day's coming when they'll pay for what they've done," Trace vowed in a stern tone.

Elise gave him a curious look. The fierceness of his tone surprised her. "Let's hope so."

It was then that the music started.

"Claire, would you care to dance?" Trace invited the older woman, glad to be distracted. Thoughts of the outlaw haunted his days and nights as it was.

Claire almost felt like a young girl again, and she blushed prettily at his invitation. "I would love to dance with you, Gabe, as long as George doesn't mind. He did buy my dinner." She looked to her companion.

"Go right ahead. I'll squire Elise around the dance floor—if she'll have me?" George said, smiling.

"I'd be delighted, George," Elise told him.

Lanterns had been hung all around the platform that had been set up for the night of dancing. The two couples made their way out onto the floor, joining the others who were already enjoying the music.

Julie and Clint sat at their table watching as more and more dancers crowded onto the platform.

"Are you ready to give it a try?" he asked.

"Yes. I'd love to dance." The sooner she got Clint dancing with Elise, the sooner she'd be with Gabe. He looked so sophisticated and worldly.

She couldn't wait to be in his arms.

"Let's go!" Clint led the way, and once they were on the dance floor, he drew her close. The tempo of the tune was a quick one, and he gave it his all.

Julie realized immediately that as a dancer, Clint was a good ranch hand. Somehow, she managed to keep up with him and not lose a toe. She had always considered herself an accomplished dancer, and she was proving it. She doubted there were many who could dance with Clint and survive unscathed.

That dance ended, and the next song was a slow one. Julie was glad. She needed some rest after the excitement of the first dance. Clint tried to hold her even closer, but she succeeded in keeping a distance between them, all the while smiling up at him in sweet innocence.

"So, when are you going to dance with Elise?" Julie asked, eager for the chance to go after Gabe.

"I don't know. Who's she dancing with now?" He looked around.

"Gabe," she told him. She noticed that a muscle worked in Clint's jaw as he spotted the other couple moving among the crowd of dancers.

"Let's head their way. I think it just might be time that I cut in on him."

Julie followed his lead as he crossed the floor and maneuvered into position near Gabe and Elise. She could hardly wait to be free of Clint and dancing with Gabe. She'd watched Gabe dancing with Elise and had seen how good he was. After Clint, Gabe was going to be heaven on earth.

Trace had enjoyed his first dance with Claire tremendously. She had been the perfect partner. She'd been light on her feet, following his rusty lead with no problem. She had even laughed at his jokes, which had endeared her to him all the more. When the tune had finally ended, he'd been sorry to let her go, but George had been waiting to claim her for his own. Not that Trace was in any way reluctant to dance with Elise. Whether he wanted to admit it to himself or not, he was looking forward to it.

"May I have this dance?" he asked courteously.

"Of course," she answered easily, going into his arms.

The slow melody brought them close together in an easy rhythm, and they moved in perfect unison as they swept about the floor.

"You're a very good dancer," Elise complimented him.

"Thank you. My grandmother insisted I learn when I was quite young, and I guess once you've learned the steps, you never forget them."

She gazed up at him, studying the lean line of his jaw. There was something so puzzling about him. Though he appeared to be such a mild-mannered gentleman, and his dancing ability seemed to confirm it, sometimes she saw a glimpse of something more. When she'd walked in on him sitting at his desk at the office with his spectacles off, he'd looked like a completely different man. Even now, as he swept her around the room holding her near, she sensed that he was much more powerful than she'd originally thought. He moved with a certain controlled grace, and beneath her hand, his shoulder felt solid and strong.

The memory of the kiss Gabe had given her when Preacher Farnsworth had declared them husband and wife returned again, and a surprising heat flushed through Elise at the sensual recollection. Maybe it was the rhythm of their bodies as they moved together about the dance floor or maybe it was the way his dark eyes caught and held hers in a penetrating gaze that left her breathless, but whatever it was, her heart was pounding a frantic rhythm.

Elise told herself her reaction was ridiculous. This was Gabe West—the man who had tripped and fallen into Preacher Farnsworth to help "rescue" her. Gabe was not exactly the most manly of men in his suits and bow ties. Still—they did dance beautifully together.

Trace had known that dancing with Elise would be enjoyable, but he hadn't expected to enjoy it this much. She fit perfectly in his arms, and as he squired her about the dance floor, it was as if they were floating on air. He looked down at her, his gaze settling for a moment on her lips. He remembered the kiss he'd given her after they'd been "married." The exchange had been heated and demanding, and he recalled every detail of that sensual encounter. Trace found that he wanted to kiss her again—to taste her innocence and passion once more. He wanted to—

The tap on his shoulder abruptly shattered his thoughts, and Trace scowled as he glanced over to find Clint and Julie standing there beside them.

"Mind if I cut in?" Clint asked.

Elise's hand tightened in Trace's. Trace wanted to whirl her away from the other man without a word, but they were trapped. There could be no escape without causing a scene, and he couldn't do that tonight, not here at the church social. Trace paused, and when he did, Clint immediately stepped between him and Elise. Without waiting for an answer, the other man claimed her for his own partner and whisked her away.

Trace was very aware of the abandoned Julie standing nearby. "Julie, would you like to dance?"

"Why, thank you, Gabe. That would be wonderful."

She went to him and was thrilled when he guided her expertly to the music. She remained quiet for a few moments, enjoying the pleasure of dancing with a man who was no threat to her physical well-being.

"So, are you having a good time tonight?" she asked finally, wanting to strike up a conversation.

"I am. I needed to get to know everyone, and this is a good way to do it."

"I hope you like living in Durango. It's a beautiful town, and the people are very warm and friendly." She added emphasis to her last words.

"So I've noticed," he agreed. He wasn't thinking of Julie. He was thinking of Elise, and her warm and friendly welcome at the stage depot.

Trace looked quickly around the crowd and saw Elise smiling as she danced with Clint. He had to hand it to her acting abilities. No one would ever have suspected her real thoughts.

Julie noticed his interest in the other woman and grew irritated. She was not used to being ignored. The auction had been hard enough to deal with, but she had no intention of being treated this way while she was dancing with him.

"So tell me all about yourself. You must have been so surprised getting caught up in all of Elise's 'wedding' plans like you did." Julie knew the best way to get a man to like you was to let him talk about himself. It was a strategy that had never failed her.

"It was certainly a far different welcome than I'd expected when I got off the stage."

"What were you expecting?"

"I didn't know anyone in town, so I thought it was going to be a rather quiet time while I established myself as the new owner of the newspaper. I had no idea that I'd be instrumental in helping Elise report her biggest story ever."

"She is a good reporter, I suppose. I hadn't paid too much attention to the news before, but now that you're here, things at the *Star* are becoming much more interesting—to me."

Trace glanced down at her, surprised by her brazenness, but her expression remained sweetly innocent. "Well, we appreciate your support."

"Where do you call home, Gabe?" Julie purred.

"Durango now," he answered.

"But you're obviously not from around here. Did you grow up back East?"

Trace had known the questions would come, and he was prepared to be as evasive as necessary to cover himself. "Yes, but I wanted to see the West. I've been traveling for some time now." He told himself that none of that was a lie. The town he'd grown up in had been east of Durango.

"And you ended up here."

"After I won the newspaper from Ben Hollins in the card game, yes. I think this will be a nice place to settle for a while."

"Just for a while? You're only passing through?" The possibility startled Julie. Ben had just up and left. He'd said he was going to take care of some family business, but now he was never going to return. She wondered if Gabe was going to be like that, too. If so, how then was she ever going to find a man who would marry her and take her to live back East, where she believed she belonged?

"I'm not going anywhere right now, but to work at my newspaper," Trace said, hoping to distract her. He didn't want anyone in Durango to suspect his motives.

"I'm certainly glad to hear that, and I'm very glad that you're here with us," she said flirtatiously.

"I am, too." Trace supposed that wasn't a total falsehood. There was no way he could have stayed in Eagle Pass or remained with Gibby any longer. Until he was physically ready for his final showdown with Harris, he would stay in Durango and keep a low profile.

"You sound like you're excited about taking over as the editor of the *Star*."

"I think it's going to be a very interesting job. It will be interesting to see what Elise comes up with for her next big story."

"She does have a flare for the sensational," Julie admitted begrudgingly. She was annoyed that the conversation had once again turned back to the other woman. She grew even more annoyed when she looked up at Trace to find him watching Elise and Clint again. "They make a handsome couple, don't you think? Clint's cared for Elise for a long time, you know." She sighed, deliberately trying to sound romantic.

"They do look very nice together," Trace responded, turning his attention back to Julie.

Across the dance floor, Elise glanced toward Gabe and Julie to see him holding her close. He was gazing down at Julie, apparently enraptured by something she'd said. The realization that he found the other woman attractive stung Elise, and the power of what she was feeling startled her.

Elise couldn't imagine why in the world she cared one way or the other what Gabe thought or did. He was her boss. *Period*. And he was definitely not her type. He wore suits and bow ties and eyeglasses, for heaven's sake. It was absolutely ridiculous for her even to give him a second thought.

Elise gave herself a mental shake and turned her concentration back to what was really important right then—keeping her feet safely out of Clint's way.

Chapter Nine

Elise was very glad when the evening drew to a close. Clint's undeterred presence beside her had kept her from relaxing and truly enjoying herself. She had had no reprieve from his company since they'd had their one and only dance.

"Can I walk you home tonight, Elise?" Clint asked.

"Well, I—"

Before she could get any further, Trace spoke up.

"Elise came with me, so I'll be escorting her home."

Clint shot him an ugly look. He'd tolerated the timid-looking newspaperman's presence all night, but he'd had about enough of him. "Why don't you let Elise decide who she's going to walk home with? She might want to spend time with a real man," he sneered.

"Clint, I'm sorry, but it's only proper that I go home with Gabe, since I did come with him," Elise said with as much dignity as she could muster.

"But—" *Proper? Manners be damned!* He wanted to be alone with her!

"Elise?" Trace stood and offered her his arm.

Clint's frustration was complete as she rose to stand beside Gabe. Except for the one dance, he hadn't gotten the chance to spend any time alone with Elise. He'd hoped he'd get to walk her home and talk to her then, but it wasn't going to happen. Clint was tempted to beat the hell out of Gabe, but they were at a church social, so he controlled himself. It wasn't easy. He wasn't a man who handled rejection well.

"Well, good night, Elise," he finally grumbled resentfully, knowing that it was going to be a while before he could get back into town again. "It was good to see you again."

"It was good to see you, too, Clint," she told him as she took Gabe's arm. She realized that she'd certainly gotten her money's worth out of Gabe tonight. He had saved her from dinner with Clint and from having to walk home with him. She'd been wondering how she was going to avoid Clint's more amorous advances if he'd been the one who'd ended up taking her home. As ardent as he was, she'd known it wouldn't be easy.

Trace led Elise off, relieved that Clint hadn't started a fight. He'd been as ready as he could be to take him on if the need had arisen, but he was glad that it hadn't. He had most of his strength back, but he still wasn't his old self.

"Thank you," Elise said to him in a low voice as they quit the grounds.

"Don't mention it. Besides, since I paid for your dinner, I figured I got the privilege of walking you home, too." He grinned down at her.

"That same way of thinking worked for me," George said with a laugh as he and Claire followed them down the street.

"Poor Clint," Claire said sympathetically. "You have to admit the man is persistent. He's been trying to court Elise for months now, and somehow he just can't understand why she doesn't encourage his affections."

"I'm sure there are a lot of girls in town who would welcome his advances," Elise pointed out. "I just don't happen to be one of them."

"Well, you got through the evening unscathed," Trace said with a laugh.

"I was worried there for a moment while I was dancing with him."

They all laughed good-naturedly at the memory.

"Did you get things worked out with Charles?" Claire asked. She had seen them talking to Ben's landlord during the evening and wondered what had transpired.

"Yes, we did. I'm going to ride out to the house tomorrow morning to collect Ben's things. Gabe has decided to come with me so he can take a look around and decide if he wants to rent it or not."

"It's a nice house," George put in. "It's far enough out to give you some privacy, but close enough that you can get into town real quick-like if you need to."

"From everything Elise has told me about it, it sounds as if it will work just fine for me." Trace was eager to get back to practicing his marksmanship and his draw.

They reached the Martin home. Claire and George bid Gabe good night and went on inside.

Trace stood with Elise on the front walk. It was quiet on the residential street. No moon shone in the night sky, so the stars seemed even more bright and beautiful.

"It's heavenly out tonight," Elise sighed as she looked up.

Trace found himself staring at her rather than the stars. He was amazed that she could be so sedate and ladylike one moment and deal with the likes of Preacher Farnsworth in the next. She looked lovely. The memory of the way she'd felt moving with him as they danced filled him with a knowing heat. He was tempted to take her in his arms and taste once more the sweetness of her kiss, but he resisted the need.

"Would you like to come in for a while?" Elise asked, turning toward him.

It was then that she caught a glimpse of intense emotion in his expression, and her heartbeat quickened. She went still, gazing up at him in the darkness. In the shadows of the night, he was more dominating and definitely more manly. Again she realized just how wide his shoulders were. He seemed to fill her very world as they stood there beneath the canopy of stars. Elise held her breath. She was certain that he was about to sweep her into his arms and kiss her just as he had at their "wedding." And she was ready. She actually wanted him to—

"No. I have to go," Trace said flatly. His voice betrayed none of his inner turmoil. He was fighting the need to take her in his arms. It was a battle his common sense had to win. He could not surrender to this desire he was feeling for her. "It's late, and we've got a lot to do tomorrow."

His words shattered the sensual mood that had wound its way around Elise's heart. She was startled by his refusal, and a feeling that could only be called disappointment threatened. Irritated and angry with herself for having even considered kissing him again, Elise tried to convince herself that it didn't matter what Gabe did. She didn't care if he stayed or left. "Oh. All right."

"I'll see you in the morning." Trace started down the walk, wanting to put some physical distance between them. She was just far too tempting for his peace of mind.

"Shall I pick you up at the hotel around eleven-thirty?" she asked. "I have to take our carriage since I'm going to bring back Ben's personal belongings."

"I'll be waiting for you."

Elise waited there, watching until Gabe had disappeared down the street. Only when he'd gone from sight did she go inside the house.

"Did Gabe leave already, dear?" Claire asked from where she was sitting in their small parlor with George.

"Yes."

"Pity. He's such a nice young man. I thought he might come in and visit with us for a while."

"I'm very tired," Elsie said as an excuse as she went to press a kiss on her grandmother's cheek.

"You have had an exciting day or two," George agreed. "But it was worth it, don't you think?"

"Absolutely," Elise answered.

She bade them both good night then and went on upstairs to her bedroom. Once in her room, she quickly undressed, donned her nightgown, and lay down. George had been right. The last few days had been exhausting.

Weary though Elise was, her mind would give her no rest. As she sought the blissful unawareness of sleep, thoughts of Gabe kept returning to haunt her. If the look on his face as they'd stood outside together that evening had been any indication of what he was feeling, he'd certainly seemed as if he'd wanted to kiss her. Elise wondered why he hadn't. The kind of man she was attracted to would have thrown caution to the wind and kissed her right then and there and never have worried about the consequences. Gabe hadn't even tried! He'd just walked off and left her standing there, all alone under a beautiful, starry night sky.

As the thought occurred to her, Elise grew angry with herself. It was ridiculous to want Gabe to kiss her! It made no sense. He was her boss! They would be working together. That would be the entire extent of her involvement with the man, and that would be fine with her.

Thinking of work and the newspaper, Elise realized that Gabe was certainly no Ben. She wasn't sure how he was going to work out as the editor of the paper, but since he was the owner, there wasn't anything she could do about it. They were going to find out soon enough, though, just what kind of newspaperman he was. Putting all thoughts of Gabe from her, she concentrated on what she really needed right then—sleep.

But even as she closed her eyes and finally started to drift off, a vision of Gabe haunted her. It was an image of him sitting at Ben's desk, his glasses off, his expression serious as he held Ben's gun in his hand.

Trace considered stopping at the saloon for a drink as he strode past it on his way back to his hotel, but he decided against it. Not that he couldn't have used a whiskey right then, but more than anything, he just needed some time alone.

Trace was angry with himself and his situation. He did not like the feelings that Elise aroused in him. He gave himself a stern warning. While Elise was a lovely, intelligent, brave young woman, he could not allow himself to be distracted from his purpose. Matt Harris had to be brought to justice, no matter how long it took. That was all that mattered in his life. Until Harris was dead or behind bars, he could think of nothing else.

Trace reached his room and went to bed. He did not rest soundly, though. His sleep was tortured with images of the outlaws' deadly ambush.

Morning came far too soon.

"It really is close enough to town, don't you think?" Elise remarked as she reined in her carriage before Ben's house.

Trace eyed with open interest the small, two-bedroom frame home that was less than a mile from the outskirts of Durango.

"It's perfect," Trace said, and he meant it. He hadn't seen a neighbor for some distance and that pleased him. He wanted some space and privacy so he could practice shooting without being interrupted. This was just the haven he needed for the next month or two. He was going to have to buy a horse, but that presented no problem.

Elise glanced at him, curiously. "But you haven't even been inside yet."

"I like the location," he explained simply. "And you're right. I will be able to get into town in a reasonable amount of time should the need arise. I'm going to have to buy a horse, though. Any ideas who sells the best mounts?"

"I'm sure David Forsyth down at the livery can help you. We can go by there later today, if you want," she offered.

"That would be fine."

"I'm glad you're pleased with the house. Charles gave me the key, so why don't you go ahead and take a look around while I start packing for Ben?"

Trace climbed down from the carriage and then reached up to help her descend. He put his hands at her waist as she rested hers on his shoulders while he lifted her down. As she leaned toward him, the sweet scent of her perfume surrounded him. It was a heady fragrance that he was determined to ignore. As he lowered her to the ground, her body slid sensuously along the length of his. Trace hadn't planned it that way at all, and his response to that contact was instant and powerful. He made a show of awkwardly setting her down and then nervously cleared his throat and fidgeted with his eyeglasses as he stepped back away.

"I'll go look around and check things out. Will you need any help packing?"

Elise looked toward the house. "I don't know. I don't think Ben had too many personal things left here, but I can't be sure until I go inside."

"Just call me if you need help."

She was bemused by the thought that Gabe was more interested in the grounds around the house than the inside. Somehow, she hadn't thought he would care at all about the surroundings. He didn't really seem to be much of an outdoorsman.

Elise let herself in and promptly began to pack all the things that Ben had left behind.

Trace strode to the rear of the property, keeping a watchful eye out. He was pleased with the small stable and corral. Living this far from town, he was definitely going to have to buy a horse, and he was glad. It was time. It wouldn't be long until he could go after Harris. He was certain of it. He headed inside, determined that the place would be his.

"Are you doing all right?" Trace called out to Elise as he let himself in.

"I'm back here in the bedroom. I've just got a little bit more to do here and then I'll be done," Elise called back.

He made his way to stand in the doorway. She was sitting on the side of the bed, emptying a drawer from the bureau.

"What do you think about the house?" she asked. "Do you like it?"

"It's just what I need. How soon did Charles say I could move in?"

"I don't know that he said any particular day, but I would imagine any time after I've cleared the place out would be fine with him."

"Good."

"So you're that tired of the hotel already?"

"I like having a little room to move around in, and there isn't much of that in a hotel room. And I like my privacy, too."

"You'll definitely have that here." She glanced over her shoulder at him and smiled. "Not many people get out this way too often."

Their gazes met across the room.

Trace suddenly envisioned her lying back on the bed, her dark hair spread out around her, her arms reaching for him.

They we alone. The teasing thought played in his mind.

"What can I do to help?" he asked, frowning as he forced himself to ignore his wayward imaginings.

Elise was completely unaware of the direction of his thoughts. "You can bring me that other drawer—and you can answer a few questions for me."

He was instantly cautious as he went to retrieve the drawer from the bureau. "What kind of questions?"

"I've been thinking. We need a lead story for the next issue, and I thought it would be good to do a feature on you—Gabe West, the new owner and editor of the *Star*. What do you think?"

138

"Don't you think everyone would find that boring?" He set the drawer down next to her on the bed.

"No, not at all. Of course, an interview with you would be no Preacher Farnsworth lead, but the folks in town will want to know more about you, and what better way to give it to them than through the paper? What do you say?"

He'd expected questions, but he had not expected to be interviewed by a reporter. Still, he knew there could be no refusing her. He hated lying, but there was no way to avoid it at this point in time. "What do you want to know?"

"Tell me about yourself."

"Well, I'm twenty-eight years old. I was born and raised back East."

"Where?"

Trace was glad that he'd traveled east several times. "I was born in Philadelphia, but my parents moved quite a lot. My mother passed away when I was young, and my grandmother helped to raise me. My father owned part of a shipping business. When he died, I sold my share of the business and decided to travel."

"And that's how you ended up here in Colorado in a poker game with Ben?"

Trace nodded, hoping he'd been specific enough about his past without going into detail to satisfy her. He didn't want to lie too much, because then he'd have to remember what he'd told her.

"What about marriage?" She paused in her packing and looked up at him.

"What about it?" he asked quickly.

"Have you ever married?" Her question was innocently put as her gaze met his.

Trace gave her a lazily seductive look as he answered, "Well, yes. I did marry once."

"Oh." Elise had not expected that answer, and suddenly all the pleasure of interviewing him left her. It had never occurred to her that he might have been a married man. She dropped her gaze from his and hoped he didn't hear the strain in her voice as she fought to maintain her professionalism. "Is your wife back East waiting for you?"

"No. My 'wife' is right here." Trace couldn't stop himself. He reached out to her and cupped her cheek to lift her face.

Elise gave a small gasp at that contact—so innocent, yet so intimate. She looked up at him to find his dark eyes warm upon her.

"I 'married' you. Remember?" He gave her a slow, knowing smile.

Elise blushed as she did remember—every detail of the kiss he'd given her so passionately at the end of the wedding ceremony. She tried to tell herself that this was Gabe, but it didn't matter. When he bent ever so slowly to her to claim her lips in a cherishing exchange, she met him fully in that embrace.

Trace had tried to deny himself, but with her open response, there could be no stopping. Her kiss was sweet and innocent, yet held an enticing promise of passion.

Mesmerized by his sensual assault, Elise leaned toward him, reveling in his nearness as his mouth moved hungrily over hers.

Desire, hot and heavy, flamed to life within him, and it was that fiery spark of desire that jarred Trace back to his senses. He forced himself to break away from her immediately.

"Gabe?"

"I'm sorry, Elise. I shouldn't have done that. I don't know what I was thinking." Trace wanted to lay her down on the bed and make love to her, but it wasn't going to happen. He deliberately made himself sound nervous and uncertain, the way Gabe West would. "It was a mistake."

She blinked up at him in confusion. She had been surprised by his kiss, and now she was even more surprised and angered by his words. *He didn't know why he'd kissed her? It was a mistake?* She frowned as her irritation with him grew. *A mistake?* How insulting could he be?

"You're right, of course," she said a bit tersely, realizing that he must not have been enjoying the kiss as much as she had, and that annoyed her, too. "It was a mistake, and it's one that we can't repeat if we're going to work together and maintain any kind of a professional relationship. You are my boss, not my husband."

Trace couldn't have agreed with her more. Kissing her again had been a serious mistake—in more ways than one. He had no time for entanglements that would only make his life more difficult in the long run. He would have to keep his distance from her. It was too easy to be distracted by her.

"It won't happen again."

141

"Good," she said firmly, using her anger to hide her confusion over her own conflicting emotions. She fought for professionalism as she tried to resume her interview. "Now, back to our interview for the *Star*. Do you want me to mention your 'marriage' in the article? It was very short-lived."

"No. You married Ben Hollins, not me."

"Exactly, so for the sake of the interview—why haven't you married?" She refused to admit to herself that she truly was curious about him.

He shrugged. "I've never met the right woman, I guess. What about you? Why haven't you married?" He redirected the question back to her.

"I'm the one doing the interview."

"I know, but I am curious. It's certainly not for a lack of suitors—look at Clint."

"Have you been talking to my grandmother?" she asked him with a laugh, her anger with him lightening a little.

"Only last night at the dinner, why?"

"Because she asks me the same question all the time. She's quite convinced that I'm well on my way to becoming a spinster." Elise sighed.

"You've never fallen in love?"

"No," she answered simply. "Somehow, Clint just isn't the kind of man I'm looking for."

"What kind of man are you looking for?"

She started to answer, then realized how he'd turned the tables of their conversation.

"I'm not sure," she hedged, "but I'll know him when I see him. What about you? What kind of woman are you looking for?"

"I'm not looking," he replied tightly.

"You don't ever want to get married and settle down?"

"Not now. Right now, I'm the new editor-in-chief of the *Star,* and that's what I want to concentrate on."

Elise had finished packing what had been left in the drawers as she questioned him, and she stood up, more than ready to get out of that bedroom. "I think that does it. I'm done here. Are you ready to go back to town?"

"If you are."

"Good. On our way, we can stop and pay Charles a visit so you can make your arrangements to move in, and then we can go by the livery and talk to David about finding you a good mount."

"Fine."

He gathered up the rest of the bags she'd packed and carried them out to the carriage for her. He waited as she locked the house, and then he helped her into the carriage. He took care not to come into any close physical contact with her. They said little on the ride back.

It was much later that night when Elise lay in bed trying to understand what had happened between her and Gabe that day. She couldn't figure out why his kiss had affected her so. Gabe wasn't the kind of man she usually found attractive. True, he had helped her out at the social by bidding for her dinner, and he had saved her from walking home with Clint, but he definitely wasn't her type.

Gabe was rather bookish and gentlemanly. Not that those were bad traits, she argued with herself. It was just that her ideal man was someone who was brave and strong. Like the men she wrote articles about—men like that sheriff from Eagle Pass.

Elise still mourned the fact that Harris had ambushed and killed Trace Jackson. In everything she'd read about him, he'd sounded like a wonderful man. His reputation as a fair and honest lawman had been known far and wide. He had been a force to be reckoned with. Not that she'd ever seen a picture of him, but it didn't matter what he looked like. It was what he stood for that was important. He was the kind of man she wanted, the kind of man she was determined to wait for. He was a white knight on a charger—a true hero.

Gabe was nice enough, she supposed, but he was no Sheriff Jackson. And that was why, even after all her grandmother's proddings, she remained unattached. No man she'd ever met had measured up to her expectations, and sadly, Elise was beginning to think that no man ever would.

At the realization, a calm came over her and sleep claimed her. It was a restless sleep, though, as memories of Gabe's kiss drifted through her dreams.

Chapter Ten

The following days passed quickly. Trace purchased a roan stallion and made his move into Ben's old house without a problem. Things went smoothly at the *Star*. The time he'd spent studying Ben's work had helped him understand what was expected of him, and with Andy's and Elise's expertise, he was quickly learning what it took to get a newspaper on the street. He had come to respect all the hard work that went into producing a weekly like the *Star*. This was not an easy job, and more often than not, it was a thankless one.

Ever aware of Elise's nearness, Trace made it a point never to be alone with her at the office. He had no reason to socialize with her after hours, so there was no danger of a repeat of the embrace they'd shared at Ben's house, and he was glad. He could not afford the distraction.

145

Unbeknownst to anyone else, Trace began to practice his shooting daily. He was glad to see that there was some improvement in his ability to draw, but he was beginning to realize that he would never again have the speed that he'd had before the ambush. Still, he knew he could train himself to be reasonably proficient, and that would have to be good enough. There were moments during his practices when, in frustration, he considered going after Harris with a sawed-off shotgun, but he held to his original plan. He was sure that it wouldn't be that much longer until he was ready.

Trace knew there was always the possibility that someone would discover what he was doing. If they did, he was simply going to tell them that since he'd heard working at a newspaper could be dangerous, he wanted to be prepared. He made sure to keep the eyeglasses with him. That way, if someone did show up unexpectedly, he could quickly assume his Gabe identity. Not that he wanted to. Lord knew, he was tired of playing that role, but there was nothing else he could do—for now. He would remain Gabe for only as long as it was necessary.

Sitting at his desk, Trace glanced into the outer office to see Andy hard at work, but there was still no sign of Elise. She had been due back nearly an hour before, and he wondered what had detained her. It was the day of their editorial meeting, when they were to pick their lead story for the next issue. Things had been quiet around town, so they were trying to come up with an interesting idea.

"Andy? Any sign of Elise yet?"

"No. I don't even see her out on the street anywhere," he called back after checking.

"All right. Just tell her to come see me as soon as she shows up."

Across town, Elise had attended a meeting of the Ladies' Solidarity. She'd hoped she would find something interesting to report on their activities, but other than the usual good deeds the women were involved in—helping to beautify the town and feed the poor—there had been nothing overly exciting going on. When the meeting ended, she'd started back to the office, detouring only for a short trip to a local mercantile.

"Good afternoon, Mr. Perry," she greeted the shopkeeper as she entered the store.

"Why, how are you, Miss Elise? And how is that grandmother of yours? I haven't seen either one of you in a few weeks," Wayne Perry, the owner, said.

"We're just fine. We've been keeping busy."

"I'll say you have. Your story about the preacher was fascinating, and now with having that new boss of yours at the *Star*, you've got a lot going on. What can I help you with today?"

"I need a few yards of material for a dress my grandmother's planning to make." She began to explain what she needed, but just then the bell jingled, signaling that someone else had entered the store, and she never got to finish.

"Excuse me one minute, Miss Elise," Wayne interrupted her as he looked up to see who'd come in. His expression grew strained, and he hurried away. "I'll be right back to wait on you."

Elise wondered who could have caused such a reaction in him. She glanced toward the front of the store to see a blond-haired young woman standing just inside the doorway. She was wearing a dress more suitable for a night in a saloon than an afternoon of shopping. It was dark blue satin, trimmed in black lace and cut quite low in the bodice. Her cheeks were heavily rouged and her lips were painted red. For all that she appeared to be a grown woman, Elise had the feeling that she was really quite young.

"Can I help you?" Wayne demanded when he reached her. His tone was almost belligerent as he glared at her.

"I needed to get some ribbon for—"

"I am completely sold out of ribbon," he declared coldly, standing to block her way into the store.

"But Fernada down at the High Time said this was the best shop in town," the girl protested.

Elise hadn't meant to eavesdrop on their conversation, but she couldn't help herself—especially after hearing the shopkeeper's undisguised hostility toward the girl. She maneuvered herself between two counters a little closer to them so she could better hear what was being said.

"This *is* the best shop in town, but I'm out of ribbon today."

"But I can see some on the counter there," she argued, pointing past him to where the dry goods were stored.

"Well, none of that merchandise is for the likes of you, so you may as well go on and get out of my store. I only want decent folk to shop here."

"But I got money!" she told him defensively.

"I don't want your money. I know how you earned it!" he said with scathing condemnation. "And I don't want you in my shop! Now get out or I'll be forced to call the sheriff and have him take you out of here!"

Elise could see the young woman's expression, which had turned haunted and pained at his words.

"But—" She reached in her pocket to show him the cash she had, but he wouldn't listen.

"Go, and don't ever come back. I don't need or want your business."

Elise watched as the young woman turned away from the shopkeeper and hurried dejectedly from the store. Mr. Perry followed her outside.

Elise couldn't believe what had happened. She couldn't believe that Mr. Perry had refused to wait on the woman. She was still stunned a few moments later when he returned to her side, his manner conciliatory.

"I'm sorry about that, Miss Elise. Some people just don't know their place in the world."

"All she wanted to do was buy something from you," she said simply.

"She's a whore! She works down at the High Time Saloon! Good folks don't associate with her kind."

"But you lost a sale." She felt sorry for the girl and thought that by appealing to the shopkeeper's business interests she might convince him to change his way of thinking.

"Like I told her, I didn't want her money. Women like her shouldn't be allowed to mix with good, God-fearing folks." He tried to maintain his dignity as he answered her, but he was still angry over the other woman's intrusion. "Now, what can I get for you?"

Elise was still a bit stunned by what had transpired, and all she could think of was the Biblical admonishment—*Judge not, lest ye be judged!* The look of hurt and despair she'd seen on the other woman's face had said it all, and Elise knew what she had to do. She quickly finished her transaction, buying the material her grandmother needed and a sizable amount of ribbon that her grandmother didn't need.

"Thank you for all your help, Mr. Perry."

"You're more than welcome, Miss Elise. You come on back now. It's always a pleasure to see you."

"I will," she said, a plan already forming in her head. She wondered if he really meant those words.

Elise hurried from the shop. She looked both ways on the street, but could see no sign of the young woman who'd just left the mercantile. She knew where the High Time Saloon was located, so she headed in that direction. She didn't even think about the fact that she was late for the editorial meeting with Gabe. The only thing that troubled her was that she was going where no good woman was ever supposed to go. She was going into a saloon to talk to the "working girls" there.

Elise worried for a moment that her reputation might somehow suffer from this adventure of hers, but then dismissed the thought. She was a journalist who was working on a story. It was important that she get all the information she needed while she could. She considered, too, that she might be putting herself in danger of some sort, but she pushed that worrisome possibility aside, too. This was no time to worry about her own safety when she'd just seen how the young woman had been treated by Mr. Perry. It was broad daylight. She was going to be fine—and she was going after the lead article for the next issue of the *Star*. There was no time for cowardice when one was on the trail of a good story.

Fernada stood at the bar in the High Time Saloon, relaxing and talking with Dan, the bartender. It was still early in the day, and it was a weekday at that, so business was slow. She'd even given several of her girls the afternoon off to get some of their personal chores done. She looked up when she heard someone come in and was surprised to see that Suzie had come back so soon.

"What are you doing here? I thought you were going shopping for a while," she asked good-naturedly. Her mood changed, though, when she saw Suzie's stricken look. "What's wrong, honey? What happened?"

"Nothing," Suzie mumbled, heading for the stairs so she could go to her room.

"Don't tell me nothing, Suzie. I wasn't born yesterday." Fernada started toward her, instantly concerned about what might have happened to her. Suzie was one of her youngest girls. She was sweet and good-natured, and as honest a working girl as Fernada had ever met. She felt almost motherly toward her.

Suzie glanced at Dan, feeling a bit embarrassed at her dilemma. Even so, she knew there was no way to avoid relating what had just happened at the store. "He refused to wait on me."

"Who did?"

"That Mr. Perry at the mercantile—and I even had cash money to pay him with! It wasn't like I was asking him for credit or anything!" The last was choked from her as her tears fell freely.

Fernada put a supportive arm around her slender shoulders and guided her toward the steps. She wanted to talk with her alone. It wasn't the first time, nor would it be the last time, that some upstanding citizen of town hurt one of her girls. She hated it, but she knew she couldn't stop it. She could only help Suzie learn how to cope with the rejection of the "good folks."

They had just started up the stairs when Fernada heard someone else come into the saloon. She didn't bother to look back, thinking it was just a cowboy wanting a drink and a game of cards.

"Miss?"

The sound of woman's voice stopped Fernada. She and Suzie both looked back. They were surprised to see a very pretty, demurely dressed, dark-haired young woman standing right there in the middle of the High Time Saloon, looking up at them.

"I'm Elise Martin," she began, addressing herself to the young woman who'd just fled Mr.

Perry's store. "I was wondering if I could talk with you for a moment?"

"Why? What do you want with my Suzie?" Fernada asked, defensively.

"I just wanted to ask her a few questions about what happened at the store."

"And why would you be interested?"

"I'm a reporter for the *Star*."

"You are?" Fernada was taken aback by this news.

"Why do you want to talk with me?" Suzie couldn't imagine what she wanted.

"I was in the mercantile when you came in to shop just a little while ago. I saw how Mr. Perry treated you. Here—" Elise approached them and held out the small bag containing the ribbon. "I bought this for you."

"What is it?"

"Look and see."

The younger woman took the offered gift, and her expression went from wary to one of pure delight as she opened it to see the ribbon she'd wanted. "You got the ribbon!" She lifted her tear-filled gaze to look at her. "Thank you. I'll be glad to pay you for it." She started to dig in her pocket for the money.

"No," Elise said, holding up her hand to stop her. "The ribbon is a gift. No one should have to endure what you just suffered in that store."

"Thank you." Her words were humble and almost a whisper. For an instant there, when she'd refused her money, she'd thought the reporter didn't want the cash for the same reason the shopkeeper hadn't. Acts of kindness

153

had been so rare in her short lifetime that she wasn't quite sure how to react.

"I'm glad I could do it for you. I was wondering—would you have time to talk with me for a little while? The scene in the store troubled me. I can't believe how cruel some people can be."

Fernada couldn't stop herself from giving a harsh, disbelieving laugh. "You ain't seen nothing if you think that was bad."

"I guess I haven't, and that's why I'd like to talk with you—both of you, if you could spare the time?"

Fernada and Suzie exchanged glances, and then Suzie, clutching her bag of ribbon, nodded.

"All right. I'll talk with you."

"Why don't we go upstairs where it'll be more private, just in case any customers come in?" Fernada suggested.

Elise nodded. "Thank you. I'd like that."

The older woman led the way to a room at the far end of the hall, and Elise followed. Elise had never been in a saloon before, let alone the private area where the girls made their livings.

This particular room was large and comfortably furnished. Fernada sat on the side of the bed with Suzie and left Elise the one and only chair to use.

"I'm Fernada, by the way, and this is Suzie."

"I appreciate your taking this time for me," Elise told them. "After what I saw at the shop today, I had an idea for a lead story for the *Star*, but I need your help."

"Our help?" Suzie repeated, surprised.

"Yes. I was offended by the way you were treated, and I wanted to write an article about what it's like to be you. Mr. Perry was very cruel."

She was stating a fact. "I don't think the public has any idea of what it's like to be a working girl."

"I don't think they want to know," Fernada countered. She'd been a working girl for years now, and she had been putting up with this kind of treatment for just as long. "It's amazing how folks can talk out of both sides of their mouths."

"What do you mean?" Elise asked.

"Well, they can talk about how sinful we are, how terrible we are, but then they come to the High Time and have a good time enjoying us and what we do here."

"I see. A lot of folks are hypocrites."

"They're what?" Suzie asked, confused by the big word.

"They say one thing and do another," Fernada explained for her.

"They also don't know where you've come from or how you came to be doing this for a living. I'd like to interview you and the rest of the young women who work here," Elise told them. "I'd like to know what your life is like working at the High Time Saloon."

Suzie gave a snort of derision. "You can find out what we do, but you'll never know what it's really like."

"Suzie, don't be so quick to judge," the older woman cautioned, "or you'll be sounding just like that shopkeeper." She eyed Elise, studying her for a moment, trying to judge the truth of her character. "Are you the one who trapped that outlaw preacher?"

"Yes, that was me."

"I see." Fernada nodded and fell silent for another moment, trying to decide how to handle this. Her decision wasn't made, though, until her gaze fell on Suzie, and she saw the bag of ribbon she was still holding. Turning back to the reporter, she asked, "Are you serious about doing this?"

"Very."

"Then I have an idea for you." And Fernada began to explain.

It was over an hour later when Elise rushed into the *Star*'s office. She was breathless with excitement.

"Andy! Is Gabe here?"

Andy looked up from his work and motioned back toward the editor's office. "Of course, he's here. He's been waiting for you for—say, two hours, but right now—" He didn't get to finish.

Elise hurried straight past his desk and in to speak with Gabe. She knew she should have felt guilty, but the story she'd come up with was too important. She was excited about selling him on the idea. If he let her do it the way she wanted, it was going to be quite an intriguing exposé.

"I need to talk with you!" she declared, striding straight into the room without waiting for an invitation.

Elise stopped abruptly at the doorway, for there, sitting across the desk from Gabe, was Julie.

"Oh. I didn't know you had a visitor," she said haltingly, shocked at seeing the other woman there.

"Hello, Elise. It's good to see you again," Julie lied. She got to her feet. "I guess I'd better go now. It looks like you have some business to conduct, and I don't want to get in your way."

"It was lovely to see you again, Julie," Gabe said, rising from the desk to walk her out of the office.

"I'll see you tomorrow night then? My mother will be delighted that you'll be joining us for dinner."

"It will be my pleasure. Did you say around seven?"

"That will be perfect. See you then." Her voice was a thick purr as she quit the building.

Trace turned away and hurried back into his office, where Elise was awaiting him.

"Sit down, sit down. Now, what happened that's got you so excited?" Trace asked as he sat down behind his desk. He wondered where she'd been and what was so important that she would be this worked up. Her eyes were sparkling and her cheeks were flushed. "Did the Ladies' Solidarity do something scandalous?"

"Hardly. They're angels—all of them. The meeting went very well. It was what happened afterward, when I was on my way back here, that got me sidetracked."

"And just what was that? And this had better be good, because I expected you back quite some time ago." He made a point of looking at his watch.

"I hardly think you were waiting breathlessly for my return," she countered. "It seems you had plenty to distract you while I was away."

The sight of Julie right there in Gabe's office with him had been quite a shock to Elise when she'd come to the door, and the emotions she was feeling, thinking of him spending time with the other woman, were troubling.

"Distractions aside, we had business to take care of, and you didn't show up," he pointed out, not even wanting to talk about how he'd just gotten trapped into going to dinner at Julie's house the next evening.

Elise slanted him a triumphant smile as she said seriously, "I've got our lead story for the next issue."

"Oh, really? And that is?"

"I want to do a story on what it's like to work in one of the saloons in town."

"You what?" He was certain he hadn't heard her right.

"I want to do a story on working girls in a saloon. I've already got everything arranged. All I need is your approval to do the article, and I can get started."

"Wait just a minute. I'm not giving my approval on anything right now. I don't even know what you're talking about."

"It's a sad story really," she began. She related all that had happened in the mercantile. "All Suzie wanted to do was buy some ribbon, and Mr. Perry wouldn't sell it to her. He all but threw her out of his store. I was right there. I saw the whole thing."

Andy had been trying to listen to what she was saying from his desk, but when she'd mentioned the High Time Saloon, he'd come to stand in the doorway. "If you need any help doing any investigating at the saloon, I'm here only to serve. I volunteer. I'll be glad to do my fair share—and then some," he offered, smiling at the thought.

"Stop it!" Elise knew what he was thinking. "I'm serious about this. Mr. Perry was downright cruel to Suzie, and all she wanted to do was make a purchase from him. I followed her to the High Time and spoke with her and the woman who runs the place. Her name is Fernada."

"You've already done all of that without permission?"

"I didn't know I needed to get your permission to follow leads on breaking stories," she stated almost angrily. How dare Gabe question her methods?! He wasn't even really an editor yet.

"It isn't proper for you to go into such a place," Trace told her.

"I can't go into the High Time, but it's all right for Suzie and Fernada to work there?" she countered quickly. "You sound a lot like Mr. Perry."

"I'm not condemning anyone or anything. I'm saying that as an attractive young woman, you could be putting yourself in a difficult situation."

"Nothing happened today."

"Good."

"But I'm not through. Here's what I want to do—and I already have Fernada's permission to do it."

"Do what?" Trace demanded, at a loss to figure out what she was planning.

"I want to work at the High Time and then write an exposé on what the life of a working girl is really like."

He stared at her in complete and utter disbelief as he told her, "No."

"What do you mean no?" she challenged. "This could be a great story."

"It's too dangerous," he argued, knowing full well what could happen to her in such a place.

"Too dangerous?" Elise repeated, giving a disbelieving shake of her head. "How can this be too dangerous? I've already dealt with the likes of Preacher Farnsworth. How can I be in danger at the High Time?"

"What exactly do you plan to do at the saloon?" Andy asked from where he stood in the doorway.

"Well, Fernada said she could help me with the clothes and makeup—"

"She what?" Trace blurted out.

"She and Suzie are going to help me dress for the work, and then I thought I'd try my hand at dealing cards and plying drinks, just like any ordinary working girl. What do you think?"

"No."

She looked at Gabe in irritation. "This will be a great story. I want to reveal what life is like from their side. Who are they? How did they get where they are? Why are they there, and why don't they leave? Some of them do, you know." Her excitement grew as she realized the humanitarian element to her story line. "When people like Mr. Perry see a girl from the High Time, they immediately judge her as being beneath them and basically of no worth. I want to change that perception. I want to show everyone the goodness in all people—no matter what their status in life."

"So write about the Ladies' Solidarity, if you want to write about good people," Trace told her sternly.

"I want to do this," she said, growing even more serious. "I promise you, you won't be sorry!"

"I already am sorry. The High Time Saloon is no place for you."

"The High Time Saloon is no place for any woman, but some women are forced by circumstances beyond their control to make a living working there. It's their story I want to tell. I want to show what their lives are really like."

He saw the earnestness of her desire. "All right, I agree—but only on one condition."

"What's that?" As uncomfortable as Gabe was with her idea, Elise wondered if he'd ever met or dealt with women like Fernada and Suzie before. Staring at him now in his eyeglasses and bow tie, she realized that a man like Gabe had probably never spent any time in a place like the High Time.

"My condition is that you don't go alone there. I want to be with you whenever you're there."

"That would ruin everything!" she protested, thinking of having him sitting right beside her as she tried to convince some cowboys that she was one of Fernada's girls.

"No, it won't. I'll keep my distance."

"You promise?"

"No one will ever have to know that I'm there to keep an eye on you."

The thought of Gabe "keeping an eye on her" made Elise smile. It would certainly be interesting to see how he reacted to the surroundings. "Do I have another choice?"

"No."

"Oh, all right." She had feared that he might not allow her to do the story at all, so she was pleased with the way things were turning out.

"When do you plan to start on it?"

"Fernada said that it didn't matter. I could do whatever I wanted to do," she said. Thinking

161

quickly and remembering Julie's dinner invitation, she added, "So I'd like to start tomorrow night. It's the end of the month, so there should be some cowboys in town, ready and willing to be parted from some of their wages. I know you've already got plans for the evening, so I can go ahead and do it by myself."

"Elise—" There was a warning note in Trace's voice. He knew how wild things could get in saloons. As sheriff, he had done his fair share of keeping things under control on payday in Eagle Pass. "I'll cancel the dinner arrangements."

"But you just made them. I hate to ruin your evening," she said almost too sweetly. "I'll be fine, really. I'm going for journalistic accuracy. That's all. I need to experience it so I can write about it," she said with dignity.

"Let's just make sure you don't experience more than you planned on," he muttered, less than enthusiastically.

"It's going to be fine. Just you wait and see," Elise assured him.

"I hope you're right, because I'm going to let Julie know I can't make dinner, and I'm going to be there at the saloon, making sure everything goes as it's supposed to."

For some reason she couldn't quite explain, Elise was pleased that he was going to be with her the next night and not Julie.

Chapter Eleven

"So you're really serious about doing this?" Fernada asked Elise when she arrived at the High Time late the next afternoon.

"Yes, I am," Elise answered, more than ready for whatever her new investigation would hold. She'd been awake most of the previous night thinking about the incident at the mercantile. She wanted the article to reflect Suzie's and Fernada's side of the story. She wanted the general public to understand their plight in a world that could sometimes be cruel and unforgiving.

"Your boss at the paper really gave his approval for you to write about this?" She was shocked.

"You sound surprised."

Fernada shrugged. "I know how the good folks of this town feel about us, and I didn't think anybody would be particularly interested."

"Mr. West is new at his job, but he trusts my judgment. I'm convinced that this is a story that needs to be told."

"How do you want to do it?"

"I want to be one of your girls for a couple of nights. You tell me what I should do, and I'll do it—within reason."

Fernada smiled at her qualifying statement. "So you don't want to experience everything?"

"Not everything."

They shared a look of understanding.

"As one of my girls, you'll be taking care of our customers. Our aim is to give them what they want—and when they come in here, they want a good time. We want them to be smiling when they leave."

"You sound like a much better businessperson than Mr. Perry."

"If I don't keep my customers satisfied, they'll go somewhere else," she explained simply. "Now, the first thing we have to do is get you some different clothes. If you're going to play the part, you have to look the part." The old woman looked her over, studying her thoughtfully. "You're on the tall side, so I think you're probably closest to Jenny's size. Let's see if she's got anything we can use."

She led her down the hall to a room near the far end and knocked on the door.

"Who is it?" a muffled, slurred voice called out.

"It's Fernada, Jenny. I need to talk to you."

A long moment passed, and the door was finally thrown open. A haggard and weary-looking woman stood before them. Her long, dark hair was in wild, tangled disarray about her face. Her eyes were bloodshot and her manner was drunken. Elise guessed she wasn't thirty yet, but right now she looked far older.

"I just got to bed a few hours ago. I was up all night. What do you want?" she asked groggily as she peered at Elise in a dull-eyed manner.

"This is Elise, the girl I was telling you about. She needs a dress for tonight, and I think she's just about your size."

Jenny remembered what Fernada had told her about the reporter wanting to work at the saloon for a few nights, and she eyed the newcomer up and down. She wondered who would believe that she worked there. There wouldn't be many men who would want her since she was on the thin side and kind of drab and ordinary looking. "It looks like she's going to need all the help she can get."

Elise felt the sting of her barb, but said nothing as Fernada spoke up.

"We just need to borrow a dress from you. I'm going to work on her hair and makeup."

"All right. Just a minute." She shut the door on them.

Elise gave Fernada a questioning look, but the other woman said nothing. They waited for several minutes until the door opened again. Jenny shoved a red satin dress into Elise's hands.

"Here. This is one of my best. See if you can fill it out and give all them good-looking cowboys a thrill."

"Are you sure you want to part with your red satin?" Fernada asked, knowing how much she liked that particular dress.

"I made me so much money last night, I'm going to get a new one," Jenny cackled in delight. She was exhausted from her long evening, but pleased with the way everything had turned out. "I got lucky last night—real lucky."

With that, she disappeared back into her room and shut the door on them again.

"Let's go on to my room, and we'll get you changed and ready."

They started back down the hall to begin her transformation.

"I take it Jenny likes this dress a lot?" Elise asked, glancing down at the vibrant red and black-trimmed satin garment she was holding. She had never worn anything like this in her entire life. She wondered what it was going to feel like to put it on. She wondered, too, how she was going to look. She tried to imagine Gabe's expression when he saw her in it the first time.

"It's always been her favorite. She must have had some very generous cowboy with her last night for her to give it up without a thought."

They entered the haven of Fernada's own private room. A large bed with a massive wooden headboard dominated the room. The headboard in particular amazed Elise, for carved into it were erotic scenes of embracing figures engaged in sensual acts. Elise couldn't stop herself from blushing at the sight.

"That headboard is something, isn't it?" Fernada bragged. "I've had that for a lot of years now. One of my best customers a long time ago was quite a woodworker."

"It's definitely . . . interesting."

"Go ahead behind the screen there and change," she directed, pointing her in the right direction. "We can keep talking while you're getting ready."

"Thanks."

Elise disappeared behind the partition, and she was glad that it provided at least a little bit of privacy. After quickly taking off the demure daygown she'd worn, she slipped into the satin dress. The slick material felt cold against her skin, and she shivered at the contact.

"Do you need some help fastening the back?"

"Yes, if you don't mind?"

"Come on out here so I can see what I'm doing."

Elise emerged from behind the screen, trying to hold the back together as she clutched the low-cut bodice to her. She turned her back to Fernada, and the other woman made short work of fastening the gown for her.

"There. Now turn around and let me get a look at you."

Elise did as she was told.

Fernada gave her a critical once-over. It was obvious the dress was too big in the bosom for her, but it wasn't because she was so small. It was because Jenny was so well endowed.

"The color is good on you—real good—but it looks like you need some help up top there," she remarked with a wry smile.

"Obviously, Jenny's much bigger than I am," Elise said, embarrassed by the way the bodice gaped open. If she went out into the saloon dressed like this, she would have few secrets from the men who were there drinking.

"Not as much as you'd think," she told her. "There are ways to make what God gave us look better than it really is. Turn around for me."

Again Elise did as she was told. Fernada unfastened the back, then went to her dresser and dug through one of the drawers.

"Here," she said, turning to her and holding out a fancy black corset. "Go on back behind the screen and put this on."

Elise looked down at her bosom again. "Do you think it will help that much?"

"It'll help some, but this will do the most for you." She took some wadded-up soft material out of the drawer, too. "See what you can do with it."

"What should I do with it?" Elise stared from the corset and stuffing to Fernada, completely at a loss how to go about the necessary enhancements.

Fernada chuckled. "You really are an innocent, aren't you? You put that corset on and stuff the material in the bodice. It'll lift you up and make you look bigger."

"Oh." Elise turned almost as red as the dress she was wearing. "It is important, isn't it?"

"The men who come into the High Time like buxom women. It'll be the first thing they'll look at when they see you downstairs."

"Doesn't it bother you to have them ogling you that way?"

"It's a part of our job. The better we look, the more money we make. We want them to notice us. The more they like us, the more they'll pay us for the pleasure of our company."

"So whoever Jenny was with last night must have really liked her."

"He liked her very much," she confirmed.

"Doesn't any of this ever bother you?"

For a moment, Fernada's expression was haunted, as if she were remembering something painful, but then the look was gone. "Honey, after all these years, nothing much bothers me anymore."

"That's not true," Elise said softly. "I saw the way you were taking care of Suzie yesterday. You were hurting for her."

"I care about my girls," she said defensively. "Suzie is still very young, but she's learning. I honestly think she believes she going to find a man who will rescue her from this—this way of life."

"Maybe she will."

Fernada gave a cynical laugh. "Even if she quit tomorrow and walked away, the good folks of this town would never let her forget where she came from."

"How can you be so sure?"

"Because there are too many people like Mr. Perry in this world."

Elise's expression darkened as she remembered the scene that had brought her to this. "Suzie really is young. How did she come to work for you?"

"She was orphaned and had no other way to support herself. She's been working for me for over a year now."

"What about Jenny? Have you known her for very long?"

"For years," she answered, a note of sadness in her voice. "And for all the time we've spent together, I've learned very little about her past."

"She doesn't talk about it?"

"Hardly ever that I can remember. All I know is that she was running from something. I tend to think it was her family, but I was never sure and knew better than to ask. Whatever it was, it pushed her to drinking. She can't make it through a day without her liquor."

"It must be a hard life, living that way."

"She's hiding from something, but we'll probably never know what. I figure if she hasn't told me by now, she ain't never going to. The only thing I've ever heard her say is when she's real drunked up, she asks me if I've seen Hunt around, but I have no idea who he is or why she wants him."

"Someone named Hunt . . . " Elise could only imagine what terrible secrets haunted Jenny's past. "What about you? How did you come to be working at the High Time?"

"I was widowed many years ago. Lost my husband to a fever, and times went from bad to worse. I had to support myself somehow." Fernada was thoughtful as she remembered the frightening days after her husband Jim's death, when she'd been close to destitute. "I met Sam Vaughn then. He took me in, and I've been with him ever since. He's the owner of the High Time, you know."

"Actually, I didn't know that. Will I get to meet him?"

"I'm sure you will. I had to make sure with him that it was all right for you to do this. He said it was all right, but he was worried that there might be trouble."

"Don't worry. I won't cause any."

Fernada laughed. "I know that. It's just that

sometimes the boys get a little wild. We'll just have to make sure you stay close to me and Dan, the bartender."

"I will," Elise promised. "Fernada, are you really happy here, living like this?"

"I'm as happy as I can be. Jim was the one love of my life. I'll never love another man the way I loved him."

"Have you ever thought of walking away from it all? Of giving it up?"

"No. Sam and I—we stay together. It's a good business arrangement, and it's the way it has to be for both of us." She paused, realizing how long they'd been talking. "Now, enough about me. You go put that corset on with the padding so we can see how it looks. We've still got a lot of work to do on you before you can go downstairs."

"You really need to do that much more to me?"

"You'll see."

Elise smiled as she held up the underthings. "And you really think this will help?"

"I know it will. A lot of girls use this trick all the time. Go ahead. Give it a try. I think you'll be surprised."

"I'll be back in a minute."

She disappeared behind the screen again to make the necessary adjustments. When she emerged and caught a glimpse of herself in the full-length mirror across the room, she stopped and stared in complete awe at her own reflection. She had never known she could look so voluptuous.

"I see what you mean—it really does work, doesn't it?"

"Beautifully. Now you look the way the men want you to look. The dress fits you much better with a little help."

Elise studied her mirror image with a critical eye. Her waist was tiny. Her breasts looked full and round and were all but falling out the top of the gown, thanks to the constricting corset. She knew it was all an optical illusion, but the men wouldn't care.

"What do we need to do next?"

"You don't want anyone to recognize you, do you?"

"No, that would ruin everything."

"Then I think you might want to wear a wig, too. If you're going to be in disguise, you may as well go all the way. I've got a blond one you can try. Sit down on the bed, and I'll help you with it." She went to her small closet to get the wig.

Within minutes, she had helped Elise put the wig on over her own dark tresses. It wasn't easy, for Elise's hair was thick and healthy, but they finally managed to get the pale wig adjusted just right.

"Take a look at yourself now and see what you think," Fernada suggested.

Elise stood up, smoothing the skirts of the red gown as she did so, and then went to stand before the mirror again. She deliberately kept her gaze downcast until she was ready to see what kind of transformation had taken place. When she looked up, she gasped out loud. She didn't recognize the woman staring back at her. If she hadn't known she was looking at herself, she would have had no idea of her identity.

"Oh, my," she breathed.

Elise

The woman standing before her in the mirror was vibrant looking, from her bright red gown to the mass of pale curls that tumbled artfully down her back. She had been transformed. She looked absolutely nothing like herself.

"And we still need to put some makeup on you. You're awfully pale."

A knock sounded at the door just then, and Fernada went to answer it. A lovely young woman Elise had never seen before stood there. She was tall, with raven hair and dark eyes. She was dressed in a dance hall outfit that fit her perfectly and showed off to their full advantage her womanly assets. Elise had no doubt that this girl was one of the men's favorites.

"Kate, come in. I want you to meet our new girl, Elise."

"I heard about you from Suzie," Kate said to Elise as she entered the room and eyed her with interest. "Say—isn't that Jenny's favorite dress?"

"She gave it to Elise to wear. Now all we have to do is help her with some rouge and lipstick, and she'll be all ready to go to work with the rest of us."

Kate stared at Elise long and hard. "Why are you doing this? You don't have to be here."

"I saw how Suzie was treated in one of the stores in town and it made me angry. I want to learn what it's like to work here, and then I want to let the public know."

"The public doesn't care about us."

"Then I want to make them care," Elise stated firmly.

"Good luck." Her comment was jaded.

"With the help I'm getting from Fernada and the other girls, I hope I won't need any."

"Just remember, Kate," Fernada put in, "tonight, when Elise is working the saloon with us, we all need to keep an eye on her. We don't want any of the cowboys getting any wild ideas about bedding her. She serves drinks only."

Elise blushed again at her blunt statement.

"All right. We'll try to keep her out of trouble."

"Now, since you're here, why don't you help me make her up? You're good at it. We need to give her some rouge and some bright lips and maybe a beauty mark on her cheek. What do you think?"

"I think that would be perfect! I'll go get some of my makeup and be right back," Kate offered.

"Sit down on the bed. That way we can both work on you at the same time," Fernada instructed Elise.

She did as she was told and waited a bit anxiously as the older woman began to paint her face. Kate was back in no time with additional cosmetics, and they both set to work on her.

"What do you think?" Fernada said to Kate as she stepped back to observe their handiwork long minutes later.

Kate studied Elise critically for a moment, making her feel like a schoolgirl again.

"I think me and the other girls are going to have some tough competition tonight. As different as you look, I don't think your own mother would know you."

"Good," Elise said firmly. "I don't want anyone to know who I am. As far as our customers are concerned, I am just one of the girls. I guess I'd better use a different name while I'm here, too." She paused thoughtfully. "I know—call me Sugar."

"All right, Sugar," the older woman said with a grin, "what do you think about the new you?"

Elise rose from the bed and turned to look at her reflection in the mirror one last time. She stared in thrilled disbelief at her image.

The makeup they'd used had heightened the color in her cheeks and brought out the green of her eyes. Fernada had painted her lips a bright red, and though it made her a bit self-conscious, the color did match the gown perfectly. She looked sensual and knowing—a far cry from the truth of her real personality.

"Well?" Kate prodded.

"You're miracle workers," she told them, her tone soft in wonder. "I wonder if Gabe and Andy will recognize me."

"Who are Gabe and Andy?"

"Gabe is my boss, and Andy works at the paper. They said they might come around tonight to keep an eye on me."

"It'll be fun to see their reactions, won't it?" Kate asked.

"Yes, it will." And Elise meant it. She was looking forward to seeing if Gabe even recognized her.

A knock at the door drew their attention.

"Fernada—it's me, Suzie."

"Come on in. We got someone here for you to see. Come in and meet Sugar."

Suzie came into the room and stopped just inside the door. "Is that really you?"

"What do you think?"

"I think you're going to have every customer in the place panting after you!"

Elise smiled, but she wasn't quite sure if that was something to be proud of or not. "When do we get started?" She looked to Fernada for guidance.

"Right now, if you think you're ready?"

"I'm as ready as I'll ever be."

"Good. The boys should be showing up any time. Since it's payday, they're going to be doing some free spending."

"And we want to help them all we can with spending their money," Kate put in, smiling at the thought.

Elise drew a deep, steadying breath as she readied herself to face the coming evening.

"Nervous?" Fernada asked knowingly. She could just imagine the thoughts that were going through Elise's mind right now, and she wanted to calm her if she could.

"A little."

"We'll stay close to you, so you won't be alone, and Dan and Sam will be there, too."

"Thanks. I appreciate it." She gave all three women a warm smile. "Let's go, then. We shouldn't keep our customers waiting."

Fernada quickly filled her in on what her duties would be. "If any of the boys start pressuring you for more than just drinks, you tell them to see me. The only thing you're serving up is liquor." She looked at her knowingly as she asked, "You are still a virgin, aren't you, Elise?"

Elise was glad that the heavy rouge she wore hid her blush. "Yes, I am."

"That's what I thought. You just stay where we can keep an eye on you. We want to make sure you stay that way. Let's go to work, shall we, ladies?"

Chapter Twelve

Elise followed Fernada down the hall toward the open staircase that led to the saloon. The saloon was one big open room. The bar ran the entire width of the back wall. Hanging over the bar was a large, framed oil portrait of a scantily clad female reclining on a sofa. An area was kept clear for dancing, with tables set up all around, and there were a few men already gathered there, caught up in a high-stakes game of poker. Dan, the bartender, was busy waiting on the cowboys and miners who had worked hard all month and were all set to enjoy some good times.

As they started down the steps, Elise looked around to see if she recognized anyone. She saw no sign of Gabe or Andy and was glad. She needed a few minutes to get used to her new personality.

One thing Elise was really happy about was that George wasn't there. Her grandmother had mentioned that she might ask him to check up on her, and Elise wasn't sure she wanted George to see her this way. She cast a surreptitious glance down at her bosom, so artfully displayed for all to see, and fought to keep from blushing in embarrassment. Her nervousness about the evening grew, but there was no way she could let it show. She just hoped that she had convinced her grandmother that everything would go just fine and that there was no reason for her or George to worry. Now she had to make sure that everything did go as planned.

As she reached the bottom step, Elise reminded herself that she was working on a story, and she had to be professional. Elise told herself to be calm, that she would be able to take care of herself here at the High Time, that she didn't need Gabe or Andy or George around watching out for her. It wasn't as if she was dealing with a desperate Preacher Farnsworth. At the saloon, she would constantly be surrounded by people. All she had to do was talk to the customers and bring them drinks. It was going to be very simple.

Standing a bit straighter, she gave a haughty lift of her chin. She was as ready as she would ever be for the night to come.

"Hey, Art! Oooo-eeee! Look who's comin' down the steps!" a cowboy named Buddy called out loudly when he caught sight of the women. He was sitting at a table near the bar with one of his friends, and his gaze was riveted on the females.

178

"Well, if this don't beat all! Evening, ladies! I know Miss Fernada, Suzie, and Kate, but who's the new girl?" Art asked, eyeing the newcomer with open, hungry interest. Red was his favorite color, and he thought she looked damned good in the red satin dress.

"Evening, Art and Buddy, it's good to see you boys again," Fernada greeted them smoothly as she started toward their table. "I want you to meet my new girl, Sugar. Sugar, this is Art and this is Buddy. They're two favorites of mine. You be good to them."

"I will. It's nice to meet you boys," Elise said. She was very aware that the two men's avid gazes were locked on her bosom as she followed Fernada to stand by them. She wondered if the two would be able to remember what her face looked like, if they were asked to describe her later. Right now, judging by their expressions, she doubted it. The thought bothered her. She wasn't really working at the saloon. She didn't have to stay there forever. She could leave whenever she was ready. But she wondered how it would affect the other girls who worked there, knowing that the men only thought of them as bodies, and not as people.

"Hello there, honey," Buddy said, finally lifting his gaze to look at her. "How long you been working here? I ain't seen you before, and I'm pretty much a regular at the High Time."

"This is my very first night," Elise answered, managing to give the man a smile. "And you're going to be my first customer."

Elise realized suddenly that Clint was a dream of a man compared to these two. Buddy was practically drooling as he stared at her. His teeth were blackened, he was missing several, and he had a scraggly growth of beard. Still, somehow, she kept smiling, but even as she did, she wondered how the other girls managed.

Buddy immediately perked up when he found he was to be her first. He reached out and started to pull Elise into his arms and onto his lap.

"Oh, no. Buddy, you're not going to be *that* kind of customer for her," Fernada said in a threatening tone, stopping him. "Sugar here will do her best to satisfy you—but only your thirst. She'll serve you whatever you want, as long as it's liquor."

"Ah, Fernada, she's one hot-looking woman. What the hell's she doing working here if she ain't putting out?" He was crude.

"Those are my rules," the older woman dictated, giving him her famous cold-eyed glare. A look like that from Fernada had been known to cow many a man. "Follow them or leave."

"You know I ain't goin' nowhere else, darlin'," Buddy said, quickly softening before her condemnation. "I just wanted to have me some fun with her, that's all."

"We can still have fun," Elise offered, getting more into her role. "What would you like—to drink?" She deliberately made her innocent question sound seductive.

Buddy's eyes glowed as he grumbled, "What I'd like and what I'm going to get are two different things."

"I know." She winked at him and gave a throaty laugh.

"I'll settle for another bourbon, since I can't have what I really want."

"Now, Buddy, don't go pouting on me," Fernada said, patting him on the shoulder. "Sugar is here to show you a good time, but if you want more than a few drinks tonight, you'll have to talk to one of my other girls."

"I don't suppose Kate's too hard on the eyes," he groused, glancing toward where Kate was talking to some of the other customers.

"Suzie's working tonight, too, and so is Jenny," she told Buddy and Art as she moved off to take care of business. "So you two enjoy yourselves."

"We will, don't worry," they answered, turning to watch the new girl as she walked back to the table with Buddy's drink.

"Here you go," Elise said.

As she leaned over to put the glass of whiskey in front of him, Buddy reached up and stuffed a dollar bill down the bodice of her gown. His fingers brushed the side of her breast as he did it. Elise was shocked by that intimate contact, but managed not to reveal her emotions.

"Thanks," she told him, giving him what she hoped was a pleasant smile. In truth, she wanted to slap him for his boldness, but she controlled herself for the sake of her story.

"My pleasure, believe me," he answered, leering at her.

She drew away from Buddy to wait on Art. "What about you? Can I take care of you, too?"

"Oh, Sugar, you can take care of me any day!" He laughed loudly at his own humor. "But I guess I'll just have another whiskey."

"I'll be right back."

"I'll be waiting."

Dan had been watching from the bar, and he was aware of everything that was going on.

"Buddy and Art are basically harmless," he cautioned Elise. "They're only out for a little fun. They don't get mean. Some of the boys won't take no for an answer, so you have to watch out for them, but you don't have to worry about that with those two."

"Thanks, that's good to know. This is going to take some practice and some getting used to," she told him with a grin.

"I don't think you need any practice at all. You've got every man in the place watching you. You should see how their heads turn when you walk by. You're going to be fine. Now, here's the drink you wanted. It's always best not to keep the customer waiting too long."

"Thanks, Dan."

He gave her a smile and a reassuring nod as she hurried off to wait on Art.

Art was ready for her when she reached his side. As she placed his glass before him, he put his money down her bodice, too. Elise was embarrassed, but didn't protest. She flashed both men a wide, flirtatious smile before turning away to wait on some of the other men who'd come in.

It was then that she saw Gabe. He was standing just inside the swinging doors, and his gaze was riveted on her. She gave him an arch smile as she continued to wait on the men who were seated at the tables.

Trace had entered the High Time and had stood there, looking around for Elise. It had taken him a moment to finally recognize her in the wig and red dress. He'd stared at her in disbelief, trying to reconcile the blond-haired, lush-figured woman with the Elise he knew. Elise was elegant and intelligent, while this blonde looked like she knew exactly what she was doing as she flaunted herself before the rowdy men. It had seemed impossible that she could be the same woman. But she was.

Trace had started forward to speak with her, but had stopped abruptly when he saw Art stuff his money down her cleavage. His first reaction had been to grab Elise and drag her out of there to safety before he throttled the other man for daring to touch her that way, but somehow he'd fought the impulse down. He'd stayed where he was, his hands clenched into fists at his sides, his expression deliberately impassive. Trace had reminded himself that she was working on a story. It hadn't been easy, but he'd done it.

"Hi, Big Guy," Kate said as she approached him. She had not seen him before and wondered what he was doing in the High Time Saloon. He wasn't one of their ordinary customers.

"Evening, ma'am," Trace said. It took an effort, but he remained in character.

"What can I do for you tonight?"

"I think I'll have a drink at the bar."

"If you want or need anything else, you let me know. My name's Kate."

"I'll remember, and thank you, ma'am." Trace headed to the bar. He needed that drink. He had the feeling it was going to be a very long night.

Elise was relieved when Gabe didn't cause a scene. She finally freed herself from the other customers and went to speak with him at the bar.

"Buy me a drink, mister?" she asked as she came to stand next to him. She turned her back to the bar and faced the room as she looked up at Gabe over her shoulder.

"What would you like, miss?"

"My name's Sugar, and I'd like a sarsaparilla."

Trace nodded to the barkeep, then glanced down at Elise. He went still. His mouth went dry, and he swallowed convulsively. He'd had no idea that she was that well endowed. As much as he told himself to look away, his gaze lingered on that exposed expanse of creamy, silken flesh. He enjoyed the view for a moment, until he realized he was behaving no better than any of the other men who were ogling her in the saloon.

"Nice dress," he finally managed, tearing his gaze away. He wanted to tell her to go back upstairs and change clothes or at least put on a shawl of some kind, but he couldn't. She was doing her job, and he was supposed to be there to help her—not make things more difficult for her.

"The girl named Jenny who works here lent it to me," she told him.

"And the hair?" He looked up at the wig.

"The hair is Fernada's." She grinned at him as she patted one errant blond curl. "It's quite a change for me, don't you think?"

He grunted and took a drink of his whiskey.

Elise noticed that he seemed uncomfortable, and she found it reassuring, after his apology for their kiss the other day, to know that he wasn't completely oblivious to her charms. When Dan served her her drink, she took a sip.

"So you didn't have any trouble canceling your dinner with Julie and her parents?"

"No, she was very understanding."

"Good. I would have hated to cause you any trouble." She had to admit to herself that she was glad he'd gotten out of it. She was glad he wasn't with Julie tonight.

"It was no problem," he responded, although Julie had pouted prettily when he'd stopped by her home to let her know that he wouldn't be able to keep their dinner engagement. "So, how is it going?"

"I've never experienced anything like this before. The men here really don't care that I'm a person. They just look at me as if I'm only a body, here to satisfy their baser needs."

"To their way of thinking, that's what you are. Just be careful."

"You sound like my grandmother."

"No, I sound like your editor."

"I hope I can do everyone justice when I write the article. There's so much sadness here."

"Well, you sure can't tell it by looking at everyone," he said as he glanced around the room.

Across the saloon, Kate was laughing loudly at something one of the miners had said. Nearby, Suzie was sitting on a man's lap, her arm around his neck, leaning toward him in open invitation. Fernada was watching over all the activities from the far end of the bar.

"They want the men to like them and want them. That's how they make their living."

"Hey! Sugar!" Buddy called out just then, interrupting her conversation. "I need another drink!"

"Coming right up!" she answered, then looked up at Gabe. "Sorry, I have to go wait on my customers."

"Is the tip worth it?"

"No, but I consider it research."

He lifted his glass to her in salute. "I'll be right here if you need me."

She nodded and went off to take care of Buddy and Art.

"Who's your friend at the bar?" Buddy asked when she reached their table.

"I think he works at one of the newspapers here in town. Why?"

"You shouldn't waste the night talking to him. We can show you a better time than he can," Art told her.

"I'll just bet you could, but I'm having all the good times I can handle right now."

"You sure you're only serving drinks?"

"Positive." She flashed him a smile to soften the meaning.

"Pity. I could take you for a ride you wouldn't soon forget."

"Why, I just bet you could, Buddy," Elise told him, glad that her rouge would hide her blush over his crudeness. "You both want another drink?"

"We sure do."

"I'll be right back with them for you."

Elise had just reached the bar, intent on getting their drinks, when she noticed another cowboy come in. Her eyes widened as she recognized him, and she quickly looked away as she went to stand beside Gabe again.

"Did you see who just came in?" she asked in a low voice after placing the order with Dan for Buddy and Art.

"I saw him. What do you want to do?" Trace asked. He was ready to help her get out of there if need be.

"It's a good thing I decided to use the name Sugar." She squared her shoulders as if preparing for battle. "I guess I'd better see if my disguise is as good as we think it is."

Trace nodded.

"I'd better hurry back with the boys' drinks. Wish me luck."

"You've got it."

She headed back to the table with the fresh drinks, focusing the entire time on not spilling them. She was nervous and her hands were shaking. "Here you go, boys. Enjoy! I'll check on you later."

"We'll be waiting for you," Buddy and Art told her.

Deliberately, Elise made her way to the table where Clint Parker had joined a poker game.

"Anything I can get for you, cowboy?" she asked, trying to make her voice as different as possible from her real tone.

Clint gave her only a cursory glance as he studied his cards. "I'll have a whiskey."

"Coming right up."

Elise breathed a sigh of relief that Clint hadn't immediately recognized her, but she still had to serve him his drink and get paid. As soon as she had the whiskey, she returned to his side.

"One whiskey, just for you."

"I appreciate it," he told her as he looked up at her. "You're new here, aren't you?"

Elise almost froze as her gaze met his, but she saw no flash of recognition in his eyes at all. "Yes. I just started."

He nodded and handed her the money, saying nothing more. She moved away, thankful that her disguise had worked so perfectly.

"Looks like your disguise is as good as you thought it was," Trace told her when she came to stand with him at the bar a short time later.

"It really must be," she said, amazed that Clint had proven so immune to her charms.

"Maybe he's not interested in any other woman but the real you," Trace said thoughtfully.

"I'll have to keep an eye out for him tomorrow at the office. He's liable to show up there at any time, since he's in town tonight."

As it happened, Clint didn't stick around at the saloon very long. He evidently lost what little money he had very quickly in the poker game and then left. Elise breathed a lot easier once he was gone. She started making the rounds of the room again.

A group of rowdy cowboys came in then, hollering and shouting. Without any warning, one of the men walked right up to Elise and slipped an arm familiarly around her waist.

"Say, honey, I know you're wanting a good time tonight, and I'm just the man you've been waiting for. Ignore all these other men who just came in with me. I'm the one you want to spend the rest of the night with."

"What's your name, handsome?" Elise

asked, trying not to squirm over his repulsive nearness.

"My name's Boyd. What's yours?" he said, pulling her closer to his side.

"I'm Sugar."

"Well, gimme a little kiss, Sugar. I've been needin' some lovin' for weeks now."

"Sorry, Boyd, but the only thing I'm giving out tonight is liquor. I'll be glad to have Dan get you a drink if you'd like one."

"What the hell are you talking about, woman? I came in here to enjoy myself, and I aim to do that—with you."

"And I'll be glad to help you enjoy yourself."

"That's what I wanted to hear. I like my women willing." He pressed a sloppy kiss to her neck, his gaze hot on her breasts. He couldn't wait to push that dress off her shoulders and get a real good look at her.

Elise stiffened at his boldness. His touch made her flesh crawl, and she couldn't help but wonder if the other girls felt the same way she did when the men pawed at them. She glanced toward Kate and Suzie, but they were smiling and looking for all the world as if they were having a wonderful time with the men they were entertaining. Elise decided that they had to be great actresses. She couldn't believe that they were really enjoying being treated this way.

"Boyd! It's good to see you again," Fernada said as she walked over to join them. She knew him well and she didn't trust him around Elise. He was a horny bastard and prone to meanness. "You and the boys in town for a good time tonight, are you?"

"You know we are, darlin'."

Fernada looked to Elise. "Boyd and the boys are from the Rocking K Ranch. You have yourself a fine time, boys, but what Sugar here told you before is right. She is only serving up liquor. That's all."

"But that ain't no fair! I'm wanting her!"

"You and at least half-a-dozen other men here at the High Time, but it ain't going to happen."

"I'll stand in line for her. She'll be worth it. I can't wait to see what's up under her skirts," he told her, giving Elise's waist a knowing squeeze and talking to Fernada about her as if she wasn't there.

"You can stand in line for any of the other girls—for Jenny or Kate or Suzie, but not for Sugar. Have you seen Jenny yet? She's probably looking for you somewhere."

Elise was beginning to feel as if she were just goods being bartered. It was humbling, and humiliating—and educational, too. The trouble was, she was learning about things that she'd never wanted to know about.

Boyd glared at Fernada. "But I want this one tonight."

"You can't have her. She's only waiting tables."

"We'll see about that," he snarled defiantly, determined to bed Sugar before the night was out.

"There ain't anything to see. Now, have a drink and relax. It's time to have some fun. It's payday for you, ain't it?"

"It sure as hell is, woman!" Boyd hooted.

"Then enjoy yourself, but keep your hands off Sugar. I'd hate for the evening to turn ugly."

Boyd was about to say something when the piano player finally started playing a raucous tune. Boyd grabbed Sugar's hand.

"Come on, little honey! We're gonna show 'em how it's done!"

There was no way Elise could resist as he dragged her out onto the dance floor.

Chapter Thirteen

From where he'd been standing at the bar watching Elise with Boyd, Trace had been hard put not to confront the lecherous cowboy and tell him to keep his hands off her. The sight of him kissing Elise's neck that way had made him furious. He watched for a sign of panic on Elise's part, but she'd seemed in control. He was amazed at how strong-willed she was, first with Preacher Farnsworth and now with Boyd.

"Want another drink?" Dan asked him.

"Yes," Trace told him tersely, turning away from the sight of the two dancing. "I could use another one."

"Sugar is something else, isn't she?" The bartender chuckled.

"She's certainly different from any woman I've ever met before," he replied honestly, surprising himself with his answer.

"I think the rest of the boys are feeling exactly same way about her. Look at the way they're watching her. Sugar is one pretty woman."

"She sure is," Buddy and Art said as they came up to the bar to get their own drinks.

"Guess you figured Sugar was going to be busy for a while, eh, fellas?" Dan chuckled.

"We gave up waiting on her. We know what Boyd's like and figured we were better off taking care of ourselves right now."

"What's wrong with Boyd?" Trace asked, glancing back toward the dance floor.

"He's one mean son of a bitch," Dan explained. "We keep a close eye on him. He's been known to get rough with some of the girls."

Trace stiffened, and a muscle worked in his jaw as he controlled his anger over this news. Any man who hit a woman was a low-life coward. Women were to be cherished, not abused.

"He gets pretty rough with everybody when he's drunk," Buddy put in. "I had a run-in with him a couple of years ago, and I don't want to have another one." He grimaced at the memory.

He and Art got their drinks and went on back to their table.

Trace took a deep drink from the refill Dan had given him, then turned his attention back to Elise. He was going to make sure she stayed right where he could see her. If Boyd even looked as though he was going to lay a hand on her in anger, he was going to have to deal with Trace Jackson first.

Elise had thought Clint was a dangerous dancing partner, but by comparison, Boyd was downright deadly. He was a big man, and she had to struggle just to hang on to him as he spun her around the floor.

"Ain't you glad ol' Boyd showed up tonight? You were just waiting for a man like me to come in and take care of you, weren't you?"

"Absolutely," she managed breathlessly as she struggled to avoid both his groping hands and his cloddish, booted feet. On top of everything else, as he worked up a sweat, Boyd smelled bad. Again, she thought of the working girls who actually lived this life, and she wondered how they tolerated it.

"I knew you were the one for me the minute I laid eyes on you," Boyd was telling her, his eyes gleaming with excitement. "I told you I wasn't letting you get away from me, and I ain't." He tightened his hold on her, bringing her against his chest as he stomped even more wildly around the floor.

Elise didn't know what to say to the man or what to do as she found herself enveloped in his bearlike hold. All she wanted to do was escape his disgusting company. His hands seemed to be everywhere as he kept her moving in no particular rhythm to the raucous dance tune.

"What are you doing with another woman, Boyd Wilson?" Jenny's voice was loud and cut through the noise of the piano player's tune.

The demanding question brought Boyd up short. The cowboy stopped dancing and turned around to find Jenny standing before him, her arms akimbo, her expression angry.

"Jenny—where you been?" he blustered, suddenly uneasy. If ever there had been a woman who could match him in his passions it was

Jenny, but he'd seen this Sugar when he'd come in and had been challenged by the prospect of trying to bed her.

"You didn't answer my question, Boyd Wilson! What are you doing with another woman? I've been sitting upstairs in my room just waiting for you to show up! I've been saving myself for you all night, and here you are! Dancing with her!" She took at step toward him, thrusting her bosom out even farther to get his undivided attention. She deliberately made a point of licking her lips as she eyed him up and down. Her gaze lingering on the lower half of his body. "I suppose I could find me another man." She looked around. "I bet there are men here who are every bit as good as you *think* you are." The last was deliberately sneered.

"Sugar was promising me a real good time, so I was going to take her up on it since I didn't know where you were," he lied. He knew how exciting Jenny could be. He'd spent many a Saturday night in her bed and had enjoyed every minute of having her. She was a wild, insatiable woman.

"Get away from my man, Sugar," Jenny told her, casting her a cold look. "Boyd is mine."

Elise quickly moved away, thrilled to be free of the cowboy. She watched as Jenny walked up to him and kissed him full and flaming on the lips all the while rubbing herself suggestively against him.

Everyone in the bar was watching, too. They'd expected Boyd to put Jenny in her place. They were shocked when, without another word, Jenny put her hand in the waistband of his pants and led him up the stairs.

Elise wasn't certain what emotion she was feeling—relief at being rid of him or pity for Jenny for having to put up with the man.

"Are you all right?"

She looked up to find Fernada at her side. "Yes, I'm fine."

"Good. Jenny always comes through when I need her."

"Does she really want to be with that man?"

The older woman gave her a meaningful look. "Boyd just got paid. Jenny cares that he pays a high price for her services—if you know what I mean."

Elise looked up the steps after them, but they were gone from her sight. She turned away, wondering what could reduce a woman to such a state in life. Of all the men in the High Time, Jenny had picked Boyd. She could have had Gabe!

The thought stopped Elise cold as she realized the direction of her thoughts. But even as she analyzed them, she realized it was true. Her gaze sought Gabe out, and she found that he was standing at the bar, watching her, his expression serious. Gabe really was the only man in the entire saloon who held any real attraction for her.

Not that Elise even wanted to be thinking about such things, but her experiences that night were forcing her to. Although her new boss was not the most dominant of men, Gabe was intelligent and civilized, and right now those two qualities meant a lot to her. He could dance, too! If only he would get rid of the bow ties, he might not be half bad-looking. The eyeglasses—well, there was nothing to be done about those. She supposed the man had to see. She gave him a slight, reassuring smile, sensing that he was concerned about her, and he returned the gesture with a nod of understanding.

"You'd better get back to work. Your other customers are waiting." Fernada's voice cut through her musings.

"After Boyd, it will be my pleasure."

Elise started mixing with some of the new men who'd come in. It was over an hour later when she finally managed to seek Gabe out at a table in the back where he'd settled in with Andy and George.

"I wouldn't have believed it, if I hadn't seen it myself," Andy said, his eyes twinkling with devilish delight at the sight of her so clad. He'd been watching her tending to the saloon's business for quite a while. He was amazed at not only the way she looked, but the way she'd been handling all the men. "You're really very good at this," he quipped. "If you ever lose your job at the paper, it looks like you've already got another job lined up."

She laughed at him, knowing he was teasing. "And I'll get you a job helping Dan the bartender!"

"No, I'm just fine where I am, thanks," he answered.

"If you really think I'm good at this and enjoying it, maybe I should take to the stage instead. Obviously, my thespian skills are honed to perfection."

"You do live an exciting life. One week, you're getting married to a man you'd never met before, and the next you're working as a saloon girl. I wonder what you're going to come up with next," Andy said thoughtfully.

"So do I," Trace said, frowning. "Something simple would be good. Maybe an exposé on the Ladies' Solidarity?"

"I know her grandmother would prefer that," George added.

"I wish she could see you now," Andy put in.

All three men laughed as they imagined what Claire's reaction would be.

"Gabe told us about Boyd. If your grandmother had been here, he wouldn't have stood a chance against her. But I'm glad Claire isn't here." George turned serious. "She'd be worried about you. This looks like it could be a rough crowd."

"Dan warned me about that."

"Do you think you've done enough research for the night?" Trace asked, ready to get her out of there.

"I told Fernada I'd work until midnight."

Trace glanced at his pocketwatch. "You've got another hour to go."

"I guess I'd better make the rounds and visit with some more customers. Jenny's still with Boyd, and Kate just took another man upstairs." The thought that the women were selling their bodies just to survive sent a shiver of disgust through her. She had always believed that lovemaking should be a beautiful experience between a husband and a wife, an expression of deep, heartfelt emotion, not a cold, calculated business transaction.

"Just keep an eye out for Boyd when he comes back down," Trace cautioned her.

"I hope I'm long gone by then."

"So do I."

The three men watched as she moved away to take care of business.

George and Andy left a short time later, once they were assured that Gabe was going to escort Elise safely home.

Trace remained observantly quiet at his table for a while longer, then joined in a poker game. He won some and lost some and was just about breaking even when midnight rolled around. He watched as Elise disappeared upstairs with Fernada. He didn't want her going home alone at this time of night, so they had prearranged for him to meet her at the back door. As Trace left the High Time to get the carriage he'd rented, he smiled to himself at the realization that this was the first time he'd ever been this glad to leave a saloon.

The alley was dark and narrow and deserted, making Trace even more glad that he'd insisted on accompanying Elise home. He didn't have to wait long for her. She slipped out of the saloon's back door and into the fresh night air as if she were making a great escape. Fernada had thought it best that she leave this way, so none of the customers could see her.

"Elise?"

"Thank heavens you're here," she said, relieved as she went straight to him. "That was one long night."

Trace stared down at her in the darkness. She was the real Elise once more in her demure, high-necked gown and wearing her dark hair sedately restrained in a bun at the nape of her neck. For just an instant as his gaze went over her, he almost missed the red satin dress that had showed off her figure to such great advantage. He grew irritated with himself for even having the thought.

"Let's get you home. I left the carriage at the end of the alley."

He offered her his arm, and she took it, allowing him to lead her down the darkened passageway.

"Are you sure you want to do this again tomorrow night?"

"I have to. I want to learn more about the girls who work there."

"It's not what you're learning about the girls that worries me. It's men like Boyd."

"Don't worry. I have no intention of going anywhere near him again, but I am beginning to wonder—is this what men are really like? Buddy and Art were bad enough, but Boyd—" She shuddered as she remembered the feel of his hands upon her.

"No. We're not all like them," he said stiffly.

"So there are still men of honor out there somewhere?" Elise said thoughtfully. "I have to admit, I have my doubts. I don't think my ideal man exists anymore."

"What's your definition of the ideal man?"

"You really want to know?" Elise looked up at Gabe. In the muted moonlight, the line of his jaw looked strong, and he suddenly seemed a powerful, fiercely determined man to her. She knew it was only the shadowed darkness that gave him that appearance, though. This was, after all, just Gabe.

"Your ideal is obviously none of the men who patronize the High Time."

"No. My ideal man wouldn't drink himself stupid at a saloon. My ideal man is strong and brave and moral. He would defend those who needed defending, and he would stand for something, like Sheriff Jackson from Eagle Pass."

"But he ended up dead," was all Trace could say. He was completely shocked by her statement.

"But he was doing what was right," she said quietly. "My ideal man would be so wonderful that he'd sweep me off my feet, and he'd protect me—even from myself."

"Now that might be a bit difficult, even for your perfect man," Trace told her with a grin. "He'd have one heck of a time keeping up with you. First Preacher Farnsworth and then with men like Boyd, and who knows what your next story is going to be about?"

"You're right." She finally managed to laugh and relax a little bit. "He probably doesn't exist anywhere." She paused, then looked up at him and gave him a gentle smile. "Thank you."

"For what?" He glanced down at her surprised.

"For staying with me tonight. It was reassuring to know that you were there in case anything went wrong."

"I won't let anyone or anything hurt you, Elise," he vowed.

They fell silent then. When they reached the carriage, Trace helped her in and climbed in himself. He took up the reins once they'd settled in.

"Your grandmother's going to be glad to see you when you get home tonight."

"Do you suppose she's waiting up for me?"

"George said she was going to. She told him she wasn't going to be able to rest until you were back home with her, safe and sound. What time do you have to be here tomorrow?" Trace asked, already trying to plan the best way to handle the next night.

"Fernada wants me to start by eight o'clock."

"I'll come to your house and pick you up."

"Are you sure you want to stay at the High Time all night?"

"I'm not leaving you there alone," he declared, then modified his statement when he realized how he sounded. "You're my employee. It's my responsibility to keep you safe."

For a moment, Elise had almost thought Gabe cared about her, but his statement had reaffirmed that he only thought of her as an employee. She should have remembered that and not have been foolish enough to let herself think otherwise. She wondered why it had mattered to her that he only thought of her as someone who worked for him. She didn't care about Gabe, other than the fact that he was her boss.

When they reached the house, she didn't wait for him to help her descend, but climbed down by herself. "Good night. I'll see you tomorrow."

"Good night." He was surprised by her hurried departure, but said nothing. He watched her until she'd gone inside before driving off.

Boyd sat on the edge of the bed and grabbed up the whiskey bottle that was sitting on the nightstand. He tilted it to his lips and took a long swallow of the powerful liquor.

"Why are you leaving me so soon?" Jenny asked from where she lay naked behind him on her bed. She'd managed to keep him entertained for the better part of three hours, and she hoped to be paid handsomely for the effort. Boyd was a brute of a man, but he did like to throw his money around.

"I want to go downstairs and have some more fun. Get dressed. I've had enough for one night."

"I haven't," she said suggestively as she reached out to caress his bare back.

"Don't!" He stood up to avoid her touch.

"You don't want me no more?"

"That's right."

"What do you mean 'that's right?'" Jenny snapped in drunken outrage.

"I've got a hankering to play me some poker. Now leave me alone. I'm getting dressed." His words were slurred from all that he'd been drinking.

"I can make you want me again," she said, leaving the bed to go to him.

But Boyd was not in the mood for her to cling to him. He was still thinking of Sugar, and he wanted to go downstairs and find her right then. He hadn't been able to put her out of his mind the whole time he'd been with Jenny, and that was unusual for him. Usually when he was with Jenny he forgot everything, but not tonight—and that was why he had to go find her. He wasn't going to let her get away from him that easily. He'd wanted her, and he meant to have her no matter what Fernada said and no matter how mad Jenny got.

Jenny came up behind Boyd as he struggled drunkenly to pull on his pants. She ran her hands knowingly over him, allowing herself free access to all of him.

"Damn it, woman!" Boyd snarled, jumping at her unexpected touch. He swung around and physically threw her on the bed. "I told you to leave me alone!"

Jenny lay sprawled before him, expecting him to be aroused and take her. It shocked her when he continued to get dressed. "But Boyd— I need you."

"You don't need anything but a big stiff one, whore! It doesn't matter who's sticking it to you!" he said viciously as he fastened his pants and tugged on his boots and shirt.

She came up off the bed at his ugly words, furious. She had just spent hours pleasing him, and this was how he treated her! "How can you say that?"

"Because it's the truth. Now get outta my way."

She blocked his path to the door. "I don't want you to go."

He dug in his pants pocket and threw a wad of bills on her dresser. "There's your money."

When he brushed past her, Jenny tried to grab him. She didn't care that he'd already told her he didn't want her. She felt sure she could convince him otherwise. The blow came with such surprising force that she was knocked across the room. She cried out as she fell heavily to the floor, her lip split and bleeding.

"Boyd—"

He didn't say another word, but stomped from the room, glad to be away from her. He heard the sounds of revelry still coming from downstairs and he was glad. He wanted to dance with Elise some more.

"Where did Sugar go?" he demanded of Dan as he went up to the bar and ordered another whiskey.

"She's gone for the night."

"Where the hell did she go? I'll go get her and bring her back!"

"No, you ain't going to do that," Fernada said, having heard his question to Dan. "She's off now."

"When she gonna be coming back?"

"She'll be here tomorrow night."

He mumbled angrily under his breath as he downed the drink Dan gave him. "Then I'll be back."

With that, he stumbled out of the High Time.

Fernada and Dan were glad to see him go. They were also greatly relieved that Elise had gone before he'd come back downstairs. The last thing they needed was a fight in the saloon, and they were certain they would have had one had he gone after Elise again. They shared a look of understanding as they realized what the next night might bring.

Chapter Fourteen

Will Campbell was tense. He had waited too long for the moment, and he had traveled too far. Heavy cloud cover blocked any light the moon might have offered, and he was glad for the shroud of blackness. He couldn't risk being seen by anyone—not tonight.

He'd reached the designated meeting place just outside the small town of Canyon Creek on time, but no one else had shown up yet. As late as it was getting, he was beginning to wonder if they would show up at all. He had received a message that they would be there, though, so he did not leave. He stayed, watching and waiting, his gun ever ready at his side.

"How the hell did you ever get to be a lawman, Campbell?" a sneering voice asked from nearby.

Will jumped and automatically started to go for his gun, but stopped. "You're here." He was relieved.

"Yeah, I'm here. Me and the boys have been watching you sweat for at least five minutes. If we'd been Indians, you'd have been dead and scalped by now."

Derisive laughter followed this remark as Matt Harris and his men appeared out of the night.

Will, however, didn't think anything about the situation was funny. "What the hell took you so long? I sent word to you like you told me to weeks ago," he demanded.

Harris stepped closer to confront him. "Where I've been and what I've been doing ain't none of your business, Campbell. I pay you. You answer to me."

"This is important! I wouldn't have tried to contact you if it wasn't! I don't want to risk—"

"I know," Harris jeered. "You don't want to risk the nice new job you got. Being sheriff in Eagle Pass must sit real good with you."

"That doesn't have a damned thing to do with it!"

"Well, then, what is this important news you've got? Is there a big gold shipment coming through? Or maybe an army payroll?" Matt's eyes gleamed with avarice at the thought that Will might really have some good news for him.

"This ain't about money! It's Jackson!"

"What about Jackson? He's rotting in his grave by now."

"No, he's not! He's alive." Will delivered the message he'd been waiting weeks to relay.

Matt's expression turned lethal at his words. "What do you mean, the bastard's still alive? There's no way Jackson could have lived through that ambush! He was dead! I was sure of it! I shot him point-blank myself!"

"Well, your aim ain't as good as you thought it was! I saw him and talked to him!" Will insisted, angry that Matt didn't believe him.

"I don't think you're funny." Matt took a threatening step toward Will.

Will didn't budge. He looked him straight in the eye as he told him, "Trace showed up in Eagle Pass in the middle of the night a couple of weeks ago."

"You're crazy. He can't be alive! He was shot at least two times before I put a bullet in his back."

"He's one tough bastard. You knew that when you started dealing with him. He came to the jail and told me everything that had happened to him. Nobody knows he's alive but me and the miner who saved him—and he wanted it to stay that way. He's alive and kicking and he's coming after you! He says there ain't nothing going to stop him from finding you and seeing you hang."

Matt was ready to shoot Will right then and there. "And you let the son of a bitch just ride away?!" he asked in furious disbelief.

"What the hell else was I supposed to do?"

Unable to control his raging temper, Harris swung at him. The blow was vicious and Will went sprawling on the ground, blood oozing from his mouth.

"Are you really this stupid?" He stared down at Will, his expression deadly. "You could have killed him! Nobody would have known! It would have saved me a whole helluva lot of trouble!" he snarled, swearing under his breath.

Harris hated Trace Jackson. He'd enjoyed ambushing the posse and putting that last slug into Jackson's back. The bastard must have nine lives, though, to have lived through that.

"Somebody would have heard the shot!" Will protested.

Matt's expression turned even more savage. "You know, there ain't a soul around here who would hear it if I put a bullet into you right now!" He found the thought tempting, but even as he rested his hand on his sidearm, he realized he still needed Campbell—for now.

Will was aware that he was treading on dangerous ground. Inwardly he was quaking. He knew how deadly Matt Harris could be, and he had no intention of incurring his wrath. "It isn't my fault it took you so long to get my message."

"Did he say where he was heading?" Harris asked. He wanted to turn the tables on Jackson and find him first. Everybody knew Trace Jackson. The lawman would be seen, and when Jackson did turn up, he would be there ready and waiting for him.

"He didn't tell me anything else. He promised he'd be in touch, but I haven't heard from him since he rode out that night. All I know is that he's planning on going after you."

Matt gave a dangerous laugh. "Jackson may have lived through the ambush, but he's a walking dead man. He just doesn't know it yet."

"What do you want me to do?"

"If you hear anything more from him, send word right away. I want him to keep thinking that everybody believes he's dead." He smiled in the darkness as he added, "The next time I see him, I won't miss."

The threat was real, and Will was very glad he wasn't Trace as he rode away from his meeting with the gang.

It was too late for him to go back to Eagle Pass tonight, so Will headed into Canyon Creek to spend the night. He needed a stiff drink. That was for sure. When Matt had threatened to shoot him, Will knew he hadn't been far from being serious.

As Will made his solitary trek into town, he thought back over how he'd become involved with the Harris gang. He'd gotten tired of being known as one of Trace's deputies. Trace had never realized just how good he was, and he'd gotten sick of hearing everybody talk about what a great sheriff Jackson had been. Will had known Matt when he was a kid growing up in western Kansas, and when Matt had approached him and offered him a bribe to look the other way during the robbery in Eagle Pass, he'd accepted. He'd believed it would make Jackson look bad if the gang managed to pull off a bank robbery in his town. He had never expected innocent people to die, though, and then when Trace had gone after Matt and left him behind and in charge, he'd suddenly realized what he'd gotten himself into.

And then the news had come of the deadly ambush.

It was true that he had warned Matt that the posse was coming after him, but he'd told him so he could get away—not so he could double back and kill them all. The men in the posse had been his friends. Granted, he had fared well since their deaths. He was now the sheriff of Eagle Pass, and Matt was still paying him for information. Everything had seemed to be going well until Trace came back from the dead.

Will's hands were shaking as he tied up at the Palace Saloon. He was worried—very worried. If Trace found out about his betrayal, or if Matt no longer thought Will could be of any use to him, he was a dead man. Contemplating his future was nerve-wracking. He needed tonight to forget for a while. No one knew who he was here in Canyon Creek, so it was safe for him to let his guard down for the night. He would worry about the rest tomorrow. Ready to lose himself in a night of drinking and women, he strode into the bar and ordered a whiskey.

Boyd was back at the High Time nice and early the next night. He had done nothing but think about Sugar all day, and he was ready to spend the evening with her. He gave no thought to Jenny. She'd gotten on his nerves the night before with all her whining. He'd paid her what he owed her and felt no need to concern himself with her at all. He only wanted Sugar, and this time he wasn't going to take no for an answer. This time he was going to have her—no matter what.

Boyd had been drinking most of the afternoon and he was ready for some good times. He was irritated when he arrived and found out that Sugar wasn't there. The night was long, though, and he didn't have anything else to do but wait for her to show up.

The minute Dan saw Boyd come in, he'd sent word to Sam, the saloon owner. Sam was angry over the way Boyd had treated Jenny the night before, and he wasn't happy to have the man back in his establishment. Still, Boyd's money was good, so he tolerated his presence.

"Where is Sugar?" Sam asked Fernada as he stood at the bar with her just after eight o'clock.

"She'll be here anytime now. I know she will," she assured him.

"What do you want to do about Boyd?"

"There's nothing we can do unless he starts some trouble. We can't throw the man out for being a drunk. If we did that, we wouldn't have any customers left."

Sam knew she was right, but he didn't like fights in his saloon. "Well, keep a close watch on things. I'll be back in my office if you need me."

"Dan and I will keep an eye out for trouble," she promised.

A few minutes later, Suzie came to tell her that Elise had arrived by the back door and was upstairs getting ready. Fernada couldn't decide whether to be glad the girl had shown up again, or to worry over what might happen now that she had. Silently, she hoped they would have a nice, normal evening at the High Time.

After seeing Elise safely inside the High Time by way of the rear entrance, Trace entered the saloon, as ready as he would ever be for the night to come. He was not looking forward to it. He had even debated strapping on his sidearm for the evening. Keeping in character, though, he had decided against wearing the gun. When he saw that Boyd was already there, he hoped he hadn't made a mistake.

"Give me a whiskey," he ordered as he went to stand at the far end of the bar. It was a quiet spot that afforded him a good view of the room.

"Here you go," Dan said as he put a glass before him and splashed a healthy amount of liquor in it.

"Thanks." Trace paid up, then turned to let his gaze sweep the room. He hoped it would be a quiet night, but he had his doubts—especially since Boyd was already there and obviously feeling no pain.

The day had been a long one for him. He'd stayed at the house practicing his shooting for hours on end. He was definitely seeing some improvement and he hoped he could soon be heading out of Durango after the Harris gang. It had been too long already. He was growing weary of biding his time.

"There she is!"

Boyd's shout interrupted Trace's thoughts, and he looked up to see Elise starting down the steps into the saloon.

It seemed that all eyes in the place turned to her as she made her descent. Elise smiled, belying the nervousness that assailed her at the sight of Boyd waiting at the foot of the steps for her.

"Evening, everyone," Elise said. For a moment, her gaze sought out Gabe's, and she breathed a bit easier when she spotted him standing at the bar. It comforted her to know that he was there, though she really wasn't sure why. Certainly, Gabe would be little or no help if there was any real trouble with Boyd.

"I knew you'd show up sometime tonight, woman!" Boyd was all but shouting as he leered up at her.

Elise had not been looking forward to the evening to begin with, and now that Boyd was there, she was dreading the long hours to come. No matter how much she didn't want to do this, though, she reminded herself that, come midnight, she could walk away from the High Time and the life that went with working there. Suzie, Kate, Jenny, and Fernada could not. She forced herself to remember that as she kept her smile from fading.

"Evening, Boyd," she greeted him.

"It's about time you came downstairs," he said loudly. "I been waiting for you."

"I didn't know you'd still be in town," she said, trying to sound as welcoming as she could.

"I stayed over just to see you again. I been missing you." He grabbed her and pulled her into an awkward embrace as she reached the bottom step.

Elise wondered again why she did such in-depth research for her reporting. Surely, realism had its limits—especially where this man was concerned.

"Can I get you a drink?" she asked, wanting desperately to be free of him.

"No, I don't want any more liquor tonight. I already had enough of that. It's you I want. I been thinking about you all day, and I been just waiting for tonight."

He ran his hands up and down her back as he held her against him. She tried to resist being too close to him, and he enjoyed her efforts. Her resistance only served to arouse him more. He was certain she would be one wild woman when he got her upstairs in bed.

"You know I only serve liquor, Boyd. There's no point in you expecting more."

"But I'll pay you real good," he whispered in her ear.

His breath was hot and moist and rancid, and her flesh crawled at that close contact.

"I'm not interested," she ground out and with all her might she shoved at his shoulders. She couldn't believe that the night had just begun and he was already causing trouble.

Elise's surprise move startled him, and it allowed her to free herself from his hold. She quickly skirted away from him, making sure to put a table between them. Boyd stared after her, the look in his eyes both angry and feverishly hungry for her.

"You can't avoid me forever, Sugar," he said, nearly drooling.

I can try! Elise thought as she smiled at him and headed in the opposite direction. She would have to keep him in sight all night so he didn't have the opportunity to sneak up on her.

Trace had been watching from his place by the bar. His grip had tightened around his glass at the sight of Boyd whispering in her ear, and he'd been ready to go to her aid when she'd managed to free herself. He was seriously regretting that he hadn't worn his gun, but there were more ways than one to control men like Boyd. He'd done it often enough in Eagle Pass.

"I'll take another," Trace called out to Dan, "and leave the bottle."

The bartender poured his refill and set the bottle on the bar before him before going off to wait on another customer.

The night passed slowly for Elise. What had been an adventure the previous evening was almost torture for her tonight. She watched the other girls and began to understand why Jenny drank so heavily. Even Suzie and Kate were not averse to raising a few with their customers, and she knew why—they were alone. They had no life other than what went on at the saloon. They had been abandoned by family and friends. They were despised by the "good" folks in town, and worst of all, they had no hope. Theirs was a very sad life, indeed.

"Hank! Watch what you're grabbing!" Jenny shrieked in delight as the cowboy pulled her onto his lap and fondled her openly.

"I am watching!" He laughed as he pressed hot kisses to her neck and the tops of her breasts.

"If you want some fun, let's go upstairs!" she coaxed, her words slightly slurred from all that she'd been drinking. The whiskey helped ease the pain from her injured face. Her lip was swollen and her cheek was bruised where Boyd had hit her the night before. Even so, she was not about to miss a night with the boys around payday. This was their most important time of the month.

"Oooh, baby, I am ready to go!" Hank stood up and swung her up in his arms. He started up the stairs, taking them two at a time.

Jenny clung drunkenly to him as he rushed toward her room upstairs. She looked back over his shoulder as he carried her off, and across the width of the saloon her gaze met Elise's.

Elise saw in the depths of Jenny's regard all the sadness and loneliness that was her life. She ached for the other woman, wishing there was some way to make things better for her. But then Jenny was gone, and it was too late to help her.

It was in that moment that Elise let her guard down, and Boyd had been watching and waiting for just this opportunity. He was beside her instantly, his arm possessively around her waist, pinning her to his side.

"Now, it's our turn," he told her, his gaze focused on her cleavage, a bit of spittle hanging at the corner of his mouth.

Elise tensed the moment he touched her, and she tried to spin free of him, but he held her pinioned.

"Let go of me! I have customers to wait on," she said quickly, trying to twist free of his hold.

"Oh, no. I'm the customer you're taking care of now—and do I ever need taking care of!" He laughed, his hand sliding up from her waist to caress the side of her breast. He could just imagine how she'd look lying naked on a bed, waiting for him. He grew hard just thinking about what he wanted to do to her. He'd been planning this all day, and he was ready. Nothing was going to stop him. If she gave him any trouble, he would pay her extra. After all, she was a whore.

"I said no!"

Elise slapped one hand away, but he just groped her openly with the other.

"You don't mean that. I'm gonna be real good to you—"

"No, you're not." Fernada's stern words got his attention. "Let her go right now, Boyd. She ain't for you."

"I'll pay her real good, don't worry." He started to pull Sugar toward the steps, meaning to follow Jenny and Hank upstairs.

"Sugar ain't selling, Boyd. Now let her go and get out of the High Time," she ordered.

"I been waiting all day for this, and I ain't waiting no longer!" he argued.

"Oh, yes, you are!" Fernada insisted.

"To hell with you. I said I'd pay!" He was bodily dragging a resisting Sugar toward the steps.

Fernada blocked his way. "Stop right there, Boyd."

Elise was struggling to free herself from the bruising grip he had on her arm. "Let me go!"

"I ain't letting you go 'til I get my fill of you, woman!" he snarled.

"Boyd, we don't want any trouble with you. Find your pleasure with Kate or Suzie."

"I don't want them! I want Sugar! Get the hell out of my way, or I'll take her right here and now in front of everybody!" he threatened, jerking her close to him again.

"No! Gabe! Help!" Elise cried, twisting and tugging to get away from him.

Boyd grabbed her by the waist with both hands and lifted her, all but throwing her on top of one of the tables. Elise landed heavily on her back, the wind knocked out of her. Boyd was chuckling with evil, lecherous intent as he started to lift her skirts and reach between her legs.

Chapter Fifteen

Trace had had enough. Again he regretted leaving his sidearm at home, but it didn't matter. He had the whiskey bottle, and he'd used one as a weapon more than once, breaking up fights in the bars in Eagle Pass. His hand closed around the neck of the bottle, and he strode straight to where Boyd was leaning over Elise.

"Sugar doesn't want anything to do with you. Let her go," Trace ground out.

"Mind your own business, city boy. She wants me! She just likes it rough, that's all." Boyd wasn't worried about anyone stopping him. They didn't dare. His reputation was too well known. Everyone in town knew you didn't mess with him. He turned back to Sugar.

But Boyd didn't know he was dealing with Trace Jackson.

His words were the last straw. Trace hit him full force with the bottle.

The pain exploded in Boyd's head. With a grunt of agony, he collapsed heavily on top of Elise.

Elise gave a shriek of horror at having his full weight upon her. Then when he was lifted off her, she scrambled from the table and stood watching stunned, as Boyd was tossed aside— by Gabe, along with the whiskey bottle he'd used to knock him unconscious.

"Oh, Gabe!" she cried, throwing herself into his arms. She was trembling in terror as she clung to him.

"Get him the hell out of here before I'm tempted to do more to him than just give him a short nap that'll leave him with a headache!" Trace ordered harshly.

The commanding tone of his voice sent other patrons of the saloon scurrying to do as he'd directed. They couldn't believe that the meek-looking man who'd been keeping to himself all night drinking at the bar had just laid a big, mean man like Boyd low with one blow—but he'd done it, and they'd seen him do it. They muttered in amazement among themselves as they dragged Boyd out of the High Time and left him lying outside in the street. As ornery as he was, they figured he didn't deserve any better.

"You all right?" Trace asked Elise, softening his tone. He could feel the shudders wracking her, and he was furious over what had almost happened.

Elise remained huddled against him, thankful for the solid, powerful strength of him. It was reassuring to know that he was there—that he had saved her. With an effort, she straightened her shoulders and leaned away from him. "Yes. I'm fine." She gave him a weak smile as she looked up at him.

"You don't look fine," he growled, seeing how pale and shaken she was.

"Sugar?" Fernada hurried toward them, with Dan and Sam close behind her.

"I guess I'd better get back to work," Elise said quickly, feeling suddenly self-conscious.

"Damn it, Elise! Don't even think about it! You're getting out of here now!" Trace was furious. She had just been attacked in front of a crowd by a vicious drunk, and she was thinking about going back to serving drinks again!

"No, I have to—"

He cut her off before she could say any more. "As your boss, I'm telling you that your days of working here are over! Get your things. We're going."

"No, I—"

At her protestation, Trace stopped caring about his Gabe image. In one smooth move, he picked her up, threw her bodily over his shoulder, and started to stalk from the saloon.

"Let me down!" she shouted, pounding on his back as he stormed out of the High Time.

Sam and Dan exchanged looks and started to go after them. They thought they were going to help Elise, but Fernada stopped them.

"It's all right. She's safe with him. It's better this way," she told them in a quiet voice.

"You sure?" Dan asked, frowning. He'd been wondering about Gabe. Fernada had told him that he was Elise's boss at the newspaper, and he had thought the man seemed to be the book-learning, mild-mannered sort. After watching him in action tonight, though, Dan wasn't so sure anymore. Gabe had known exactly what he was doing when he'd gone after Boyd with that whiskey bottle.

"I'm sure," Fernada answered. Then, turning to the men who'd gathered around to watch what happened, she shouted, "Drinks are on the house! A free round for everybody!"

A cheer went up as the patrons rushed forward to get their free drinks. Dan hurried off to wait on them.

With all the men at the bar, Suzie went to stand with Kate in a quiet, deserted place near the front of the saloon.

"Did you see that?" Suzie asked in amazement, peeking out the window to see where Gabe had taken Elise.

"I saw it all right. Can you believe it? He actually carried her out of here over his shoulder!" Kate had never seen anything like it in all the years she'd been working there.

"Do you think he cares for her?"

"It certainly seemed that way. Why else would he save her from Boyd and carry her off like that?"

"It was very romantic, wasn't it?" Suzie said, a half smile curving her lips. "Maybe one day, a man will come along who'll rescue me."

Kate glanced over at her and saw the dreamy look on her face. "You better grow up, Suzie, and forget all your stupid, childish fantasies. There ain't no man going to show up at the High Time and sweep you off your feet."

The momentary look of innocence that had haunted Suzie's expression disappeared. She glanced down at the low-cut, satin dress she was wearing. "You're right, I know—but wouldn't it be wonderful?"

Suzie walked slowly away, leaving Kate standing alone wondering.

"Put me down!" Elise demanded, hanging on to Gabe for dear life as he made his way to where he'd left the carriage. She was furious at his high-handed ways, but she was helpless to do anything about it.

Trace wasn't about to put her down because he knew she'd just try to go back into the saloon. She could have been seriously hurt tonight. She had no business going back in there—ever. He was still seething when he reached the vehicle and put her on her feet beside it.

"Get in!" he dictated tersely.

"No, I need to go back. I need to get my things."

"They're not going anywhere. Now get in. I'm taking you home."

In a huff, she started to climb in, but found she was a little unsteady from all that had happened.

When Trace thought she was moving too slowly, he took her by the waist and lifted her into the conveyance. He climbed in beside her, but didn't say another word as he took up the reins.

Elise sat rigidly beside him. She occasionally cast a glowering look at him, but he ignored her, and that bothered her even more.

In angry silence, Trace drove straight to her house. He was concentrating only on getting her as far away from the High Time and Boyd as quickly as he could. When the drunk came to, he was going to be in one helluva mood, and Trace didn't want Elise anywhere near the man. He drew to a stop in front of her house, only to find that the whole place was dark.

"Where's your grandmother?" he asked worriedly, wanting to make sure she would be safe. "Has she gone to bed already?" It was only ten P.M., and he was surprised at how empty the house looked.

"She had a meeting at church tonight."

"You go inside and lock the door behind you, do you understand me?" He was dictatorial as he climbed down and then reached in to lift her out.

"Who do you think you are, trying to tell me what to do? You're not my bodyguard!" she declared in angry defiance as she looked up at him.

"Do you have any idea how close you came to being seriously hurt tonight?" He glared down at her, his patience with her stubbornness at an end. Though it was true that she was a very brave and smart woman to do the things she did as a reporter, there were obviously still some things about life she just didn't understand.

Elise stormed up the walk. The wig had come loose, so she snatched it off, freeing her own thick, dark mane in the process. Trace stayed right beside her. When she reached the porch, she opened the front door and turned on him defiantly.

225

"All right," she bit out. "You can leave now. I'm home."

"Not until I'm sure it's safe here," he declared. He knew men like Boyd. They were mean and unforgiving. If the man found out where she lived, there might be more trouble tonight.

"I am fine!" she insisted, her eyes sparking fire, her cheeks flushed. "Go on! If anything happens, I'll handle it, just as I could have handled everything at the saloon on my own! I had everything under control!"

"You had everything under control? You were handling it?" He repeated, his expression mirroring his disbelief at her words as he followed her inside to stand in the darkened hallway. "Don't you realize what Boyd planned to do to you right there in the middle of the saloon?"

"I would have gotten away from him." Even as she said it, though, she realized she had been helpless before Boyd's brute strength, pinned down as she'd been by his heavy weight. She tossed the wig on a nearby table and faced him.

"Like hell you would have!" Trace swore, close to losing his temper. He found it hard to believe that Elise honestly thought she could have escaped a man like Boyd. Even now, she wasn't completely safe. Once the man regained consciousness, he was really going to be mad. "You're just lucky I got you out of there before anything more serious happened."

"I didn't need your help! I was working!"

"You were working all right! Just like Suzie and Kate!"

Her temper flared even higher at his remark. "I was doing research for my story! I can't write about it unless I've experienced it!"

"Good old Ben might have let you put yourself in harm's way, but I am not Ben! I am your new editor. I own the *Star*! No story is worth getting hurt over."

"You're right about one thing—you're not Ben! You're not really an editor, either! I know what makes a good story, and you just ruined everything by interfering with your high-handed ways!"

"Interfering? I saved you from being attacked!" he growled, closing on her. "Or maybe you really wanted to do *all* the research and make your story completely accurate!"

"Why, you—" Elise was hurt and angered by his insinuation. Without thought, she slapped him.

The last of his iron-willed self-control snapped, and he reached back to push the door shut. "Since you think I interfered with your work and you want to do more research, let me help."

Trace took her by the shoulders and dragged her to him.

As Elise gazed up at him in the darkness of the night, Gabe looked different to her. No longer was he the mild-mannered boss. Tonight, he looked as he had that day she'd come upon him sitting at Ben's desk. He appeared as some fierce, avenging warrior, and she gasped softly as his mouth claimed hers in a demanding kiss.

Elise resisted for a moment, angered by his daring, but then his kiss gentled. Instead of dominating her, it became persuasive, coaxing. His lips moved seductively over hers, evoking a response that overruled her outrage.

She told herself that this was Gabe. He had just carried her bodily out of the saloon. She knew she should be furious with him, but in the back of her mind, the haunting realization came to her that Gabe had rescued her. He had saved her from Boyd and from herself, when she had wanted to stay at the saloon and keep working. Gabe was a mysterious man, a perplexing man. And his kiss aroused her as no other man's ever had.

When he parted her lips to delve into the sweetness of her mouth, she gave a low moan of sensual surprise, even as she met him tentatively in that more passionate exchange.

Trace had been beyond angry with Elise, but at the touch of her lips on his, his fury had turned to something else—something far more potent. He wanted her. The realization shocked him even as he deepened the kiss.

Instinctively, he tightened his arms around her, drawing her closer. It seemed as if she fit to him perfectly. Her breasts were crushed against his chest, her hips firmly nestled against his. The shock of that intimate contact jarred him. He softened his kiss, wanting to gentle her. He began to caress her, his hands moving over her body in a fiery path that ignited the flames of her desire as he sought out her pleasure points.

Elise had never known that a man's kiss and touch could arouse such feelings within her. She whimpered as she pressed herself more fully against him, seeking more, wanting more.

The revulsion she'd felt at Boyd's touch was forgotten as Gabe's caress swept her away in a haze of sensual reverie. Her thoughts grew confused and jumbled as she gave herself over to his practiced ministrations.

Her unspoken surrender sent a jolt of awareness through Trace. He lifted her in his arms and made his way into the parlor to lay her on the sofa. He drew away for a moment, but she lifted her arms to him in invitation and he was lost. He followed her down, covering her body with his, fitting himself to her, reveling in the heat of her sweet curves pressed so tightly against him.

The red satin dress slipped easily from her shoulders, and he unlaced her corset to bare her breasts to his touch. He paused to look down at her. She was beautiful. He bent slowly to press hot, hungry kisses to that sensitive flesh.

Elise closed her eyes and arched in passionate welcome to the touch of his lips. Where the gropings of the men at the saloon had made her flesh crawl, Gabe's touch was ecstasy. She had never known that a man's caress could affect her this way. She held Gabe close, delighting in his nearness. Excitement built within her womanly depths. When he rose over her, she looped her arms invitingly around his neck and innocently moved her hips against his. Rapturously, she whispered his name.

"Oh, Gabe—"

Gabe. Trace went still for an instant as reality returned with a vengeance. This was Elise, and she was offering herself up to him in the throes of her desire. He knew he had to stop her, for she was an innocent who didn't understand the consequences of her actions. He was certain she would come to regret anything that happened between them tonight.

He kissed her, but his passion was tempered now as he struggled to bring his own desire under control. Trace remembered how she'd talked about her ideal man. He did not want to be her ideal man. He did not want to be the hero who swept her off her feet. He knew he could have her right then and there—Lord knew he wanted to—but if he allowed himself to take her, he would ultimately just end up hurting her.

There was only one thing that was important to Trace, one thing that drove him endlessly—and that was finding Harris and exacting his revenge. There could be no future for him with Elise. He didn't even know if he had a future, if he would survive his encounter with Harris. He could afford no relationships, no ties. And that included Elise.

He ended the kiss.

"Gabe?" Elise was stunned that he'd stopped kissing her. Being in his arms was exciting.

Trace stood and moved away from the sofa. He glanced back at Elise once, and he immediately regretted doing so, for the sight of her lying half-naked before him sent a white-hot shaft of heat throbbing through his body. He wanted her, but he would not, could not, allow himself to make love to her.

"Cover yourself," he growled as he turned his back on her again and strode farther away.

"Oh—!" Elise was suddenly all too aware of her situation. Humiliated by his rejection, she quickly sat up and pulled her bodice back into place.

"Make sure you lock the door after me."

"You're leaving—now?"

"It's best that I go. We both know this shouldn't have happened." His tone was flat and emotionless. "Even if I was helping you research your story."

She was grateful for the cover of the darkness. It hid her embarrassment—and her hurt—from Gabe.

"But—" she began, confused and wanting to know why he was leaving her so abruptly.

Trace cut her off, knowing there was nothing he could say that would change anything. For her own well-being, whether she realized it or not, this was the way it had to be. "I don't think Boyd knows who you really are or where you live, so you should be safe, but I don't want to take any chances. Lock this door."

He let himself out and quickly climbed back into the carriage. He took up the reins, but waited until he heard the lock turn in Elise's door before he drove away.

Trace was glad to disappear into the night. He would have gone back to the High Time for another drink, but he didn't want to answer any questions and he didn't want to risk running into Boyd. He couldn't guarantee how he would react to the man if he saw him again.

Elise sat alone in the darkened parlor for some time, then slowly got herself together and went to her room to change. She laid the red gown on her bed as she donned her nightgown and wrapper. She paused as she brushed out her hair to stare at the satin garment. Wearing it had taken her into a world she hadn't known existed, and right now she wasn't sure whether that was good or bad. Sometimes innocence was a wonderful thing.

The confusion she was feeling left her restless, so she got some paper and her pen and ink and went to sit at the kitchen table. She started to write her article for the next edition.

"What are you doing home so early?" Claire asked as she came into the kitchen to find her so diligently at work.

Elise had been so caught up in the article that she hadn't even heard her grandmother come in. She looked up, a bit startled, then smiled at her. "Things got a little out of hand tonight, but I got out of there safely enough."

"What do you mean by 'a little out of hand'?" Claire pinned her with a knowing grandmotherly look.

Elise would have liked to avoid talking about any of it, but it was better her grandmother heard it from her than anyone else. "One of the men at the bar decided he liked me a little too much. Gabe managed to get me out of there before anything bad happened."

Claire smiled gently as she thought of him. "Gabe always seems to be there when you need him the most. He's turning out to be quite the hero, isn't he?"

"Gabe?" She stared at her grandmother in surprise.

"Well, he saved you from Preacher Farnsworth, and now from this Boyd. I'd say he's quite a good man to have around."

"I suppose," Elise said noncommittally, but silently she hated the fact that her grandmother was right. Gabe had saved her tonight. She had all but thrown herself at him, and he had walked away. She supposed she was glad that he had. Lord only knew what would have happened if he hadn't stopped when he did.

"Are you sure you're feeling all right, darling?" Claire went to her side and put a gentle arm around her shoulders. "You are looking a little pale."

"I'm just a little tired, I guess," she lied.

"Then why don't you go on to bed and get some rest? You can finish up your article in the morning."

"There are a few more things I need to get down tonight, while I'm thinking about them, so I'm going to work a little longer."

"Well, don't work too hard. I'll see you in the morning." Claire pressed a soft kiss to her cheek and headed up to bed.

"Good night."

Elise stared after her, lost deep in thought. Her heartbeat quickened as she remembered the sweet heat of Gabe's kisses and caresses. Pleasure flushed through her body at the memories of what it had been like to be held in his arms. And tomorrow she would have to see him again.

Elise couldn't decide if she was glad or nervous at the prospect of facing Gabe. After the way they'd parted, she wondered if he would even want to talk to her again. She supposed, too, that she owed him an apology. As much as she hated to admit it, her grandmother was right—Gabe did have a knack for getting her out of trouble, and he had protected her from harm at Boyd's hands tonight. She would go to Gabe tomorrow and tell him how much she appreciated his help and how sorry she was that she had slapped him.

Picking up her pen again, Elise went back to work. It was early morning by the time she finally went up to bed, and when she did, she didn't sleep.

Chapter Sixteen

When Claire came downstairs early the next morning, she found Elise up and dressed and ready for the new day.

"You're up bright and early this morning," Claire remarked as she began to make breakfast.

"I've got to get down to the office so Gabe can proofread my article."

"You finished it last night?" She was surprised.

"Yes. After all that happened, I was too excited to sleep. The ideas were flowing so I just kept writing. I hope he'll be pleased with it. I'm tentatively calling it 'Fallen Angels'."

"Can I read it before you go?" Claire asked, truly interested in what she'd written.

Elise handed her grandmother the handwritten copy and sat down across from her at the kitchen table. Claire read slowly, not wanting to skim over a thing. When she finished reading and looked up at her granddaughter, she had tears in her eyes.

"Is it that bad?" Elise asked nervously.

"No, darling, it's that good," Claire said softly. "This is very poignant. You did a fine job. I think Gabe will be most pleased with your efforts, and I hope the community responds in a Christian manner. There are any number of ways we could help these girls."

"Thanks. I wanted it to be good. I wanted everyone to understand what difficult lives the girls lead, and how hopeless it is for them once they're caught up in it."

"You did just that—and more. In fact, I think I'll bring it up when I speak to the other ladies at our meeting next week. Surely, there is something we can do to aid these young women, some way we can help them."

"That would be wonderful." Elise thought of Suzie and hoped there was some way to help her start anew.

"It's our duty. We should help the less fortunate. Not everyone has a good home or a comfortable way of life."

"I love you," Elsie said with heartfelt emotion as she went to hug and kiss her grandmother. "Now, all I have to do is get the article past Gabe, and our lead story is ready to run."

"You're sure you don't want any breakfast before you go?"

"Not today. I'll see you later this afternoon."

She gathered up her article along with the carefully wrapped dress that Jenny had lent her and Fernada's wig, and left the house. She wanted to be at the office first, so that when

Gabe came in, they would have a few minutes of privacy to talk before Andy showed up.

An hour later, with Andy already there and working, Elise was still waiting for Gabe to arrive.

"Andy? Did Gabe say anything to you about coming in late today?"

"No. In fact, I'm kind of surprised that he isn't here yet—especially with him needing to check over your lead story."

"Well, I think I'll go down to the High Time now, while it's quiet."

"You're going back there? Why? After last night, I'd think you'd never want to go back again."

"I have to take back the things they lent me and pick up the clothing I left there."

"If Gabe shows up, I'll make sure he stays here until you get back."

"Thanks."

Elise got the parcel and left the office. The High Time was deserted when she entered, and she was glad. Only Dan stood at the bar. All was quiet and peaceful—a far cry from the night before.

When Dan saw her, he smiled. "It's good to see that you're safe and sound. Me and Sam were worried about you last night, but Fernada said you'd be all right."

"Gabe took care of me," she told him with a smile. "Is Fernada or Jenny around? I need to return the dress Jenny lent me."

"Fernada's in back. Let me get her for you."

He went off to find her. Moments later, the older woman appeared and hurried over to hug her.

"I am so glad you're all right, but I had a feeling your Gabe was going to get you out of here without a scratch. He was pretty impressive last night, taking care of Boyd like he did. Who would have thought it? He certainly doesn't look the type, does he?"

"Gabe isn't 'my' anything, but he is a surprising man." Elise remarked.

"I've got your clothes all bundled up for you upstairs. Do you want me to give that to Jenny for you when she gets up?"

"Please, and tell her I said 'thanks'."

"I will. Did you get your article written?"

"I worked on it last night, but I still have to show it to Gabe. I'm not sure what he's going to say about it."

"I'm sure you did a good job."

"I hope so. If it changes one heart, then it will all have been worthwhile. Did you see any more of Boyd last night? Gabe was worried that he might come back in and cause some more trouble for you."

"He came back in, all right. I don't think I've ever known a meaner, more vile drunk than Boyd." Her expression turned grim as she remembered what had transpired after Elise had gone.

"What happened?"

"He tried to bust things up pretty good around here. He was threatening to kill all of us at one time or another. Said he was going to find that 'Sissy-pants coward who hit him when he wasn't looking,' and teach him how a man fights."

"Do you think he went looking for Gabe?" she asked.

A sudden inkling of fear ran through Elise. Gabe had yet to show up at the office when he should have been in hours before. She wondered if Boyd could have tracked him down. The thought frightened her. Gabe had been expecting trouble in the saloon last night, and that was why he'd been able to save her. But if Boyd caught him out at his house all alone, she didn't know if he'd be able to defend himself.

"Hard to say. Sam and Dan threw him out and told him never to come back. He slunk off into the night like the low-life that he is. I was glad to see him go. I don't want his kind in my place. There's no reason for men like him to get all drunked up and try to hurt people. It's stupid."

"I think 'stupid' is a very accurate description of Boyd."

"Let's just hope he stays away."

They shared a look of understanding.

"I'd better go now."

"It's been a pleasure to meet you, Elise."

"You, too, and thank you, Fernada. I couldn't have done this without your help." She hugged the older woman, appreciative of all that she had done for her. "Thank Suzie and Kate and Jenny for me, too, will you?"

"I sure will, honey. Let me go get the rest of your things for you," Fernada said hurrying off to get Elise's clothes.

Once she had them, Elise returned to the newspaper office, hoping that she would find Gabe there.

"Is he in his office?" Elise asked Andy anxiously as she came through the front door.

"No. I haven't seen or heard from him yet this morning. And look at this!" He held up a telegram for her to see. "Word just came in that the Harris gang has struck again. This time they robbed a bank in Canyon Creek!"

"Did they kill anybody?"

"Looks like a teller was shot, and they got clean away again, just like they always do!" He knew she had been following the Harris gang's activities.

"It seems as if they keep working their way closer and closer to us. I hope to God they stay away from here."

"You're not the only one. I like printing exciting news, but I can do without those kinds of headlines."

"I'm concerned about getting Gabe's opinion on this article, so I'm going to ride out to his house and see what's keeping him." She considered telling Andy about her fear that Boyd might have gone after Gabe, but told herself that there was probably no real basis for her concern. Andy would probably think she was just being foolish to be so worried about him. If Gabe had decided to come in late to work, that was his business. He did, after all, own the *Star* and could set his own hours.

"Do you need me to go along with you? Are you worried about riding out alone?" he asked, frowning as he looked at the work stacked up on his desk.

"It's daylight, so I should be all right. You go ahead and keep working. I'll be back as soon as I've finished talking to him."

Elise tried not to seem too anxious as she left the office with her article and telegram in hand. She managed to drive out of town at a calm pace, when all she wanted to do was whip the horse to a faster trot. She wondered why she was so worried about Gabe. He was the one who was always saving her. It wasn't the other way around. Still, Boyd's threat rang hauntingly in her thoughts, and she wanted to let Gabe know about it, along with the news of the Harris gang's new robbery.

Although it was a short trip out of town to Gabe's house, today it seemed to take an eternity. As Elise drew near, she was surprised to hear the sound of gunfire in the distance. Her fear for Gabe's safety grew even more at the thought that Boyd might be there at the house right now, attacking Gabe. She slapped the reins on her horse's back and rushed up the lane to his house. She reined in out front, but saw no sign of Gabe anywhere. After taking her small derringer out of her purse, Elise climbed down from the carriage. She hurried up to the front porch and knocked on the door, but there was no answer. As she was standing there, the gunfire erupted again around back.

Elise followed the sound to the rear of the house. She kept close to the shrubs, not wanting to show herself, just in case it was Boyd. If he was there, she would have to do whatever she could to help save Gabe. Her little derringer was only a two-shot, but if she came up on him by surprise, she might be able to get off a clear shot at him.

The sight that greeted her as she left the shelter of the bushes shocked her. Gabe was standing some distance away with his back to her. He was naked to the waist, having shed his shirt in the heat of the day, and he was holding a six-gun as if he knew what he was doing with it.

241

Elise stood in silence, looking on as he holstered the gun, then drew and fired at three tin cans he'd set up about fifty feet away. His aim was accurate as he hit all three and sent them flying. He slid the gun back into the holster and turned slightly, allowing her to get a better look at him. It was then that she realized he wasn't wearing his glasses.

Elise stared at him in disbelief, trying to reconcile this man with the Gabe she knew. She couldn't believe that they were the same. This man was all man. He exuded a sense of power and command. His shoulders and arms were thickly corded with muscle. When he moved, the muscles rippled across the powerful width of his back. She could see the sheen of sweat on his sun-bronzed skin as he continued to practice his draw, and she was amazed that he was tanned. She hadn't even considered that Gabe would ever take his shirt off, let alone look like this when he did.

Gabe hadn't seen her yet, and she wasn't ready to say anything. She wanted to wait and see what he did next. She moved a little closer, drawn to him, needing to get a better look at him.

It was then that Elise was able to make out the scars on his back, and she went still. The scars were obviously from bullet wounds, and they weren't old ones. Gabe had been shot!

The knowledge was a complete and utter shock to her. *Gabe? Shot? Why would anyone want to shoot Gabe?* He had never said anything about being in any trouble in his life. They must have been grievous wounds. She wanted to reach out and touch the scars, which she knew must be vivid reminders of his pain. She swallowed tightly at the thought, then frowned slightly. *How many secrets was this man keeping from her?*

The reporter in Elise awakened. The questions that couldn't be easily answered stayed with her. This was the same man who had saved her from Boyd. This was the man who had kissed her and caressed her just last night. She didn't understand why he wore the glasses when he obviously didn't need them. He was shooting very accurately, and his draw was fast. It occurred to her then that whenever he wrote he used his right hand, but for shooting now he was using his left. Her gaze focused again on the vivid scar on the right side of his back. The wound had been serious, almost deadly, yet he had survived. Who had shot him in the back? And why?

She took a step forward. She needed to understand. She needed answers.

"Gabe?"

At the sound of her call, Trace turned quickly toward her. He was surprised by her presence, and his expression was guarded and wary. "Elise? What are you doing here? Is something wrong in town?"

She wasn't about to be distracted from what she needed to know about him.

"You were shot," she said as she stepped forward, drawn to Gabe, wanting to be closer to him.

He shrugged, not replying as he grabbed his shirt off the fence post where he'd hung it.

"How did it happen?"

"It's a long story, and it all happened a long time ago."

"The scars look new."

"They're not." His answer was curt and his gaze hardened as she came even closer. He didn't want her too near. He turned his back on her and had just started to shrug into his shirt when she reached his side.

Elise couldn't help herself as she stopped before him. She reached out to him, her hand just skimming his back near the scar.

Her touch sent a shock of awareness through him, and Trace almost groaned out loud. He had passed a long, sleepless night thinking of her. The memory of her touch and kiss had left him aroused and wanting more. He had paced the house like a caged animal until dawn, and he had deliberately stayed away from the office this morning just so he wouldn't have to see her. He hadn't been sure that he could keep his hands off her.

Now, Trace stepped away, consciously distancing himself from her. He took his glasses out of his shirt pocket and quickly put them on. He needed to be Gabe right now. Gabe was the one who had had enough control to walk away from her last night. Gabe was the one who'd told her that their kisses should never have happened.

"What are you doing here, Elise? Is there a reason you came out here this morning?" he asked again, trying to keep his voice cold as he changed the topic.

Elise could not explain the disappointment that filled her as Gabe shifted away from her, physically and mentally. Certainly, she couldn't admit to him that she'd come out to the house because she feared that Boyd had come after him.

"I came for two reasons, really," she began. "First, I came to apologize for last night. I shouldn't have slapped you, and I'm sorry. You were right to get me out of the saloon when you did."

"It's not necessary for you to apologize. You have nothing to apologize for."

"Well, I felt that I did owe you one. It could have gotten even more dangerous at the High Time, and I should have realized that. In fact, earlier this morning when I went back to the saloon to get my things, Fernada told me that Boyd did come back in after we'd gone. He'd threatened everybody—you and me included."

"I had a feeling that he'd be back. What did they do with him?"

"Dan and Sam threw him out, and Fernada is hoping that he never comes in again."

He nodded and didn't say anything as he worked at the buttons on his shirt.

Elise was watching him closely. She realized that he was changing back into the Gabe she knew before her very eyes, and she was puzzled by his two personalities.

"The other reason I came out here to see you was because I finished the article, and I thought you would want to give it a quick read-through."

"Why would I want to do that? I'm not an editor. You said so yourself." His words were harsh.

Elise did manage to look a bit shamefaced. "I told you that I was sorry, and I meant it. I'd like you to read over it and see what you think. Oh—and before I forget, Andy got word this morning that the Harris gang robbed another bank, this time in Canyon Creek."

At her words, Trace went still. "They struck that close to Durango? How long ago?"

"Just a few days. One teller was shot."

Unconsciously, Trace's hand settled on his sidearm. "Did the law go after them?"

"I don't know. That was all the wire said."

His expression turned stony, revealing nothing of what he was feeling as he thought about Harris. Soon, he would go after them—very soon.

Elise studied the change in him, wondering how he could seem so different, so quickly. "Gabe? Why were you out here practicing with a handgun?"

"As you said, you never know what kind of trouble you might run into, being the editor of a newspaper. I wanted to be ready—especially after our run-in last night with Boyd."

She knew his reason was logical, but somehow she just didn't believe him completely. "Well, from the looks of things, you're already ten times better than Ben was. I know I offered to give you shooting lessons a few weeks ago, but I can see you don't need them. I think you might be able to teach me a few things—especially a fast draw. How long have you been practicing?"

"Since I moved into the house."

She knew he hadn't gotten that good that fast, but she said nothing more. "Do you want to read my article?"

"Where is it?"

"I left it in the carriage. I'll go get it."

Trace let her walk on ahead of him. Then, as he started to follow her, he realized he'd made a big mistake. He found he couldn't look away from the gentle sway of her hips as she headed back to the house.

"On second thought, don't bother. Let's just go in to the office, and I'll read it there." He did not trust himself to be alone with her in the house right now. She was far too tempting.

"Are you sure?" Elise stopped to look back at him, puzzled by the change in him.

"I'm late already."

"I can give you a ride, if you want," she invited him innocently.

Trace stared at Elise, knowing she had no idea what she'd just offered him or how badly he wanted to take her up on that 'ride'. He knew, too, that if he was truly a gentleman, he would never even have had the thought, but the memory of their passionate embrace the night before was seared into his soul. He wanted her desperately, but he would not give in to his need.

"No, I'll follow you in a few minutes. You go on ahead," he told her, staying where he was, keeping the distance between them.

"I don't mind waiting for you."

"I've got a few things to finish up around here. I'll see you in town."

Elise didn't wait for his help, but climbed into the carriage and drove off. As she rode away, her reporter's instincts were taking over. She wanted to learn more about Gabe West.

"Your article is fine. Run it as is," Trace said to Elise as he came out of his office later, her papers in hand. "We may offend some of the those in town with finer sensibilities, but overall, I think your exposé will sell papers."

"Good, and thanks." She looked up from her desk, where she was writing the story on the Harris gang.

"There's no need to thank me. The article is well written, and we both know you have your facts straight."

"I've almost got this article on the Harris gang done. Do you want to see it?"

"Have you learned anything new since that first telegram?"

"No."

"Then there's no need. Run it. And for the next few days, I want you to be in charge while I'm away."

"You're going somewhere?" Elise was completely taken by surprise.

"Where are you going?" Andy asked, looking up from his work.

"I'm going to Canyon Creek to see what else I can find out about the gang's whereabouts."

"If anyone's going to Canyon Creek, it should be me!" Elise spoke up.

"You're staying here at the paper. I'm going alone," Trace stated.

"We could go together," she insisted, wanting to be in on any story about Harris.

"It would be inappropriate for you to travel with me."

"Why? We'd be going as newspaper reporters, not as anything else." There was a note of challenge in her voice as her gaze met his across the room.

"I seriously doubt that your grandmother would approve of such a trip."

"I'll ask her. Maybe she could go with us—if you think you need a chaperone."

He glared at her. "I said no, Elise, and I meant it. I am your boss, and I need you here with Andy to take care of things. I won't be gone long, and if I find out anything important, I'll wire you the information so you can print a special edition."

"Are you taking the stage or riding?"

"I'm going to ride. It'll be faster that way, and I can come back whenever I'm ready."

"You're sure you won't reconsider taking me with you?" she asked again, hoping against hope that he might change his mind.

"No. I'm not going to reconsider. You make sure you put out a good paper this week, and maybe I'll have the lead story for you next week."

"I thought you were the editor of the *Star*, not a reporter," she countered in irritation.

He handed her the article on the High Time and started from the office. "You're right. I am your editor, but let's just say you've inspired me."

With that he was gone, and she was left staring after him, her expression thunderous.

"I'm the one who should be going to Canyon Creek," she said hotly to Andy.

Andy only shrugged. "He's the boss."

"I know."

Trace was glad to get out of the office. He hadn't been lying when he'd told Elise that she'd inspired him. She'd inspired him all right—inspired him to get out of town and away from her for a while.

Trace didn't know if he would learn anything new about the gang's whereabouts, but he was going to try. He would be riding out of Durango soon on the final journey of his quest to bring Harris down, and he was going to need all the help he could get to locate the murderer and his men.

Chapter Seventeen

Ben stood at the bar in the Mother Lode Saloon in Canyon Creek, enjoying a beer and relaxing for a while. Since he'd lost the paper in the card game, he'd finished taking care of his family's business and had been just roaming from town to town. He had arrived in town earlier in the day and had decided to stay over after hearing all the talk about the robbery by the Harris gang. Even the working girls in the saloon had been frightened to discover that the bad men had been able to move through their town so quickly and with such deadly force.

"It's just a shame that that sheriff from Eagle Pass didn't get them all those weeks ago," Lottie Lawson, one of the saloon girls, remarked to her friend Sissy.

Sissy Perkins looked at her and smiled secretively. "From what I heard earlier tonight, he still might."

"Trace Jackson's dead," Lottie scoffed.

"Maybe, maybe not."

"What are you talking about, Sissy? He's dead and buried. What do you think is going to happen? His ghost is going to come back and haunt Harris?" she chided her derisively.

"You may think he's dead, but I'm not so sure. A week or so ago, I had a cowboy in here who got pretty drunked up before we went upstairs. He was talkin' kinda crazy-like while we were upstairs together, and he said Jackson was still alive."

"Who was he?"

"I don't know. He never told me his name and he rode out of town early the next morning. He paid me real good, though."

"What exactly did he say?"

"Something like, 'They think Trace Jackson's dead, but he ain't. I saw him. I talked to him.' "

"And you believe that?"

"Why else would he talk about it? He was real drunk, almost passed out."

"It'll be interesting to see if he was right."

"I hope it's true. I'd like to think Jackson is still around. The Harris gang scares me. They are one dangerous bunch, what with killing the teller at the bank and all."

"If Jackson's really alive, he'll get them."

The two women moved away from where Ben was standing at the bar. He stared after them, lost deep in thought.

Trace Jackson might be still alive?

The possibility was mind-boggling—and

exciting. The newspaperman within Ben was alive and well, and Ben knew exactly what he had to do. First thing in the morning, he was going to wire Elise and let her know what he'd heard. He knew how interested she was in the Harris gang, and she would be really excited to learn that Sheriff Jackson might not have been killed in the ambush—that he might still be alive and going after the gang.

Ben grew even more excited. If Elise wrote an article about Jackson's survival, the gang might get nervous and make a few mistakes and get caught. Ben couldn't think of a better place for those robbing murderers than at the end of a hangman's rope. They had been terrorizing the state for years now, and it was time to see them brought to justice.

Ben believed, just as the women did, that if any lawman was going to catch Harris, it would be Jackson. Jackson's reputation had been real. If he really had come back from the dead to seek his revenge, all the better. Ben knew it couldn't happen to a more deserving bunch.

Elise was still irritated with Gabe the following morning when she made her way to the office. She and Andy had worked hard the day before, getting the paper ready, and they were pleased with the results. She was eager to see if the community would respond to her story as her grandmother had. She hoped so. It would be good to know that she could make a difference in some lives.

When she reached the office, she discovered

that Andy hadn't shown up yet, so she let herself in and settled in at her desk. This edition was done, so it was now time to start thinking about next week's paper. If she had gone to Canyon Creek, she could have been working on a report on the Harris gang, but stuck here as she was, there was nothing new she could write about the outlaws. She was going to have to come up with a whole new idea for the lead article. She hoped an inspiration came to her soon.

It was almost an hour later when Pete from the telegraph office came hurrying in. "I got a wire for you, Miss Martin."

"Thanks!" Elise was excited as she took the telegram from him. She reasoned that it was from Gabe and that he'd learned something important. She still wished she was the one who'd gone to Canyon Creek, but she would do whatever she could to report the news. She opened the wire as soon as Pete had gone and eagerly began to read.

> *Elise. When I was passing through Canyon Creek, I heard talk that Sheriff Jackson from Eagle Pass survived the Harris ambush. Saloon girl named Sissy at the Mother Lode seemed reliable. See what you can find out. This could be big news for you.*
> *Ben.*

Elise stared down at the wire, her eyes wide in shock. *Sheriff Jackson had lived through the ambush? He wasn't really dead?* She couldn't believe it. Excitement filled her. She was going to Canyon Creek!

Stuffing the telegram in her purse, Elise locked up the office and rushed to the stage depot to check departure times. The next stage to Canyon Creek pulled out in less than two hours. She could be there by late that afternoon. Elise bought a ticket and hurried back to the office to let Andy know.

"Thank goodness you finally got here!" Elise exclaimed as she came through the office door.

"Why? Did something exciting happen?" Andy looked up at her expectantly.

"Darn right, something happened! I'm going to Canyon Creek! Now! Today!"

"Did you get a wire from Gabe?" he asked, surprised by her excitement.

"No. It's even better than that! I got a wire from Ben!"

"Ben?" Andy was confused.

"Yes! It seems Ben was in a saloon in Canyon Creek and heard talk that Sheriff Jackson survived the ambush. So, I'm going there to interview the bar girl at the saloon and find out just exactly what it was that Ben heard. Then, I may even go looking for Jackson myself," she declared.

"You'd better think this through, Elise."

"I already have," she stated firmly. "I've got my ticket and I'm leaving town in a couple of hours."

"Why don't we just send Gabe a wire and let him look into it?" he reasoned.

"If we knew where he was staying, we could, but he didn't say when he left and we haven't heard from him."

"Still, I don't think—"

"Andy, I'm going. This story is too big!" Her expression grew even more delighted. "In fact, I think we should put out a special edition right now!"

"What are you talking about?"

"There's time. I'll help you. Here—"

She sat down at her desk and began to write. Within ten minutes she was done with a news release.

"See what you think." She handed Andy her article.

BREAKING NEWS

SHERIFF TRACE JACKSON SURVIVES
DEADLY AMBUSH!

Word just in—reliable sources have confirmed that Eagle Pass lawman Trace Jackson did not perish in the ambush by the Harris gang, but is still alive and on their trail. We will be reporting more details as they become available.

"Let's run this now, so you can get it on the street. I want to take one with me to give to Gabe when I get to Canyon Creek."

They set to work, not stopping until the type had been set and the copies of the special edition were finished.

"I've got to go home, so I can talk with my grandmother and pack a few things for the trip. I'll see you when I get back," she said, heading for the door, a copy of the paper in hand.

"How long do you think you'll be away?"

"I'll send you a wire," she promised. "Do you

think you can handle things here on your own?"

"I think we're about to find out," he answered, giving her a semi-confident smile.

With that, Elise quit the office and headed home. She wasn't quite sure what her grandmother was going to say about her plan, but she wasn't going to let anything stop her. Sheriff Jackson's survival was too big a story. She couldn't ignore it.

To Elise's surprise, her grandmother was not at the house when she arrived. She went on to her room, packed a small traveling bag, and got some money to take with her for expenses. When her grandmother still hadn't returned, she sat down at the kitchen table and wrote her a note explaining everything. A short time later, Elise was on the stagecoach heading to Canyon Creek. She hoped her grandmother would understand why she needed to make the trip.

Elise was excited. It wasn't just that she was making the trip. It was that she wanted desperately to believe Ben's news was true—that Sheriff Jackson had survived. She knew it was almost too much good news to hope for, but she clung to it anyway. Dwelling on the Eagle Pass lawman, she wondered, as smart a sheriff as he'd been, how he'd ever managed to get trapped by the gang that way. She wondered if he'd been betrayed in some way, but she had no idea by whom or why. If she ever met him, she was going to be sure to ask.

For some reason, Gabe slipped into her thoughts then, and she grimaced inwardly. He was not going to be glad to see her when she showed up in Canyon Creek. She was certain that their reunion would not be a pleasant one, but she didn't care. This was big news. She wanted him to know what she'd found out, and she wanted to investigate Ben's source and see what else she could learn about Jackson. The only way she could do that was by going to Canyon Creek. She hoped Gabe approved of her special edition. She thought that once he got over being angry with her for coming to Canyon Creek, he would appreciate her efforts.

Elise frowned at nothing in particular as her thoughts lingered on Gabe. So many things about him were a mystery to her. She still hadn't been able to figure how he'd been shot, or why. He was an interesting man, a compelling man, but he was also a stubborn man. She was going to have to figure out how to handle him, and soon, if she was going to get to the bottom of this story on Sheriff Jackson. She knew how interested Gabe had seemed to be in her articles on the Harris gang, and she hoped he didn't try to interfere and ruin her chances to follow up on Ben's lead.

The stagecoach trip couldn't end soon enough for her. She was eagerly looking forward to her arrival in Canyon Creek.

It was late in the afternoon when the stage finally pulled into the station. As they rolled to a stop, Elise remembered her first encounter with Gabe at the stage depot in Durango. She couldn't help but smile at the memory of her desperation that day. Now, here she was descending from a stagecoach in a town where she knew no one, just as Gabe had done all those weeks ago. At least here in Canyon Creek there was no stranger waiting to hustle her off to a fake wedding.

From the stage Elise made her way to what looked to be the best hotel in town and went in to get herself a room.

"Will you be staying long?" the clerk asked after pushing the registration book across the counter for her to sign.

"For a few days, at least," she replied. "Tell me, is there a Mr. Gabe West registered with you? He would have arrived yesterday."

"He sure is. Mr. West is in Room 212, but he's not in right now. He went out earlier this morning, and I haven't seen him come back in since. Would you like to leave him a message? I can give it to him for you when he comes through."

"No, thank you. I'll just wait and catch up with him myself."

The clerk turned the registration book around and after reading her name, said, "Here's your key, Miss Martin. You're in 217. Up the stairs and to your left."

Elise took the key and disappeared upstairs. She was eager to seek out the saloon girl named Sissy at the Mother Lode, but considering what she now knew about how saloons worked, she decided it was too late in the day to go. It was almost evening, and no doubt business at the Mother Lode would be booming. She would stop in early the following morning when things would be much quieter.

Elise let herself into her room. It was clean

and comfortable, and that was all she required. She wasn't going to be spending much time there anyway. She had a lot of work to do, but before she could start anything, she had to talk to Gabe and tell him the big news.

Trace sat across the desk from Sheriff Lewis, his notebook and pencil in hand. "And do you have any idea where they went when they rode out of town?"

"I wish I did, Mr. West," the lawman snarled his frustration. "I'd be there right now, arresting the bastards and bringing them in. Two of his men were killed during the robbery, and I was glad. It's just too bad Harris wasn't one of them. I got a posse together right away. We chased them for a good two days, but a gully-washer came through and wiped out every trace of the trail. We stayed another day and a half, just trying to pick it up again, but it was gone."

"That's the truth," Deputy Miller put in from where he was standing at the office window.

"That must have been some storm," Trace remarked. "Where exactly did you lose the trail?"

"Why? You thinking about trying to find it again?" the deputy asked.

Trace shrugged as he answered evasively, "Couldn't hurt to take a look around."

Both Sheriff Lewis and Deputy Miller chuckled at the thought of this reporter trying to find a cold, washed-out trail.

"We lost it out by Pinnacle Pass, but if you think you're going to find it, you're sadly mistaken," Miller told him.

"We had Ol' Mike with us when we were on

their trail. He's the best tracker in the county, but after that downpour he couldn't find a damned thing."

"It was the worst storm I've seen in years," Sheriff Lewis said in disgust, "and wouldn't you know it would come when we were chasing Harris."

Their laughing at him annoyed Trace, but he kept his emotions hidden. He knew there was no point in trying to pick up a washed-out trail. If they hadn't been able to find it then, he certainly wouldn't find it now. "Can you think of anything else pertinent to the robbery that I need to know to write this article?"

"No, that's about it. Just let it be known that Harris had better never show his face around here again or he'll be a dead man. We'll be shooting first and asking questions later," the deputy vowed.

Trace completely understood the sheriff's bloodthirsty sentiments. "I appreciate you both taking the time to talk with me."

"I wish there was more we could tell you," Lewis said. "Just let the folks in Durango know that they're damned lucky the gang hasn't struck there yet."

"We know it, believe me," Trace assured him.

"You got a good marshal there in Jared Trent. Next to Trace Jackson, I'd say he's about the best around. Hell, he probably is the best, now that Jackson's dead. I never got the chance to meet Jackson, but from what I heard about him, he was one good lawman."

"Well, thanks for all your help."

"If anything we've told you helps to bring the

gang in, we're glad to help."

Trace rose and shook their hands, then left the office. He was as frustrated as ever as he headed back to the hotel. He'd made the trip to Canyon Creek in hopes of learning something new that would help him track down Harris. Despite all his interviews today with the bank employees and the lawmen, though, he had turned up nothing. He'd been planning to ride out and pick up the gang's trail, but after talking to the sheriff and the deputy, he knew now there was no point in even trying. It was a dead end.

As he strode back into the hotel, Trace grimly made up his mind. He would start back to Durango first thing in the morning, but his days as Gabe West were numbered. As soon as the Harris gang struck again, he was going to be on their trail. Nothing was going to stop him this time—nothing.

Trace didn't even think about eating dinner. He was in no mood for food, and so he went straight to his room. He thought only of getting an early start back to Durango in the morning and seeing if there was any new word in on Harris.

Elise had gone out for dinner at the small restaurant nearby. The food was delicious, but she was too excited to enjoy it to the fullest. She could think only of the coming morning and her interview with the saloon girl. Over and over in her mind, she replayed the questions she would ask her as she tried to get to the bottom of the story on Sheriff Jackson.

When she'd made the short walk to the

restaurant, Elise had kept a look out for Gabe, but she'd seen no sign of him. She returned to the hotel, wondering if he'd returned or not.

"Miss Martin?" the desk clerk called out.

"Yes?"

"I wasn't at the desk when he came through, but I did see Mr. West going up the stairs a short while ago. He should be in his room now."

"Thank you," she told him, then quickened her pace up the steps.

She wanted to get her copy of the special edition of the *Star* before she went to speak with Gabe. She was certain he was going to be angry, so she wanted to have a good reason to show him why she'd followed him to Canyon Creek. It took her only a moment to grab the paper, and then she was heading down the hall to Room 212, her mood excited but cautious. There was no telling what kind of reaction she was going to get out of Gabe.

Trace was lying on his bed, trying to rest. The night was hot and sultry, so he'd discarded his shirt before stretching out. He'd left his glasses on the bureau and was staring at the ceiling, willing himself to sleep, but not succeeding.

Trace's mood was tense and frustrated. Nothing was working out the way he'd hoped it would. He had come to Canyon Creek to find a lead to the gang, but he'd come up empty-handed. True, he had every intention of going after them the next time they committed a robbery, but someone else might be killed before he could get to them. Enough innocents had already lost their lives because of Matt Harris.

His thoughts drifted to the following day and

his return to Durango. Elise would be there, awaiting his return, angry at him for leaving her behind. He smiled in spite of himself at the thought of her. She was different from any woman he'd ever known. She was smart and brave—and beautiful. Despite his best attempt to control his thoughts, the memory of that night in her parlor returned.

Trace drew in a ragged breath. Elise aroused feelings in him that he'd never known before, and that troubled him. He wondered if he loved her, then brought himself up short. He couldn't love her. His life was too complicated for him to risk becoming involved with her. Still, even as he tried to banish the memory of Elise from his mind and heart, the sweetness of her embrace and the beauty of her kiss stayed with him, leaving him even more restless.

The knock at the door startled Trace. Only the sheriff and the banker knew where he was staying, so whoever it was, it had to be important. He got up quickly, and grabbing up his shirt, he shrugged into it, not bothering to button it. He put on his glasses and hurried to open the door.

Trace's shock was real when he found Elise standing there. For a moment, he imagined that he'd conjured her up just by thinking about her.

"Gabe! I'm glad you finally came back to your room. You can't imagine what happened! I need to talk to you!" Elise said quickly without waiting for him to react to her presence. She had meant to look up at his face, but she found herself staring at the broad width of his chest. She was again amazed by the hard, corded muscles there, and she had to give herself a mental shake to keep herself from reaching out to touch him.

"Elise! What are you doing here?" Trace immediately started to work at the buttons on his shirt to cover himself more fully. Trying to sound like Gabe, he said quickly, "I specifically told you to stay in Durango and take charge of the paper."

"I know that, and that is precisely why I'm here. This is all about the paper! I've got something important to show you. May I come in? We have to talk."

"Well, I—um—" He couldn't decide what to do. It was most inappropriate for her to be in the room of a single man. "Is your grandmother here with you?"

"No. I came alone. This was too important to wait. I had to get here as quickly as I could to show you what I'd learned."

"It couldn't have waited until I got back?"

"I didn't know when you were coming back, and you didn't let us know where you were staying. My reason for being here is strictly business," she declared with dignity.

"What is it that's so important?"

"I received a telegram early this morning. It was from Ben."

"Your old boss? Why would he be contacting you?"

"Ben will always be a newspaperman, even if he doesn't own the paper anymore. I guess when he heard this, he had to let me know. Anyway, he's right. The minute I read the telegram, I knew I had to run a special edition of the *Star*!"

"This had better be good."

"It's fantastic! Wait'll you see! I was certain that you would want to see the paper right away, knowing how interested you are in the Harris gang—"

"Did they rob another bank?" he asked, suddenly focusing on what she was saying.

"Not yet, and the news isn't specifically about the gang."

He was growing frustrated with her. "What is it, then?"

"It's Sheriff Jackson—that lawman I told you about from Eagle Pass."

Trace suddenly went very still and took a step back. "What about him?" he asked cautiously.

Elise took his move as an unspoken invitation to enter his room, so she strode right on in.

"Look at this! He's still alive!"

Chapter Eighteen

Elise handed Gabe the single-sheet edition of the *Star* as she stepped farther into the room. She was so proud of herself. She'd made the trip to Canyon Creek all alone. She'd found Gabe without too much trouble. Now all she had to do was convince him that Sheriff Trace Jackson was still alive, hiding out somewhere nearby, and they could start trying to locate him. She could just imagine it—an interview with Sheriff Jackson! And what an interview that would be! She could hardly wait.

Trace watched her move past him, then glanced down at the special edition.

BREAKING NEWS
SHERIFF TRACE JACKSON SURVIVES DEADLY
AMBUSH!

266

The headlines screamed at him.

Trace went cold. He swallowed tightly and kept reading. Fury filled him. When he'd finished, he looked up at her, his expression black.

"Well, what do you think?" she asked anxiously. She had expected Gabe to be as excited as she was at the news, but instead of exciting, the look on his face was almost frightening. She was suddenly uneasy. "Gabe? What's wrong?"

"Where did Ben learn all this?" he demanded in a low, strained voice as he pinned her with an icy glare. He realized then that the door was still standing open, and he reached over to push it shut behind them.

Elise looked from Gabe to the closed door and back. She had a sudden sense of foreboding. "According to his telegram, he overheard two saloon girls talking about Jackson here in Canyon Creek in the Mother Lode. The one was named Sissy. That's why I followed you here. I thought I could go to the saloon and talk to her. Maybe she could help me find Sheriff Jackson, and I could get an interview with him. An interview with Sheriff Jackson would be big, Gabe, real big—"

"How many of these did you print?" he asked tersely, cutting her off.

"Andy and I got out over two hundred," she said tentatively.

Gabe swore violently under his breath, his expression turning even more thunderous. "Damn it, woman!"

She blinked, completely shocked by this reaction from him. "What is it? What's wrong? We thought you'd be pleased."

It was then that she glanced around the

room for the first time and saw his gun and holster on the chair and a rifle leaning against the wall next to it. It struck her as unusual that Gabe would have come to Canyon Creek to do interviews so well armed.

"Pleased?" he ground out. "I should be pleased when you've just ruined everything?"

"How did I ruin anything? I just printed the truth," she said, confused.

It was then that she saw his saddlebags on the floor in the corner. Hand-tooled on the leather flap were the initials *T J*.

Elise stared at them for a minute as everything finally came together for her. Gabe practicing his quick draw—the bullet wounds on his back—saving her from Farnsworth and from Boyd—and now his barely controlled fury.

She didn't say a word, but walked straight to the saddlebags and picked them up.

"*T J?*" she said softly, staring down at the saddlebags.

Elise couldn't stop herself. The reporter in her had to know the truth. Opening one flap, she reached in and took out an item wrapped in a handkerchief. She glanced back at Gabe to find him watching her, his gaze searingly intent upon her. She unfolded the handkerchief and stared down at the sheriff's star she held in her hand.

"Oh, God—it's you," she breathed in a strangled voice. She lifted her gaze to stare straight at Gabe. Her eyes were wide in astonishment. "You're Trace Jackson."

Trace grimaced, knowing there was no more

denying it. "You're damned right I am, and you can't imagine what damage you just did by publishing this!"

"I didn't know—"

He threw the paper down in disgust and took off the glasses, tossing them carelessly onto the nearby table. "Harris thought I was dead! I was going to go after him as soon as I had my strength back."

Elise stared at him with new understanding. All the mysteries of "Gabe" now made sense to her, and he transformed himself right before her very eyes. No longer did he seem retiring or bookish. Trace Jackson was every inch the man she'd thought him to be. He stood before her, tall and darkly handsome, filling her whole world, radiating power and command.

Gabe was Trace!

Elise's heartbeat quickened as the truth sank fully into her consciousness. The honorable lawman whose death she'd mourned was really alive and standing right here before her. Why hadn't she realized it sooner? Why had she been so blind to the truth about Gabe? She laid the saddlebags and star aside and went to him.

"What happened to you and the posse?"

"Harris caught us on a mountain trail. We didn't stand a chance," he told her, his voice tight with emotion.

"How did you make it through the ambush? All the reports I got said that you'd been killed."

"I wanted it that way. A miner named Gibby saved me. I'd been shot three times. How I lived through that, I'll never know. Gibby nursed me back. He wanted to let the people in town know that I had survived, but I told him to tell everybody that we had all been killed. I wanted to have an edge on Harris. I wanted to surprise him." Trace smiled a cold, deadly smile. "I was going to enjoy seeing the look on his face when I finally caught up with him."

"I'm sorry."

"So am I."

"You'll still catch him. I know you will," she said with confidence.

"I'm planning on it," he said fiercely.

"Gabe—er, Trace—if the miner was the only person who knew you were alive, how did the saloon girl here in Canyon Creek find out? Would he have told her?"

"I don't think it was Gibby, but I'm going to find out before I leave. There was one other person who knew I was alive, and that was Will Campbell, the man who took my place as sheriff in Eagle Pass. He was one of my best deputies. He was the only one I've talked to besides Gibby since the ambush."

"But why would he have talked about you to a saloon girl?"

"I don't know. That's what's troubling me. Will gave me his word that he'd keep quiet about it. He wants Harris brought in as badly as I do."

"We've got to find out who revealed your secret."

"You go on back to Durango in the morning. I'll talk to the saloon girl and see what I can find out."

"No, I want to stay here with you and find out who betrayed you."

270

"It doesn't really matter who did it, although I do want to know. What's really important is that the truth is out, and once Harris hears that I'm alive, he'll be looking for me."

"Is there any way for you to track them down now?"

"I talked to the sheriff earlier, before you got here. He said they'd followed their trail for almost two days, but lost it after it was washed out in a bad storm."

"So there's no way for you to go after them now?"

"No. Not until I hear that they've struck again."

Elise was actually relieved at this news. She didn't want Trace to ride out after the gang. She feared that if he did, she would never see him again. He had become a big part of her life. Even as Gabe, she'd been fighting her attraction to him. He had drawn her to him with his kisses and his fierce protection, and now to discover that he was Trace Jackson . . .

"We could find some way to work together to find them," she offered, wanting to do anything she could to help.

"Why? Because it's such a good story, and you'll sell a lot of papers reporting on it?"

"No. Because you matter—to me." She went to him and, unable to stop herself, reached out to touch his arm. The warm, solid strength of him sent a shiver of awareness through her.

"You don't even know me," Trace said seriously, trying to ignore the feelings that her simple touch generated within him. "You don't know anything about me."

271

"Oh, yes, I do," Elise said softly, looking up at him, her eyes filled with all the wonder of the emotions she was experiencing. "I know that you saved me from Farnsworth and from Boyd—and you saved me from myself."

Elise couldn't resist. She rose on her tiptoes and pressed her lips to his. She wanted Trace to know everything she was feeling in her heart. She knew this was dangerous. She knew she shouldn't be kissing him, but she didn't care.

For an instant, Trace met her in that kiss. He wanted to kiss her. Lord knew he did. He hadn't stopped wanting her since that night at her house, but he wasn't going to let it happen— not here, not now. With all the inner strength he could muster, he took her by the wrist and put her from him.

"No, Elise." He was firm as he fought down his own desire for her.

"But Trace—" She said his name in a soft voice, loving the sound of it.

He stifled a groan at her unknowingly seductive ploy. "You need to go back to Durango."

"And you need to go with me. Durango is your home now, too. It's where you belong."

Brazenly ignoring the way he was holding himself away from her, she went to him.

"Kiss me, Trace."

Trace stared down at her, seeing how beautiful and trusting she was. She stirred emotions in him he'd never known before. She always had, even from their very first encounter. He remembered how worried he'd been the first day he met her that Farnsworth might harm her, and then at the High Time, he'd been furious at the sight of Boyd's hands on her.

He loved her.

The realization came to Trace, amazing him in its simplicity—and its complexity. Ever since she'd thrown herself into his arms at the stage depot wearing her wedding gown, he had known she was special. Elise was innocence and beauty. She was everything that was missing in his life.

Trace knew, though, that he had no life, no future. Harris wanted him dead. Even as he told himself to stay away from Elise, he was unable to deny himself that which he wanted most. He bent to her and claimed her lips in a searing kiss.

Elise gave a throaty purr as his mouth moved over hers and his arms came around her, crushing her against him. She responded to him as a blossom to the sun, fully and openly. Looping her arms around his neck, she reveled in his nearness. She had been drawn to Gabe, but now she understood the truth. Her instincts had known that beneath his glasses and without the bow ties, Gabe had been as strong as any man. And he was. He was Trace—the man she'd always admired even without knowing him. He was honorable, and dedicated, and courageous.

And she loved him.

The truth did not surprise her. Her emotions where he was concerned had always been volatile and now she understood why.

"I love you, Trace," she whispered when they finally broke apart.

He gazed down at her, seeing the truth of her

devotion in her eyes, and he kissed her gently. "I love you, too."

They stared at each other in silent awe.

"You'd better go back to your room now," he said, trying to be strong. Until he was through with the Harris gang, he could make no lasting promises or commitments. He wanted her, but he loved her enough to deny himself.

"Trace?" Elise looked up at him, hurt by his apparent rejection.

"It's best that you leave now, Elise."

"You don't want me?" She wanted to be with him. She wanted to love him. She knew she shouldn't, but it felt so right being in his arms, kissing him.

He gave a low laugh that was half a groan. "I want you very much, but I love you. I don't want to hurt you, and I'm afraid that's what might happen if I don't send you away."

"I want to stay with you, Trace." Her voice was a gentle whisper.

He closed his eyes, trying to find the strength to turn her away. "But I can't promise you a future, Elise."

"I only want what you can give me now— here—tonight," she said softly, lifting one hand to caress his cheek. "I want to love you, Trace."

He turned his head to press a kiss to her palm. Her touch was a balm to his tortured soul. He had been alone for so long, but in her arms he knew he could find peace for at least a little while.

Logic told Trace to send her away, to save her from the torment the future might hold for both of them, but his heart refused to listen.

"Ah, Elise," he groaned. Then he cast all caution to the wind as he gathered her near.

Trace held her to his heart, cherishing her nearness. He had come to Canyon Creek to escape his feelings for her. He had thought that if he put distance between them, he would be able to forget her and concentrate on the Harris gang. But she'd followed him and captured him with her innocence and excitement. She was everything he'd ever wanted in a woman— she was intelligent and beautiful, and he never wanted to let her go.

Without another word, Trace lifted her in his arms and carried her to the bed. He lowered her upon its welcoming softness, then left her for a moment to lock the door. They would be safe now. This would be their haven from reality. This would be their time to love and be loved, until the dangers that they faced beyond the door forced them apart.

Elise watched Trace and smiled as he returned to her side. She lifted her arms in welcome to him, and he went to her without reservation. He covered her body with his, searing her with the heat of his need. She gasped at the contact, thrilling at having him so close.

His mouth covered hers, tasting of her sweetness, parting her lips to delve within. Hungry for him, she met him in that exchange. When his lips left hers to seek out the sweetness of her throat, she arched toward him as delight coursed through her.

Trace began to caress her, his hands skimming over her slender curves until she was moving restlessly beneath him, urging him on in her innocence. He drew back to shed his shirt, then reached out to unfasten the buttons at her bodice.

Elise helped him, eager to be rid of any barriers between them. She remembered all too well the glory of his caress, and she longed to feel him touching her again. His touch was heavenly, and she knew she would never have enough of him. When Trace helped her slip out of her dress, she finally lay before him clad only in her chemise. She felt a bit shy, until he came to her and kissed her.

As their lips met, all thoughts of shyness were banished. This was Trace. He loved her.

Elise offered herself up to his loving expertise. She reveled in his kisses and caresses, learning from his touch, becoming brave enough to caress him in return. At first, her touch was tentative. She stroked his back, her hands gliding over him, sculpting his muscles, thrilling at the hard heat of him. He stiffened as her hands moved over him, and she immediately stopped, fearful that she might somehow have injured him.

"Did I hurt you?" she asked worriedly.

He gave a low laugh as he pressed a kiss to her throat. "No, darling, you didn't hurt me—far from it. Don't stop."

Emboldened by his response, she began to caress him again, exploring his chest and back even more brazenly. She loved the feel of his hard-muscled body beneath her hands. She trailed her fingers along the waistband of his pants and smiled to herself at the way he tensed at her exploration.

Hungry for more of her, Trace brushed the straps of her chemise from her shoulders and bared her breasts to his kisses. She was as beautiful as he remembered, and he pressed heated caresses to that tender flesh.

At the feel of his lips upon her, Elise was lost. Caught up in his lovemaking, she became only a creature of the flesh, ruled by the fire he'd created within her. She clung to him, wanting to know more, needing to know more. A great emptiness filled her and drove her to move her hips against his. Elise knew only Trace could ease the ache that throbbed deep within the womanly heart of her. When he stripped away the chemise and she lay unclothed before him, she delighted in the burning look in his dark-eyed gaze as he stared down at her.

"Do I please you?" she asked.

"You more than please me," he answered in a passion-strained voice. He moved away from her then, leaving her only long enough to rid himself of the rest of his clothing.

Elise watched him as he returned to her, her gaze widening a bit at her first sight of a nude man. She thought Trace beautiful. He seemed perfectly proportioned, from his wide shoulders to his narrow waist and long, powerful legs.

Trace joined her on the bed again, enfolding her in his embrace, fitting himself to her. She gasped and lay still at that intimate contact.

"Easy, love," Trace told her, gentling her.

With the utmost care, he began to kiss and caress her. He could sense her nervousness, and he wanted to calm her fears.

And he did.

As he stoked the fire of her need, rousing her to a fever pitch, Elise began to move instinctively beneath him again. He reached down and lifted her hips to his, and she shuddered at the primal feeling of passion that surged within her. Trace sought the center of her desire and began to enter her, slowly, sweetly.

Elise went still as he pushed forward, intent on claiming her for his own. When he came to the barrier that was proof of her innocence, he paused, fearful of hurting her.

"Trace?" she whispered his name, wondering why he was holding himself back.

"This may hurt you, but it will only hurt once," he told her, kissing her softly. With utmost care, he pressed on, piercing her maidenhead and making her his.

Elise tensed at his invasion, so foreign to her. He began to move against her then, setting his rhythm as he caressed her, rousing her passions. With each touch and kiss, she relaxed a little more until she had accepted him fully and was glorying in his possession. She strained against him, seeking a thrilling release that she knew would only come from him. The fire of their passion flamed ever higher until they reached the peak of ecstasy together, and she was swept away, caught up in the pure rapture of Trace's love.

They drifted back to reality together, wrapped in each other's arms. They lay, their bodies still joined, not speaking, only feeling, savoring the beauty of their union.

"I hope I didn't hurt you," Trace said in a low growl.

Elise gave a throaty laugh. "Loving you was worth it."

At her words, he rose over her to press a cherishing kiss to her lips.

"And you did say it would only hurt once,"

she whispered, linking her arms around his neck to draw him to her as she wriggled her hips against his.

Trace was surprised that she would want him again so soon, but he was also delighted. He hardened immediately at her sinuous ploy, and he was more than willing to oblige. "Are you sure?"

"Ummm, I'm very sure." Elise drew him down to her for a hungry kiss.

Trace needed no more encouragement.

It was a long while later that they lay together, exhausted and finally sated.

Chapter Nineteen

Trace had thought the night hot and sultry before Elise had come to him, but now he knew the true meaning of heat. He smiled into the darkness at the memory of her fiery passion. She had branded him with her love.

Trace looked over at Elise as she slumbered beside him. She was curled against him, her hand splayed possessively across his chest. He knew then that he never wanted to let her go. He hadn't meant to fall in love with her, but he had. He wanted to stand with her before a preacher—and not Preacher Farnsworth. He wanted to claim her as his bride.

But as long as the Harris gang was free, he couldn't do it. By marrying Elise, he would make her a target for Harris's hate. He would be putting her in danger. If anything happened to her because of him, he would never be able to forgive himself.

The thought of Harris hurting Elise drove Trace from the bed. He slipped quietly away to stand at the window. He stared down at the deserted streets of Canyon Creek, wondering where Harris was and how he could get to him. He wondered, too, if the outlaw might see Elise's special edition and come to Durango looking for him. He would have to be even more careful now.

The last few months had left Trace feeling helpless, and he hated feeling helpless. His hands clinched into fists at his sides. He was a man of action, a man who fought for justice, and now, against Harris, he felt powerless. Hell, he couldn't even find his trail to go after him! Trace raked a hand through his hair in an impatient gesture. He wanted to put an end to Harris's reign of terror. Only then could he get on with his life.

"Trace?" Elise whispered his name as she came awake to find him gone from her side.

"I'm here," he answered, not turning toward her as he fought with his emotions, his voice flat and strained.

Elise knew something was wrong. She rose from the bed and went to him. She came up behind him and encircled him with her arms, closing her eyes and resting her cheek against him. He was so warm and strong, and she loved him so. Elise opened her eyes after a moment, and she could see the scars that marred the sleek male beauty of his back. Pain stabbed at her as she imagined the horror of that day with the posse. Wanting to ease his torment, she pressed her lips to a scar.

"I'm sorry they hurt you. I'm sorry any of this had to happen to you," she told him in a hoarse voice.

At the touch of her lips upon him, a shudder wracked Trace. He turned away from the window, taking her in his arms. He held her close to his heart. He knew they might never have another night like this. He knew their happiness could be fleeting, but he was determined to cherish it for as long as he could.

"I love you, Elise." The words were torn from him as he lifted her and carried her back to bed.

With all gentleness, Trace made love to her. He held his raging passion in check, wanting to give her all the pleasure he could, wanting to remember this moment forever. Elise responded to his gentleness with wild abandon, and when at last they had reached the heights of passion together, she rested in the haven of his embrace, never wanting the night to end.

It was a long time later when she finally stirred and rose onto one elbow to look down at him. There was no hint of Gabe in him now. Compellingly handsome, Trace was the fierce, powerful man she'd caught glimpses of during their earlier weeks together. She wondered how she could have been so blind.

"What were you worrying about before?" she asked quietly, not sure that he was ready to talk about it, but truly wanting to know. She wanted to help him in any way she could.

"I was thinking of the Harris gang," he answered flatly, his frustration obvious. "I was trying to figure out how to stop them before anyone else gets killed. There has to be a way I can get a lead on them. I must be overlooking something, missing some clue that will take me to them."

"Maybe you're going about this the wrong way. Maybe instead of chasing them, you should try to draw them to you." Elise knew that nothing was more important to Trace than bringing the gang to justice. She couldn't bear the thought, though, that he might ride away one day to go after Harris and never come back. She had been desperately trying to think of a way to keep him with her. She hoped she'd come up with the perfect solution.

"Sure, I'll just take out an ad in all the newspapers around the state, telling Harris that I'm in Durango."

"No, nothing like that. This is something we could do together—like exposing Preacher Farnsworth. I know Marshal Trent will work with us. He wants the gang almost as badly as you do," she told him, hoping he'd come to see that her way might work. "All we have to do is set a trap with bait they can't resist."

"That's what I'm afraid your special edition on me was."

"There's no guarantee that Harris will even see that. We only got out two hundred copies. No, we need something big, something as big as Farnsworth, that'll get the whole area talking. If we set it up, we would be in control of the whole confrontation."

"What did you have in mind?"

"We know they're after money—and they like lots of it. What if we printed news in the *Star* that would entice them to come to Durango? What do you think?"

"I don't want you anywhere near Matt Harris. I don't want you in any danger," he declared.

"I won't be in any danger." Elise leaned forward and kissed him tenderly. "You'll be with me the whole time. You've already saved me from Farnsworth and from Boyd, and with any luck you won't have to save me from Harris, too."

Trace deepened the kiss at the thought of her in Harris's hands. "He's a deadly man, Elise. Farnsworth and Boyd were nothing compared to Harris."

"And that's why we have to do this. Everyone in the whole state is in danger right now with that gang running free," she argued. "From the way things have been going lately, they could strike anywhere, any time, and get away with it. But if we did it this way, luring them to Durango, we could be ready for them. We would be in charge. We would set the time and the place. There would be no surprises. It will work, I know it will."

Trace knew Elise was right. It made more sense to try to lure the outlaws to him than to try to track them down, never knowing when he would come face-to-face with them. After that day with the posse, he knew he wanted to be in control the next time he confronted Harris. He didn't want any surprises.

"We can't use a gold shipment or an army payroll," he said thoughtfully. "The movements of those shipments are always kept highly confidential, and they're heavily guarded."

"I know. I was thinking of something a little more creative, a little more believable. A few years ago, when I first went to work for Ben, he made a special trip to Denver to see some British royalty who were there for a visit. He was quite impressed with all the pomp that went with their tour, and as I recall, he did go on quite a bit about the jewels the women were wearing." She paused, lost deep in thought for a moment; then a slow smile curved her lips. "Of course—"

"What are you thinking?"

"I've got our lead story for next week! We at the *Star* have just learned that Lord and Lady Winston will be arriving by train later in the month to tour the area. Lady Winston is known for her fabulous family jewels."

"Lord and Lady Winston?" he asked with a half smile.

Elise's laugh was almost childlike in delight as she let her imagination run away with her. She answered, "Oh, yes! Real British royalty coming to Durango. What do you think?"

"And just where do you plan to find your Lord and Lady Winston?"

"I have the perfect couple in mind—"

"Elise—" He had a sudden fear that she was planning on the two of them pretending to be the royals.

"Don't you think George and my grandmother would make a perfect lord and his lady?" she asked, her eyes aglow at the thought.

Trace was relieved at her suggestion, but concerned about their safety. "Do you think they'd do it?"

"I think they would. Grandmother was certainly excited about the 'wedding' and Preacher Farnsworth. If she thought she could help bring down the Harris gang, she'd be thrilled."

Trace gave a low chuckle as he thought of the older woman. He lifted one hand to cup Elise's cheek and draw her near for a kiss. "I know where you get it from then."

She gave a soft laugh as she met him in that exchange, knowing he was right.

It was a long while later before they bothered to to think about the paper or the gang again.

"We need to talk to the saloon girl first thing in the morning," Trace said, holding her close, yet knowing that they would soon be facing daylight and reality.

"And then head back," she finished for him, her tone sad. "I don't want to go back. I want to stay right here, like this."

He kissed her again, letting her know he felt the same way. "Elise," he began softly, "when this is all over, I want to see you again in that dress you were wearing at the stage depot."

She lifted her head to gaze down at him, tears burning in her eyes as she smiled. "I love you, Trace Jackson or Gabe West or Ben Hollins or whatever your name really is. I knew you were the man for me the minute I saw you climbing down off that stage, and I promise you, you'll have a much better wedding night next time."

"I'm looking forward to it," he told her with a rakish grin.

They came together one last time, treasuring their love and their privacy.

The sky had just begun to lighten when Elise finally slipped back to her own room. Her heart was singing as she let herself in. She couldn't believe so much had changed in just one night, but it had. Her whole life was different now.

Gabe was Trace—and she loved him.

The realization still stunned her, even as she embraced the knowledge happily. Everything she'd ever imagined about Trace Jackson had proven true. He was brave and honorable and dedicated. His fierce need to right the wrongs the gang was wreaking on the state only made her love him more.

And he loved her.

She sighed contentedly as she began to prepare herself for the interview to come. It was important that they find out who revealed the truth of Trace's survival.

Sissy Perkins was not pleased when someone pounded on her door that morning. She had worked late into the night and the last thing she wanted to do was get up early.

"Who is it?" she demanded, pulling the covers over her head.

"It's me, Lottie! Get up! There's some people here want to talk to you."

"Well, I don't want to talk to them! Tell them I'm busy!"

"I will not!" Lottie declared, trying her door and finding it unlocked. She let herself in. "This is important. Get up, Sissy!"

Sissy groaned and buried her head in her pillow. "I want to sleep!"

"You can sleep later," Lottie told her. "It's a man and a woman, and they say they're from a newspaper in Durango. They want to interview you about something."

"They're from a newspaper? What would they want with me?"

"I don't know, and that's what I want to find out! So, get up!"

Sissy only groaned. Her head was still aching from all the liquor she'd drunk the night before with the wild cowboy who'd spent most of the night with her. She'd had a fine time. She'd enjoyed every minute, but right now, she was regretting having had so much fun.

"Go away," she muttered. "I'll be down in a few minutes."

"Good. I'll go tell them you're coming. Don't take too long!"

Sissy moaned as Lottie slammed the door behind her on her way out. It took an effort, but she threw off the covers and sat up. She immediately caught a glimpse of herself in the mirror and shook her head in disgust. The sight certainly wasn't pretty. Getting to her feet, she staggered to her washstand to start repairing the damage. It wasn't going to be easy, but she couldn't go downstairs looking like this. One of her customers might see her!

Trace and Elise sat at one of the tables in a corner, waiting for Sissy to come downstairs. They knew the bartender and the other working girl were watching them, curious about the reason for their call on Sissy, but they pretended to be above it all.

"The Mother Lode has a lot in common with the High Time, don't you think?" Elise remarked, trying not to grin at Trace.

"Let's hope not. The last thing I want to deal with this morning is another Boyd."

"He was interesting," she said, her eyes sparkling with humor.

" 'Interesting' is not a word I'd use to describe him," he growled.

"Thank you, again, for helping me that night," Elise said softly, remembering Trace coming to save her. He had been her avenging warrior, her guardian angel. She would have kissed him right then and there, but she thought the barkeep might offer her a job. The thought made her smile.

"What are you smiling about?" he asked, wishing they were alone so he could kiss her.

"Nothing that we can talk about," she informed him primly.

He bit back a groan of sensual awareness as he looked at her across the table. She looked every bit the proper lady, but he knew first-hand the passionate woman she really was. He wanted to pick her up and carry her out of there back to his hotel room, but he managed to control the impulse. "It's too early for a drink," he muttered to himself as his mind conjured up the image of her in her red satin dress and blond wig.

"What?"

"Nothing."

They finally heard someone coming down the stairs and saw a tall, voluptuous blonde wearing a low-cut black dress making her way into the room.

"They're over there, Sissy," Lottie called out to her, pointing toward the table where they were sitting.

Sissy nodded and headed toward the two strangers.

"This damn well better be good," she complained out loud. "You interrupted my beauty sleep." She stopped at the table before them. "I'm Sissy Perkins. You want to talk to me?" she said curtly.

"Yes, we would." Trace stood and pulled out a chair for her in the most gentlemanly fashion.

"Oh." Sissy got a good look at him and wondered who he was as she slipped into the chair. She knew she'd never seen him before. With those glasses and bow tie, she would have remembered him. She wondered vaguely if he would be any fun upstairs. She decided maybe getting up early hadn't been such a bad thing. "Thank you. A true gentleman is a rare thing here in Canyon Creek."

"My pleasure, Miss Perkins." Trace gave her a winning smile as he sat back down.

She practically melted at his smile, and she batted her eyes at him.

For the first time in her life, jealousy flared within Elise, and she was startled by it. She found herself speaking up, wanting to distract the other woman from Trace. "We appreciate your taking the time to talk with us."

Sissy was irritated by the woman's presence and looked over at her coldly. "So who are you and what are you after?" She looked back at the man and smiled, ignoring the woman again.

"I'm Gabe West, Miss Perkins. I'm the owner and editor of the *Durango Star*, and this is Elise Martin. She works for me at the paper," he told her smoothly.

Lucky girl, Sissy thought.

"Please, Gabe," she said, emphasizing his name, "just call me Sissy. Everybody does."

"Well, Sissy—"

When he said her name, she practically cooed, and Elise gritted her teeth at the display.

"—we're here because we received word that you might know something about one Sheriff Trace Jackson," he explained, smiling at her again.

Sissy looked a bit surprised by his statement. "How'd you hear about that?"

"A good newspaperman never reveals his sources," Trace said easily in his most charming manner. "But if it is true, we'd definitely like to know more about it."

"Sheriff Jackson was the best lawman in the state," Elise put in. "If there's a chance he's alive, the public needs to know about it!"

"Well . . . " Sissy hesitated, and then thought, *why not?* "All I know is that a cowboy came in to spend some time with me, and he got to talking while we were upstairs."

"And?" Elise pressed her.

"He said something like, 'They all think Jackson's dead, but he ain't. I saw him. I talked to him.'"

"Who was this man? Do you know his name? We'd like to interview him, too."

"No. I'd never seen him before that night, and I ain't seen him since."

"What did he look like?"

"He wasn't real tall. Had blond hair and was a little on the heavy side. He looked like he'd been in a fight and had come out on the losing end, too. Will that help you?" She looked at the man named Gabe and gave him her most inviting look.

"Yes, thank you. And you think he was serious?"

"He had no reason to lie to me," she said with a shrug.

"Did he say where Jackson might be?" Elise asked. "We'd like to find him and talk to him, if we could."

"No, he didn't say any more than what I just told you."

"Well, we appreciate all your help, Sissy," Trace said.

Totally ignoring Elise's presence, she gave him her most hungry look. "It may be early, but sometimes a little fun in the morning can set the mood for the whole day," she offered. "You want to come upstairs with me for a while?"

Trace stood and took her hand. "We appreciate all your help, but we really have to be going." He kissed her hand.

Sissy nearly fell off her chair at his gallant gesture. No man had ever treated her that way before. She watched speechlessly for a moment as he offered his arm to Elise and started to escort her from the saloon.

"You can come back later!" she called out. "I'll be right here!"

Trace smiled at her one last time as he disappeared outside with Elise.

Inside the Mother Lode, Sissy sat staring after them, her heart pounding.

"What was that all about?" Lottie asked as she came over to join her.

"He owns a newspaper in Durango, and somehow he'd heard that I knew something about that Sheriff Jackson." She was still staring after him. "Damn, Lottie, maybe we should head for Durango and go to work at a saloon there. He sure was special."

"I like my men to be more manly," Lottie said, thinking the man had looked a bit like a sissy in his spectacles and all.

"My instincts are never wrong, girl. For all that he looked like the book-learning type, that man was a stud. I wish he'd had more time. He could have serviced me, and I could have showed him a good time, loosened him up a bit." She paused, a sexy smile curving her lips. "That would have been fun—loosening him up a bit."

"Go back to bed," Lottie advised her. "You need some more rest."

"Not now I don't," she complained. "He done woke me up."

Sissy hurried to the swinging doors to see if she could catch sight of the man named Gabe West, but he and the woman had already disappeared from sight. Disappointment filled her. She went to the bar.

"Give me a whiskey, Harry Lee. It's going to be one long day."

Chapter Twenty

Trace's expression turned grim as soon as they'd walked away from the saloon.

"What's wrong?" Elise asked, seeing the sudden change in him.

"It was Will," he stated flatly as they started back toward their hotel.

"The man who was your deputy?"

He nodded, lost deep in thought, wondering how Will had come to be in Canyon Creek and why he'd chosen to talk about him to a whore. "It doesn't make sense that he was talking about me, unless there had been some talk of the Harris gang earlier in the evening and he just got too drunk to know what he was saying. It's strange, though. As long as I've known him, Will was always able to hold his liquor."

"What are you going to do about it?"

"There's not much I can do now. I'll just send him a wire and remind him that we were going to keep it quiet until the time was right. It was probably just a momentary lapse on his part. He's a good man."

"I'm sorry it had to happen, but I'm glad it's that easy to resolve for you. I'm also very glad that I got you out of the Mother Lode when I did."

He looked down at her, his mood lightening as he slanted her a wicked grin. "Why? Were you remembering your working days at the High Time?" He had a mental image of her as she'd looked those nights.

"No, I was remembering what women like Sissy like to do with their customers to earn their money." She tightened her grip possessively on his arm. "And if you're going to be anybody's customer, you're going to be mine, Gabe West—all mine."

"Sissy was a temptation," he teased, "but I like my saloon girl from the High Time the best." Trace was suddenly wishing they were back at the hotel already and not walking down the sidewalk in broad daylight. It wouldn't do for him to stop and take her in his arms right there in front of God and everybody—not that the thought didn't have appeal.

"I was hoping you'd say that." She gave him a smile that let him know that she was just as eager as he was to return to the hotel as quickly as possible.

They quickened their pace, glad that they hadn't checked out yet. It seemed to take an eternity to get back to the lobby. They managed to control their need until they'd made it up the stairs.

Elise was thankful that there was no one else in the hallway, for the moment they were out of sight of the lobby, Trace dragged her into his arms and kissed her. It was a powerful, hungry kiss, and she matched his desire. She'd wanted him desperately, ever since she'd watched the other woman flirting with him. When they broke apart, Trace unlocked his door.

They slipped inside his room, and before Elise could even speak, he began unfastening the buttons at the back of her dress. Elise couldn't wait to be free of the barrier of her clothes. As soon as he'd loosened the last button, she slipped out of the offending garment, took off her shoes and the rest of her underthings, and went into his arms. She started to unbutton his shirt, but he couldn't wait any longer to have her. He took off the glasses and tossed them aside. He wasted no time removing his own clothes. Lifting her, he turned and backed her against the wall. Freeing himself, he linked her legs around his waist and sought the sweet depths of her.

Their mating was a heated, frantic coupling. They strained together, desperate to give each other the ultimate pleasure of their union. When at last ecstasy burst upon them, they clung to each other, weak yet sated from the splendor of their loving.

Without speaking, Trace carried her to the bed. They lay together in enraptured silence, treasuring the fierce wildness of their passion.

"Will it always be like this?" Elise finally asked, her heart still pounding an erratic rhythm from the thrill of their joining.

"Yes, love, between us it will be. I promise," Trace said softly as he pressed a gentle kiss to her lips.

She sighed and relaxed against him, savoring his nearness, never wanting to let him go. She loved him.

They remained together, exploring each other with tender touches and sweet whispers until reality forced them to awareness.

"We'd better get up," Elise said reluctantly. She would have loved to stay in Trace's arms for all eternity, but she knew they could not hide there in the hotel room forever.

"I know," he agreed with less than enthusiasm, rising over her to kiss her one last time.

She looped her arms around his neck and pressed herself against him.

It was a gesture of wanton innocence, and one that forced Trace to move away from her—quickly.

"Trace?"

"Darling, if you keep kissing me like that, we'll never get back to Durango."

She gave him a seductive smile. "Would that be so bad?"

Trace was tempted. His body was certainly urging him to return to her side and spend the rest of the day loving her, but he forced himself to discipline his wayward desires. "There's nothing I'd like to do more than make love to you for hours on end."

"I'd like that, too," she sighed, slowly getting up and moving to pick up her hastily discarded clothes.

"Need any help getting dressed?" he offered,

his eyes glowing with the rising heat of his barely controlled need.

"No. You just stay right where you are, or we may never get out of town."

He knew she was right, so he stayed across the room from her. Still, he did manage to enjoy every minute of watching her slip back into her clothing. Only when she was finally fully dressed did he allow himself to go near her again.

"Is that better?" Elise asked as he crossed the room.

"No, it's not better, but I guess it wouldn't do for you to take the stage to Durango dressed—or should I say, undressed—the other way."

She smiled up at him, thrilling to the newly discovered power of her femininity. "It all depends. If there were only the two of us onboard the stage . . ."

Trace drew a ragged breath at the thought and donned the spectacles. "I'll finish packing and meet you at your room."

"I'll be waiting." Elise let herself out. She was smiling as she returned to her own room and gathered her few things together.

A short time later Trace was there, looking very Gabe-like. They paid their bills at the front desk and then headed for the telegraph office.

"Can I help you, sir?" the operator asked.

"I need to send a wire to Sheriff Will Campbell in Eagle Pass."

"Here you go," the man pushed a pad of paper and a pencil toward him. "Just write out what you want me to send."

It took Trace only a minute to jot down the few lines.

Elise

Sheriff Will Campbell—

Regarding our private conversation in your back office, the information discussed there was to remain confidential. A recent report out of Canyon Creek seems to indicate otherwise. If there is a problem, you can reach me in Durango.

Gabriel West

"This is everything," Trace said, handing the operator back the paper.

"I'll get it out right away for you. That'll be two bits."

Trace paid him.

"Thank you, Mr. West."

They left the office and went to the stage depot. The next stagecoach was leaving for Durango in less than an hour.

"Will you be riding back on your own, or will you ride with me?" Elise asked in all innocence.

Trace's eyes darkened as he remembered her idea for an enjoyable trip back in the stage. "I'll ride with you," he said in a low voice, letting her know that he hadn't forgotten her words.

She blushed and turned away as she tried to collect her thoughts. Elise had always prided herself on being in control of her emotions at all times. But with Trace, she was finding that she had become a creature of the flesh. He had only to look at her, and she was weak with wanting him. She had always known that when she fell in love it would be wonderful, and it was. She had never dreamed it would be so exciting.

Trace went to get his horse from the livery and settle his bill there, then returned to meet her at the depot. His hopes were soaring as he found that Elise was the only person waiting there for the stagecoach. His gaze met hers as he rode up, and heat settled low in his body as he imagined the long, private, uninterrupted ride back to Durango.

"It seems we're destined to meet at stage depots," Elise told him as he came to join her where she was awaiting the stage's arrival.

"It's the ride home I'm looking forward to," he said in a voice meant only for her to hear.

Elise tried to ignore the way her pulse quickened at his words, but there was no way. Just his very nearness set her heart to racing. She wanted to reach out and touch him, to kiss him and caress him. She brought herself up short, forcing herself to think of other things—of her grandmother and Andy and the office and how blue the sky was.

"The weather certainly is nice today, don't you think?" she asked, deliberately trying to distract herself and him.

"It won't matter what the weather is like once we're alone in the stage," he said quietly.

It was then that they heard the stagecoach pulling in, and the sexual tension between them grew even more intense. In a matter of minutes they were going to board the stage, and then they were going to be alone on it for hours. The thought left Elise positively breathless, for she knew that once they were back in Durango they would have little or no time for intimacy. There would be no privacy for them.

They shared a look of longing and desire as the stage rumbled ever nearer. Soon, very soon . . .

And then the stage pulled to a stop before them. The door opened and three of the four passengers descended. One little old lady remained on board.

"You can go ahead and get in," the driver called down to them. "Mrs. Warson is going all the way to Durango with us."

Elise and Trace exchanged disappointed glances as their excited anticipation died a painful death. Trace handed Elise into the stage, making sure he didn't take her by the waist to lift her in. He wasn't sure he would be able to let go of her if he touched her that way. Elise couldn't believe how disappointed she was that they were going to be so thoroughly chaperoned for the entire trip.

"Good afternoon," she said as she settled in opposite the woman.

"Hello, dear," the old lady greeted her happily. "I'm Mrs. Warson."

"I'm Elise, and this is Gabe," Elise responded.

Trace climbed in and sat down beside Elise. The coach was so small, there was no avoiding contact with her, and he found his leg pressed thigh to thigh with hers. He wanted to groan in misery at the torment he knew awaited him for the next few hours, but he controlled the urge. He smiled at the little old lady.

"Are you two married?" Mrs. Warson asked quickly, eyeing them with interest.

"No, we're not," Elise answered, glancing up at Trace. "Gabe and I work together."

301

"Ah," Mrs. Warson said knowingly.

Suddenly, Elise feared that her emotions had been too easy to read, but she said nothing more. She tried not to think about the hard heat of Trace's thigh pressed so tightly against her own. She tried not to think about the long, hot exciting hours they'd just passed in each other's arms. She stared out the window, wondering if there was any way the driver could make the trip in half an hour instead of three or four.

"I'm going to see my grandchildren in Durango," Mrs. Warson chirped. "I haven't seen them in almost a year, and my son just invited me to come and stay with them for a whole month."

"That's wonderful," Elise and Trace agreed. They were miserable, but they made sure it didn't sound in their voices.

From there on, Mrs. Warson performed a monologue, telling them everything they had never wanted to know about her life and her grandchildren and the scenery and the way the stage was so uncomfortable as it hit every bump—although Trace himself was rather enjoying the bumps, for they brought him closer to Elise. Neither Elise nor Trace had to worry about making witty conversation with the woman. They couldn't have gotten a word in edgewise if they'd wanted to. Finally, after a good solid hour of her ramblings, the elderly lady nodded off.

Elise was afraid to take a deep breath for fear that it might wake her and start her chatting endlessly again. She glanced up at Trace to find him giving her a knowing, humorous look. She reached out and gently covered Trace's hand with her own.

Trace had managed to lose himself in the elderly woman's ramblings, but at the touch of Elise's hand, his carefully banked desire threatened to reignite. He lifted her hand to his lips to press one sweet kiss to it, his gaze meeting hers as he did so.

Their eyes locked, and they each knew the other's most heartfelt need. Elise gave him a trembling smile and withdrew her hand. They sat quietly together, neither of them speaking for fear of rousing their companion, remembering the last twenty-four hours and enjoying the simple contact that they were allowed in the close confines of the coach.

They began to think that the trek would never end, and they were relieved when at dusk the coach arrived in town a little behind schedule. Providence had been looking out for them, though, for Mrs. Warson had managed to sleep for a good two hours, at least giving them some peace and quiet.

"Maybe one day we can take another trip, and we'll be the only passengers," Trace said to Elise as he held out his hand to her to help down. Mrs. Warson had already been met by her family and had disappeared down the street with them.

"I think I'd like that," she said sweetly, deliberately leaning into him as he aided her descent.

Trace let her sweet body slide down the length of his as he helped her down. He knew it was a mistake, but he didn't care. Now that they were back to Durango, things would have to be different.

"Shall we stop at Marshal Trent's office before we take you home? Your grandmother's not expecting you at any particular time, is she?"

"No. I didn't say when I'd be returning in the note I left her."

Trace was very tempted to take her home with him that night, but he knew better. Her reputation was on the line. He would not do anything to harm her.

"Then let's talk to the marshal. We need to fill him in on everything so we can start making our plans for when Harris shows up."

Trace left instructions at the depot for his horse and their luggage to be delivered to the *Star*'s office, and then they headed off to speak with the lawman.

Jared Trent sat at his desk in the marshal's office, enjoying the fact that it had been a very quiet day. Nothing illegal or dangerous had gone on, and he was grateful. A little peace and quiet was a wonderful thing. He heard voices outside and looked up to see Gabe West and Elise Martin coming into his office.

"Evening. I didn't expect to see you two tonight. Last I heard, you were in Canyon Creek."

"We just got back into town and came straight here to talk to you. We're just glad you're here tonight," Trace told him.

"Is there some kind of trouble?" Trent was instantly alert, fearful that something might have happened down at the *Star*'s office. "Did you find something out about the Harris gang or Sheriff Jackson?" He had learned from Andy why the two of them had left town.

"No—at least, not yet," Trace began. "Are we alone? We've got a few things to tell you that need to be kept quiet."

"I'm the only one here. There's one deputy on duty, and he's out making the rounds. What can I do for you?" He looked expectantly from Gabe to Elise.

"There's something you need to know," Trace began slowly.

"Gabe is really Trace Jackson, Marshal Trent," Elise finished for him.

Jared's expression betrayed his shock. "You're Jackson?"

Trace nodded. "I was left for dead in the ambush. Only two people knew I'd survived. I kept it quiet so I could have an advantage on Harris when I'd recovered enough to go after him."

"No wonder you knew exactly what to do with Farnsworth!" He was grinning as he rose from his desk to shake hands with Trace. "I'm damned glad to meet you, and damned glad you survived the ambush."

"So am I," he answered. "Elise heard from Ben that the word was out in Canyon Creek that I was alive. I'm sure you saw her special edition of the *Star*."

"It's been the talk of the town for the last couple of days, but no one even suspects it could be you."

"Good, and we want to keep it that way," Trace said fiercely. "Here's what we'd like to do, but we're going to need your help."

Elise explained their tentative plan to use the news of royalty and jewels to draw the Harris gang into the area.

"Have you talked to your grandmother or

George about this yet?" the marshal asked.

"No, you were our first stop. We just got to town on the late stage."

"I think it will work, but only if we're very careful," Jared said, trying to calculate the danger involved.

"I don't want anyone else to die at their hands," Trace stated flatly, his determination unyielding.

"How many people are going to know the truth about you, Sheriff Jackson?"

"Just call me Trace, but better yet, we ought to stick with Gabe until this is all over."

Jared nodded in agreement.

"We'll have to tell my grandmother and George and Andy," Elise said. "They should be the only ones who really need to know. To everyone else, he'll remain Gabe until this is all over."

"And the end can't come soon enough for me," Jared told them. "I've been waiting a long time for the chance to see this gang brought to justice."

"Let's do it," Trace said.

"We can run a special edition about the 'royalty' and their fabulous jewels coming through town," Elise said.

"Then it's a matter of waiting and praying that Harris hears about it and comes after them. We'll have to be ready and watching for them," Jared pointed out.

"Don't worry. We will be," Trace declared.

The two men shook hands on it.

"How soon do you want to pull this off?"

"Next week?" Elise suggested.

"We'll be ready. Just let me know the details as soon as you've worked them out."

"We will."

They left the marshal's office and went straight to Elise's home. They were delighted to find that George was there with Claire.

Claire looked suitably upset with her granddaughter as Elise came through the door.

"Well, young lady, I hope you have something to say for yourself," she huffed. "Do you know how worried I've been?"

George reached over and patted her hand to calm her. "We *have* been concerned about you, Elise."

Elise managed to look a bit chagrined, but answered, "I think once you've have heard what we've got to say, you'll understand why I did what I did."

"I'm listening," Claire said with cool dignity.

A few minutes later, she was staring at Trace in amazement.

"You're Trace Jackson? But—!"

Trace grinned at her. "I know. Elise felt the same way, but taking up this disguise was the only way I could keep the secret that I'd lived through the ambush by Harris. Now that I've recovered, it's time to go after him, and that's where you and George come into it."

"We do?" George looked up questioningly.

Elise quickly explained their plan. "Don't you think the two of you would make fine British royalty?"

George and Claire exchanged a look of shock.

"You want us to pretend to be some lord and lady?"

"That's right. We going to lure the Harris gang right here to Durango, and then Trace and Marshal Trent can trap them. It will work. I'm sure it will. After all, we got Preacher Farnsworth," Elise told them with confidence.

"But Matt Harris is far more dangerous than Preacher Farnsworth," George cautioned.

"That's exactly why we're doing this, George. We want him locked up, and by bringing the gang to us, we can control the confrontation. Will you help us?" Trace asked.

George looked at Claire, and she smiled and nodded tightly.

"All right," he said. "We'll help you. Whatever you want us to do, we'll do."

Chapter Twenty-one

Will sat at his desk in the sheriff's office, staring down at the telegram in his hand. It took an effort on his part, but he managed to keep his expression schooled into one of only moderate interest as he read the wire.

"Who's it from?" Fred Carson, his new deputy, asked.

"An old friend I hadn't heard from in quite some time. He's up in Durango now. It's good to know that he's settled in somewhere."

Fred shrugged in response, not really caring. It was just unusual for them to get any telegrams unless there was something important going on. "Well, I'm going to go take a walk around town. I'll be back in a little while."

"I'll be right here."

As soon as Fred had gone and he was alone, Will laughed out loud in triumph. He had been waiting and hoping for just this moment ever since his last encounter with Harris. Now he was going to show the outlaw leader just what he was worth. Since Harris hadn't been able to shoot straight in the first place, he was going to finish the job for him. Not that he would phrase it exactly that way when he finally sent word to Harris that he'd taken care of Trace permanently, but that was what he was feeling. Will was still angry that Harris had blamed him for Trace still being alive. He was going to change all that now. He was going after Trace, and he was going to see him dead. He would notify Harris of that bit of good news just as soon as he returned to Eagle Pass from Durango. He would handle this by himself, and when the time came, he was going to enjoy letting Harris know how he had done it all on his own.

Will's smile was feral as he began to plan the trip. He would have to be gone for almost a week, but Fred could cover for him. There would be no problem getting away. He was going to take care of this unfinished business once and for all.

Trace lay awake and alone in his bed late that night. He was tired and needed sleep, but memories of loving Elise would give him no rest. He tossed and turned, seeking some kind of comfort, but it eluded him. He had known that giving in to his desire for her would only make things more complicated for him, but he had never realized it would be this difficult to stay away from her. Keeping his hands off her was going to be one of the hardest things he'd ever done.

Trace groaned as he realized just how much he missed her. He wanted her with him—beside him—beneath him.

The last mental image made him smile, but he quickly pushed the thought away. He couldn't dwell on how perfect it had felt to bury himself deep within her. Thinking about it was only going to make his return to celibacy that much more torturous.

Getting up, Trace stalked out of the bedroom and went to stand on the small front porch. The night breeze was cool and helped ease his torment.

As he stared up at the star-studded night sky, he wondered where the Harris gang was hiding out. Only when they'd been arrested and brought to justice would he allow himself to marry Elise. Only then would he feel it was safe to take her for his wife. He knew how much Matt Harris hated him, and he knew the man would stop at nothing to hurt him and anyone who was important to him.

The thought of Harris possibly harming Elise sent a sense of cold dread through Trace. It erased any and all thoughts of desire and focused him on what he needed to do. He would not, could not, rest until he'd caught the gang.

Andy stared at Trace in disbelief as they stood together in the *Star's* office late the following morning.

"Are you serious?" Andy demanded.

"I'm deadly serious." Trace confirmed what he'd just told him—that he was really Trace Jackson and that they were planning to set a trap for the Harris gang, working with Marshal Trent.

"Damn." Andy shook his head and grinned at his boss. "I liked you as Gabe and I'm sure I'll like you even more now that I know who you really are."

"You're one of very few who know, and we want to keep it that way."

"Yes, sir, Mr. West," he told him.

"We're going to start on a special edition of the paper today announcing the coming visit by the British Lord and Lady Winston. We want to make certain it's widely known that Lady Winston owns a magnificent collection of jewelry."

"But are they really coming to town?" Andy was confused.

Trace quickly explained the deception, and Andy grinned again.

"Your plan is brilliant."

"Let's just hope it works."

"Even if it doesn't, at least we haven't really lost anything. The danger will be only if the gang does show up. Does Marshal Trent know what we're going to do yet?"

"Not yet. Elise and I are still working on the details. Right now, we just need to get the word out."

"The word about what?" Elise asked as she came into the office.

"The Winstons' visit."

She smiled at Andy. "So Gabe has told you the truth?"

"Yes, he has, and it's wonderful news."

"That it is," she agreed, her gaze meeting Trace's across the room.

She'd passed a long, sleepless night wanting him and missing him. Given half a chance, she would have ridden out to his house and begged him to take her back to Canyon Creek so they could be alone together. The thought had appealed to her in those dark hours of the night, and it was even more appealing now that she was staring at him. He was so handsome. He was everything she'd ever dreamed of in a man.

The urge to back Trace into his office and shut the door so they would be alone was very tempting. She wanted to—

"Well, let's get to work on our special edition!" Andy said. "What kind of jewelry is Lady Winston famous for? Any ideas? We need to know the who, what, when, where and why of their visit."

Andy's journalistic musings interrupted Elise's erotic daydream. She gave Trace a quick smile as she followed Andy to his desk. It was time they went to work on the story.

Trace had just started back to his own desk when the main door opened and Julie swept in.

"Gabe! I'd heard that you'd gotten back, and I just had to come and see you!" she exclaimed. Her gaze was focused solely on Gabe as she marched into the office, a big picnic basket on her arm.

"Hello, Julie," he greeted her, surprised by her unexpected appearance.

"I've brought you a surprise. Do you have a few minutes so we can talk?" she asked, looking up at him and smiling.

"Well, I—uh," he began.

She didn't bother to wait for his invitation, but walked right past him and on into his office. Elise looked up, watching Julie's brazen entrance with keen interest.

"Wait until you see what I've got for you," Julie said as she put the basket in the middle of his desk and turned toward him, giving him a look that spoke volumes.

Mentally, Trace groaned. He could just imagine what she had in mind, and he wanted no part of it. "We're putting out a special edition of the paper today, so we are very busy."

"Oh," she said with little interest. She was not about to be put off from her goal of being alone with Gabe for a while. "I promise not to stay any longer than you want me to."

Trace didn't even glance toward Elise and Andy. He just mentally squared his shoulders for the encounter to come and followed after her.

"She sure is something, isn't she?" Andy remarked, staring after her. He'd long thought Julie was one beautiful woman, but she'd never given him a second look.

"I think that describes her very accurately," Elise agreed, making sure to keep her tone sweet.

Sweet was not what Elise was feeling, though. Especially not when Julie closed Trace's office door behind them. It was all Elise could do not to throw the offending portal wide and go in after her. She wanted to drag the other woman out of there by her hair.

Control yourself, Elise dictated to herself, and she managed not to act on her impulse. It wasn't easy.

"Let's get to work," she finally said, turning her attention to the matter at hand. Try as she might, though, she could not ignore the fact that Julie was alone with Trace.

"We missed you at dinner the other night," Julie purred as she stood with her back to the closed door. She finally had Gabe West right where she wanted him—alone!

"I'm sorry I had to miss it, but it was important that I get to Canyon Creek as quickly as I could," Trace said.

"Did you find out anything new about the Harris gang that will help you?"

"I wish I had. I was hoping to get a good lead from the sheriff there, but he'd lost their trail in a bad storm two days after the robbery and ended up calling off his posse."

"Pity," she said dismissively. She was actually glad that the lawman had failed. If they had know where the gang had gone, Gabe would probably have tried to go after them, and she didn't want him out running around, tracking down outlaws. She wanted him safe and sound right there in Durango with her.

"So what brings you here to the office?"

"I wanted to see you—and to bring you this picnic lunch, since we didn't get to have dinner." She opened the basket as she was talking and began to take out the food, arranging it on his desk. "I remembered how much you seemed to enjoy the pie at the social, so I made one just for you."

Julie didn't tell him that her mother had actually been the one who'd baked it for him.

What mattered was that she'd brought it to him. After they married would be soon enough for him to discover that she didn't know how to cook and had no desire to learn.

"I appreciate the thought, Julie. It's very sweet of you, but I really don't have time to do this today," Trace told her, knowing he had to be firm with her.

She looked up at him, almost shocked. "You're that busy?"

"Yes, we are. In fact, Elise and Andy are working on the final draft of our special edition. We have to start the press just as soon as they're done."

Her expression altered to a pout as she moved toward him. Pouting always worked with her father, and she believed it would work on Gabe, too. "You're going to have to stop and eat sometime, you know."

Trace had always suspected that Julie could be persistent, but he hadn't realized just how persistent until she closed in on him. He realized she was much like a predator, and he was the quarry she was after.

"You know, Gabe, if you don't have time for lunch right now, that's all right. There was something else I wanted to ask you." She stopped before him, gazing up at him with an undisguised look of hunger in her eyes—and what she was hungry for wasn't the food in the picnic basket.

"What's that?" he asked cautiously, not wanting to encourage her. If he was going to be locked in his office all alone with a woman, it was Elise he wanted to be with, not Julie.

"Well," she said softly, moving even closer

and running one finger along the front of his suit coat. "Weston's Wild Texas Stampede is coming to town next week, and I was wondering if you'd like to go with me. I've never been to a Wild West show before, but I think it would be fun."

Julie ever so slowly ran her hands up the front of his chest until she had linked her arms behind his neck. She gazed up at him, knowing exactly what she wanted from him.

Trace stiffened at her ploy. "Julie, this isn't—"

"Shhhh," she whispered as she stood on tiptoe to press her lips to his.

The contact startled Trace. He immediately took her by the forearms and put her physically away from him.

"Julie, I appreciate your kindness in inviting me. I am very flattered that you thought of me, but I won't be able to make it. We're very busy here at the *Star*, and I can't just take off whenever an opportunity comes along."

"Why not? You're the boss," she asked, her logic simple and direct.

"That's precisely why not. I have to be here to make sure everything is running smoothly. I'm sure there are a lot of young men in town who would be delighted to escort you to the Wild West show, but I am not going to be able to make it."

Julie took his refusal with good grace. "It would have been fun, but maybe we can go another time. By the way, what is this special edition about that you're working so hard on? Did something exciting happen that I haven't heard about yet?"

"As a matter of fact, it did. We just got word that British royalty will be coming to town. A Lord and Lady Winston will be arriving in the next few weeks."

"How exciting! Perhaps we can attend one of the social functions for them. With luck, you'll be all caught up with your work by then."

"We'll see how things work out. I don't know the details of their visit yet. We only know that they are planning to come through town. Now, Julie, you'd better be going. It really isn't proper for us to be in here unchaperoned this way with the door closed."

She smiled archly at him as she ran the tip of her tongue over her lower lip. "I was hoping you wouldn't prove to be such a gentleman."

"I respect you too much not to be," he said gallantly.

Her heart fluttered at his words.

"I'll leave all the food for you. Come see me when you get time," she said sweetly as she picked up the basket.

"Good-bye, Julie," Trace said, relieved that he'd managed to get rid of her without a scene.

Julie practically floated out of his office. She didn't bother to speak to Elise or Andy as she passed them. She was smiling too widely. She adored Gabe West and was too caught up in her fantasies about him to even think of acknowledging the others. She had kissed Gabe! Her day was almost perfect!

Elise watched the other woman go, but said nothing. At that particular moment, seeing the ecstatic expression on her face, Elise was not wishing Julie any good things in her life.

318

"She didn't stay very long," Andy remarked.

"She would have liked to, but we've got too much work to do," Trace said, coming to stand by their desks. Then, changing the topic, he asked, "How's the story coming?"

"We're almost done," Elise told him. "I'll bring it in for you to proofread just as soon as we finish the final draft."

He nodded and went back into his office. The scent of Julie's perfume lingered, reminding him that she'd been there, adding to his irritation with his whole situation. He cleared her food off his desk and sat back down.

It was only a few minutes later when Elise and Andy appeared in his doorway.

"We've got the story ready for you," Elise told him.

"Good, come on in and sit down," he said, gesturing to the two chairs before his desk. "And if you want any of the food that Julie left, help yourselves."

They both declined to eat any of it. They were too excited about seeing his reaction to their article to worry about food. They sat before his desk watching his expression as he went over their story.

BRITISH ROYALTY COMING TO DURANGO

Lord and Lady Winston of London, England, will be arriving in town next week. They will be passing through as part of a cross-country tour that has included stops in New York, Philadelphia, St. Louis, Denver, and now Durango.

The Winston family made their fortune

in the diamond trade. Their jewels are legendary and second only to the Queen's.

Current plans call for them to stay in town for at least two nights. We will keep you updated as we learn more about their itinerary.

"It's fine," Trace told them. "Let's go with it."

"Good. Now all we have to do is brief the 'Winstons'," Elise said with a slight smile.

"I wonder how the public is going to feel when they discover that we made this all up?" Andy said thoughtfully.

"When they realize we used the paper to help set a trap for the Harris gang, I believe they'll be glad," Elise said, feeling certain that the ends justified the means. "It'll be worth it, you'll see."

He nodded, wanting to believe her. Certainly, Elise's plan to catch Preacher Farnsworth had worked, and her exposé on the saloon girls had seemed to help them. He knew for a fact that Mrs. Martin's church group had established a fund to help the working girls, should they decide to leave their chosen profession. If this false story about the Winston jewels did draw the Harris gang in so Trace and Marshal Trent could catch them, he supposed it would definitely be worth the risk.

"What are we going to tell the other papers in town? They'll want to print articles about the visit, too."

"We'll tell them everything we know—which, right now, is just what's in this article. We'll worry about the last-minute details early next week, when we figure out exactly how we want to set everything up," Trace told him. "If anyone pressures you for more details, direct them to me or Elise. Now, let's get these run off. The sooner we get the word out, the better chance we have of making contact with Harris."

Andy took the handwritten copy and hurried out to start typesetting the edition, leaving Elise and Trace alone in the office.

"Do you really think this will work?" she asked, lifting her gaze to his.

"It has to. We've got to stop them some way," he said fiercely. Then, realizing that they were actually by themselves, he gave her a half smile and moved close enough to her to touch her cheek in a gentle caress. "I'm sorry about Julie."

"There was nothing you could do about it." Elise trembled at that simple touch of his hand, but she tried to sound as if Julie's visit with him hadn't bothered her.

"She wanted me to escort her to a Wild West show that's coming to town next week. I told her no." He took a step even nearer, wanting to take Elise in his arms yet struggling to fight down the urge, for he knew they could be interrupted at any time.

"I'm glad," she said in a low voice.

"So am I." He grinned at her. "There's only one woman I want to be alone with in my office with the door shut. You don't suppose we could—?"

He glanced suggestively toward the outer office and Andy.

"I'm sure Andy would think something was wrong," she whispered back.

Trace looked up again, and right then he couldn't see Andy anywhere. In a daring move, he backed Elise one more step farther out of sight of the outer office and swept her up in a heated embrace. His mouth covered hers in a passionate, dominating kiss that lasted only a few seconds but left them both breathless in its wake. They stared at each other, amazed by the power of their need.

"I liked being in Canyon Creek better," she said regretfully.

"You're not the only one," he growled, aching to hold her close again.

Elise was tempted to throw caution to the wind and go back into his arms, but instead she started from the office. "I'd better go help Andy. The sooner we get done, the sooner . . ." She gave him a hopeful look.

Trace followed her to help. He wanted to speed things up, too.

They went to press within the hour and had copies on the street by late that afternoon.

Chapter Twenty-two

It was a long two days' ride for Will, but he finally reached Durango late in the afternoon. Things had gone smoothly for him in Eagle Pass. No one had questioned his need to take a week off. When asked where he was going, he'd deliberately been evasive, and he'd been glad when no one had pursued the question. He wanted to slip into Durango unnoticed, take care of his unfinished business, and head back home.

Will knew there was no better place to find out what was going on in a town than the saloons, so he stopped at the first one he saw. After two drinks, he grew frustrated, though, for no one there had heard of Gabriel West. He left that establishment and rode farther, stopping finally at another saloon called the High Time.

"Whiskey," Will told the bartender as he strode up to the bar.

"You're new in town, ain't you?" the bartender asked, making conversation as he poured the drink.

"Just passing through," he answered easily. "Kind of a quiet town you got here."

"Yep, and we like it that way. Biggest excitement we got going right now is that Weston's Wild Texas Stampede is in town and next week some royalty is going to pay us a visit."

"Royalty?"

"Yeah, the *Star* newspaper reported it first that some English lord and lady will be coming through. I don't care one way or the other, but some of the folks are getting all excited about it."

"You ever head of a man name of West? Gabriel West?"

"Yeah, he's the new editor of that newspaper, the *Star*. Why? Do you know him?"

"A friend of mine told me to look him up while I was here."

"Well, the office is just a couple of streets over. You can probably find him around there, if you've a mind."

"Thanks."

Will downed his whiskey and signaled for another. He took his time with the second drink. The later it was, the better. He didn't want any witnesses when he went after Trace.

When he finally strode from the saloon, Will's mood was determined. He mounted up and rode toward the newspaper office, wanting to check out the area and see just how busy it was.

Elise

The streets of Durango were quiet this night, and Will was glad. He located the *Star*'s office without too much trouble and rode slowly past it. There were lights on, and he could see several people moving around inside.

Will's smile was savage. With any luck, one of them would be Trace Jackson. He kept on riding, disappearing around a corner, where he reined in and dismounted. He moved quietly down the alley that ran behind the office, wanting to assess all the avenues of escape. Once he was satisfied that he would be able to get away without incident, he led his horse to an area near the back of the office and tied it up there. Then he strolled back to the front of the building. He stayed out of sight, but managed to look in the window. Inside he saw a young man, a very pretty young woman, and another bespectacled man wearing a suit and bow tie. Where the hell was Trace?

Will frowned, then for some reason glanced back at the man wearing glasses. In that instant, he realized it was Trace in disguise. Obviously when he'd taken the name Gabriel West, he'd also taken on a new way of dressing.

Will smiled again. He was ready now. Ideally, he would like to follow Trace home and confront him away from other people, but he was going to do whatever was necessary. He'd waited too long for this moment. He was going to show Matt Harris that he was capable of taking care of things for him and that he was worth every penny the man paid him.

Will stayed in the dark cover of the shadows, watching and waiting.

* * *

Elise sighed happily as she looked up at Andy and Trace. "I think we've got all the arrangements made for my grandmother and George."

"And they're really willing to do this?" Trace asked again.

"Oh, yes. They're very excited about helping us out."

Trace nodded. "Then all we have to do is to meet with Marshal Trent and set up the best way to work with him and his deputies to guard their 'precious jewels' while they're staying at the hotel. It's too late to go find him tonight, but I'll plan on meeting with the marshal first thing in the morning."

"I'll go with you," Elise offered. "I want to know everything that's going on."

"Let's meet here in the morning at 7:30, and we'll head over to see him."

"Fine."

"Are you ready to call it a night?" Andy asked Elise.

"If you are."

"I'll walk you home. You're planning on staying here until this is over?" Andy asked Trace.

They had discussed the danger of him living alone that far out of town, and Trace had decided to start sleeping at the office.

"I'll be bedding down here tonight, so you'll know where I am if you need me."

"We'll see you tomorrow."

Trace and Elise exchanged a look of longing that was immediately masked when Andy looked their way.

"Good night," she said in a soft voice, wishing Trace were the one to walk her home and not Andy.

They left the office and started toward her home. Trace watched them from the door until they were out of sight and then pulled the shades down to give himself some privacy.

Elise was surprised to find that George's horse was tied up out front as they reached the house.

"Would you like to come in for a while? It looks as if George is here for a late visit."

"No, thanks. I'm calling it a night. I'll see you tomorrow."

Andy watched until she was starting in the front door, then moved off down the street.

Elise was weary as she entered the house, but her weariness changed to complete and utter surprise when she walked in on her grandmother and George sitting in the parlor, locked in a passionate kiss.

"Elise!" Claire said her name quickly, nervously, as she hurriedly tore herself from George's embrace.

"Grandmother?" Elise said in disbelief as she moved farther into the room. Her grandmother was quite a stickler about appearances, and yet, right now, her hair was in disarray and she was blushing.

"I didn't expect you back quite so soon," Claire blurted out, embarrassed.

Elise almost said "obviously," but she held her tongue. She only smiled and stared at the two of them.

Claire was feeling more guilty than a young

girl caught with her first beau. She couldn't believe that she felt so young and carefree. "Elise, there's something George and I have to tell you!" she finally said, speaking nervously as she went to her.

George got to his feet and went to stand at Claire's side. "Yes, there certainly is," he confirmed.

She looked expectantly at the two of them, scarcely able to imagine what it was they wanted to tell her.

"Sweetheart," Claire began, casting a loving look at George before continuing, "I am thrilled to tell you that George has proposed, and I've accepted. We're going to be married right away—in fact, tomorrow, if we can arrange it."

"Married?" Elise repeated, in shock. Not that she shouldn't have expected it. They had been seeing each other for years now. It had just never occurred to her that they were anything but happy with the way things were between them.

"That's right," George said with pride, slipping an arm around Claire's waist. "I love your grandmother, and this trip that we're going to be taking together made me realize just how much. If we're going to be pretending to be married, I thought for the sake of her reputation that I should do the honorable thing, and make sure that we weren't just pretending."

He smiled down at Claire, and her blush deepened.

"What are you planning?"

"We're going to speak with Reverend Ford tomorrow and see if he'll marry us."

"You are happy for us, aren't you?" Claire

asked, worriedly.

At last, Elise broke into a wide smile. "Of course I'm happy for you. This is wonderful news! I'm just surprised, that's all. I guess it never occurred to me that you two might really get married, but I am thrilled that you are."

She immediately hugged her grandmother and then embraced George.

"Thank you, sweetheart," Claire said, tears filling her eyes. "I am so ecstatic. I love George so much."

She looked up at him, all the love she felt for him shining in the depths of her gaze. Unable to help himself, George kissed her. It was a gentle kiss that spoke of devotion and love.

"You're making me a very happy man," he told her.

They shared a secret knowing look.

"Well, what do you say we go down to the office and tell Trace the good news?" Elise suggested. "I'm sure he's going to be interested in hearing about this."

"Let's go. I want to tell him," Claire insisted.

The three of them left the house excitedly. They could hardly wait to let Trace know of the upcoming nuptials.

Will had waited until the woman and the other man had disappeared from sight before he even thought about venturing into the newspaper office. He'd considered waiting until Trace came out, but as the minutes passed and he'd shown no sign of leaving, Will knew he had to take action. He didn't want anyone to see him standing there in the shadows and grow suspicious of him.

As ready as he would ever be, Will headed toward the office. He tried the door and found it unlocked. He was pleased at the discovery, for it meant he would have the element of surprise on his side. He stepped inside and shut the door silently behind him. He wanted to catch Trace unawares.

Walking softly, Will rested his hand on his gun as he approached the door to the back office.

"Hello?" he called out, not wanting to seem too sly by his entrance.

"Who is it?" Trace settled back in at his desk. He'd just set his glasses aside and had opened the bottom desk drawer to get himself a drink when he heard the man's voice. He'd planned to use the whiskey to help him forget about Elise being so close, yet so far away, but now it looked as if he wasn't going to be getting a drink at all. He looked up as Will appeared in his doorway.

"Hi, Trace," Will said in a slow, easy voice as he came face-to-face with him for the first time.

"Will?" Trace was surprised to see his old deputy. "Well, I'll be damned. What brings you to Durango?" He smiled widely in welcome.

"I got your telegram and wanted to come and see how you were doing."

"I'm glad you did. How are things in Eagle Pass?"

"Everything's going fine. How are you doing?" he asked. He noticed that Trace wasn't wearing a gun, and he was pleased by that discovery. The other man hadn't been expecting trouble tonight.

"Things are better. I own the *Star* newspaper now, so I don't have to be as worried about confronting outlaws as I used to be." He was surprised by Will's unexpected visit, though, and wondered at the true motivation for it.

"I'm just glad I found you again. I'd been wondering where you'd disappeared to after our last meeting."

"I've been working here, keeping quiet about things."

"So I noticed," he said, irritated that it had taken him this long to find him and correct things.

"What have you been up to?" Trace asked.

"Just working, like you."

"Did you come to town for business or pleasure?"

"It's going to be a pleasure trip for me, I assure you."

"Oh?"

"That's right. I'm going to be very pleased when I'm staring down at your dead body." He drew his gun, fed up with Trace and wanting him out of the way. "Get up real slow, and let's get out of here."

"You low-life son of a bitch," Trace said in a low, threatening voice, but remained where he was. "Why the hell were you talking to that saloon girl about me?"

"I was drunk, and I was angry because you weren't dead. I'm going to correct Harris's mistake tonight, though."

"So you were in on the ambush—" The revelation was a painful one for Trace. He had trusted Will. He had considered him a friend.

"And the robbery," Will told him as he gave him a smug smile. "A man's got to do what a man's got to do."

"You're not a man! You're Harris's puppet!" he shot back at Will, his thorough disgust obvious in his tone.

"I'm my own man," Will told Trace. "And don't you go worrying none about Harris. He doesn't even know I'm here tonight. I'm doing this on my own—cleaning up his mess."

"So, I'm Harris's 'mess', am I?"

"Yep, so let's go." Will took a step back and gestured toward the door again with his gun.

Trace's mind was racing. He had never been so glad that he'd been practicing his left-handed draw as he was right then. Will thought he was right-handed, and Will knew he wasn't armed right then. What Will didn't know was that he had Ben's gun in the drawer on his left side, safely tucked away with the bottle of whiskey.

"Just where is it that we're going?" Trace asked.

Will smiled thinly. "Quit talking and start moving," he ordered, his gaze narrowing on Trace.

Trace knew he was staring death in the face. If he walked out of that office, he didn't stand a chance. He had to make his move right then, but as closely as Will was watching him, he didn't know if he would make it or not.

It was in that instant that main office door was thrown open and Elise came in with her grandmother and George.

"Trace? Oh, do you have—"

She stopped the instant she saw the gun.

Will was startled by the interruption, and he glanced their way.

It was in that moment, as Will was distracted, that Trace knew he had to make his move. He had no choice. Elise and the others might be hurt if he didn't stop Will now. He grabbed Ben's gun out of the drawer and fired.

Will was just turning back toward Trace when the bullet took him full in the chest. He got off one shot, but it went wild as he staggered and fell. He was staring at the deadly gun held in Trace's left hand as he collapsed. The look on his face was one of complete shock and disbelief.

"Trace!" Elise cried out in terror. She ran to him, fearing that he'd been hurt.

Trace swept her into his embrace and clasped her to him. "You're all right?"

"I'm fine," she said, trembling as she clung to him. "What about you?"

"He missed," Trace said tersely. He looked up to where the older man had his arm around Claire, helping to support her. She looked pale and was obviously shaken by the incident. "George?"

"We're fine, just scared—that's all," George answered, glancing toward the dead man.

Certain that no one had been hurt, Trace put Elise from him and went to check on Will. He was kneeling down and staring grimly at the lifeless form of the man he'd once believed to be his friend when Jared Trent came charging through the door, his own gun in hand.

"What's going on? I heard shots." He stopped immediately at the sight of Trace and the dead man. He slowly holstered his sidearm as he went to kneel beside Trace. "Who was he?"

"His name was Will Campbell," Trace said slowly. "He was one of my deputies in Eagle Pass. He took over my job when they thought I was dead."

Elise gasped, shocked by the news. "But why was he trying to kill you?"

Trace and Jared slowly got to their feet.

"Evidently he'd been working for Harris, and they still wanted me dead. He said he was here to 'clean up Harris's mess'."

"Oh, God." She looked stricken and went into his arms again.

George and Claire shared a knowing look as they watched Elise with Trace. They had not realized how much Elise had come to care for him, and they hid their smiles at the thought.

Marshal Trent looked up at Trace, his expression black. "That explains your posse getting ambushed that way."

Trace nodded tightly.

"Exactly what happened tonight?" Jared asked.

Trace quickly explained all that had taken place. "When Elise came through the door, I had my chance, so I took it."

"Thank heaven we got here when we did," she said softly.

The lawman took Will's gun and went through his pockets. He found his sheriff's badge and muttered something unintelligible under his breath.

Trace pulled out of Elise's embrace and he went to see what Trent had found.

"It's his kind that give lawmen a bad name in some towns," Jared said as he stood up again and showed him the badge. "I'll go tell the undertaker that he's here and have him come for him."

"How do you want to handle notifying Eagle Pass?"

"I'll take care of it," the lawman said. "How much time do you need to set up the gang?"

"Another week."

"You've got it. For now, as far as anyone knows, he was a drifter who broke in and tried to rob you. Report it that way in the paper. Word will get out, so you'll have to write something."

They all nodded in agreement.

Jared left to notify Jehosaphat Jones, the undertaker. Trace and the others waited in the outer office. A short time later, Mr. Jones arrived and removed the body. Elise and Claire looked the other way as he was carried from the office. Only when the undertaker had driven off with the body in his wagon did they all breathe a sigh of relief.

"There was a reason we were coming to see you tonight," George said, wanting to brighten their mood.

"Why did you come back?" He looked from Elise to George and Claire. "Is something wrong?"

"Actually," George began, "something's very right."

Trace waited expectantly, needing some good news after what had just happened.

"Claire and I are going to be married."

The tension of the moment vanished at his declaration.

Trace smiled widely. "Congratulations!"

"Well, I couldn't very well travel with her as my 'lady', if I wasn't her 'lord'!" George said, laughing heartily.

"He's protecting my honor as a true gentleman should," Claire told Trace with delight.

"They're going to speak with the reverend in the morning and see if he can marry them tomorrow afternoon," Elise explained.

"If he can," George continued, "we'll take a trip to Denver as our honeymoon, but when we return late next week, we'll come back as Lord and Lady Winston."

"Your plan sounds great."

"It's a shame that it took the Harris gang to make me realize how much I wanted to marry Claire, but it doesn't matter now that she's said yes. The good news is we are finally getting married. She is going to be my bride."

"And you're going to live happily ever after," Elise supplied dreamily.

"Yes, we are," Claire assured her. Then she added, teasingly, "Of course, on such short notice, our wedding won't be as exciting as yours and 'Ben's' was." She gave Trace a knowing look.

"I don't think many weddings are as exciting as that one," Elise remarked.

"But, you know, as 'Ben', I had a lot less notice than George does," Trace told them with a smile. "He's got a whole day to prepare. I only had about twenty minutes."

They all laughed at the memory.

"Well, we'd better be going. It's getting late, and we've got a lot to get ready for tomorrow."

George started toward the door, ushering Claire before him.

"Elise? Are you coming with us?" Claire asked as she started from the office.

"I'll be along in a little while," she said, unwilling to leave Trace just yet.

"You'll see her home?" George asked Trace.

"That I will."

Claire and George nodded. "We'll see you later."

They closed the door behind them and headed back to the house, thrilled that they were going to have a few moments more alone.

"Did you see Elise with Trace?" Claire asked.

"I had no idea she cared for him. The way she's always acted around him, I thought she only considered him her boss."

"That's what I believed, too, until tonight. Maybe there's going to be another wedding in the not-too-distant future." Her eyes were sparkling at the thought. Even when she'd thought of him as Gabe, she'd suspected that he was special, and now she knew she'd been right.

"Once this trouble with the Harris gang is over, I think we just might see that happen."

Claire took his arm and they continued on into the night, eager for their few stolen moments before Elise returned.

After Claire and George had gone, Elise couldn't restrain herself any longer. She went to Trace and put her arms around him, holding him tightly. She almost sighed out loud when he hugged her back just as fiercely.

"I was so afraid he was going to shoot you!" she said, her head resting against his chest so she could hear the powerful pounding of his heart.

"He would have done it, too, if you hadn't come in when you did," Trace told her. "I'm very thankful for George's timely proposal."

He grinned down at her.

Elise looked up at him and smiled gently. This was the man she loved. She had no doubt in the world. He meant everything to her. "I love you, Trace Jackson."

"I love you, too, Elise. And as soon as this is over, we're going to be paying the Reverend Ford a visit, too."

"Will I be marrying Ben, Gabe or Trace?" she asked in a throaty voice.

"Take your pick," he answered, willing to be anyone to please her. Will's threat to her had only convinced him all the more of the depth of his love for her.

"You," she sighed. "Only you."

And then Trace kissed her.

Chapter Twenty-three

Reverend Ford performed the ceremony the following afternoon. It was very private, with only a few of Claire's and George's closest friends in attendance. Several people expressed their surprise at the sudden nuptials, but all were delighted at their marriage, seeing how happy Claire and George were as they exchanged their vows.

"I now pronounce you man and wife," Reverend Ford said. "George, you may kiss your bride."

Claire looked up at George, all the love she felt for him shining in her eyes. She blushed prettily as he bent and kissed her with tender devotion.

"I am so happy for you!" Elise said as she hurried forward to hug them both.

Trace followed Elise to speak with them. He shook hands with George and kissed Claire's cheek. "Congratulations, George. You not only got yourself a beautiful bride, you married the best cook in Durango."

Everyone laughed.

"She's not going to have to cook for a while, though. I'm taking her on a long honeymoon. We're heading out on the eastbound train first thing in the morning."

"How romantic!" Mildred Andrews, one of Claire's dearest friends, sighed as she came up to congratulate them. "I can't believe you two have finally gone and done it—and after all this time!"

Claire smiled sweetly at her and then looked up at George adoringly. "Sometimes, you just know when the time is right."

They left the church a short time later after visiting with everyone and accepting their well-wishes. They would be spending their wedding night at George's home and leaving from there for the train depot in the morning.

Trace and Elise watched them ride off in George's carriage.

"I'll need to change clothes before we head back to the office," Elise told Trace after the others who had attended the wedding had departed.

"I've got a better idea," he said, his gaze warm upon her. "Let's forget about the *Star*. Let's take the night off and go out to dinner."

"I'd love to," she accepted eagerly and took his offered arm.

They made their way to one of the better restaurants in town that was located not far from the office. They were both looking forward to the evening to come. They would be alone, completely unchaperoned for the first time since they'd returned from Canyon Creek. Food was not the main thing on their minds as they entered the restaurant.

Trace immediately realized that he'd made a terrible mistake when he heard someone call out his name. He looked up to see Julie Stevens waving to him from where she was already seated at a table with her parents.

"Gabe! It's so good to see you! Come join us!" she invited.

Trace felt Elise's grip tighten on his arm, but knew he had to go and exchange pleasantries with them. He led the way to their table.

Lyle Stevens immediately stood up and offered his chair to Elise as they drew near. "Miss Martin, please, you and Gabe be our guests for dinner."

"We wouldn't want to intrude," she insisted.

"Nonsense. Gabe was supposed to have dined with us a few weeks ago, but things didn't work out. We'd be thrilled to have your company tonight." The banker wouldn't take no for an answer.

They were trapped, and they knew it.

"You are very kind, Mr. Stevens," Elise answered gracefully as she begrudgingly let go of Trace's arm and took the offered seat.

"Lyle, please." Lyle pulled up an extra chair for Trace and positioned it next to Julie, then got another one for himself.

"This is an unexpected pleasure," Adele Stevens spoke up, smiling warmly at Gabe. She thought he would make a very good match for Julie, and she was glad to have the opportunity to visit with him some more, so she could get to know him better. She was glad now, too, that her daughter had worn her nicest gown this evening. It was deep blue in color, and though it was high-necked and long-sleeved, it showed off her figure to advantage and brought out the highlights in her hair.

"For us, too," Trace replied politely, glancing at Julie as he spoke.

She was gazing at him, focusing only on him and him alone. "I'm sorry you couldn't keep our date before," she said with a note of hurt in her voice. "I was really looking forward to it."

"I apologize again, but if you read the next edition of the *Star*, you'll know exactly where I was the night I had to miss dinner. I was working on a story at the High Time with Elise," he told her.

"Yes," Adele said, a touch of disapproval in her voice, "that was a very interesting exposé on the lives of the soiled doves. Whatever possessed you to do that, Elise?"

"I was in one of the mercantiles when one of the girls from the High Time came in. The shopkeeper wouldn't wait on her. In fact, he was downright cruel to her. I thought it was important to make everyone realize that the women who are forced into a life like that are real people with real problems."

"And you enjoyed working at that saloon?" Julie asked with disdain, thinking that Elise must be something of a tramp to have done what she did.

"I enjoyed telling people the truth about the girls' lives. That's what good journalism is all about. I wanted to tell everyone what is really going on in the world. I want to help right wrongs. I want to improve things for everyone."

"Very noble goals, my dear, but I hardly think the erring sisters from the saloon are a worthy topic for polite dinner conversation," Lyle said critically.

"Well, we hope a few of the 'erring sisters' will be encouraged by Elise's work and find the strength to leave that profession behind and begin life anew," Trace defended her.

Julie didn't like his championing the other woman. She leaned toward him and, without anyone seeing, rested her hand on his knee. The tablecloth draped long and low, so she knew her brazenness wouldn't be detected by anyone but Gabe. When she felt him tense at her touch, she fought back a smile. It was good to know that she could affect him in that way.

"Well, I'm just glad that you came in tonight while we were here," Julie told him, looking up at him innocently, when all she wanted to do was climb onto his lap and kiss him.

"We just left quite a joyous event and were coming here to celebrate," he explained.

"Oh? What happened?" Adele looked from Gabe to Elise. "Tell us and we'll celebrate with you."

"My grandmother and George Lansing were married this afternoon," Elise answered.

"My dear, that's wonderful!" Adele remarked, but immediately wondered why they'd married so oddly and without all the usual fanfare.

"But it was so sudden, wasn't it?" Julie asked, puzzled too.

"They'd been seeing each other for a long time and just decided that this was the right time to marry."

"We're very happy for them," Lyle said, although truth be told, he really didn't care one way or the other. "Now, what's the latest news on the royalty that's coming for a visit?"

"We haven't heard a lot more. They're due to arrive in town the middle of next week."

"Are they truly as wealthy as you reported?"

"Wealthier, I do believe," Elise answered, enhancing their story even more.

"It will be interesting to meet them. Do you suppose they'll be staying long?" Julie asked. She tightened her hand on Trace's knee.

"They haven't said. I know they'll be here at least two nights, but other than that I don't know anything," Trace answered. He tried to ignore her caress and focus on the conversation. He was greatly relieved when the waiter came to take their orders.

"You say it's just the lord and lady who are coming? They don't have any children, do they?" Adele asked, thinking that as much as she liked Gabe, she certainly wouldn't mind Julie marrying into royalty if she got the chance.

"If they do, I haven't read anything about them," Elise answered.

"Well, we'll just have to be happy knowing that we've got an honest-to-gosh lord and lady in our midst," Lyle declared.

Elise was miserable, although no one could tell because she kept up a good front, smiling and making small talk with Adele and Lyle. She had come into the restaurant eagerly anticipating a quiet dinner with Trace and then having some time alone with him. She had been aching to kiss him and had been hoping that they might get their food quickly so they could leave all that much sooner. But now, all her plans had been upset by Julie and her parents.

From beneath lowered lashes, Elise watched as Julie monopolized Trace. Jealousy ate at her and she wished they were anywhere but there. If she could have, she would have pleaded a headache and asked Trace to take her home, but she knew she couldn't. She would just have to suffer in silence. The only reassuring thing that kept her from being too upset was the occasional glance that Trace cast her way, letting her know by a single look that he was feeling exactly the same way she was.

Julie was unaware of the unspoken communication between Gabe and Elise. She thought she had his undivided attention. She moved her hand a bit higher, but immediately regretted it when Gabe reached down to take her hand in his. He gave her hand a gentle squeeze and put it back in her own lap. She couldn't decide whether that was a good move or a rejection. After a moment's reflection, she decided to take it as a good move. Obviously, she'd been exciting him with her touch, and he'd been hard put to control his desire for her. The thought thrilled her, and she couldn't wait for the chance to be with him again at a social event so she could dance with him again. She loved being in his arms, being close to him.

The next hour passed agonizingly slow for Trace and Elise. When at last the meal was over, Trace made their excuses.

"Elise and I had better be going now. We've got a newspaper to get out first thing in the morning. Thank you so much for your hospitality," Trace said to Lyle. He smiled at Adele, and nodded to Julie as he rose.

Elise could hardly believe she and Trace could finally leave. The previous hour had felt like one of the longest in her lifetime. "Yes, thank you so much for dinner."

"It's our pleasure," Lyle told them as he stood to shake Gabe's hand. "I'd like to see more of you. Don't make yourself so scarce, son."

Trace grimaced inwardly at his familiarity. "I appreciate your kindness."

With that, he led Elise from the restaurant. He was aware that every moment Julie's gaze was upon them. They escaped outside into the night's welcoming darkness. Trace didn't speak until they were a good distance down the street from the restaurant.

"I'm sorry," Trace said, and he meant it. "If I'd known they were going to be there, I would never have gone in. I wanted to be alone with you tonight."

Elise cast him a sidelong glance as they walked down the dark street. When they passed a deserted alley, she grabbed his hand and pulled him into the darkness.

"We're alone now, Trace," she whispered as she drew him down for a flaming kiss.

Trace gave a low groan as he deepened the exchange, tasting her sweetness. "I've wanted to do that all day."

"So have I," she said in a low, sensuous voice.

They stood there, wrapped in each other's arms for a moment longer, then finally tore themselves apart. They knew they were in the middle of town and that someone could come upon them at any time, despite the lateness of the hour. They started for her home at a quickened pace, knowing what pleasure awaited them there.

They couldn't cover the blocks fast enough as far as they were both concerned. When at last they reached the front porch, Trace took the key from Elise's trembling hand and unlocked the door for her. Inside, the house was warm and dark and welcoming, and they didn't bother to light any lights.

"If you want me to go, say so now," Trace told her, trying to control his raging need for her.

Elise came to stand before him. She lifted one hand to caress his cheek.

"I don't ever want you to leave me," she said softly, and then rose onto her tiptoes to press her lips to his in precious, unspoken invitation.

He broke off the kiss only long enough to lock the door behind them; then he swept her up in his arms.

"My room is upstairs," she told him, looping her arms around his neck.

He took the steps two at a time and kicked her bedroom door open wide so he could carry her in. He laid her on the bed and followed her down.

"I need you, Trace," Elise whispered.

Glorying in his nearness, she surrendered to his passion. They hurried to strip away the clothes that kept them apart and came together in a blaze of desire. Each needed what only the other could give.

347

Theirs was a rapturous mating, a joining of body and soul. They shared pure ecstasy as they sought to please each other. With each kiss and caress, they showed the depth of their devotion until, in that perfect moment, they reached the peak of love's delight together. Clinging to each other, they soared to the heights, treasuring the bliss that was theirs, knowing that what they shared was special.

They loved through the night, savoring this time alone. It was just hours before dawn when Trace left Elise's bed and began to dress.

"Do you have to go?" she asked regretfully, already missing having him by her side.

"You know I have to," he said, pausing to go to her and kiss her one last time.

"I wish you could stay with me forever," she said in a passion-husky voice.

He groaned inwardly at her invitation. There was nothing he wanted more than to make her his own in all ways. And he would, just as soon as he'd dealt with Harris. The incident with Campbell the day before had only emphasized to him that he needed to settle his past before he could plan his future.

And Elise was his future.

He kissed her gently one last time and quietly left the house, making sure his passage went unnoticed. He did not want to put her reputation at risk.

Trace returned to the office and tried to get some sleep on the makeshift bed he'd set up there. Thoughts of Will's betrayal and of Harris left him restless and tense, though. He was glad when the sun finally came up and he could start another workday. The sooner this next week passed, the sooner his confrontation with Harris would come. He was ready—more than ready—for this to be over. He was looking forward to it. It was payback time.

The following days passed in a blur of activity for Trace and Elise, and the nights passed in a haze of heated passion.

As the day of Claire's and George's return neared, Trace grew more and more tense and watchful. Elise noticed the change in him.

"Everything is going to work out, you'll see," she encouraged him as he sat at his office desk going over the plans yet another time.

"I hope so. We've gone over every detail often enough. Between you posing as a maid in the hotel and Trent's deputies stationed nearby, we're going to be watching the entire building. There's no way the gang could get in or out without one of you seeing them."

"So you need to relax and quit worrying. Grandmother and George are going to show up looking quite unlike themselves, and I know they'll have come up with a perfect case for the family jewels," she told him smiling. "All we have to do is sit and wait."

"That's what I don't like. I like being in control. I don't like surprises."

"This time the surprise is going to be on Harris and his men. Our plan won't fail. It's too perfect!"

Trace knew she was trying to make him feel more confident, but he also knew that the moment you let yourself get too confident, mistakes happened. He didn't want anyone hurt. He just wanted Harris brought to justice.

"You spoke with Fernada about keeping an eye out for strangers in town, didn't you?"

"Yes, and I even gave her an extra copy of the Harris gang's wanted poster, so she could show the other girls and tell them who to look for."

"Good." His mood was grim, but he was satisfied that they had done everything possible to make this work. "Now, all that's left to do is pray."

Elise smiled at him. "I've already been doing that for days."

Chapter Twenty-four

"Well, what do ya think?" Terp Wilson asked Matt Harris as they sat in their hideout up in the mountains. "That lord and lady showing up is all the talk of Durango." He had just passed through Durango and had stopped at a saloon long enough to hear the news about the royalty and their family jewels coming to town.

"We ain't never paid a visit to Durango before. I think I'd like to stop in and see these royal folks, what about you?" Harris gave an evil chuckle.

"Sounds good to me. Those jewels they'll be bringing with them must be worth a lot of money."

"I know," Harris said, his smile cold and determined. "This could be fun."

"And we ain't had much fun lately," Terp said, smiling back.

"Who's the law there?"

"Jared Trent, last I heard. He's a pretty good lawman from what I understand."

"I guess we ought to find out just how good he really is," Harris said thoughtfully, already planning the robbery. "What do you think?" Harris looked at his two other men, Al Brown and Tom Edwards. Max and Jim had been killed during the escape from Canyon Creek, and he still missed them.

"Let's do it!" Al and Tom agreed quickly.

"All right, we ride for Durango first thing in the morning. We'll have to be careful when we get there. Al, Tom, one of you boys will have to go in and take a look around. We don't want to risk being seen before we make our move."

Al and Tom nodded in agreement. "Whatever you want us to do, we'll do."

"Good. Tomorrow, we're heading for Durango."

The train carrying Lord and Lady Winston to Durango was right on time.

Trace, Elise, and Andy were at the train station eagerly awaiting their arrival. They were there only as newspaper reporters. A good number of curious townsfolk had shown up hoping to get a glimpse of them, along with Mayor Brown, who planned to greet them with Marshal Trent.

Elise wasn't surprised by their presence, considering the amount of excitement the story had generated. She was just glad that she didn't know many of those who had turned out. She was concerned that George and her grandmother might be recognized and ruin everything before they even got started.

Elise soon discovered that all her worries were for naught. When Claire descended from the train, aided by George, Elise gasped in surprise along with the rest of the crowd. She barely recognized either one of them. George was wearing a very lifelike fake dark beard and mustache, and he had somehow managed to make himself look much heavier. It was almost as if he'd padded his stomach. The changes in her grandmother's appearance were equally amazing. She was wearing an auburn wig and had taken a hint from Trace and donned eyeglasses. Her disguise was perfect.

George moved into the crowd, escorting Claire on one arm and carrying an ornately carved chest, which everyone could see was securely locked, under the other. As planned, they wanted everyone to believe that it contained the Winston jewels.

George and Claire smiled politely and nodded to those gathered there.

"Welcome to Durango," Mayor Brown greeted them. "We are honored to have you here."

"Thank you," George answered in a reasonable copy of an English accent.

"If there's anything you need, just contact Jared Trent, here—he's our marshal—or get in touch with me," the mayor offered.

"It's nice to meet you both," George said, giving the lawman a bland smile. "We appreciate your generous offer."

They exchanged pleasantries a moment longer, and then spoke in passing with the others who had come to meet them.

"We appreciate your warm welcome," Claire said with dignity, her accent as convincing as

George's. "We'd heard that the Dorchester Hotel was one of your best—is that true?"

"Yes, ma'am," one of the men told her. "It's right on down Main Street a few blocks."

"Thank you so very much."

They moved gracefully off in the direction of the hotel, leaving the crowd excitedly staring after them.

Once they'd registered, they retired to their room.

"It worked!" Claire told George in a hushed yet thrilled voice when they were safely alone.

"I couldn't believe it! Did you see Elise's and Trace's expressions? They were quite impressed with us, my dear Lady Winston," George intoned in his best British accent.

"I'm quite impressed with us!" she insisted. "We actually did it! We had everyone convinced that we really were a lord and lady from England."

"Well, so far, so good. I'm sure Trace and Marshal Trent will be showing up soon to let us know what to expect next. According to the itinerary we've set, we're only staying in Durango for two nights, so whatever is going to happen is going to happen soon."

Claire paled at the thought of the possible danger they faced. "I'm so afraid something bad is going to happen."

George went to her and put his arms around her to comfort her. "Don't think that way. We're going to have Marshal Trent and his deputies close around us twenty-four hours a day. Not to mention the fact that Trace is here. We'll be protected. Everything is going to work out just fine."

"I hope you're right."

Silently, George hoped he was right, too.

The balance of the day passed quickly. George and Claire left the hotel to walk the streets of Durango, seeing the sights and enjoying the town. They returned to the hotel to find Trace and Elise waiting for them in the lobby.

"Lord Winston? Lady Winston?" Trace said as he approached them.

"Yes?"

"I'm Gabe West, and this is Elise Martin. We're with the *Durango Star* newspaper, and we wondered if you'd have time for us to interview you."

"Why, of course," George deigned to speak with them. "We'd be delighted. Would you care to come upstairs to our room?"

"We'll do whatever you'd like."

"Come, then. We can relax better there." George led the way up the staircase with Claire on his arm.

They made general small talk until they were safely in the room. As soon as they were certain no one else could hear them, Elise hugged her grandmother.

"You are so wonderful! Both of you!" She looked over at George as she held her grandmother close.

"You think so, do you? I make quite a lady, don't I?" Claire asked.

"I never had a doubt, but the wig and spectacles are a touch of genius! No one's even had an inkling about your true identities. It's amazing."

"We've been practicing our accents," George told them.

"And you've done a fine job."

"Let's just hope this all pays off," Trace said solemnly. "I've arranged everything with Marshal Trent. He's going to have deputies out front and in back of the hotel, along with one man in the lobby all night. Elise has volunteered to work as a maid, so she'll be 'on duty' in disguise until midnight. Is there anything else you need to know? Anything else I can do for you?"

"It sounds as if you've covered everything," George said thoughtfully. "I've got my sidearm in my suitcase. I'll keep it handy just in case all the precautions aren't enough."

"And what about your jewels?" Elise asked, a twinkle in her eye. "Do you have the fabulous Winston jewels with you?"

"Yes, my dear, we do," George said pompously. "Come here, and I'll give you a look at our treasure chest."

He had left the chest on the bed, and he went to it and unlocked it.

"Come, have a look at our priceless gems."

He lifted the lid, revealing a white satin lining in the chest. Within the confines of the box were a magnificent assortment of jewels unlike anything Elise had ever seen before.

"Oh, my," she said softly. "Where did you find these?"

George's eyes were twinkling with devilment as he watched her reaction. "The same place we found the wig, beard, and mustache. We got them from a troupe of actors in Denver. We were quite fortunate to meet up with them. They were most helpful."

"Indeed they were," Claire agreed.

"The jewels are paste, Elise, but unless one is truly knowledgeable about precious gems, there's no easy way to tell the difference."

"You'll have to wear some of these to dinner tonight," Elise told her grandmother. "We want the townspeople to see them and start talking about them."

"I'll do whatever you want me to do if it will help you," Claire offered.

Later that evening, Claire and George dined in the hotel's dining room. Claire wore a sparkling, 'diamond-encrusted' heart-shaped pendant, huge 'diamond' earrings, and what looked to be a diamond ring at least three carats in size. They were aware that everyone was watching them, and they enjoyed playing out their little charade.

When they'd returned to their rooms to retire for the night, they found Elise hovering near their room, disguised as a maid. They invited her in for a few moments to talk some more.

"What do you think? Does everyone still believe we're royalty?" Claire asked.

"Oh, yes. It's going great. Just make sure you keep this door locked tonight. We'll be close by outside, keeping watch over you."

"Good night, Elise," Claire told her as she hugged her close.

"Sweet dreams." Elise was smiling as she left them. They were, after all, still newlyweds.

Lord and Lady Winston retired for the night as Trace took up the watch outside with Marshal Trent.

"It looks like everything's in place," Jared told him. "Now, all we have to do is wait."

357

"This is the hardest part," Trace said in a low voice. "I've been waiting months for a show-down with Harris. I hope this draws him out."

"I hope it does, too. I want to stop the Harris gang once and for all."

They remained where they were and kept watch in companionable silence. They were the best of the best, these two lawmen, and they were determined to get their man.

It was decided that Tom Edwards would make the trip into Durango. He was the least well known of the gang, and that would give him an advantage as he moved around town.

Tom stopped at the first saloon he could find. He made himself at home at the bar, drinking quietly and not doing anything to draw undue attention to himself. When the talk in the bar turned to the rich English folks who were in town, he listened closely. By the time the locals were done talking, he even knew the hotel where the Winstons were staying, and he knew that the townfolk thought the jewels were locked up in an ornate wooden chest they saw the lord carrying as he came off the train.

No one seemed to notice as Tom finished off his drink and left the saloon. He rode on far-ther into Durango, looking for the hotel they'd mentioned. He needed to find out just how dif-ficult it was going to be to get to the jewels. If the hotel was quiet, and it looked as if they weren't expecting trouble, it would be a simple thing to break into their room the following day and take the jewels. Tom just had to be sure that it really was going to be that simple before he could go back to Harris with a plan.

Tom rode past the hotel, studying the area. He couldn't see anybody, but he had the feeling that there was someone around watching everything that was going on. He rode onward, acting as if he was just passing through.

When he was out of sight of the hotel, Tom reined in and tied up his mount. Silently, on foot, he entered the alley that ran behind the hotel. He stayed to the shadows, ever cautious, as he approached the two-story building. He was only half a block away when he caught sight of the deputy guarding the back entrance. The man had taken up a place in a darkened area near the back door. If Tom hadn't actually been looking for him, he would never have seen him.

The presence of the guard around back convinced Tom that he'd been right about the feelings he'd had out front. This hotel was being very heavily guarded. He began to wonder if their idea to rob the royals of their jewelry might be a bad one. They'd lost two men on the last robbery in Canyon Creek. There were only four of them left now. They couldn't afford any more deadly trouble.

Determined to try to convince Harris to give up the idea of stealing the jewels, Tom returned to his horse and mounted up. He would meet Harris at their agreed-upon meeting place and explain everything he'd seen. It was not going to be as easy as they thought, robbing the lord and lady at this hotel.

The long hours of the night passed slowly for Trace. He was tense and anxious as they watched and waited, but it was a quiet night.

There were no surprises. Things remained calm. He had watched as Andy escorted Elise from the hotel when her shift as a "maid" had ended, and he'd been glad to know that she was safe.

As the sun finally edged above the eastern horizon, Trace stirred from his vantage point and stared out across the landscape, trying to judge the new day.

"That was one long night," Jared said.

"I'm glad it's over, but it only makes me worry more about the rest of the day and tonight," he returned. "I'm going to head on back to the office now and try to get some sleep there. If you need anything, just let me know."

"I'll be in touch, but plan on doing the same thing tonight. I'll meet you here at sundown."

"All right."

When Trace got to the office, everything was locked up and quiet. Though he was ready for trouble if it happened, he didn't want any unwelcome surprises. He was tempted to go to Elise, but held himself back. He needed some sleep if he was going to be alert all day, and he definitely wouldn't be getting any sleep if he went to see her.

Trace smiled at the thought of waking her up this early in the morning to make love to her. He denied the desire that urged him to go and locked the office door behind him. Soon, he would make Elise his lady, and then they would never have to spend another night apart.

The cot he'd set up in his office offered little in the way of comfort, but he was too tired to care. He fell asleep quickly, but it was a restless sleep. He kept waking up, his heart pounding, tense and in a sweat. He knew he was worried about Harris, but this was different. There was something he was missing, and he couldn't figure out what it was.

"So you're saying the place is too heavily guarded?" Harris repeated back to Tom.

"There were guards everywhere. It's almost like—"

"Like a setup?" Matt supplied, his gaze narrowing at the thought of all the lawmen watching the visiting royalty and their hotel real close.

"Yeah."

"But that's what makes it perfect." Harris laughed.

"What are you talking about? There's no way we could get out of that hotel with the jewels without getting shot up bad."

"Who said anything about the hotel?" he sneered. "The reason we're so damned good is because we're a whole helluva lot smarter than those dumb-ass lawmen. We ain't going after the jewels. We're going to do what we do best. We're going to rob the bank."

Tom, Al, and Terp all smiled savagely at the thought.

"That's perfect! They're gonna be watching the jewels. They ain't gonna be thinking about the bank."

"That's right. We're going to be making a withdrawal from the Bank of Durango—a big withdrawal!"

The gang was hooting with laughter as they got ready to ride.

* * *

It was late morning when Trace finally got up. What little sleep he'd gotten had not helped. If anything, he was more tense now than when he'd retired. He'd always trusted his instincts, and he wasn't about to ignore the feelings that were driving him now.

"I'm going to find Marshal Trent. I'll be back later," he told Andy and Elise as he came out of his office.

They had both shown up for work on time, but had taken care to keep things as quiet as they could to let him sleep.

"Is something wrong?" Elise asked worriedly, seeing his dark expression.

"No. I just want to check with him and make sure that we've thought of everything. I don't trust Harris, and I wouldn't put anything past him."

He started to leave, then went back into his office. When he came out again, he was wearing his gunbelt. He strode from the newspaper office, a look of grim determination on his face.

Jared was already at his desk when Trace came in.

"You had the same kind of night I did," the lawman said, taking one look at him.

"It wasn't pretty," Trace told him with a grimace that didn't pass for a smile. "There's something I think we need to take a look at. How many deputies are working today?"

"Right now, two."

"While we've been so busy worrying about the jewels, the banks are doing business as usual."

"You think they might go after a bank?" Jared went still at the thought.

"It's a possibility. Harris is smart. That's why he's stayed alive this long. If he thinks we're watching the jewels, he'll go after the bank."

Jared was on his feet and starting from the office. "Let's go take a look around."

Chapter Twenty-five

Harris had enjoyed every minute of the robbery. They'd ridden right into Durango under the nose of Marshal Trent, and nobody had even noticed them. There had been no extra guards at the bank, and they'd taken full advantage. They would have made it out of town without firing a shot if the stupid bank president hadn't gone for a gun. They'd left him lying, bleeding, on the floor. Now Harris had the money and they were getting out of town. Harris charged through the front doors of the bank with Tom, Al, and Terp following close behind him.

Trace and Jared were nearing the area when they heard shots ring out and saw four masked men come running out of the Bank of Durango. They drew their guns instantly as they raced straight toward the action, firing as they went.

Harris was angry that they'd been discovered, but they still had the loot, and they could still get away. They'd done it often enough before. He fired back in the general direction of the gunmen, who were shooting at them as he swung the money-stuffed saddlebags across his horse's back.

Al was running close beside Harris. He gave a sudden scream as hot lead slammed into his back. He fell writhing on the ground, crying out in agony for help from his friends.

"Don't leave me!"

Harris cast only a quick glance at his wounded comrade as he mounted up. They had long ago agreed that if any of them went down, the others would keep going.

Tom and Terp looked Al's way, too, but they did not go to his aid. They leaped on their horses.

Trace and Jared kept firing, hoping to hit another of the outlaws.

Harris turned to shoot back, and it was then that he got a look at the two men coming after them. One had a marshal's badge on his vest, so he knew that had to be Trent. The other man looked like a dude. He was wearing a suit and had eyeglasses on. In spite of the fact that he looked so different, Harris thought there was something familiar about the man. He frowned, but couldn't waste any time on it now. They had to get out of there.

"Let's ride!" he shouted as he put his spurs to his horse's sides. He leaned low as he led his men from town at top speed, firing indiscriminately.

Tom and Terp were riding close behind him. They followed him out of town, shooting at anything and everything that moved.

"Damn!" Trace swore violently as the outlaws made their getaway. He stopped shooting as they disappeared around a corner on their way out of town. "How fast can you get your deputies ready to ride?"

"As fast as I can get to the horses."

"I'll meet you at your office."

Jared hurried inside the bank to check on things there before going to organize his posse.

Trace ran toward the newspaper office to get his horse and let Elise and Andy know what had happened. He found the two of them already out of the building hurrying in the direction of the shots.

"What happened? What were all the gunshots about?" Elise cried out as she ran to him. She had feared that something had happened to him or to her grandmother and George when she'd heard the eruption of gunfire.

"Harris and his men just robbed the bank. We're going after them," Trace said tersely.

They ran back into the office, where he threw off his suit coat and glasses.

As Andy and Elise both looked on, Gabe transformed himself, once and for all, into Trace Jackson. He walked back into his own office, and when he came out, he was carrying his saddlebags and rifle and had his Stetson on. There was no mistaking him for Gabe now. He looked every inch the fierce lawman they knew him to be.

"I don't know when I'll be back," he told Elise solemnly, "but I'm not coming back without Harris."

Elise went to Trace, not caring that Andy was there, and kissed him. "Be careful. I'll be praying for you."

He nodded grimly, then looked up at Andy. "Keep an eye on her," he told him.

Trace strode from the room. He did not look back. If he had, he would have seen Elise standing in the doorway watching him leave, tears running down her cheeks.

Trace reached the marshal's office, and the other deputies looked at him strangely.

"Men, I'd like you to meet Trace Jackson," Jared told them.

Their shock was obvious. "You're Sheriff Jackson?"

"That's right," Trace said.

"Then that report in the *Star* was right!" another said.

"Yeah, the last time I saw Harris, he shot me in the back and killed the rest of the men in my posse. That isn't going to happen this time," he told them with savage determination. "We're not stopping until we've brought him in."

"They wounded Henry Jergens over at the bank," Jared added. "The Harris gang's days are at an end—as of now. Let's ride."

Jared left one deputy behind to take care of things, and the rest of the men rode with them. They were ten heavily armed, very serious lawmen. They were prepared for whatever it would take to bring down the Harris gang once and for all.

The gang's trail was fresh, and the posse rode steadily, doggedly, after them. They never wavered in their pursuit, but they were always watchful of the surrounding area. They were taking no chances, giving Harris no opportunity for an ambush. They had long hours of daylight ahead of them, and they were not about to give up.

"Who the hell is leading that posse?" Harris demanded as they continued their flight into the mountains.

"It must be that Marshal Trent we heard about."

"He's one helluva tracker," Harris complained. "They look like they're gaining on us."

"We'd better move faster," Terp said, worried. He, too, had noticed the way the posse had come quickly after them and had not lost their trail, not even when they'd ridden over rock and through several creeks. These men were good—real good.

They stopped talking and concentrated on making their escape, moving ever higher into the mountains.

The posse stayed with them. Their pursuit was relentless. Harris and his men were not going to get away from them. They knew every inch of the area surrounding Durango, and they were determined to catch them before they got too far away. They wanted no surprises from these outlaws. They knew just how deadly they could be. The lawmen stayed on their trail, moving ever more quickly, their eyes always watchful, always suspicious.

"Up ahead about two miles, there's a steep-walled canyon with a single trail up the far end," Jared told Trace as they rode side by side at the head of the posse.

"Will we be able to get any shots off at them before they get a better position on us?"

"If we ride harder, maybe. We can split the posse and send half of the men around the long way. It's several miles longer, but if we stay on them and manage to slow them down in the canyon, they could get to the far end at about the same time Harris and his men are riding out."

"I'll do it," Trace volunteered, wanting the chance to face down Harris.

"You sure?"

"Positive."

"We won't be able to make a run at them when they're up on that trail. There won't be much cover for us, and I don't want to risk losing any men."

"Do what you can. We'll ride our horses into the ground if we have to. They're not getting away again."

Jared reined in and signaled to his men. "I want you four to ride with Trace and take the long route. The rest of us will stay after them, and try to drive them to you—if we can't stop them completely."

Trace and the deputies headed out in the other direction. The deputies explained to Trace why they were glad that Harris and his men had chosen this particular canyon for their escape route. It was tricky terrain, but they were all familiar with it. They didn't know how well the outlaws knew the lay of the land, but right now things seemed to be going their way.

Hours passed. The sun sank lower in the western sky, but still the gang rode on. They could not stop. They could not rest. They could not shake the posse.

"Who the hell are these men?" Terp complained, growing more and more exhausted with each passing mile. "We ain't been chased like this since Jackson was after us that day in Eagle Pass."

"Whoever they are, they're good, but they ain't gonna catch us," Tom said, determined not to give in to his own fear.

"Jackson!" Harris said as if he'd had a revelation, and then he suddenly started to swear out loud.

"What's wrong?"

"It was Jackson! That's who the hell it was with the lawman in town!"

"What are you talking about?" Terp demanded, thinking he'd lost his mind.

"We now know where Trace Jackson's been hiding out all this time. I saw him in Durango. He was one of the two men shooting at us when we came out of the bank. He was the one wearing the eyeglasses!"

"Why would he be doing that?"

"How the hell am I supposed to know?" Matt snarled. "But it was him, and the whole thing was a setup!"

"What do you mean?"

"Jackson probably made up that whole story about the jewels just to draw us into town. And now they're staying on us so close. No wonder they're not giving up or backing off. We gotta find a way to trap them, to turn the tables on them. We got to take them out, just like we did with his posse from Eagle Pass."

"I don't think there's any way to do that up ahead. We can try to get some shots off at them when we start up the trail, but if they stay out of range, there's nothing we can do."

"We'll just see about that when we get there," Harris told them, furious.

They rode as quickly as their tired horses could carry them, but every time they looked back they could see the dust of the posse. When they finally reached the end of the canyon and started up the trail that led to the rim, the posse hung back, taking care not to give them anything to shoot at.

"Harris!" Terp called out to him when he saw that the posse was half its original size.

"What?"

"Look! Half the men are gone! They must have split up and sent half the posse to catch us on the other side."

Harris cursed even more violently and kept riding. They were going to get out of this. He was Matt Harris. No one was going to bring him in. It just wasn't going to be easy or simple. It was going to be savage and bloody. He might have missed killing Trace Jackson the first time, but he wouldn't miss again.

Jared was frustrated with his vantage point. He wanted to slow the outlaws' flight and give Trace and the other deputies the time they needed to be ready and waiting for them on the other side. He moved his men in as close as they could get and then ordered them to start firing at the gang as they made the trek to the top of the canyon.

The gang didn't return their fire, but kept riding, their pace slowed as they tried not to give their pursuers any clear or easy shots. They knew they didn't have far to go to escape, and they knew they had to move fast to get away before the rest of the posse showed up.

Harris and his men finally reached the crest and hoped that freedom was just a few miles and a few hours away. If they could elude the posse until sundown, they could sneak away during the night and be long gone by the next morning. They just needed a little luck right now.

But this time, luck was on Trace's side.

As Harris, Tom, and Terp rode the crest and started down the trail they thought would lead to freedom, shots rang out around them.

Trace and the deputies had ridden like the wind to get there before they did. Trace had feared running their horses into the ground, but he knew this was the best place to trap Harris, and he had to do everything he could to make sure the outlaws did not escape them.

At the sound of the shots, Harris, Tom, and Terp spurred their horses on. They tried to get to cover, but bullets were flying around them. Screams erupted as Tom and Terp were both shot. They fell and lay unmoving on the narrow, rocky trail, leaving Harris on his own.

Harris threw himself from his horse's back and dodged into the nearby rocks to hide. He was furious at being trapped this way and desperate to escape. There was no going back. He knew that. Half the posse would be riding up the trail from the canyon now. He couldn't go forward, for Jackson and his men were waiting for him.

Harris looked around, frantically searching for a way out. Behind him was a sheer drop-off of nearly fifty feet to the rushing river below. There was no escape. He was trapped. Jackson had done it. Jackson had won!

The thought left Harris even more enraged. He refused to die easily, though. If he could, he was going to lure Jackson out, so he could at least kill him before he himself was gunned down.

"Throw out your guns, Harris. It's over!" Trace shouted.

"You go to hell, Jackson!" he returned and fired blindly in his direction.

"I've been there already. Now it's your turn."

Harris couldn't tell exactly where Trace's voice was coming from. It disconcerted him, and he tried to decide whether to charge forward and take them all on, or wait it out in hopes that he could pick off a few of the other deputies riding up behind him.

He never got the chance to make a choice. A shiver of terror went down the hardened killer's spine as Jackson's voice spoke up from near by.

"I told you to throw down your gun," Trace snarled as he stood up close to Harris, his gun trained straight at the middle of the outlaw's chest.

Harris had been so distracted trying to think of a way to escape that Trace had managed to crawl forward and get this close to him without being seen.

Harris glared at the lawman, hating him more than he'd ever hated anyone in his entire life. He wanted to shoot him, to try to take him out one last time. He refused to be taken in by a damned posse of lawmen—and especially not by Jackson.

Trace was ready for him, though. When Harris lifted the gun to fire, Trace shot first, hitting him in the shoulder. Harris's gun flew from his hand.

"You bastard!" Harris swore at him. The outlaw stumbled backward, trying to get away.

"You're going in. I'm going to watch you hang!"

Harris continued to back away from him, clutching his shoulder, which was streaming blood. He was dazed and disoriented. He looked back at the edge of the cliff and then back at Trace. Harris smiled an evil grin, then turned and jumped from the cliff, screaming as he plunged more than fifty feet into the raging river below.

Trace lunged forward, trying to grab him before he went over the side. But he was too late. He looked down, praying that he could see Harris below, but there was only the rushing water. There was no sign of the wounded outlaw.

"What happened?"

The other deputies were beside him in an instant.

"I wounded him in the shoulder, but then he jumped."

They looked, too, but couldn't see him anywhere below.

"The other two are dead," Jared said as he and his part of the posse joined them. "You say you shot him?"

Trace nodded. "Then he looked straight at me and jumped."

Jared looked over the edge. "There's no way he could have survived that fall."

"I want to believe that, but I'm going to ride down and check on him anyway. I don't trust Harris. He's got as many lives as a cat, and I'm not taking any chances."

"All right," Jared agreed. "Take half the men with you. We'll wait for you back in the canyon."

Trace and the deputies mounted up and rode down to the river. It was a slow, tedious trail, hard for even the most sure-footed of horses. They had less than an hour of sunlight left when they reached the bottom, and they started to search for Harris immediately. The only trace they could find was his battered, sodden hat on the riverbank. Otherwise, there was no sign of him anywhere.

"I'm going to stay the night here and search for him again in the morning," Trace told them. "I don't trust this bastard. If there was any way to live through that fall, Harris did it. Any of you who want to head back and meet Marshal Trent, go ahead. I'm going to stay here and go over the area again at daybreak."

Two of the deputies decided to return to Jared with word of his plans, while two stayed on. Trace told them to tell the marshal that he would see him back in town the following day.

They made camp for the night, but decided to post a guard, just in case. They knew how deadly Harris could be, and they wanted to be ready, no matter what.

Jared and his deputies tied the bodies of the dead outlaws to their horses and rode for town once they'd heard from Trace. They managed to travel for about an hour before it became too dark and the horses were too tired to go on. They, too, made camp for the night. They would return to Durango in the morning.

Chapter Twenty-six

Elise passed a miserable night. Her grandmother and George had come back to the house to stay with her, but even their loving presence had not helped to lessen her fears about Trace's safety. She knew Trace had meant it when he'd said he wouldn't come back without Harris. She knew it might be days, even weeks, before he returned. But being logical didn't change the way she felt. Trace was going after a vicious murderer who'd tried to kill him once before. She would not be able to relax until he was safely back in Durango with her. Morning found Elise up before dawn, restless and tense.

"Sweetheart, are you all right?" Claire asked when she found her in the kitchen.

She gave her grandmother a tight smile. "I'm as good as I can be."

"Trace will be back. I'm sure of it."

"So am I. I just wish he was back now."

"Are you going to work at the paper today?"

"I'd better." Elise knew work was the only thing that could keep her distracted from her worries. She smiled more brightly at the thought. "Andy and I can start putting together a special edition on the robbery and on Trace!"

Claire completely understood her need to keep busy. "Well, if you hear anything, let us know right away."

"I will. What do you want to do about Lord and Lady Winston?"

"George and I were discussing that. Do you want to reveal everything about the fabulous 'Winston jewels' in your story?"

"Yes, there's no need to keep up the charade any longer."

A short time later, Elise was at the office writing her story. When Andy showed up, he was impressed that she had arrived so early, but he knew the truth.

"You couldn't sleep, could you?"

"Not a wink," she admitted, getting up to look out the window, her expression forlorn and strained. "I just wish I knew where Trace was."

"Don't we all," Andy agreed.

They set to work writing their respective stories, so they could get the issue out as soon as possible.

It was near noon when a man passing by opened the door to shout at them that the posse was riding into town and that they had dead bodies with them.

With a cry of relief, Elise left her desk and ran into the street. Andy stayed right with her as they hurried toward the marshal's office. When they reached the corner and could see the office, Elise stopped dead in her tracks. Marshal Trent was there, and so were some of his deputies, but there was no sign of Trace anywhere.

"Andy?" she said his name in a strangled voice and grabbed his arm. "I don't see him. Where is he?"

"I don't know," he said, as troubled as she was by Trace's absence.

It was then that she caught sight of the two dead men thrown over the horses' backs, and she gasped out loud.

"Oh God! No!"

She started running forward, stricken by the fear that Trace was one of them. Terror ate at her. Her heart was pounding a violent rhythm. *Trace couldn't be dead! He couldn't be!* She loved him too much for him to die this way. She needed him with her. She wanted him near her. She couldn't lose him! Not now when she'd finally found him!

Andy tried to stop her, but she broke away from him and hurried toward the lawmen.

Jared Trent heard her cry out, and he turned to see her coming. "Elise!"

She looked away from the dead bodies and to him.

"Trace is all right." He'd understood her moment of panic and wanted to calm her.

"What?" She was stunned, and then slowly realized that Trace was not one of the dead men.

"These are the last two of Harris's men, but Harris was only wounded."

"Where is he?"

"He jumped off a cliff into the river. The fall probably killed him, but Trace wanted to find his body and make sure. He's got two of the deputies with him. They were going to search the riverbanks this morning and bring Harris back with them.

"Thank God he's all right! I thought—"

"I know," he sympathized. "But no one in the posse was hurt."

"You were most blessed."

"That we were. I expect Trace and the others will be back here by sundown."

She nodded. "Where did you finally catch up with the gang?"

Jared quickly told her and Andy all that had happened. He promised to let them know the minute Trace got into town.

Elise went to tell her grandmother and George what had happened while Andy returned to the office. She met him there a short time later, and they went back to work on their special edition.

Trace was frustrated and worried as he strode along the rocky riverbank, searching for Harris. They had been looking for the outlaw since dawn, but had found nothing.

"He's got to be dead," one deputy said flatly.

"If that's the case, we should have found his body," Trace pointed out.

"The current is damned fast here. There's no telling how far he might have washed downstream," the other lawman said.

Trace swore silently to himself. He realized that they were probably right, but his gut instincts would give him no rest. Harris was out there somewhere, he was certain of it, and he needed to find him.

Trace lifted his gaze to the craggy hillsides. He wondered if the outlaw had been strong enough after being shot and falling so far to drag himself out of the river to safety. An ordinary man would have been killed— but they all knew Harris was no ordinary man.

"Let's keep looking and let's check farther up the banks. Harris is one tough bastard. I don't put anything past him."

The deputies did as Trace directed. It was well past noon when Trace finally called off the search. They had found no clues to Harris's whereabouts.

They started back to town, their mood guardedly triumphant.

Trace was watchful and cautious on the trek back. He wondered if he would ever truly believe that Harris had been killed.

Elise and Andy were holding the press until Trace returned. They wanted to make sure they had all the pertinent information on Harris in the edition. It was just dusk when they heard the office door open. They looked up to see Trace come in.

"You're back!" Elise cried in delight and ran into his open arms.

"We just rode in here a few minutes ago," he said slowly, holding her close.

"Did you find Harris?" she asked, leaning back to look up at him.

At her question, his expression darkened. "No. We never did find his body."

"But you're sure he's dead?"

It was the question that haunted him more than he cared to admit. "I hope so."

"So do I," she said fiercely. "We've just about got the paper ready to go. We were waiting for you to get back before we went to press."

"Do you want to go with our headline?" Andy spoke up. "HARRIS AND HIS MEN DEAD! OUTLAWS' REIGN OF TERROR OVER!"

"Print it," Trace said firmly.

As Andy went to work, Trace took Elise by the hand and led her into the privacy of his own office. Only then, when they were alone, did he kiss her.

"I was worried about you when the marshal came back and you weren't with them," she whispered to him as she held him close.

"I'm sorry, but I wanted to make sure Harris really was dead."

"It's all right. All that matters is that you're here with me now," she sighed, resting her head against the broad width of his chest.

They stood wrapped in each other's arms, savoring the beauty of the moment. The terrible threat that had haunted Trace's life was over. He was home. He was safe.

"If your grandmother and George could put together a wedding in less than twenty-four hours, how long will it take us?" Trace asked. She fit so perfectly against him that he never wanted to be away from her again.

She gave a throaty chuckle. "You're absolutely sure about this?"

"I'm sure." There was no doubt in his voice at all. "I told you—I want to see you in that dress again."

"And I want to be in that dress again," she told him, gazing up at him adoringly.

"Do you want to have a traditional wedding?"

"If you don't mind." She had always dreamed of coming down the aisle in her gown, to be joined forever with the man she loved—with Trace.

"I'll do whatever you want me to do. I love you, Elise, and I want to spend the rest of my life making you happy."

She lifted her lips to his. "I'll talk to my grandmother tonight. We'll start making the arrangements right away."

"It can't come soon enough for me," he said ardently.

"I feel the same way." She sighed blissfully. "I'm glad your nightmare is over, Trace."

"So am I," he answered, but even as he said it, he wondered if it really was.

After they got the copies of the *Star* out, Elise and Trace returned to the house to tell George and Claire and to start making plans for the wedding. The older couple was delighted with their news. They planned to meet with Reverend Ford the next day and see how soon they could have the ceremony.

With the threat to him over, Trace moved back into his own home. George and Claire were to stay with Elise as chaperones until the wedding, after which they would move into George's home.

The wedding was perfect. They took four weeks to plan the ceremony, and it was even more spectacular than Elise's first 'marriage' to 'Ben'.

"I believe I heard talk that you two have done this before," Reverend Ford quipped with a smile as they came to stand before him.

Elise was resplendent in her white gown and veil, and Trace was handsome in his dark suit.

"This time it's for real, though," Elise told the reverend, smiling up at Trace.

"Good," the preacher said. Then he began, his mood more serious. "Dearly beloved, we are gathered here today . . . "

He recited the vows that would bind them as man and wife for all eternity, and they repeated them faithfully.

Seated among the crowd of well-wishers, Julie fought hard to keep from scowling as she watched Elise and Trace profess their undying love for each other and then pledge to forsake all others until death did them part. It had been difficult enough thinking Elise was going to marry Ben during the first wedding, but this time, Elise really was marrying Gabe—or Trace.

Julie was still confused by all that had been going on, but she had to admit, Trace Jackson was one exciting man. She had thought him wonderful when he'd been Gabe West, and now that she knew who he really was, she was even more impressed. Julie had to hand it to Elise— she had found herself an even more exciting husband the second time around.

Husbands. The thought was wearying to Julie, and she suddenly wondered if Clint had really been as bad as she'd thought that night at the church social.

* * *

"I now pronounce you man and wife. You may kiss your bride," Reverend Ford told Trace.

It was the moment they had both been waiting for. Trace turned to his bride, his gaze warm upon her. She was the most beautiful woman in the world, and he knew he couldn't live without her. Ever so gently, he cupped her face with his hands and kissed her sweetly on the lips.

Elise sighed rapturously at his tender touch and kiss. This was Trace. He was her husband. They were going to live happily ever after.

"Ladies and gentlemen, allow me to present to you Mr. and Mrs. Trace Jackson," the preacher announced. Everyone cheered happily for the newlyweds.

The reception followed on the grounds. Trace and Elise could hardly wait for the opportunity to slip away. It seemed an eternity since they'd last been alone, and they were truly looking forward to their wedding night. George and Claire had already moved out of the house, so it was all theirs now. There would be no interruptions tonight.

They stayed on at the reception for several hours, but finally managed to disappear without too many people noticing. Trace had parked the carriage around back, and he helped her into the vehicle and then climbed in beside her. It was quiet, so he gathered her in his arms and kissed her thoroughly.

"I think you'd better hurry up and take me home," Elise told him, her heart pounding a wild rhythm in anticipation of their night of bliss to come.

"That's exactly what I plan to do."

He slapped the reins on the horses' backs and rode for the house. He could never remember being this happy before. He glanced over at Elise as he drove. In the moonlight, she looked even more beautiful, and deep in his heart, Trace knew he would love her forever.

When they arrived at the house, Trace made short order of tying up the horses. He then lifted Elise down. He didn't put her on her feet, though, but carried her up the steps and across the threshold. She looped her arms about his neck and clung to him, enjoying every minute of being in his arms.

Trace put Elise down only long enough to lock the door behind them, and then he scooped her up again and carried her upstairs to the bedroom. This time, he kicked the door shut and then put her on her feet.

"I love you, Elise," he said in a voice hoarse with emotion as he lifted his hands to the back of her dress and began to unfasten the small buttons on the gown. "I've wanted to do this ever since I first saw you in this gown."

"And I've wanted you to do it," she murmured excitedly. Every fiber of her being was alive with the thrill of being with Trace.

Elise began to work at the buttons on his shirt. Then she parted the garment brazenly caressing his hard-muscled chest. She smiled at his sharp intake of breath.

"Kiss me, Trace," she whispered.

It was all the encouragement he needed. He stripped away her gown and undergarments and lifting her in his arms, carried her to the bed. He left her only long enough to undress himself, and then returned to make her his own in every sense.

"You are so beautiful," he told her, his gaze going hungrily over her, visually caressing her full breasts, the sweet curve of her waist and her long, lovely legs.

"So are you," she responded.

Elise ran her hands over the powerful width of his shoulders and then down his chest, slipping ever lower until Trace groaned and clasped her to him. He rolled her beneath him and moved to make her his.

They came together in a blaze of glory. Giving and taking, pleasing and pleasuring, until rapture burst upon them in a crescendo of passion's delight.

They rested only a moment before the embers of their desire were stoked to a blazing fire again. With each touch and kiss, they explored one another. They gave freely of their love, expressing through this physical closeness all the beauty and depth of their emotions.

From that first day when Trace had walked off the stagecoach and into her arms, it seemed that they had been meant to be together—to be one.

And now they were.

They finally slept, but only when the eastern sky brightened with the promise of the new day. It was the beginning of the rest of their lives.

Chapter Twenty-seven

The following days and nights passed in a haze of loving glory. It seemed Trace and Elise couldn't get enough of each other, and they loved long into each night, seeking the joy that could only be found in cherishing each other.

Elise was ecstatic. She had never known being in love could be so wonderful. It seemed her every thought was of Trace. He had become the center of her existence. She wanted to be with him, listening to the sound of his voice, touching him, loving him.

It was when she awoke to find him gone from their bed in the middle of one night that she first realized something was troubling him. She got up to search for him and found him standing in the darkened parlor, staring out the window at the street beyond.

"Trace, are you all right?" she asked quietly as she went to him.

He turned to her, and even in the darkness she could see the strain in his expression.

"What is it?" Elise went to him and slipped her arms around him. He was solid power, all male.

"I just couldn't sleep."

"Why?"

He shook his head to discourage any more questions, but she would not be put off.

"Tell me," she insisted.

Trace drew a deep breath and started back to the bedroom. He put one arm around her waist as they walked. "I've been uneasy lately. It's almost as if things are too good."

"They are too good," she said in a throaty voice that held a hint of loving to come.

He stopped to kiss her, then went on. "It's Harris," he finally admitted flatly.

"What about him? He's dead."

"I hope to God he is."

She understood his fears, but wanted to ease them. "I know that without seeing Harris dead, it's hard for you to accept, but wouldn't he have shown up somewhere by now if he'd lived through that fall?"

"I'd like to think so, but there are no guarantees."

"Well, he's not here tonight. Come to bed with me. I think I have an idea of how to get your mind off him."

She gave him a smile that sent a jolt of sensual awareness through Trace. He needed no further encouragement to return to their mar-

riage bed. And he did manage to forget about
Harris for several long, hot hours.

Later that night, however, when Elise was
fast asleep, Trace got up and got his gun. He
put it in the drawer of the small table next to
his side of the bed.

It was in the early morning hours over a week
later that Trace came awake with a start. He had
been sleeping lightly, but was suddenly wide
awake and very tense. He did not know what
had awakened him, but he slipped from the bed
and pulled on his pants before grabbing his gun.
He went to the bedroom door and stood there in
silence, waiting and listening. He wanted to
know what had jarred him awake that way.

He heard nothing unusual, but he still felt as
if something wasn't right. He went to the bed
and knelt beside Elise to whisper in her ear.

"Elise," he said her name in low, barely audi-
ble tones.

Her eyes flew open and she looked up at him,
questioning and fearful.

"I heard something outside. I'm going out to
check on it. You stay inside, no matter what."

She snatched up her discarded nightgown
and tugged it on. "What did you hear?"

"I'm not sure, and it may prove to be nothing, but I've got to check."

She smiled at him as reassuringly as she
could, then gave him a quick kiss. "Be careful."

Trace nodded, then told her, "Lock the bedroom door after me."

With that, he was gone.

Elise remained where she was for only a few

moments, then realized there was no way she could just sit there and wait while he was in danger. She pulled on her robe and then opened the door and started down the hall toward the steps. The first thing she was going to do was get her derringer; then she was going to help Trace. Whatever danger he was facing, she was going to be by his side.

Trace made his way downstairs silently. He stayed in the shadows, keeping careful watch, trying to figure out what had awakened him. A quick look around the main floor of the house revealed nothing. No one had broken in; nothing was disturbed. Whatever had bothered him had come from outside. It was then that he glanced toward the kitchen and saw the shadow moving across the wall. Someone was on the back porch!

With utmost caution, Trace slipped out the front door. He made his way around the house, staying to the shadows, watching and listening. He held his gun at the ready, prepared for whatever might come.

The black-clad figure moved soundlessly off the porch and started around to the front of the house.

"Hold it, right there!" Trace ordered.

"Die, Jackson! Like you were supposed to the first time!" Harris shouted, and he fired at Trace, wanting him dead, wanting to see him facedown in the dirt again.

But it wasn't to be. Trace was ready for him. He threw himself to the ground, firing at Harris and hitting him full in the chest. "I don't think so, Harris. Now, it's your turn to die," Trace said in a low, lethal voice.

Harris gave an agonized cry as he crashed backward, fell, and lay still. Trace moved to stand over the outlaw. He kept his gun trained on him. When he saw Harris trying to lift his gun to get off one last round at him, he savagely kicked the gun out of his hand.

Harris looked up at him, his lips curling into a hateful sneer. "I'll see you in hell, lawman," he said harshly as the last of his life's blood drained away from him.

"Trace!" Elise could no longer restrain herself. She came flying out of the house, her derringer in hand.

"I'm back here," he called out to her.

She was trembling visibly as she reached his side. She looked down at the Harris's lifeless body and then back up at her husband. "You were right all along! He did survive that fall into the river!"

Trace nodded, but didn't say anything. He just held her close, knowing that his only haven was in her arms.

Several of the neighbors came running to see what was going on. "What happened?"

"It's Matt Harris," he answered tightly, gesturing toward the body.

"We thought he was dead!" They were shocked at the news.

"He is now."

One man ran to get the marshal.

Trace drew Elise with him away from the scene of the carnage.

"You're all right?" she asked, still trying to understand all that had taken place.

"I am now that you're with me," he told her solemnly. "It's over, Elise. It's finally over."

Epilogue

TRACE JACKSON GETS HIS MAN!
MATT HARRIS DEAD!

Previous reports stating that Harris had been killed during the shoot-out with Marshal Trent and the posse were in error. Harris returned to Durango late last night in an attempt to murder Trace Jackson. There was a shooting at Jackson's home, and Harris was killed by Jackson during the incident.

With Harris's demise, all known members of his gang are now dead. The state is well rid of their violence.

"Amen," Elise said as she finished rereading the article. "What do you think?"

"I think that's the best headline I've ever

read," Trace told her, coming to read over her shoulder.

"I'm glad you approve," she turned toward Trace and smiled archly up at him as she rested one hand on his chest. "I like it when you approve of my work."

"I always approve of your work," he growled as she let her hand drift a little lower to rest near his belt.

"You know, it's rather late, and we are alone here in the office right now," she said suggestively. "I don't expect Andy back until tomorrow morning."

"I'm glad he's going to be busy all night," Trace said, needing no further encouragement from his wife. "You know . . . "

He paused to kiss her passionately.

"You were saying?" she asked with a grin.

"I've gotten a lot of use out of Ben's desk, but I always wondered . . . "

He pushed the door to his office shut and lifted Elise up to sit her on his desktop.

"Wondered about what?"

"I always wondered how it would feel to make love to you here."

"Let's find out, shall we?" she offered, lifting her arms in welcome to him.

He answered her with a kiss.

And then they did their research.

WESTON'S *Lady*

BOBBI SMITH

There are Cowboys and Indians, trick riding, thrills and excitement for everyone. And if Liberty Jones has anything to say about it, she will be a part of the Wild West show, too. She has demonstrated her expertise with a gun by shooting a card out of Reed Weston's hand at thirty paces, but the arrogant owner of the Stampede won't even give her a chance. Disguising herself as a boy, Libby wangles herself a job with the show, and before she knows it Reed is firing at her—in front of an audience. It seems an emotional showdown is inevitable whenever they come together, but Libby has set her sights on Reed's heart and she vows she will prove her love is every bit as true as her aim.

___4512-5 $5.99 US/$6.99 CAN

THE LADY'S HAND
BOBBI SMITH
Author of *Lady Deception*

Cool-headed and ravishingly beautiful, Brandy O'Neal knows how to hold her own with the riverboat gamblers on *The Pride of New Orleans*. But she meets her match in Rafe Morgan when she bets everything she has on three queens and discovers that the wealthy plantation owner has a far from gentlemanly notion of how she shall make good on her wager.

Disillusioned with romance, Rafe wants a child of his own to care for, without the complications of a woman to break his heart. Now a full house has given him just the opportunity he is looking for—he will force the lovely cardsharp to marry him and give him a child before he sets her free. But a firecracker-hot wedding night and a glimpse into Brandy's tender heart soon make Rafe realize he's luckier than he ever imagined when he wins the lady's hand.

_4116-2   **$5.99 US/$6.99 CAN**

BOBBI SMITH

Rapture's Rage. Renee Fontaine's cascading black hair and soft, full curves draw suitors like bees to spring's first flower, but the dazzling beauty has eyes only for the handsome lawyer who scorns love. The innocent young woman can't get him out of her mind—and she knows that he is the one man she will ever want.

___52238-1 $5.99 US/$6.99 CAN

Renegade's Lady. Sheridan St. John sets out for the Wild West in search of the perfect hero for her new book. The man she finds fulfills every requirement for a fantasy lover—half Apache, all dark dangerous male. And the wildfire attraction between them destroys her reservations, leaving her with one burning need—to become the renegade's lady.

___4250-9 $5.99 US/$6.99 CAN

Dorchester Publishing Co., Inc.
P.O. Box 6640
Wayne, PA 19087-8640

Please add $1.75 for shipping and handling for the first book and $.50 for each book thereafter. NY, NYC, and PA residents, please add appropriate sales tax. No cash, stamps, or C.O.D.s. All orders shipped within 6 weeks via postal service book rate. Canadian orders require $2.00 extra postage and must be paid in U.S. dollars through a U.S. banking facility.

Name_____

Address_____

City_____State_____Zip_____

I have enclosed $_____ in payment for the checked book(s).

Payment <u>must</u> accompany all orders. ❏ Please send a free catalog.

BOBBI SMITH

The LADY & the TEXAN

"A fine storyteller!"—*Romantic Times*

A firebrand since the day she was born, Amanda Taylor always stands up for what she believes in. She won't let any man control her—especially a man like gunslinger Jack Logan. Even though Jack knows Amanda is trouble, her defiant spirit only spurs his hunger for her. He discovers that keeping the dark-haired tigress at bay is a lot harder than outsmarting the outlaws after his hide—and surrendering to her sweet fury is a heck of a lot riskier.

___4319-X $5.99 US/$6.99 CAN

HALF-BREED'S

Lady

BOBBI SMITH

To artist Glynna Williams, Texas is a land of wild beauty, carved by God's hand, untouched as yet by man's. And the most exciting part of it is the fierce, bare-chested half-breed who saves her from a rampaging bull. As she spends the days sketching his magnificent body, she dreams of spending the nights in his arms.

___4436-6 $5.99 US/$6.99 CAN

Dorchester Publishing Co., Inc.
P.O. Box 6640
Wayne, PA 19087-8640

Please add $1.75 for shipping and handling for the first book and $.50 for each book thereafter. NY, NYC, and PA residents, please add appropriate sales tax. No cash, stamps, or C.O.D.s. All orders shipped within 6 weeks via postal service book rate. Canadian orders require $2.00 extra postage and must be paid in U.S. dollars through a U.S. banking facility.

Name_____

Address_____

City_____ State_____ Zip_____

I have enclosed $_____ in payment for the checked book(s).

Payment <u>must</u> accompany all orders. ❑ Please send a free catalog.

CHECK OUT OUR WEBSITE! www.dorchesterpub.com